Holly —
Hope you guys like it,
Thanks for always being
so damn cheerful!

Best

Advanced Praise for William Hanlin's Civil War

". . . A very promising start to an overdue series on the real Civil War . . . the point of view and voice are very well done . . ."~ Richard Slotkin, *The Long Road to Antietam*, 2 time National Book Award finalist.

". . . Funny, poignant, completely different from the standard Civil War book . . . it appeals on many levels . . . visual, visceral with wonderful dialogue, it would make a great TV series along the lines of Boardwalk Empire . . . ~James Marshall Reilly, *Shake the World*

". . . A unique blend of detective-style noir and Civil War history . . . Hicks draws the reader in quickly with character-driven drama that also manages to be darkly comical. William Hanlin, the soldier and state's attorney, tells the story though a first-person narrative that is compelling, and weirdly funny. . . A great ride- funny, cutting, and intense, with a terrific central character. ~ Nate Fey, *The Whiskey Predicament*

History, Humor and Humanity . . a great read for women too. I expected to be entertained with war facts and reminders of American history. Well, I was — But the bonus was finding myself engaged with characters that were funny, real and able to show a dimension of the Civil War era that left me ready for the next book" ~ D.D. Dauphe

"A wonderfully engaging real life tapestry of adventure; a personal depiction of a military survivor who trains a regiment while a dark family secret unravels. ~Charlotte Fields

THE HANLIN SERIES

THE CEREMONY OF INNOCENCE
THE FALCON (SUMMER 2014)
A WIDENING GYRE (FALL 2014)
THE CENTER CANNOT HOLD (JANUARY 2015)
THE BLOOD DIMMED TIDE (SPRING 2015)
PITILESS AS THE SUN (SUMMER 2015)
THE ROUGH BEAST (WINTER 2015)

NON-FICTION

2 SOUPS & A FISH
(A MULTI-MEDIA MEMOIR OF SORTS, COMING WINTER, 2014-15)

Cover Image – At the Front, 1865, by George C. Lambdin, 1866, courtesy Detroit Institute of Art

THE

CEREMONY

OF

INNOCENCE

A Novel in Seven Parts

RR HICKS

For more information on the author, the Hanlin Series, essays, and future writing projects please go to:

Rolandrhicks.wordpress.com

To Contact the author:

rolandrhicks@gmail.com

Also:

Look for RR HICKS on Facebook

This is work of fiction, some characters are real, some are not, none are alive today. Historical characters often speak in their own words, when they do not every effort has been taken – while juggling the needs of creativity and fictional flow – to keep them within the realm of the speakers' beliefs and attitudes.

Unless otherwise noted, all images are courtesy of the Library of Congress; the image on page 81 is from the collection of the New York Historical Society.

FORLORN HOPE PUBLISHING

ISBN - 13:978-1500857615
10:1500857610

TO KM
Regardless, and Because

CITY OF HARTFORD, CONN.

The Meadows

River

Cemetery

The Capitol

Courthouse

The Colledge

The Park

Hartford Club

William's House

The Wadsworth

You smug-faced crowds with kindling eye
Who cheer when soldier lads march by,
Sneak home and pray you'll never know
The hell where youth and laughter go.

~ Siegfried Sassoon

PROLOGUE

April 1917

We were called together a few hours after Wilson asked Congress to declare war. Our editor, a dyspeptic runt of a creature, half-drunk most of the time (all drunk the rest, my colleagues added with annoying frequency– annoying because as there was no evidence to the contrary, it was simply redundant) decided our readership would be fascinated with filler pieces exploring local connections and impact of what was sure to be Congress' affirmation - when they got around to it.

Crammed in a smoke filled, body heat hot conference room the size of a closet we squirmed while he staccatoed ideas with the confidence of a man utterly aware, and at peace with, the fact that while his position may have demanded attention his presence cultivated contempt and gulped-down derision. Ideas flowed fast, furious from his tobacco stained lips, some would have been hackneyed during the McKinley administration, some were vaguely viable, all promised to be a pain in the ass and reeked of make-work while the real news of the day was handled by the wire services

We traded raised eyebrows, knowing looks, rolled eyes, suppressed grins and yawns, played with our pencils, and internally tried to gauge who would be assigned what and how long it would take to polish off and get back to real reporting or our homes and/or local taverns. I was on the verge of dozing off when he got to the last of the interminable items.

"I wanta' interview with a Civil War veteran - an' not a fucking drummer boy who was fourteen at Appomattox, an' didn't see shit. A real soldier, a hero, if you can dig one up —"

"Should we take that literally there, Lindy?" Harrison, our elder, as avuncular as he was sarcastic, crowed with hope.

"Huh?" The wary reply.

"Jesus Christ, Boss," O'Riordan, free to fully exhibit exacerbation now that Harrison had broken the silence – the only condition by which he would speak - hoarsed out, "your hero hafta' be in his eighties."

"So what?" Lindy was genuinely perplexed, "You think all eighty year olds are senile?"

"Actually, yeah."

"Ignorant snot," Lindy hissed a time worn epithet, "listen, you guys go through the rolls –"

"What rolls?" Harrison demanded.

"The rolls, wherever, whatever, go to the Old Soldier's Home in Rocky Hill, just get me a distinguished, cognizant vet for one a you to interview, and get him yesterday."

That was it, as was his wont he was not going to elaborate, he was not going to listen to more discussion, never mind questions, he was not going to be dissuaded. We had no choice but to indulge. The ensuing research was convoluted, involved, and, above all, tedious. Two-thirty a.m., we had our answer - 'Hanlin, Wm, 21st Conn. Vol. Rgmt' was the highest ranked Connecticut officer alive and in state. Most likely, that is, for tedium seldom equates thoroughness and most certainly did not in our case.

There was both consternation and hope with the discovery. Consternation in that Hanlin lived in the tiny village of Norfolk, deep in the north-central hills, a miserable day trip from Hartford; hope that the ever parsimonious Lindy would take one look at our terrifying prophecies of immense expense accounts and settle for someone further down the list – the aforementioned and discounted former drummer boy, sixteen at Five Forks, living in Newington, a short hop away.

That hope faded and died a quiet death with the look on his face when he heard the result of our late night, numbingly dull search. "So, it's Hanlin, eh?" He asked, rhetorically, surveying our saddening faces, "Thought it might be …. Well, one a you is going up there to see him," he smiled savagely, feasting off the misery

ii

he was about to inflict on one of his crew, "Draw lots, whatever, lemme know who's up," he took a moment to look each of us in the general direction of the eye for a heartbeat before snarling, "Whoever goes, you give it your best effort – hear me?" He did not wait for our reactions, spun unsteadily on his heels and tottered off to his standing 9:30 am date with the contents of his desk's lower right hand drawer.

Straws it was and I truncated all suspense going first and pulling the short one. I was the youngest in the room, by far, and had more than a sneaking suspicion I had been cheated. A few minutes later, still pondering that possibility, I entered the peppermint fragrance of Lindy's office, stood before his desk, an expense request for a car and draw limply hanging from my fingertips, and stared into his red, rheumy eyes.

"You volunteer or draw the short straw?" Drunk or half-drunk, his eyes always grabbed mine and there was no denying the naked intelligence behind his.

"Short straw."

"O'Riordan run it?"

"Yes."

"They set you up, he cheats."

"I figured," I mumbled, always great to have the feeling one has been cheated verified by a man so besotted his socks never matched.

"But you're going to put up with it anyway?"

"I am."

"Well, could be your lucky day, then," he brightened, inasmuch he was capable, "if you have any proper newspaper instincts, that is."

No real response possible on that score considering I had worked for the man for six years and written a few hundred articles, I gritted out a "Sir?"

"You get Hanlin to talk to you, who knows where it will end up," he smiled a half-cocked strangely wistful grimace, "'cause the man's got a lot to say, if he'll only say it before he dies."

With that I helped myself to the tattered, tobacco stained chair reserved for senior staff or those who had broken a big one, he started to say something – undoubtedly about the sudden lack of protocol – until I said, "You know him." He blinked the answer, I suppressed 'how's that for newspaper instincts you drunken bastard?'

"Knew," a sigh corrected the tense, "thought he was alive, didn't know for sure, but we woudda' run his obit in a prominent place."

"So this whole thing's a come-on, isn't it?" I leaned back, the chair creaked a protest, Lindy looked to the transom for his answer.

"Whaz' a come-on?"

"Old vet talks about America's new war, spouts all sorts of patriotic vitriol while reminding us his generation was a thousand times tougher than ours … that kind of come-on… you've got something else in mind with this guy, right?"

Lindy regarded me with what a more secure man would take as fleeting respect before answering, "First a all, his generation was a hell of a lot tougher than yours, second, he's the last guy in the world who'll spout patriotic anything," he considered his jagged, yellowed fingernails, "The story's legit, tho', good reading with all this patriotic shit flying about." He made a move to gnaw on a cuticle, thought better of it with an audience present.

"But?"

A short chuckle, "But, yeah, there could be more with this one, lots more, actually," he glanced at his drawer, "lotta' people thought he'd be governor afta' the war, there was a scandal late sixties early seventies, somewhere 'round there, and he faded away. Took a lotta' answers with him, that I know."

"How?"

"How what?"

"How do you know?"

"Never fucking mind," spat with decent muzzle velocity.

"Fine," I spat back, too quickly.

"Fine is right, you stay outta' the morgue," he accurately read my mind, "For your own good, you go up there thinkin' you know something – which you won't, no matter what you might read –

and you'll come back with nothing. The man was a great trial lawyer, he'll eat you alive."

"Alright," said with little enthusiasm.

"Bullshit, alright, I'll be calling the morgue right now to let them know you're taboo until the story's filed, now go see Hanlin," he waved for my paperwork, I leaned over, dropped them on the rounded pile of clutter that was his desktop, "and for fuck's sake, don't tell him you work for me."

"Why?"

"Out!"

◊

By next morning the Senate passed Wilson's resolution despite Senator LaFoyette's courageous, politically foolhardy, two hour soliloquy against war. The House due to vote in hours; the country officially to be at war by the end of daylight; I chugged up the road to Winsted in a cold, sporadic rain-sleet (or sleet-rain depending on the elevation), the exact, perfect, amount to make it completely miserable without giving me excuse to stop, or better yet abort.

I made it up Connecticut's highest hill, slid down to the glen below and into Norfolk, a normally

Norfolk CT, 1917

charming village little changed over the past hundred years or more, now gray, cold, wet, and made infinitely worse with my mood. The house was easy to find, right on the trim green, a white (of course) Colonial off a long walkway through a wide patch of neat, dead grass. A discreet, brass nameplate by the door confirmed, 'William Hanlin, Attorney at Law'.

Two steps up the three stepped stairs, the door opened and a man not nearly as elderly appearing as I expected stood in the

V

doorway. He was tall - three, four inches taller than my five foot eight - large shouldered despite whatever age he was, closed cropped gray-white hair speckled with flecks of reddish brown. Clean shaven - a surprise, one always expected Civil War Veterans to sport prodigiously overgrown beards - his blue eyes were sharp, proving his faculties were intact. Under errant wisps of the fine, silken hair of the ancient, high over the left temple, a pucker of prune like, faintly bluish, relief map like skin a half-dollar in diameter, veiled and unveiled in the gentle breeze.

I stood stock still, momentarily taken aback: I had not announced my visit and yet he stood in the doorway as if awaiting me. Worse, I had expected an ursine, gnarled, little old man happy to be getting some long overdue attention and was instead being received by anything but; my preconceptions, the ban of my reporting existence (if I were forced to be totally honest), were eviscerated before my first words.

He made it easy, though, with the greeting of a man comfortable with himself. I introduced myself simply as from *The Courant*, a fact he accepted without comment, as if I were there to renew his subscription. He shook my hand, barely glanced at my notebook, and led me into and through his hundred and fifty year old home. He limped noticeably – painful looking even at a casual glance – all the way to the study in the rear of the house.

I was awed, almost intimidated, by the elegance of the room: two walls floor-to-ceilinged with overflowing bookcases, roaring fire in a stone fireplace bigger than the car I had come up in; a mahogany partner's desk illuminated by a low burning Tiffany lamp piled high with papers and files dominated the center of the room. Impressive as that was, it was the wall behind the desk that drew me in, captured my immediate, tunnel-vision attention: the entire area was covered with framed photographs, maps, letters, drawings, more, so close together, of such diversity of shape, color, size, it was kaleidoscopic.

I was inexorably drawn to it. William – he scolded me into using his first name – bade me leave to inspect, and, with audible relief sat, hard, behind his desk, leaned back, and bemusedly watched me … explore.

Which I did, with propriety-tinged abandon, carrying on a running commentary that William responded to with polite measure:

"That's the 21st Connecticut?"

"July, 'Sixty-one, just about where the Statehouse stands now."

"And below, who are they?"

"Look at the faces and tell me."

Long pause, the light was, after all, dim, "Jesus ...."

"Exactly," he muttered, picked up a battered file, began to sort through papers.

Later, over a plainly framed, fading photograph.

"Is that you with –"

"Yes, better days for both of us, I think."

At a beautifully framed, large, crumpled, stained onion-skinned telegram I blurted, "This can't be the original."

"Certainly is."

"Shouldn't it be somewhere... I don't know, safe?"

"It is somewhere safe."

I was at the wall for a half an hour, at least, while William indulged me with half-answers and guileful evasions, it was like trying to pin down a live eel in an oil barrel. It ended, though, when I moved toward a column of pen and ink profiles of beautiful young women along the far side of the wall.

I was a sidestep away when William, in an altogether different voice, one that did so much command as expect obedience said, "Not now, let's see how well we get on, first, then, who knows."

If he meant to intrigue me, further, it worked. I took a seat on an overstuffed, ancient, Chesterfield in front of his desk, and mortifyingly stuttered, "Yyyou, must be wondering why I'm, well, ah ... here."

"Had crossed my mind," slow smile that never neared his eyes, "tell me, you like books?"

"Of course I do," I replied in surprise.

"Convince me," another order, despite the reasonableness of the tone, but an order I was more than happy to comply with. I launched into a free ranging, completely disorganized, at times fumbling, dissertation on a few of my favorite authors. I was saved a bumbling soliloquy when he joined me and we embarked on a marvelous discussion on Twain, Zola, Tolstoy, dozens more that lasted until I became aware of the early spring sun setting behind the Litchfield Hills.

William noticed as well, stopped abruptly, and simply stared at me for the few seconds it took before I, without hesitation or artifice, told him everything, including my editor's name and his demand for anonymity – two facts he took with aplomb, tainted, perhaps, with a dollop of contempt – though that could have been me.

Done, he studied me for long seconds, then, in a soft, magnanimous voice, "Well, let's get the nation-goes-to war horseshit out of the way first, shall we?"

"First?" I was somewhat baffled

"First."

With that, as if he had been writing puff pieces for years, he led me through a quick, perfectly professional interview that avoided jingoism while setting just the proper tone of cautious optimism and support for the fighting man. He smiled at our mutual fatuousness when 'we' finished, then made the offer that changed my life: "write my story".

Like that. No preamble, as if he conjured the idea out of the air. He followed with a concise, so concise it sounded long rehearsed, explanation that it 'might well' be time for him to tell it, in detail. That was it, an unexpected offer dazzling in its promise and perplexing in it being offered to a man he had known for a few hours.

I moved to make reply, was stopped by a long, thin, age spotted hand, "No answer now," he said kindly, "tell the prick you work for you got the story, go to the archives, study up, then let me know if you want to do this. Door's always open, don't phone, I hate the thing."

He escorted me to the door, I took every step in numbness, mind areel with calculations, wonderment. At the front door, he offered his hand, I took it expecting a quick shake, instead he squeezed with mystifying strength, held my eye in a cold-blue gaze and answered my unspoken question, "The piece you did on the

Red Sox pitcher last fall, the Ruth kid – you showed real humanity ... pretty damn rare ... now."

I was released and dismissed in one motion, the door shut against the now steady rain before I reached the bottom of the stairs.

◊

I was back in three days, would have been sooner but at some point I had to sleep for a solid four or five hours. I borrowed a car and drove up on my own dime after begging off work with feigned illness and concern for the well-being of my co-workers. I had spent all my waking hours in the morgue and would have run back to Norfolk if I had to, such were my findings.

This time there were no preambles or pleasantly idle talk. We retired directly to the study where a fetching young woman with radiant red hair appeared with a tray of coffee and sandwiches, fussed over William with great affection, and retired, unintroduced.

William started as she gently closed the door. He would tell his story, in full, to me, at our mutual convenience. He would tell it his way – without interruption. Over the years he had written down long, unconnected narratives, he would use them as an outline as he went along, I was free to take them when he finished. For my part, I could come whenever I could and listen, trusting he would explain it all at his pace. For his reasons. I was not to interrupt, I was not to ask for clarification or explanation, it would come – or I was free to consult with the Official Records of the War of the Rebellion, all 53 volumes of it. It was, he iterated and reiterated, the first time he had spoken of most everything he had to tell me; some of it was going to be intensely personal, painful in fact ... it had to come as it came. Later, we could discuss. At length.

There was one more condition and it was his most ardent. If I was in, I was in all the way; if I was going to tell the story, I was going to tell it all. Without amendment, comment, expurgation, censure. Period.

I agreed as he stated the terms. I could do little else and he knew it. We shook on it there and then. Knowing I was going to be drafted in any event, I quit the paper, moved into his attic and spent the next four and one half months in William's company … listening. Months I would trade for nothing for so many reasons.

J.A.W.
Norfolk, CT

BOOK I: THE BODIES

It was delightful to share in the heroic sentiment of the time,
and to feel that I had a country —
a consciousness which seemed to make me young again.

~Nathaniel Hawthorne

1

Hartford, Connecticut
April 12, 1861

The girl and the country died the same day. That may sound prosaic or seem a poor attempt at Dickensian grandiosity, might well evoke Edward Bulwer-Lytton, I do not much care – it would not make it any less true.

It started with the girl. She was nude, grotesquely – yet precisely – splayed under the shadow of a headboard so huge, so baroque it made the petite, pale body below tinier, more forlorn, more ... broken. She was young, maybe twenty, violated in every manner and cut in the fourteen places I could count without touching. I knew with the confidence of previous experience we would find another fourteen when she was turned over.

The wounds were obscenely, clinically clear for not a smudge, drop, or faint suggestion of blood marred her alabaster skin. The sheets under her were unwrinkled, tucked in squarely and eggshell blue except where tinged with blood, a dark edging of rust brown outlining white flesh. Not as much blood as I would have expected, a fact that may have been attributed to the opulence of the bedding employed by the exclusive brothel I stood in – for the first time.

She was almost identical to the three other corpses my investigator, Osgood, and I had attended to since Election Day. Young women pretty even in death, cleaned, and left interred in luxurious surroundings. The major difference this day: the body had been found by chance, we had not been directed to it by an infuriatingly articulate note.

Three hours into the morning, I leaned against an open window and watched in silence and relative impotence while Osgood moved slowly around the ark of a bed. His hard, unblinking black eyes registered every detail while his hands methodically, delicately, inspected the body. Not a sound in the room, we seldom spoke while he performed his specialized duties, now, with four identical bodies in five months, there was little to say in any case.

I had performed, more than adequately, one of my two primary duties hours earlier when I cleared out the gaggle of Hartford cops who had rushed to the call on Asylum Hill to jam in around the corpse. My jokes, threats, subtle touches, and unsubtle elbow left Osgood unencumbered to work while sparing the gawking flat footers utter destruction from his obsidian eyes the, inevitable, moment one of them offered a comment or, infinitely worse, observation.

Osgood took no notes, had no need, he could recite the details of any crime scene accurately upon request. Better still, for my purposes, he could draw it from memory with an expertise that would elicit envy from the illustrators at *Harpers*. I knew of no time limit to either talent.

The scene well in hand, there was one remaining task to perform that unhappy morning and she was pacing as obviously as possible in the hallway outside the bedroom door. Madam Petrovsky, the proprietress, waiting to give a statement. Tall, regal, competent in every sense of the word, she was by any measure the most successful woman in the state. Aside, perhaps, Harriet Beecher Stowe, she was probably the most successful woman in New England.

A woman to be dealt with tactfully, if indeed one had no way to avoid her in the first place. Mishandled she was a screeching halt to the career of anyone not of her social standing – a standing shared by less than thirty men in Connecticut, Osgood and I most emphatically not among their number. With the body discovered at her house at six-thirty on a Friday morning, avoidance was not, regrettably, an option. Interviewing the good Madam had to be done as a matter of course despite the more than evident pitfalls and that task fell to me and me alone through stature and by nature. Osgood was a great many things, tactful was nowhere on the list.

I was less than eager to get to it and would gladly have tarried all morning at my comfortable post had not Osgood begun a series of 'why-are-you-still-there' glares. On the fourth such challenge, that one accompanied by a thorough throat clearing, I pushed off the sill and crept toward the door. I loitered there for a moment swallowing trepidation, let out an audible groan that intensified Osgood's glare, and stepped out into the devil's lair.

Two steps in Petrovsky, her back to me, stopped as if sensing prey. She pirouetted gracefully and stood stock still projecting the aura she had been kept waiting – which indeed, she had, and if I had had my way, would still be. I stood like an idiot until it occurred to me *I* was required to cross the gulf between us. I did so, acutely aware with each step that although in her late forties, my senior by at least a dozen years, she was stunning.

Unfettered brunette hair cascaded around the sharp, clear features of a face of classic beauty, dominated by sharp nose and perfect mouth. Shallow lines accentuated her crystalline azure eyes, adding to the overall effect in an unexpected and entirely pleasing manner. Those pretty, deadly cool eyes were, at least momentarily, reassuringly benign.

"Madame Petrovsky," I started, immediately distracted – despite the fact I stood just over six foot two and was inured, if not always comfortable with the fact I loomed over most contemporaries, she was perilously close to eye level, "I'm —"

"State's Attorney Hanlin," she interrupted, her voice ripe with silky knowledge, "please call me Olga."

"William," I replied by rote. In something akin to abject terror, I saw she was standing under a startling realistic oil of a nude reclining. I fought to regain eye contact and feign calm, "while I appreciate the promotion, it's Assistant State's Attorney, so —"

"So I am a tad premature, William,' she unleashed a knee buckling smile, "but we all know it's only a matter of time, isn't it?" That last accompanied by her right hand exerting brief yet compelling pressure on my left forearm.

While I mulled over the many implications of the 'we all' my eyes, entirely of their own volition, strayed to the dangling nude, now my personal sword of Damocles. I fought to pull them away, concentrated on Olga's patrician nose, focused on the sharp, sensual point, breathed evenly, knew I would not stray again. And did. She noticed.

"You like the portrait?" She asked in an insinuating tone that was far from unpleasant.

"It's ... beautiful," it occurred to me, too late to help in any way, that she had purposely positioned herself below it.

"You have good taste, William, it's a —"

"Thomas Cole," my turn to interrupt, a fact that did not go unregistered,

"You know his work?" She marveled, I took it as a general comment on her opinion of civil servants.

"That and I can read," I proudly pointed to the lower right hand corner, safely away from the incriminating details – there were towns in Connecticut that would still pillar one for displaying such an anatomically correct work of art, "I'll wager it was painted in 'forty."

Her laugh was delightful and as light as air, "Well done."

"I thought," I said, showing off for the pretty lady now, "he only did landscapes?"

"With some rather private commission work as well," something clicked behind eyes that were not sharing in the quick smile she bequeathed me, "more of a favor, really, for a good ... friend." She stared, left eyebrow minutely arched, waiting for my comprehension.

Which was longer in arriving than it should have been, "It's you," I kept the exclamation point to myself.

"I am sorry to think it so long ago you do not recognize me," She answered with measure.

"To tell the truth, Olga" I said sheepishly, "I haven't looked at the face yet."

This time the laugh was deep, lusty, and accompanied by a painful punch to my shoulder. She laughed long enough for me to not so surreptitiously study the beautiful face above the perfect breasts. Unmistakably Olga. Furtively, I hoped, I wondered how much of the Venus-like body survived under the morning's conservative, high-necked dress.

Olga recovered, pointed to a settee down the hallway, safely under a seascape, "Well, William, I suppose we should get to it."

I followed her, our footsteps muffled by a Persian rug that cost more than the combined annual salaries of the six people who worked for me. She insinuated herself into a corner, I blundered onto the opposite end, teetering on the silky edge. Thinking our foreplay at an end and reasonably sure I would not slide off, I started, "I take it she was not one of yours?"

Even before she snapped, "Of course not!" I knew I had erred, grievously.

"I've offended you," was out before she finished.

She nodded curtly, "I would not be sitting here calmly," her voice crystallized into ice, "had it been one of my ... associates."

I met her gaze for an uncomfortable moment before intoning, "Most women wouldn't be sitting calmly anywhere after finding a body, regardless of their familiarity with the deceased," that said with a cool I did not feel.

She regarded me for a heartbeat or two before stating the obvious, "I am not most women."

"So I have noticed."

"As I have noticed you have not apologized for the slur."

"I apologize for my error," I tendered, her eyes noted the change of noun.

She made me squirm through a significant silence, finally nodded solemnly, "Accepted, you would not know any better," she saw my look, hastened to add, "not being a client, of course."

"Of course."

"For we are a family here."

"Of course."

"I have no idea who she is ... was . . . pretty girl," she sighed, looked up at the seascape, "first time I saw her was like that, when I walked in this morning."

"You found her?"

"Yes," a nod that could be taken for cautious, "would not have if the door had not been wide open."

"Why's that?"

"The doors are closed at the end of business; they certainly were when I walked through last night."

"How late was that?"

"Just after midnight, early nights for us, but then Thursdays are slow. Particularly so yesterday."

"All your clients at the Republican gala for Buckingham?" I hazarded.

"Weren't you?"

"I am neither a Republican, nor do I travel in the same circles as our Governor."

"You are a Democrat?" She startled.

"You make that sound like a disease."

"Right now I would say it is," she astutely, almost kindly, pointed out.

I smiled thinly, "For the record, I am a member of no party."

"Curious."

I answered her arched eyebrows, aware that while no explanation was required, one was certainly expected, "At present, I find myself with an aversion to fanaticism in all its forms."

"Curiouser."

Intent on maintaining some semblance of control over the discussion, I returned to the matter at hand, "So, you closed at midnight, woke at six-thirty, did a tour around the house, discovered the open door and walked into ... that?"

"Yes."

I mulled that over for a good ten seconds while she studied her perfectly manicured fingernails, "You found her?"

"As I stated," she threw with a whisper of suspicion, "why do you ask again?"

"It's just that now I'm curious."

"Are you?" An altogether different smile flicked across her face, "Then ask."

"It's more of an observation, really."

"Then observe."

"When I arrived this morning I had to wade through a sea of black just to get a glimpse of the body."

"And?" It was not the good kind of 'and?'

"There were Hartford cops ten deep in there, men with no chance of ever getting in here, all reveling in the moment."

She shook her great mane at the foolishness of the common man, pushed deeper into the corner of the settee, and fixed me with a gaze that could in no way be described as benevolent, "So what, William?"

"So," I took a deep breath, plunged in where circumspect public employees interested in career advancement fear to tread, "with you discovering the body I would have thought that by the time I got here the only one in the room would have been the Police Commissioner, Mayor, Secretary of State, anyone but a bunch of gawking cretins."

With narrowed eyes and slightly gritted teeth she iced, "I sent a maid, she panicked and ran into the Asylum Street station instead of carrying out my instructions."

"Which were?"

"Not carried out," her eyes found mine and bored in, "I am concerned with your tone William, after all no one in this house could possibly be suspected."

"No?" I affected to smile, it died an early death.

"No, first there is the matter of all that semen," she said almost gleefully.

"There is that," I agreed tiredly, sensed what was coming.

"And, of course, we have alibis for the other murders, as well."

I nodded, examined a small paper cut on my left index finger, "There are, maybe, three people in the city that know about the murders, Olga."

"Really? Huh," She lost ten years, at least, toying with me, "I'll bet there were no police at the other scenes - just you and your friend in there . . . right?"

"Right."

"Because you were directed to the sites by notes?"

"Yes."

"Get a note this morning?"

"No," I sighed, "it's early, maybe he made a mistake this time."

"Leaving the door open," some of the chill left her eyes, "she was found too early."

"Exactly," I said distractedly, "Who told you about the murders, Olga?"

"I believe you have a one in three chance of answering that yourself," she beamed.

I shook my head in open admiration, "At least tell me who has access to the house at night."

"Outside of the occasional sleep-over –very expensive," she winked, "no one who does not live here. Overnight guests are locked in."

"No one last night, of course."

"No one."

"Any clients with keys?" I asked with hope.

"God, no!" She yelped in a highly becoming manner, "We would have randy politicians and the like running through here all hours looking for unbilled liaisons."

I made some kind of sympathetic noise in commiseration with the trials of running one's own business, "I don't suppose anyone knocked on your door in the wee hours carrying a body over his shoulder seeking sanctuary?"

"Sorry, no," she shook her head in what was either amusement or disgust looked down the hall, "Do you think she was dead when he put her here?"

"I'm thinking no," I said absently, following her look. The same question had been rattling inside my head since I walked into the room, "but there's not all that much blood, so I couldn't say for sure."

"Seemed like a lot to me," she averred without emotion.

"You'd be surprised how much blood is in the human body."

"And you are not?"

I shrugged, smirked uncomfortably, she accepted my response without expression, "I have to believe if she were killed like ... that," her expression did not match the stutter, "someone would have heard something."

"Some people are heavy sleepers, especially after ..."

"Men after," she allowed a laugh to exist for a brief moment in time, "we're all light sleepers – comes with the profession – no one in this house heard a thing last night."

"Aren't these rooms ..." I trailed off.

"Aren't my rooms what?"

"Well, I ... ah, assumed ... well, oak doors, thick walls, heavy bed hangings ... seems – to me –it's designed to contain the, ah, noises that emanate..." feeling the fool, I dropped it.

She did not, "Normal, ah, noises from our normal course of business," she mocked with a mischievous glint, "but screams and ... whatever, I think not." She uncoiled, stood, "but why speculate ... wait here," she commanded and glided down the hall.

I watched her go without comment, made no move to get up –I saw no need to warn her of Osgood's presence for precisely the same reason I saw no need to warn him of her approach. Instead, I sat and tried, in vain considering my impossible angle, to make out the details of the portrait down the hall. With great difficulty and self-congratulations on my iron discipline, I resisted the impulse to walk over and give it the consideration due a work of art.

The urge was further blunted when the bedroom door gently closed. A short minute later a series of muted grunts, moans, yips, wails, and screams of varying intensities and lengths wafted down the hallway. They receded, stopped, the door reopened and Olga floated back to me.

"Hear anything?" She asked lightly.

"On and off, how loud were you yelling?"

"Rather louder than one would in the act of sex," she glowed, "softer, I would guess, than one being stabbed. Having only experienced one of the two, it is only a guess, mind you," she nestled into her corner, eyes half veiled, my face squarely in her crosshairs, suddenly all allure and come-hitherness. I was smart (lucky?) enough to recognize that, in a pinch, when it really mattered, that recognition would do me no good whatever.

"Regardless," I managed not to stutter, "I heard you from here," I observed.

"You did?" She perkily asked, with bewildering interest.

"I did."

"Well, then" she smiled a smile of pure avarice, "there are clients I could charge just to sit here for an hour an evening."

"There are?"

"You would be surprised what men will pay for," she purred.

"No doubt," I smiled meekly, rose, "I need to speak with Osgood for a moment, if you will excuse me."

"Certainly," she sang out. I felt her eyes on me with every step, I stared intently at an inoffensive vase at the end of the hallway lest I glance at the beaconing nude. William Hanlin as Ulysses lashed to the mast.

I was right under it when Olga's voice rang down the hall, "William?"

I turned, eyes on the rug, "Yes, Olga."

"I hope my manner does not offend you."

"Why would it?" I asked in all sincerity, "I find it refreshing."

"Why thank you."

I avoided the oil, entered the bedroom to Osgood's steely glare – the combined residue of two unprecedented, unthinkable interruptions in the space of minutes. He turned it off, returned to his inspection of the body, I breathed easier without those twin searchlights of malevolence leveled at me.

"How loud did Madam yell? I asked, quietly.

"Ran the gamut, high, low, loud, soft," he did not pause or look up, "quite a woman, that," he nodded toward the hallway, "comes in, introduces herself, scouts out a spot on the bed without blood on it, sits down, lays back, starts making noises?"

"She take the time to explain her behavior?"

"No . . . women like Olga are not one's to offer explanation – but, I figured it out."

"Shock you?" I asked with hope.

He moved his head just enough to insure I saw the look of utter derision, "Unlike you, I am quite used to beautiful women making loud noises in bed next to me."

"You're an astoundingly unfunny man," I uttered a well-worn mantra, slowly surveyed the room once again. Despite the wide open windows the musty-rust smell of blood lingered. The girl's eyes were still open.

"Osgood —"

"I know, I'll shut them in a minute."

"Sorry."

"No matter," he waved it away.

"Anyway," I moved to a window, stared at an ancient maple that showed no signs of spring, "I heard Olga pretty clearly down the hallway."

"I should think you would have heard part of it down by the docks," he growled, gently touched the cold flesh about the mouth, "but I get the point." I watched his movements, deft, sure, and it hit me, for the hundredth time that long, long morning, she had been very pretty. As had they all. In different ways.

"Any sign of a gag?" I wondered aloud.

"Hard to tell, no bruising ... yet," he answered with gruffness, "we'll see in a few days."

I nodded, Osgood had noticed over the years that corpses bruised after death. Neither of us could interest anyone in conducting studies to determine how best to utilize that knowledge. The response was unvaryingly the same: murders were committed by friends, spouses, siblings, and/or off spring... how hard were they to solve when all one needed was a family tree?

"Wrists? Ankles?" I added.

"Not a mark."

"Think she walked in here?"

"That require an answer?"

"No, not really," I sighed, "gagged, maybe, but not further restrained," I summed up our total knowledge to date.

"Appears so."

"Drugged?" I asked as the idea hit me.

"Drugged?" He repeated with an edge.

"Drugged," I nodded.

Osgood leaned close, nose inches from the dead girl's mouth. He sniffed loudly, met my eyes and shrugged, "It would put our man in a new light."

"Would indeed," I agreed, "Is it me, or is there not all that much blood on the bed?"

"It's not you," he looked up, "what are you thinking?"

"He carried her here, maybe gagged, certainly sufficiently incapacitated that her mobility was not a concern."

"Which would mean what?"

"I think we may have another crime scene – where he started – before finishing her off in the lap of luxury."

"Again."

"Again," I agreed, "man likes opulent surroundings. We need to rethink the other murders, they may have started in the same spot, finished off in another."

"Does not seem like too big a leap to make, but how's that help us?"

"There may be a common site – where he starts- find it, we find him," I was talking more for my benefit, a verbal habit of reasoning things out I had had since childhood and one Osgood was long inured to, "you know, moving a half dead, nude, bleeding body through our sleepy town has to add to his risk of —"

"Catching cold, pulling a muscle?"

"Getting caught," I snapped.

"Strange way of thinking," he stopped working, "focusing on his fucking up rather than our finding him before he kills off half the female population of Hartford."

"I'll take any way of nailing the bastard," I confessed, "he fucked up this time – albeit slightly – maybe it's a sign he's getting sloppy."

"You don't believe that," he reached over, gently closed the girl's eyes, "I just hope he sends his next note too early and we shoot him in the act – save unnecessary complications."

"Like a prolonged and well attended trial."

"Exactly."

My response died in my throat when Olga sailed into the room. Her eyes took in the corpse for a heartbeat with nary a flicker, "I thought we could finish our conversation here, William," she announced in a voice that did little to invite dissent.

"Sorry I abandoned you," I muttered without thought, though it was obviously the response she was looking for.

"It's fine," her posture indicated otherwise, "I am sure you have much to discuss."

I nodded, "Whose room is this Olga?"

"No one's, it's solely for entertaining."

"Who would know that?" I asked, already knowing.

"Clients," her terse confirmation.

"And clients," I began to an icy blast from her narrowed eyes. Osgood, my political litmus paper, loudly cleared his throat, "know that Thursday's are traditionally slow."

"Yes ... William," her voice was as flat as a chopping block, "although any fool would know we would be empty with the

Republican's throwing a party."

"You don't have a single Democrat?" I had to ask.

"Find me one in this state with influence above that of street cleaner right now and I'll consider him," she shook her head ruefully, "they have gone the way of the Know Nothings."

"Had a lot of them?"

"At first, but they were so consumed with the immigration issue they could not keep it up . . . it became a mutually frustrating relationship."

"So, the —"

"We have the few who joined the Republicans – something about abolition hardened them," she smiled wickedly, "When John Brown took Harper's Ferry they were lined ten deep downstairs."

I chuckled dutifully, plunged back into harm's way with single minded abandon, "And your client list," her smile, indeed her face, froze with the last two words. The frog in Osgood's throat worsened, "is, what, a few hundred?"

The response came with infinite slowness, "Perhaps," said with an edge any sane man would avoid.

"I suppose their prominence requires the utmost confidentiality?" I was seldom accused of complete sanity.

"Without ... a ... doubt," she staccatoed, "and they receive it."

"I'm sure of that," I happily agreed, "and —"

"William," Osgood interrupted.

I ignored him, "That would not leave them receptive to discreet questions from a very personable State's Attorney concerning their whereabouts last night, would it?"

"Oh, William!" She laughed in what appeared to be genuine amusement, "You are adorable – if I gave you my client list in inverse order of importance you would be unemployed before you hit number five," her smile widened, "I hope you do not take that as a threat, my dear."

"No, Olga, I take it as gospel," her eyes acknowledged the complement, "tell me, if a member of your staff heard anything this morning they would have told you right away, right?"

"Surely."

"And, out of respect for you, none of them would talk to me

without your approval, right?"

"William," she throated, "you are the chief law enforcement officer –."

"Please, Olga," I truncated the civics lesson, "as a practical matter."

"In that case," her laugh reasserted itself, "of course not."

"You're telling me no one in this house saw or heard anything last night?"

"Nothing, sorry."

"It would be a waste of time then for me to speak with your staff."

"Why no," she surprised, eyes aglitter, "they are quite lovely, very bright, it would be time well spent."

"I —"

"And, if you don't mind my saying so, I think you could very much use the diversion," she patted my shoulder. Osgood suffered a consumptive coughing fit. My face reddened, I shot a glare at him that would have melted glass. He shrugged it off unapologetically.

"Well, then," I struggled to salvage my remaining dignity, "unless you have anything to add, I think we are done."

I expected her to bolt for the door to get on with the free enterprise system, instead, she stood stock still and looked slowly from Osgood to the girl and to me. She sported a look that she wished to make a comment but needed to be invited to do so.

"Olga?" I did so.

"Well," she pursed her lips as if making a hard decision, "I know you do this all the time ... and you have probably already noticed ... oh, I am probably thinking out of turn," she threw her dimples at us.

We stared for a three count before Osgood broke the silence, "Coyness does not become you, Olga," I turned in surprise tinged awe, Olga snapped her long neck around, was undoubtedly as close to slack-jawed as she was capable.

"Osgood," she rallied with a withering smirk, "I did not know you spoke in complete sentences."

"That's good, Olga," he smiled back through gritted teeth, "What do you have for us?"

"It is my ... guess," she nodded toward the body without taking her eyes off Osgood, "she's German. Hair, nipples, skin ... hips, legs that will . . . would have turned heavy in a few years. Eyes – thank you for closing them – I would look for a missing girl from the South End."

"That all, Olga?" I gaped.

She acknowledged with a half-smile that accepted the compliment while disparaging its delivery, "No, not all, she's no working girl, not with that pubic hair ... I will bet she has factory worker hands."

Osgood beamed confirmation, nodded his approval.

"You can't deduce her address - can you?" I gave it a shot, she scowled her answer. I added hastily, with proper diffidence, "Very helpful, thank you. You know your women."

"Ah, but I know men so much better," a more than appropriate Mona-Lisa-smile firmly in place.

"I find that disconcerting," I inadvertently muttered aloud.

"I should think you would," she lilted, to a renewal of Osgood's chest problems, "Are we done, gentlemen?" She held out a slim hand to prompt the correct answer.

"Yes," I took it in a firm, warm grasp.

"I hope you both," she spoke breezily, squeezed my hand harder, stared down at Osgood, "come by again under better circumstances ... anytime," then swept out of the room.

To his credit and my surprise, Osgood waited over three seconds before commenting, "You really know how to conduct an interview."

I was about to reply, nastily, when Olga's voice floated from the hallway, "Oh, and William, I expect the bed cleared and room in order by noon. Friday is a busy day."

I nodded absently to the doorframe, Osgood dissolved in laughter.

2

I paced the narrow porch outside the oppressive finery of Olga's house and basked in the cool sunlight of a perfect April morning. On the corner of a tree lined street of similar brick homes,

 bordered by high hedges and overgrown trees, hers was an island of privacy in an ocean of insurance executives. Her neighbors were prosperous, but not prosperous enough to join the elite further up the hill. Theirs to take

comfort they could hear the chimes of the clocks in the army of steeples on the crest, a distance above that could not, for them, be measured in mere yards.

I leaned against a smooth rail, let cold, dry air purge the lingering smell of blood and considered that Olga had chosen well - good house, good street, well shielded by nature and the neighbors' natural desire to climb the social ladder and, therefore, more than willing to turn a blind eye to the foibles of their social betters.

Further ruminations were interrupted when Osgood walked wordlessly past. I jogged to catch up, we walked together without acknowledgment through a cast iron gate and out into the cobblestone street where our driver and rig waited.

"Through these gates have passed generations of Hartford's, nay, New England's finest," Osgood intoned.

"No doubt", I agreed without enthusiasm, "I'm walking

downtown."

"Excellent."

"Mr. Phelps," I yelled up to our driver. He was slouched on his perch, reeling from a combination of a late night with cronies and whiskey bottles, and our outrageously early call for his services. Phelps made a subtle, barely perceptible movement indicating he was both alive and had heard, "Osgood and I are walking downtown, I have an errand for you, after which you may feel free to pursue whatever it is you … pursue when alcohol is not involved."

"Very good, Boss," he replied languidly, a temporary rasp across his normal baritone, "In tha' case I'll be a needin' a sizable advance as I'll be spendin' tha' rest of the day here."

"They prefer clients who bathe occasionally, Charlie," Osgood observed to a look of mock hurt.

"Pithy as always, Osgood – wha's the errand, Boss?"

"Get to Hartford Hospital, tell the coroner to come out immediately and remove the body … tell them to make sure they take all the linen and save it. And, Charles —"

"Boss?"

"Make sure they're aware of the address and the need to be discreet, fast, and, for once, respectful. By noon, latest."

"Christ, Boss, if it's tha' important, I'll jus' tell 'em tha' Madam ordered it an' leave ya' right outta it," he struggled to something approximating an upright position, "more impact tha' way." He flicked the reins with an exquisite movement of his wrist and was gone.

I watched the gig recede, muttered, "The man has an unmatched grasp of the political and social realities of this city."

"Does indeed," Osgood quickly agreed, "almost matches his insolence and indolence."

"Which are unparalleled."

We walked briskly watched by platoons of maids banging out rugs, sweeping porches, shouting across the short distances between homes. One by one they fell silent as we passed. Another strata of Hartford's classes: Italian, German, Irish, Hungarian, the refuse from Europe's famines and failed revolutions gainfully employed in jobs no proper Connecticut Yankee would be caught dead performing.

"They know we're not clients," Osgood doffed his hat to a red haired maid who tilted a strawberry eyebrow back and unsuccessfully stifled a smile, "else we would not be walking."

"Or out in daylight."

"No," made in something between a snort and a sigh, "I did a quick sketch upstairs, I will ink it out when we get back."

"Then dig up a Smith or a Brown who used to be a Schmidt or Braun and send them through the South Side in mufti," I added, needlessly.

"Think that will make a difference?"

"Outside chance," I tried to convince myself, "with a missing girl out there maybe people will talk."

His grunt said it all - it was an impossible task and we both knew it. Virtually the entire Hartford Police Department had joined the Know-Nothings in their heyday. While things had settled down since that brief and not so shining moment of American political history, community perceptions and enmity had not - no one with a hint of Old World in their speech, a whiff of garlic or cabbage on their clothing, would approach the law and with it the prospect of subjecting themselves to apathy. At best.

"We need to talk about the girl now?" I asked, hoping.

"No," answered flatly.

"Good, later then."'

"Much."

"How much?"

"After a few days drunk."

"Fair enough."

We crossed a remarkably lightly trafficked Asylum Street and walked along the usually serene, this day remarkably non-malodorous, Park River. Across that optimistically named stream was Hartford's sprawling, unnamed, always almost finished great park, ten years in the making. I had been told, repeatedly, the tenements that had covered the grassy hill a few hundred yards off had emitted a miasmic effluence that had made the walk impossible for anyone without a cast iron stomach or severe nasal congestion.

A few more steps before I broached a subject that merited

discussion," What did you think of Olga?"

"Much," he answered without hesitation.

Three steps before I realized he had no intention of expounding further, "That was remarkably concise."

"She's a force of nature, what more do you want?"

"She is that ... I would've loved to have met her twenty years ago."

"You could not have afforded her."

"You know that I could."

"I stand corrected," he corrected, "in that case, she would have killed you."

"You're a vicious bastard, you know that?" I asked rhetorically.

He answered anyway, "I revel in it."

I pretended to become engrossed in the flight of an early season robin, asked with studied indifference, "You happen to notice the painting by the bedroom?"

"Am I breathing?"

"Get a good look at it?"

"It could, perhaps, account for my delay joining you on the porch."

"Long look, then?"

"Not long enough," he laughed, "what is your point?"

"Long enough to sketch it?"

"You have no business entrusted with public office."

"That is extraordinarily well established," I agreed wholeheartedly, "so ... can you?"

"Was planning on starting it this evening," he snickered to my snort, "we'll work out a commission schedule later."

We moved at a good pace on uncommonly sparse sidewalks, the train station looming. It was deserted but for half a dozen or so black porters and stevedores lounging in front of the freight entrance. They were talking with great animation and gesturing of arms, hands, eyebrows, until they saw us. Immobile as one, they turned to stare.

As was my wont I stared back. I connected with an older porter, very dark skinned, close cropped salt and pepper hair, neatly trimmed beard. He nodded as if in deep thought, slowly touched his cap. I nodded back, raised my hand.

Osgood touched my arm, "There is respect there, William . . . well earned, too."

"I didn't do a thing," I said simply.

"You attempted —"

"And lost."

"You attempted," he would have none of my self-pity, "the unheard of and that's something, particularly to them.

"I tried," I muttered, "then I lost."

"As you knew you would when you started," he snapped, "and by my count, that brings your total losses to one – so quit bitching, the attempt was significant."

"You're wrong on this one," I corrected without malice, "I really did think I could nail the bastard."

"You scared the living piss out of him, not your fault the marshals stepped in."

"Pricks."

"South Carolinians," he pointed out with less venom than most north of Delaware would have employed, "though surely not acting on their own."

My shrug adequately summarized the episode: two years ago a rich, connected (I never learned how or to what extent) businessman from Charleston came to meet Samuel Colt. He came convinced Connecticut was not only indistinguishable from our radical neighbor to the northeast, but merely a fawning extension of abolitionist Massachusetts. He came grim, resigned and ready to meet Satan himself in the streets around the Colt Armory.

He found the Evil One a good deal earlier than anticipated – on his first steps on New England soil, in fact. From the unanimous accounts of the many witnesses, it went like this: The Southern gentleman never envisioned freemen porters plying their trade and, in any event, was not used to paying a black man for personal services; the porter in question – aptly named Freeman Smith, from three generations of freeborn blacks – was equally unused to being cheated out of honest wages by anyone, regardless of birthright; the gentleman expressed his opinions about the North and its less than obsequious black population quite freely, with volume; Freeman, with little, if any, tolerance for insulting language of any regional dialect - regardless of how colorful - found a blunter, more direct way to express himself; the traveler from South Carolina had even less tolerance for slurs concerning his parentage and sexual habits with one or both; Mr. Smith was restrained by innumerable conventions, including a hard earned respect for the law, from advancing the dispute beyond words; the southern gentleman was bound by innumerable conventions to exercise his autocratic privilege and employ violence as a means to a justifiable end.

The gentleman dispatched Freeman with three blows from the pocket pistol he kept for just such an emergency (he was, apparently, some sort of pistol whipping virtuoso). Smith suffered a fractured skull that left him unconscious for the better part of a week. When he miraculously awoke he had lost the use of his left arm and half his face was frozen.

A few hours after the assault, Freeman's continued existence very much in doubt, I issued a warrant for the gentleman's arrest. It was served, perhaps unintentionally on my part, by two sheriffs who by virtue of well-known membership in certain Associations despised all things Southern. They arrested him as he sat down to supper at the Goodwin Hotel ... I do not believe his subsequent treatment did anything to disavow him of his opinions of New Englanders.

I was able to hold him on attempted murder charges for all of six days, after which U.S. Marshals from Columbia appeared, habeas writs in hand, and away he went, as untouchable as if snatched by Barbary Corsairs. I got to watch him step smugly on a train while a Marshal big enough to pull the damn thing south by himself loomed over me and suggested, strongly, I stay out of South Carolina for the remainder of the century.

The event caused a stir for some weeks; Buckingham lauded my boss as a paragon of abolitionist virtue without inquiring as to whether I had consulted with him first (I had not); the newspapers had a field day twisting the story to fit their views on a myriad of national issues. The story might have had serious legs had not John Brown chosen that particular moment to listen to the voices in his head and seize the armory at Harper's Ferry. The story vanished under far more dramatic copy.

My (bitter) memories were truncated by Osgood's growl, "Stop thinking about it, it's done, he might as well be in another country."

"That may be literally true any day now," I answered. We passed the passenger's entrance – few people in evidence - and crossed into a pleasant block of upscale shops. Out of habit, I stopped in front of the Brown & Gross bookstore.

"Too bad the old bastard's not there," Osgood, reading my mind.

"I even miss the dead possum on his head," my friend and long-time denizen of the store, Gideon Welles, sported the most ridiculous wig in the annals of male baldness.

"I do not miss that," Osgood chuckled, "but I do miss his acidic wit, it is no fun reading the *Evening Press* anymore."

"Acidic – that sums him up nicely," I resumed walking," I'm not sure the paper survives without him."

"Nor I, wonder if the Navy Department survives with him."

"You've doubts?"

"Has he ever even seen the ocean, never mind dipped a crusty old toe in it?"

"Think it matters?"

"Could not hurt."

"He'll get the job done, see that the right people are hired – John Knox was a bookseller in Boston, if memory serves he did quite well as Washington's Chief of Artillery."

"Well, similar physiques, in any event," Osgood stopped, touched my forearm, "You know, it is a Friday morning, the first decent day in weeks, and I can hear our footsteps in the busiest street in the city."

I glanced for confirmation I did not need, the dress shop next door was closed – as were the stores across the street, "Where the hell is everyone?"

Osgood peered down the street, "There is a great deal of activity by the State House."

I could dimly make out figures moving rapidly toward the square defined by the confluence of a mass of wires - the one place in town literally connected to the world outside Connecticut.

"News," I spit, upped our pace.

"Big news," Osgood echoed.

We glanced at each other on the trot, "Sumter," said as one.

We raced by the Goodwin Hotel, crossed Trumbull Street, heaved up a slight rise to Main Street and stopped dead: every manner of

The Statehouse 1861

horse drawn conveyance was chaotically jammed together, abandoned, their drivers and passengers packing into the square where hats undulating like a wheat field in high wind.

Going across we made the acquaintances of a half dozen unhappy horses, each quick to express its displeasure with snot-filled snorts and non-playful nips. Across in one piece, Osgood took control of the move into the teeming mass of humanity. With my height and a fairly solid one hundred and eighty pounds and Osgood at, perhaps, five foot six, one hundred and forty pounds (fully clothed in a torrential downpour), the casual observer might find it incongruous Osgood led the way. Easily explained – I was big, Osgood radiated menace.

Osgood effortlessly cut a swathe through the mob, I followed in his wake, scanned flushed faces for acquaintances, heard our first – and only – hunch confirmed by countless intonations of 'Sumter' chanted with disturbing reverence. A reverence that could only mean one thing.

I recoiled when a still damp broadsheet smacked into my hand and Osgood nudged me toward an ancient oak in the center of the square. He cleared the bench at its base with a quick, intense scowl; we stepped up, stood with backs against smooth bark, and looked out over a sea of heads. Secure above the fray, I looked down at an extra-edition of *The Hartford Courant,*

'FORT SUMTER FIRED ON!!!!'

screamed off the masthead, the largest, blackest headline I had ever seen. Below, in type normally reserved for stories of major national import,

'Bombardment Begins at 3:30 AM!
The Flag Still Flies!'

and, slightly smaller, in type normally only employed for juicy murder trials and/or political peccadilloes,

'No Word on Anderson or the Garrison'
'All Charleston on Hand to Watch'
'Experts Say Anderson Putting up Bully Fight.'

The headlines took up half the sheet, fortunate because there was little more to relate. The 'stories' were nothing more than clever repetition of the basic facts with a dash of pure speculation and a handful of irresponsible conjecture added for spice that was not needed. Still, I marveled at reading news of an event that had occurred only eight, nine hours earlier, however sketchy.

Osgood tugged at my sleeve, yelled over the crowd noise, "What do you think?"

"It's done," I yelled back, a few upturned faces showed we had been overheard, "the rest," I brandished the broadside, "is all we're going to get until it's over."

"Over?"

"Over ... and soon."

"Over how?"

"Can only end one way, Anderson will fire back, try to keep the men safe, make a show of it for a solid twenty-four hours then surrender. The time honored routine for futile positions ... for anyone not named Travis or Roland."

Osgood nodded, whatever he was about to utter was cut off

when something hard struck my left instep and I yelped, "Goddamn it!" Pain rising, I looked down and saw the cause of my discomfort was a short, bespectacled, heavily bearded man three feet away brandishing a dark, knotty cane.

"I think that bastard hit me," I said, awed by the ridiculousness of it all.

While I stood in shock, he seized the moment, "You, sir!" his high-pitched, quivering voice cut through the steady drone of the crowd, drawing looks with every syllable, "How dare you impugn the courage of our army!"

Before I could move a muscle, Osgood leaped down forcing the little man to step back into the craning, slightly quieter crowd that bent back and allowed a clearing to form. I stepped down, made sure to keep a good distance between the interloper and my considerable temper – which was rising at the same rate as the bruise on my foot.

I took a deep breath, flicked over the inquiring stares of the onlookers and cursed, not for the first time, the fact I was, however peripherally, a public figure, "I was not aware, Sir, I had impugned the honor of anyone or anything in a conversation you were not a party to .... Sir."

Some would have taken my words and the heat under my general demeanor as a warning, some a threat, the perceptive, a promise. My anointed pest chose none of those. Instead, I inspired him to greater stridency, "But you, Sir, are speaking treason – and on this day! Regardless to whom you direct your remarks, treason it is, treason it remains."

Our amateur production of *Julius Caesar* was capturing the attention of the multitudes, those nearest backed a little further off, the oval got larger, more irregular, the more to leave space for the shedding of blood – I could feel the crowd's collective wish to see this end badly. Pure obstinacy on my part, allied with Osgood's knowing, warning looks, kept it in the realm of civility.

As for Osgood, unnoticed by all save the pickpockets in the throng he gently bumped into the man, practiced hands exploring his clothing. Done, he stepped away, smiled viciously, slowly shook his head, made a subtle motion to indicate 'he's unarmed and all yours'. Unsportingly, I hoped Osgood managed to relieve the cretin of his wallet in the process.

My response not immediately forthcoming, the beard with legs pointed a long, bony finger and emoted, "Explain your treasonous statement, sir," he took a breath, parted his overgrown, untended beard in a hideous caricature of a smile and appealed to the crowd, "All the world waits!" That received a smattering of applause sprinkled with 'well dones', he had the temerity to take a slight bow.

I stepped closer, he showed himself poorly attuned to his environment by holding his ground, "I believe," I began in a courtroom-summation voice I hoped would begin to cower him, "no, I know, it's 'All the world wonder'd'," I leaned into him, dropped my voice so only he would hear, "and if you continue to point that digit at me I will see you make a meal of it." The gap in the beard closed and he took a step back.

I straightened, made a conscious effort to keep my words measured, "I'm sorry you seem to have inferred some sort of .... defeatism in your eavesdropping," I scanned the square for a friendly face, found none among the quieting onlookers, "I merely offered the opinion that Major Anderson's defense is all the more valiant for he knows he is defending the indefensible.

"He knows better than any his position is untenable and yet he will persist as long as honor demands. To my mind, that certifies him as a most courageous man."

A ragged chorus of agreement greeted that, I had a fleeting, if foolish, hope the matter was closed. The nasty little gnome, however, perhaps impelled by the sure knowledge it was his first and only appearance in the public eye, held on like a bull terrier, " You assert," he pirouetted with a flourish, happily including the crowd in his passion play, "this brave man and valiant garrison, will be defeated by a rabble?" Asked as if I had averred the sky was green.

The crowd turned in an instant, "Yes, tell us!", "Explain yourself," more, called out in a hundred different voices, Osgood's very definitely among them..

I took a deep breath (yet again), exhaled softly, "Very well ... very well," too lowly, men craned and let me know they could not hear, I cleared my throat, "You all know Anderson left Fort

Moultrie to move to Sumter. Moultrie's less than half the size of Sumter and —"

"How do you know that?" A voice, not Osgood's at least, rang out from deep in the masses.

"I've been to both," I answered simply, loudly, to a collective gasp and something then approaching silence. My antagonist was visibly rocked – nothing like reality to put a damper on an ill-informed opinion, "Anderson doesn't have enough men to properly man Sumter's guns – not that that makes a difference as they are assaulted on three sides while they defend a fortress designed to stop incursions from the sea, the only direction they are not threatened from."

I hit my stride, began to make eye contact with those on the ragged edges of the oval – my jury – the little man had ceased to be as far as I was concerned, "Also, worse, as we know from the debates in Washington, Anderson has not been supplied since New Year's."

"That's all well and —" the troll began, spine-tingling strident now.

"Lastly," I flicked him off, dismissing him forever, "Major Anderson faces no rabble, Pierre Beauregard opposes him – a highly decorated soldier and, to boot, Anderson was his artillery instructor at West Point. He won't insult him by being anything less than ruthlessly efficient."

"You do not know —"

"But I do," I answered to the crowd, "the fort is lost, it's a moot point ... we should pray for the safe return of Anderson and his men, and prepare for what's sure to follow," with that I brushed by the bearded gnat, pushed through a sea of compliments and unappreciated thumps on the back and sought refuge in the clear.

Limping from the now shoe tightening welt, back sore, probably bruised, breath in short gasps, I broke out into blessedly open air, turned to see some lower level abolitionist hack mounting my deserted bench to start in on God's will. I enjoyed a brief moment alone, caught my breath, gave thanks I was too far away to hear the rising diatribe - redundant, in any event, as of a few hours ago, I had to believe.

Osgood stepped in beside me, "So much for perfect solitude in the crowd, eh?"

"Spare me the Emerson," I grunted, "and thanks for your support," I trailed off, mesmerized by the wild gesticulations of the ad hoc speaker.

"Just one among many," he grinned, "I must say you handled that very much like an adult."

"Thank you ... I think," the speaker-cum-charismatic was about to go into a religion fueled seizure, "you expect me to hit him?"

"Tell me you did not contemplate it."

"Not after the first minute . . . or two."

"Or about how long it took me to insure he was unarmed."

"Please," I waived him off, "by the way, did it occur to you the cane might hide a blade?"

"Harmless," he snorted, "I could only hope he would brain you with the thing."

Before I could form and deliver a suitable reply a short, plain woman, in a plain, black dress, her hair pulled back so severely I doubted she could close her eyes, plodded unattractively by passing out flyers, one of which Osgood gleefully snatched out of her plain hand.

"Look," he announced in mock surprise, "an informational tract, I wonder what it is about?"

"I'll wager," I rose to the challenge, "it is an abolitionist flyer."

"My God, sir, you are a psychic! Please, go on.

"Well, let's see," I affected effort that pretty much disavowed a lifetime around the damn things, "start with a quote from *Uncle Tom's Cabin*, then an essay proving slave owners – individually and as a class – are the Antichrist, follow with a passage from Frederick Douglass' autobiography, a mercifully short section of a Sumner speech ... and, of course, end it with a Phyllis Wheatly poem, 'some view our sable race with scornful eye' or some such shit."

"Not a fan of hers?"

"Oh, she's fine," I waved off my current misanthropy, "I grew up with her being held up as some paragon of great poetry only to find she was basically copying Milton and Pope – decent poet, not fair to make her more than she was because of what she was, what she overcame .... Ah, hell," I pushed the memories away, "how'd I do anyway?"

"Nailed everything except Sumner's speech."

"Really? What took his place?"

"John Brown's last words."

"Hebrews Nine Twenty-two?"

"And here I thought you were a pagan."

"But not ignorant . . . . am I right?"

"'Without the shedding of blood there is no remission of sin'," Osgood confirmed.

"Let's settle it with blood, nice sentiment."

"But accurate . . . as of today, at least."

I nodded, "Judging by the mood down there," I pointed back to the square, if anything it looked more crowded, "they're —"

"And the millions like them."

"Yes, we —"

"On both sides."

"You make my point for me."

"More efficiently, too," slight sneer, "this really goes only one way from here, right?"

"One way, yes."

"In that case, I do not see you continuing your courtroom duties much longer – do you?"

That stopped me dead for an instant, I had not considered the personal implications of the news, yet my answer was immediate and automatic, "No, not really."

"Then we need to make plans."

"We? How old are you?"

"Forty-six, as you fucking well know," he snapped with an irritation that arose only when his age was mentioned, a subject that always put a smile on my face, as it did now, "what does that have to do with anything?"

"Unless someone with no sense of esthetics gives you a commission, I think there's little chance you need be bothered."

"Well," he considered that for a long moment, "I do have a soft spot for rebels."

"But, not for slavery."

"There is that," he sighed with melancholy, "shame to waste a perfectly good rebellion."

"Shame," I agreed wholeheartedly.

4

The courthouse was abuzz - somehow I had expected different, either from an overdeveloped sense of decorum or in the cynical expectation the Hartford Bar was flooding the Square with thoughts of starting or bolstering political careers. Instead, the normally somber marble halls were crowded with tight groups of wool encased men excitedly sharing the news, the moment, speculation, placing blame, making threats, promising vengeance for as yet unknown harm. They did all that with an ardor that belied the fact they were each armed with one, identical, piece of information.

With no wish to join fools rushing in after the way my day had started, I avoided eye contact, weaved through the halls and barricaded myself in my book-lined offices. I hid there, Osgood in the antechamber writing up his notes, until dusk when, the courthouse mercifully clear, we left. We walked alone, footsteps echoing off the gas lighted streets to the Hartford Club and our Friday night dinner.

We ate in comfortable silence, the only patrons – some sort of rally was being held out by the Colt Levee, as our sullen waiter reminded us every chance he had. By the main course he had made it crystal clear we were infringing on what amounted to an unofficial holiday. In return for his less than effervescent company we quite willingly tortured him by ordering dessert, brandy, and cigars before taking our leave.

A full moon was rising over the Connecticut River when we reached my home. My house, the last survivor of a late-Colonial merchant's row of homes built by the men who had reaped the benefits of the pre-steam river trade. Two stories, built of mica flecked stone, slate roof, eight fireplaces, a wide, teak porch, it enjoyed an unobstructed view of the river. As well as an equally unobstructed view of the approaching wall of high, brick, cookie-cutter office buildings replicating themselves mercilessly and inexorably toward the anachronism that was my home.

Oil lamps were burning in the first floor windows, I could smell a fire, ample evidence Phelps had made it back – always something of a surprise. We stomped up to the porch, slipped into the foyer, Phelps' usual baritone rang down the hallway, "Note there for yer, Boss, 'onna table."

"Jesus, how does he do that?" I asked the portrait of Franklin over the table.

"He's at least half terrier," Osgood answered for him.

"At least," I muttered, picked up an envelope that had my name scrawled in far too ornate script:

> *Hanlin:*
>
> *With the import of today's news, the uncertainty of the immediate future, as well as the need for unity of community through these coming hours, we, the ruling board of the Hartford Blues Base Ball Club, feel it inappropriate to engage in our favorite pastime.*
>
> *We are sorry for the late notice while sure you understand, agree with, and respect the sentiment behind this.*
>
> *God Bless the United States of America.*
>
> *Yours,*
> *Robert Stately Hughes.*

I handed the note to Osgood, took a direct line to my sitting room and a decanter. I was tired, emotionally drained in any number of ways, and now I was, however irrationally, irate I was not going to be playing base ball on the first Saturday the Meadows north of town was dry enough to give it a go.

"Leave it to your friend Hughes to say in eighty words," Osgood started as he grabbed the decanter, "that which could so easily be said in three – 'tomorrow is cancelled'," he crumpled the note, tossed it into the fire, "but, of course, that way he risks us missing the breadth of his eruditeness and the depth of his intellect."

"Couldn't have that, could we?" Snifter in hand, I walked to a high backed chair in the corner, furthest from the fire and collapsed inward, slouched into smothering comfort, low lamp over my shoulder casting shadows. I rooted around a side table piled high with books and journals I was behind on before deciding this was not the time to catch up.

"Imagine," I took a sip of a particularly well healed cognac Osgood had brought back from his last trip abroad, "sitting through one of his classes at Trinity? Something particularly riveting, like logic and rhetoric?"

"I cannot," he moaned, added an extra dollop to his snifter, "I cannot look at him, never mind endure his presence," he shuffled to a chair in the opposite corner, "that neck . . . . his head gets there five minutes before the rest of him – man's a giant praying mantis."

"He does have certain insect-like qualities," I agreed.

"The way he ogles and rubs his hands together . . ." he was obviously unsatisfied with my mere agreement, "I swear to God I can see the day I'll have to shoot him and claim self-defense."

"I can guarantee you'll not be prosecuted," I assured him with alcohol fueled bravado.

"I do not imagine,' Osgood went on, he was unusually loquacious on the subject of Hughes, "he has any athletic ability . . . inasmuch any are needed for that interminable sport you enjoy so much."

"He who does not know base ball—"

"Cannot know the American mind," his voice dripped derision, "De Tocqueville only said that to confuse the hell out of the rest of the world, drive them crazy trying to figure out a senseless game . . . typical nasty Frenchman."

I rolled my eyes at the fire, "I realize that to you a sporting event is neither sporting nor an event unless someone is maimed or, better yet, killed. So, I can see you having an aversion to a beautiful, intellectual game."

"I play chess, you ass."

"In a manner," I smiled at the barb, he ignored it, "though you pretend your men are killing the other side."

"Makes it more fun, that's all," he muttered defensively.

"Uh-huh," I tentatively agreed, "Hughes does have his uses – he is an able administrator and a keen observer of our limitations and shortcomings."

"He good at it?"

"You have to ask?"

"Yes."

"Outstanding, in fact."

"That's something, anyhow," he mumbled in to his snifter, cold black eyes beamed over the rim, "though I find it hard to believe you put up with it."

"I concern myself with playing the game, not the inane, petty politics of those who cannot play."

"I believe," the snifter came down revealing first the black, drooping mustache, then the nasty smile beneath it, "you just more than adequately summed up your life."

"Thank you."

"I am not sure that was a compliment."

"Well, it probably sums up my political philosophy."

"You have no politics over which to philosophize."

"Exactly," I took a good sized, blasphemous gulp of cognac.

He did not appear as pleased as I at the rhetorical exchange, he stared for a long moment, carefully put his snifter on the table, intoned, "You need to start . . . . now."

"Start what?"

"Philosophizing – this war will change things."

"Most wars do."

"Your last war put a general in the White House."

"Sure did," I yawned, "another ran for president, a colonel became Secretary of War, hosts of congressmen, senators, I get your point."

"Do you?"

"I saw it first hand, I don't think you have to lecture me, do you?"

"On history? No," unperturbed, he merely continued to glare, "the self-preservation realities of local politics? Most definitely."

"You think that?"

"I know that."

"Then give me an example in this time of national crisis, o' great oracle of Adriaen's Landing," I reached for my like-new copy of *Bleak House*. We both knew it was an empty threat, but I felt better for the effort.

"Let's start with your Mr. Hughes," he intoned with solemnity.

"Hughes?" My surprise was real, "He's nothing more than a —"

"What does he teach at Trinity, William?" It was clear he knew the answer.

I idly thumbed through the five pound tome on my lap, then played along, "Want to tell me?"

"Rhetoric, logic, as you know," he nodded as if to a precocious pupil, "as well as history and military science."

"Great," I said amiably. I had no question Osgood was correct – he knew a great many things, however acquired, but I could not fathom his interest in Hughes.

"He is a dean of Trinity as well, is he not?"

"If you say so."

"I do."

"You know, Osgood, sitting here on a Friday night discussing Hughes is rather pathetic for us while flattering to him."

"What a pretty turn of phrase," he managed to infuse his praise with contempt, his look was either one of amusement or he had just made the decision to slit someone's throat –in almost ten years together, I still could not tell the difference, "but it will not stop me from making my point."

"What would?" I asked with hope.

"Mock away," he flicked his hand dismissively at my corner of the room, "but men like Hughes will soon find themselves in vogue —"

"Oh, please."

"No please. Proven administrators with specialized knowledge at a time when even the appearance of such knowledge is perceived as vital will be indispensable in short order."

"Very insightful," I flipped the book open to page one,

probably the hundredth time I had done so since buying the damn thing at Welles' bookstore.

"William!" I made no attempt to hide my pleasure at his irritation, "look, you will be enlisting when this is official, and —"

"Not enlisting, per se, so much as allowing myself to —"

"Oh, for fuck's sake, you will be joining up, right?"

"Yes," I said sideways, took an inordinate sip, read the first line, though I had it memorized.

"Tell me, then, how would you feel with Hughes as your commanding officer?"

A cognac fueled snort made my eyes water, before I gasped, "That's utterly ridiculous . . . . he has no training and less experience, he's —"

"A mason, a Republican, and through long standing family ties is considered a rising star of the abolitionists – sound familiar?"

"Vaguely."

"I have your attention now?"

I nodded, he continued, "This is a man who with a little battlefield experience – better yet a nice flesh wound – is a future governor."

"Of Connecticut?"

"I am not trying to amuse you —"

"Then take it as a bonus."

"I just want you thinking ahead as this thing progresses," he tilted his snifter in my general direction, "lest you walk into a situation not suitable for your talents or temperament."

"Worried about my temper?"

"Constantly," he sneered happily, "but there are greater considerations here."

"You think if I fail to promote myself I'll get lost in the shuffle, end up behind a Hughes and he'll either get me killed or take credit for my actions," I said with the authority derived from dozens of like conversations.

"Pretty much."

"You sound like my father."

"Sorry."

"Look, Osgood," I dropped my tone, it tended toward stridency whenever I spoke of my father, "this is the one time your instincts are off . . . way off. Because you think what's coming will be orderly. You think army and you conjure images of ancient regiments and long, precise, red lines."

He regarded me with stern attention, "And your army now?"

"Couldn't defeat Greenland, especially with the Southerners leaving in droves."

"You are starting from scratch."

"Pretty much . . . it will be the states who'll be charged with raising regiments for Federal service. They'll need all the professionals - professionals, Osgood, not amateurish, unbloodied college professors - they can get."

"But men like Hughes —"

"Will be exposed, the more talking he does, the more rope he'll provide to hang himself with," I smiled at the image of Hughes swinging.

"That's more like it," Osgood's mustache twittered wickedly, "my only concern, then, is to get you in front of the people who count . . . unless, of course, you are willing to do some boasting of your own for a change?"

"No need," I stifled a wide grin, "the telegrams will do it for me."

"Telegrams?" Rare puzzlement suffused Osgood's face.

"Telegrams," I enjoyed it for a long moment, "every governor has a list of West Point graduates handy, telegrams will be flying over the next few days."

"And one will be landing here."

"One?" I laughed into the dregs of my snifter, "I make the over-under three, Osgood, care to wager?"

His answer, a salute of his snifter.

.

5

By nine-thirty, Monday morning, it was clear no work was going to be attempted, never mind accomplished, under any circumstances by anyone in the judicial system. We, myself most certainly included, were suffering from a hangover of national consequence. Like everyone in Hartford – high and low born, freeman, native, immigrant, both untouchable ends of society – Osgood and I slogged to our unfinished city park at dusk Sunday, summoned by every church bell in a city rife with steeples.

Downtown Hartford

Sumter had fallen after thirty-five hours of 'intense bombardment'. Anderson made what was left of the country proud when he fired a fifty-one gun salute to the United States and paraded out of the wrecked fort, tattered flag still firmly in his possession. I could infer that Beauregard made his new country just as proud by so chivalrously allowing Anderson those honors but, for once, kept that opinion to myself.

The promise of war packed the park, great bonfires lighted the twilight, dew formed under our sodden feet, and our breathes mingled together in a low hanging cloud. Bands were in abundance involved in some unwritten contest to play 'Yankee Doodle' and 'Dixie' (not yet co-opted by our missing brethren) loudest and fastest. Fireworks burst in unpredictable, intermittent bursts, scattering celebrants when it became clear three quarters of the way through 'oohs' and 'ahs' that the glowing embers were coming straight down into their midst.

The Governor's Horse Guard, resplendent in red coats and

black dragoon hats wheeled out an ancient, glistening brass twelve pound cannon with dazzling pomp. Their subsequent fumbling of the gun, powder, tampon, leader – every possible step, really – was a source of great hilarity to everyone behind them and well expressed – if not vulgar – apprehension from everyone in a forty-five degree arc down range. I attributed their troubles to the vast variety of brews freely bestowed on them by every frenzied patriot within fifty yards. Finally, mud caked from pratfalls on the sopping sod, they managed to fire a symbolic – and I dearly hoped blank – charge southward.

Scripted speeches studiously rehearsed to appear impromptu were delivered throughout the evening by various and sundry notables and those wishing to join their ranks from an obviously hastily constructed platform. They were watched in rapt fascination. What the speakers undoubtedly took as support for the staunch prosecution of the upcoming war, the forced reunification of the nation, and the hanging of Southern blackhearts - P.G.T. Beauregard chief among them – was most assuredly morbid curiosity on the load capacity of the shaking tiers.

Deep into the night until, the speakers hoarse, spigots dry, fireworks exhausted, bands out of repertoire, the House Guard out of powder and passed out around their piece, the crowd disbursed, reeling through the park on numb, sodden, uncertain feet.

And now we paid for the night's excesses. The docket canceled, everyone migrated to the marbled great hall. For reasons I could not immediately fathom I joined them and ended up standing against a cool wall next to Judge Alexander Hamilton Crompton. Short, plump, thick, wispy white hair flying wildly whenever he moved – which was constantly – Crompton was my favorite authority figure. I could ask for no better companion to slouch next to and listen to court denizens trade incrementally creative rumors and outright invention. Crompton had a ready wit and busied himself with highly scatological refutations of each and every comment within earshot.

I listened, nodded, laughed, and grimaced along with the judge while I waited for ten o'clock and Osgood's messenger bearing the three telegrams that had arrived over the weekend – each one received with a sly smile from me and a deep scowl from Osgood. Crompton was on a roll when a commotion by the massive front doors brought a halt to conversation and several men gathered around a diminutive figure. Some frantic movements, the group broke to scan the hallway, searched faces, settled on mine, pointed, then pushed a short, gasping youth in my direction.

Down he plodded, the hall dead quiet. When he reached me, he half rasped, half shouted as if in discovery, "William Hanlin, Esquire."

"In the flesh," I replied, noted the thinness of the fool scrap in his hand.

"Telegram, sir, 'Extremely Urgent'," he announced to the assembly, every eye now riveted on the mechanics of the trade of my tip for the telegram.

The boy, emboldened by the spotlight, added, in an appalling breach of telegram etiquette, "It's from Governor John Andrew, sir!"

There was an audible snap as every head in the room turned at the mention of the fire breathing, avenging angel of the abolitionist's movement. No one save the boy moved, he pocketed the tip, skipped down the hall and out the doors leaving me the centerpiece of inspection, the fool scrap a flaming torch in my left hand. My colleagues maintained their silence but made their curiosity obvious in the very attempt to conceal it.

I stared at the telegram and realized my machinations with Osgood had been for naught, Andrew always had a superb sense of timing. A tug at my sleeve, I looked into Judge Crompton's wide, red face. It beamed bemusement and concern, "You need to be alone, William?"

"I'm fine, Judge," I mumbled, "I think I know what it's about," looked down and read:

April 15, 1861

William Hanlin, Esq.

Mass. immediately raising regiments. Have arranged for

division strength shipment Enfield Rifles, etc. from Britain. Commission Colonel readied. If acceptable, report to Warren Island for rgmt'l assignment.

This is the time for all Mass. sons to return and do their duty. God Bless the United States.

Yrs.

J. Andrew
Governor Commw'lth Mass.

I stared at the thin sheet for a long moment, while I had expected the content, it managed to stir me still.

"You alright, Hanlin?" Crompton broke my reverie.

"Yeah . . . ., Judge," I handed him the flimsy paper, studied the ceiling.

He scanned the sheet at least twice, looked at me quizzically and shouted to the galley, "Nothing doing here boys, return to mongering your rumors," he grabbed my arm, whispered, "my chambers . . . now."

I followed his short bulk to the back of the hallway and into chambers, an immense, vault-like room with a spectacular view of the Connecticut River that was as doomed as the one from my house, for the same reasons. He went to a battered, black leather, well-worn chair, and threw himself into it, 'Where the hell does that come from, Hanlin"?

"Massachusetts. . . . Your Honor," I smirked.

"I can cite you for contempt in here as easily as in my courtroom, you know."

"Sorry, Judge," I took refuge in a deep, comfortable side chair, "Andrew's reaching out to Massachusetts's West Point appointees."

Crompton stared at me for several heartbeats, a question mark formed on his white, bushy eyebrows, "Goddamn it, William, I don't know where to start . . . . . I had no idea you were from Mass . . ." he paused, indicated with a meaty hand I should fill in the blank.

"Boston."

"Boston," he chewed on that unpalatable word, "and West Point?"

"Class of Forty-six."

"Forty-six," he mulled over the implications of the year, "next you'll be telling me Andrew is your uncle or some such horseshit."

"Of course not," I said . . . too quickly.

"But, what?" Not for nothing was he the top jurist in the state.

"To be completely honest," I lied, "Andrew is a particular friend of my mother's....."

Understanding suffused Crompton's ruddy visage, "Your mother resides on Beacon Hill."

"I prefer reigns."

"Indeed," he shook his head like an English sheepdog confronted by a heard of gnus. "I should have put that together years ago, but you lack the accent".

"Thank you," I replied with ardor, his eyebrows rose to exclamation points.

"And you certainly lack your mother's political ..."

"Acumen, instincts, aspirations, zeal?" I, helpfully, offered.

"Oh, yes," he agreed with an evil little sneer, "so, you're a West Point graduate, Andrew wants you to take a regiment, and your mother is an abolitionist leader – you hiding much more, Hanlin?"

I shrugged a well-rehearsed shrug that he took with an obvious show of suspicion, "Well, I'm sure you have your reasons for keeping it to yourself, and I will, of course, respect your privacy."

"Thank you."

"Unless you feel compelled to unburden yourself to a kindly old man."

"Why, you know any?"

He blinked that away - as he did with most of my sarcasm, "People say I'm an excellent listener."

"People say that's what you're paid for, Judge."

He smiled thinly, "While I respect your right to privacy, I feel compelled to pass the news of the offer – and the reason for it – to the Governor . . . . . . you are desperately needed here, I should think."

"Fine with me."

"You'll put off responding to Andrew?"

"Certainly," I said with the sincere, complete magnanimity of a man agreeing to refrain from juggling rattlesnakes.

"I am to lunch with the Governor this afternoon —"

"Are you?" I asked with measure.

"I am," his eyes narrowed, tone now one normally reserved for a lawyer bending the rules of evidence without the opposition objecting, "I'll see to it he sends for you . . . . . quickly."

"I'll be in my office," I offered helpfully.

"I'm sure you will," said with a trace of suspicion.

"If he thinks he may need my services."

"Our Governor, my friend, would dearly like to think himself as prepared and full of piss for the cause as Andrew, he'll be eager to snatch you away ... while wondering how he missed you sitting under his nose."

"I'd say Andrew is intent on winning the war by himself – God knows he worked hard enough to get it started. . . . unless Buckingham's been tapping a secret slush fund and buying arms from the French, snatching me away is not going to do a hell of a lot."

"It'll be a start," Crompton smiled, "nice speech, though, reminds me of one I heard the other day by the Statehouse. I should have guessed listening to you then, I just attributed it to the fact you always have your head buried in a book or newspaper."

"Glad you liked it," I rose, headed for the door.

"Surprised you didn't tear the little shit's head off," he said behind me, "perhaps you are maturing."

"Doubt it," I carped over my shoulder, hit the hallway and dodged through the still jabbering crowd to my office. The antechamber was empty, Osgood sat behind my desk, feet up on my window sill.

"Guess you won't need a messenger to bring you these now," he threw three telegrams on the desk.

"Andrew came through with exquisite timing."

"And you thought he forgot you."

"I should have known better, when it comes to war

mongering, the man's the gold standard."

"I was not three steps into this place before ten people told me about the telegram and you were in Crompton's chambers."

"Great."

"He still having lunch with Buckingham?"

"Sure is."

"Nice when things work out."

6

I sat with six middle aged gentlemen, each dressed identically in dark suits, restrained vests, gold watch chains taut across growing bellies. Each of their white, manicured hands nervously kneaded a hat while they scanned everything in the room save each other's eyes. The very embodiment of men without appointments.

William Buckingham

Clocks within and without the building struck six, the door swung open, six heads craned, one could cut the hope with a knife. A balding head the size and consistency of an overripe pumpkin teetering atop an insubstantial body blinked at us from the doorway.

"Mr. Hanlin, the Governor will see you now," it spoke in a cross between a croak and a rasp. I stood, with every step I took twelve eyes tried to sever my spinal cord.

The Governor stood in front of a barn sized desk, hand extended, "Mr. Hanlin, how good of you to join us."

"An honor, Governor," his grip was surprisingly strong.

He nodded in agreement, "Been awhile, hasn't it, Counselor," he made a show of conjuring our one and only meeting out of the white ceiling, "Two years? When you tried to arrest the lout from South Carolina."

"That would be it . . . Sir," he instantly sported the 'there-I-told-you-I-remembered' look of smug satisfaction indigenous to politicians, "just before John Brown's raid."

He further acknowledged with a tilt of the head, then smiled widely, "If only, heh? If he had succeeded it would be all over by now," said wistfully with no apparent thought to the irony of supporting one insurrection while mobilizing to crush another.

He led me to a heavy, unyielding couch in front of a mammoth fireplace blazing forth hot enough to forge steel, above which hung a Trumbull portrait of, well, another Trumbull. The scale of the place was clearly designed to aid the individual in understanding one's relative standing in the matters of state.

I sat as far from the fire as possible, Buckingham took one of a pair of more comfortable looking wing chairs to my right, motioned toward its mate. It held a six foot three praying mantis with google-eyed head resting on long, thin hands atop long, thin arms. When our eyes met it unfolded, rose slowly, crossed the physical gulf between us in two long strides, extended a hand that encased mine in uncomfortably moist membrane.

"Nice to have you here, Hanlin," Robert Stately Hughes said in a tone that sounded rather as if he had summoned me, an insinuation I knew he would pay for before the meeting ended.

I mumbled something, set about the problem of my right hand trapped in his talons, he showed no sign of letting go as he continued to drone, "Best striker in New England, Governor."

Buckingham blinked in non-comprehension, I deigned to enlighten, "Base ball, Governor, Robert's president of our team," I tore my hand away when Hughes acknowledged his title with a short bow.

Buckingham dismissed the small talk with the flick of a bushy eyebrow, got down to matters directly, "I'm sure you know why you're here, Hanlin, Judge Crompton regaled me at lunch with news I could not believe I was hearing for the first time – you're a West Point graduate," said with a smile and an air of 'how dare you keep it to yourself.'

"Class of Forty-six."

"My good friend John Andrew has the temerity to try to poach you from us," Buckingham's smile widened while his eyes hardened.

"To be fair, Governor, I was appointed from Boston, so he surely feels he's well within his rights," I reached into my breast pocket, pulled out a sheaf of onionskins, "though Rhode Island, Maine and New Hampshire had the same idea – without Andrew's claim."

I slapped the telegrams on the table between us, Hughes and the Governor stared at tangible proof they were not only not the only game in town, they were well behind.

"No Vermont?" Hughes broke the silence with a sarcastic gleam.

"I believe they are of the opinion only Vermonters are fit to command Vermonters," I opined to their ready agreement - outside of Vermont, Vermonters were considered hopelessly idiosyncratic. I thought that their appeal, which left me a minority of one in Southern New England,

"So, William," Buckingham began – brandish evidence of your worth to a politician, earn first name status, "Crompton's timing was perfect, Hughes and I were meeting tonight to put a plan together . . . Robert has graciously taken a leave of absence from Trinity to assist in our military undertaking."

Hughes moved his head sickeningly forward in studied, modest, martyr-like acknowledgment.

"How?" I asked, reasonably enough.

"How?" Buckingham did not agree, "Well . . . ," a long pause that proved only that he had not asked the question himself, "by offering his expertise, I suppose."

"Expertise?" To my credit I kept a sneer out of my voice.

"His military expertise," Buckingham, losing patience with the game, "Hughes is a prominent military science professor, quite the reputation . . . we've been talking for hours, he has ideas."

"I'm sure he does," I chuckled, "regaling the Governor with tales of Cannae and Agincourt, Robert?" His unintentionally self-deprecating smirk and slight blush confirmed my guess.

"We've been discussing forming . . . regiments," Hughes valiantly regrouped, "organizing, officering, as soon as possible," he made a gruesome attempt to smile patronizingly, "naturally, we would like you to have a part in the process, an important part."

"What would that be, Robert?" I asked, quietly, "Officer,

civilian liaison, oversight committee?"

"Why, we . . . ah," he looked to Buckingham, realized no help was coming from that direction and blundered on, "we rather thought you would prefer a line officer's commission."

"And get shot at!" I yelped in mock horror.

"Well . . . . ah . . . ."

"Relax Hughes," Buckingham came to his rescue, "I think Hanlin is having us on . . . I presume to make a point."

I saw no need to couch it, "You brought Hughes in here because he teaches military science and you've brought me in because I went to West Point and you really have no idea to what end – either of you – beyond the need to throw some regiments together and get them to Washington in one piece."

"I don't think that's fair, Hanlin," Hughes, strident and hurt.

"Really?" I replied with equal measure, "How many militia companies, National Guard units are you planning on incorporating into the first regiments?"

"We're not sure, but —" Hughes stammered, Buckingham sat back in his chair.

"Where we training?"

"We have several ideas, and —" poor Hughes answered without a clue that he had lost Buckingham.

"Ideas don't make a warehouse, commissary, procure arms, medical facilities," no answers were forthcoming, I did not really wait for them in any event, "what are we doing for uniforms, shoes, powder, minie balls – I assume we'll be using rifles?" The sarcasm was registering, "We have any lists of former officers, veterans, especially NCOs? Do you have anything at all, Robert?"

"Be fair, Hanlin," Hughes pled while the Governor reappraised me with a long, steady gaze, "no one's had time to do any of that, this is only a few days old."

I stopped him with a wave of Andrew's telegram, "Please, this has been in the works for months, you know that – Massachusetts has rifles from Britain on the way, are already training under professionals.

"So," I held the Governor's eye, "don't tell me it's too early, you're behind, you're panicking, and all you have is theory."

"Pretty blunt, Hanlin," Buckingham said without hint of

pique.

"Hanlin —" Hughes started before Buckingham's upraised hand stopped him cold.

"Though your point is well taken," the Governor spoke to the fireplace, "we are not prepared . . . . I take it you have concerns about serving with Hughes?"

"In the field?" I asked.

"In the field," Buckingham confirmed.

"No concerns, Governor, because that won't happen."

Silence save for the crackling fireplace, before Hughes, "Then we have a problem, Hanlin," no hint of offense, as was appropriate in a man comfortable in his patronage, "because we are forming a regiment immediately as a model for the rest and I will be serving in it."

He blinked at the Governor and me in turn. When he saw that neither of us showed any inclination of interrupting he went on, "Over the weekend we had an offer from Seth Arnold – I'm sure you know him," my blank stare did nothing to reassure him, "to raise that regiment, all expenses paid, best of everything."

"Then that's the regiment to join," I stated the obvious.

"Precisely," Hughes triumphed, pleased his slow student was catching up, "we envision it with Seth as it's titular head, myself as lieutenant-colonel, strictly as administrator, and you major, de facto commander, particularly when battle offers." He finished well satisfied and oblivious to my look of utter incredulity.

"Where are you and Arnold 'when battle offers', in a committee meeting?" I snapped, "'When battle offers', Robert? We're not being invited to a fucking joust, we're going against men with rifles."

"No need for profanity —" Hughes tried.

"Precisely the time, I'd say," I corrected.

"Doesn't look like Hanlin's comfortable with that arrangement, Robert," Buckingham, with gross understatement.

"But, but, surely," Hughes persisted, not getting that his political anchor had just set him adrift, "major must be a higher rank than any you previously attained?"

"Sure is," I agreed amiably, "and a hell of a lot higher than any you or Arnold have held as well." Buckingham chortled.

Hughes, however, was undaunted, "What was your rank when you left the army, William?"

"Lieutenant."

"Not so high and mighty," he barked triumphantly, showing a lack of sportsmanship I would not have previously attributed to him, "Maybe we should —"

"Though I was brevetted to captain during the Mexican War," that captured his attention.

"Brevet?" Buckingham asked.

"Temporary promotion to rank for the remainder of a conflict," Hughes could not stop himself from explaining, "usually awarded for bravery under fire or some such conspicuous service. I congratulate you."

"Thank you."

"You were under fire, Captain?" Buckingham used my former rank in an obvious attempt to flatter me, a strategy that worked, "and you led, what?"

"A regiment."

"A regiment," he repeated as if invoking, "I think that changes things . . . what do you want, Captain?"

I did not pretend to think it over, "I assume Arnold is an indispensable political ally?"

"He is," a smile for my political naïveté.

"He'll spare no expense?"

"None."

"He is aware he is a neophyte, a rank amateur?"

"Very much so."

"Does he want to learn, be a martinet, raise the regiment and go home, what?"

"You'll find he wants to serve, is as far from martinet as can be imagined, and is a fast learner."

"You going to form a committee to oversee this thing?" I asked while staring at a somber Hughes.

"Of course," Buckingham, happy to have a positive to reply to, "you want to sit on it?"

"Sure, Hughes would be perfect for it too," Hughes smiled wanly at the mention of his name, "it's the one place an academic can't hurt anything."

"Agreed," Buckingham smiled at Hughes in an effort to soften the consolation prize, "and you'll serve with Arnold?"

"I'll agree to be his executive officer, lieutenant-colonel, at least through training and into federal service . . . unless I feel Arnold is deficient, at which point you will allow me to take my own regiment."

"Done," the Governor pounced.

"I'm not," Buckingham's only reaction a slightly raised eyebrow, "I pick all staff officers and I have right of first refusal on company commanders."

"Well, I —"

"Lastly," I interrupted a man who was so seldom interrupted he could only gape in response, "Hughes is not an officer, he thinks he knows everything and he'll be an enormous pain in the ass during training."

"That is slander, sir," Hughes did his best to sound outraged, his heart clearly not in it.

"Far from it, Robert," I said, not unkindly, "I'd be glad of your company - we could discuss the campaigns of Hannibal, Montcalm, Napoleon —"

"Yes, but —"

"But you need to learn from the bottom up . . . I invite you to start as an enlisted man," the invitation did little to brighten his continence. I looked to Buckingham, "we all set on this?"

I had rehearsed my 'demands' all afternoon, was fairly sure I would get what I wanted, but it was still something to watch the cogs behind the Governor's eyes while he calculated: Arnold was an important political ally, therefore his success in the field was important – if not vital; he needed him to be at least a semblance of a war hero, he needed him to be efficient and protect the lives of untold voters in the ranks. A fairly simple reality.

A brief smile, decision reached, "Hughes, set up the committee, Lieutenant-Colonel Hanlin will chair it, you will be a civilian overseer," a visibility deflated Hughes nodded slowly, "if I were you I'd take Hanlin's advice and enlist – I envy you the adventure," he beamed at Robert with paternal warmth that was wasted as Hughes carefully studied his shoes.

"So, Lieutenant Colonel —"

"Lieutenant-Colonels are addressed as colonel, Governor," Hughes quietly corrected him.

"Thank you, Hughes – anything else, Colonel?"

"Yes sir, I'd like my investigator appointed my aide with the rank of captain . . . . he is a most competent man."

"He is indeed," Buckingham readily agreed, "Osgood's a captain," he shot a look to reinforce the fact he had not come to the meeting as unprepared as it seemed.

I nodded, "How soon can I meet Arnold?"

"Tomorrow, breakfast at the Goodwin, we'll meet you there at eight,"

"No offense, Governor," I said slowly, with measure, "we're to serve together, I'd like to meet him alone."

"I understand," he may well have but his face did not convey it, "I'll send Seth my regrets," he rose, headed to his desk, beckoned I follow. He reached into a cavernous drawer, pulled out a rolled parchment tied with Connecticut's colors, blue and white, "your commission, Colonel," he smiled broadly and handed it to me, "a pleasure, William."

"I suppose I shouldn't be surprised," I took the scroll, an electric shock running through me as I did – had I remained another twenty-five years, I might have attained such exulted rank in the seniority obsessed regular army. Might have.

"You weren't leaving here without it," Buckingham said with authority.

I nodded toward the desk, "Got one in there for major as well?"

"I have no idea what you're talking about," he said without inflection and escorted me to the door. As we made our farewells I had a last glimpse of a dejected Hughes slumped in his chair, staring into the fireplace.

7

I walked through a foul April morning – gray, dreary, cold – in a fouler mood. I had slept, if it could be called that, fitfully, lingering over the Buckingham meeting and filled with ever growing trepidation over the implications of my deal, i.e., serving 'under' a political appointee alongside yet more political appointees.

My mood was in no way mitigated when I was met at the door of the Goodwin by two obsequious waiters who insisted on escorting me to 'Mr. Arnold's Booth'. I had lived in that over-decorated slag heap for almost six months and there had never been a 'Mr. Hanlin's Booth'.

I was in danger of muttering to myself by the time I neared a booth in the back corner and a burly, wildly whiskered man leaped from the gas lighted shadows. He was on me before I could take another step, grabbed my right hand in both of his, pumped as if to raise water, proclaimed to the room, "William Hanlin, my salvation!"

"Mr. Arnold," I mumbled, nothing worse than having a perfectly good bad mood stomped to death by a man in a great one. I braced myself, prayed that a hug was not forthcoming.

"Seth, man, it's Seth," he roared, threw me into the booth, slid in opposite, jolting the table in the process. He signaled for a waiter while I assessed my assaulter - just under six feet; lively brown eyes; mop of brown hair flecked with gray-white; long untrimmed muttonchops framing a thick mustache; big without quite being fat – although it was easy to see how he would someday soon, the war notwithstanding.

That was the formality of our meeting and as formal as it ever was between us. He ordered much needed coffee – a sip lightened my mood considerably – mapped out an intricate breakfast and handed me an envelope with the Governor's crest on it, "That's from Bill, for you and your man Osgood . . . get outfitted out at Blake's – I was there yesterday, they've stocked some superb uniforms."

"Thank *Bill* for me," he blinked at my irony, "that's something we need to do right away - clothe the men . . . make them feel like part of a unit from the start. It'll help strip away the sense of entitlement that comes with being born in Connecticut."

"Well in the works," he laughed into his coffee, "I've appointed a quartermaster," he took evident notice of my reaction, "I know, I know, rash of me, but it's on an interim basis subject to your approval," I nodded appreciative acknowledgment, "Simon Wycroft – he runs my mills . . . a genius with supplies, ledgers, all that - but you decide."

"Can't wait to meet him."

"Good, because he's going to meet us at the armory after breakfast . . . I thought a tour would be worthwhile, see what we have to start with," I shrugged non-committedly – my expectations as to the contents of the Hartford Armory were abysmally low.

Further discourse was interrupted when seemingly the entire Goodwin staff teamed together to bring us a breakfast stunning in its complexity. Thanks to tremendous coordination, acute senses of size, angles, and outstanding depth perception, they covered every square inch of the table with a dozen dishes.

"Who's joining us?" I asked.

To a look of brief bafflement, "Oh, no, this is for us," he spread his arms wide, "breakfast is the key to the day."

"I won't be in any shape to move after this".

"Nonsense . . . eat up, William. I need you sharp, you have to teach me enough to raise me to the level of imbecile," he laughed and crushed a tiny bird in one satisfying, crunchy bite.

"Somehow, I have the feeling you catch on quickly," I kept the hope out of my voice, cautiously eyed something out of the mollusk family.

"I try and I'll do whatever I need to get a working understanding . . . . I don't pretend to know everything about my mills, yet they are paragons to efficiency," he had no issue with the mollusk in question, he speared it expertly, flipped it into his mouth whole and never missed a syllable, "I'm very good at picking men to delegate to and better at allowing them to work unimpaired, even when it kills me to do so."

"There's a difference between sitting back while making money and entrusting others when your life's in the balance," I observed. If I thought I was going to put a damper on his good cheer, I was mistaken.

"My God, you know that little about Yankee businessmen?" He roared, receiving looks from the other diners. Another mollusk met its fate, "I know my limitations, I compensate for them by picking the right men, and I stand by them in all regards."

"You didn't pick me... Seth," I pointed out the obvious, chewed on freshly squeezed orange juice and contemplated its cost in mid-April Connecticut.

"No," he nodded vigorously, eyed the spread with the cold eyed professionalism of a big-game hunter, "you're God sent." Decision made, another tiny bird was run through with swiftness and delicacy, "I finally put my money where my mouth has been all these years, had to, really," he held up a hand, dispatched the bird with a shattering, crunching bite.

"A minute after Bill accepted my offer I was in a panic over my utter lack of knowledge. Terrified I'd bungle it," with casualness born of long practice, he flipped a chop neatly from its serving tray to his plate, began to dissect it with surgical precision, "I don't fail and I abhor failure in others.

"But then," with machine like intensity, he chewed a silver of chop so fine it would have dissolved if left alone, "a day later I'm told that State's Attorney William Hanlin, who I admired for his stance on that scandalous railroad assault, is - wonder of wonders - a West Point graduate and Mexican War veteran. The miracle I needed," in went another infinitely thin slice, "now I can rest assured our regiment will be fine."

"It will," I had no choice but to agree, the man's sincerity was contagious. My last vestiges of unease left in a great rush, leaving me famished. I began a search of my own.

"We're going to get on well, William, aren't we," his bushy

eyebrows knit together as he tried to coax a cheesy omelet onto his plate, "our regiment will be an exemplary model for the others."

"They'll be many and they'll be close behind," I absently ladled fried potatoes onto my plate. He watched as I then successfully solved the omelet problem. I looked up from the steaming ova, caught his eye, "that worry you?"

"What, that I could screw up all of Connecticut regiments doing this wrong?"

"That's it," I took a large bite of potato and onion and let him ruminate.

"God, no, not when I have a professional soldier to blame!" He roared again, I spit out my food and joined him. Although my laugh had elements of choking involved.

"Nicely done, Seth . . . nicely done," I gasped.

"As long as we know where we stand, Colonel," he reached a hand across the table.

"We do," I took it in a hard clasp, "by the way, what are we calling ourselves – Arnold's Rifles, the Rose City Regiment?"

"No,' he chuckled, poked suspiciously at a hitherto unknown species of breakfast animal, "I'd like to go with the Twenty-first Connecticut Volunteers – nice ring to it and twenty-one is my lucky number."

"There may be a few militias getting called up for three month duty – but only a few," I smiled in return, "but twenty-one - "

"I know, I know," he alsmost seemed embarassed, " I talked to Bill, I . . . need twenty-one and I think we can all agree there is no way possible Connecticut will have to supply anywhere near twenty-one regiments before this is over."

"Perhaps not," I answered slowly, twenty-one thousand men from Coonecticut serving in one army did seem outrageous.

"See," he laughed, "when the war's over, we'll stand out!"

"Twenty-first it is then," I had to agree.

"Great," he roared, "so, you know the Meadows?"

"Of course."

"I've asked the governor to cede it to us as our training camp."

"Those are our base ball fields!" I jumped.

"Well, hell, William," he pretended to glare, "how much ball do you think you'll be playing over the next few months?"

"They're perfect," I muttered, realized I should have thought of it first, "just leave a diamond or two alone for off-duty - good for morale."

"For them or you?"

"A happy Colonel makes a happy Regiment."

"Consider it done," he beamed, "Wycroft - should you accept him- is meeting with the railroad this evening about building a siding there so we can construct our own station and warehouse."

"Very good."

"You see," he winked conspiratorially, "Bill may be the consummate politician, but he does care."

It took me a minute before it clicked, "You met with him after I left," I surmised a day late.

"Five minutes, tops," a mollusk found itself homeless, weightless, and in-flight to Seth's maw.

"You were that sure you'd get your man."

"Well . . . we had a pretty good idea."

"I'm that easy to read?"

"We were that desperate to get you."

"That's what being woefully unprepared does."

"Indeed," a half a pound of freshly drawn butter was forcibly united with several dark pieces of toast, the dispossessed crumbs sought refuge on my plate, "I believe he is already acting on everything you mentioned," he looked up from his plate, "you're quite the politician, you know."

"No one," I laughed, "has ever accused me of that."

"You certainly removed Hughes from the picture–neat and quick–poor bastard never saw it coming," neither did a boiled quail's egg.

"I got the idea that Buckingham found himself saddled with him and was looking for reason to excise him."

"Did you?" He confirmed.

"Why didn't he do it himself?"

"Not politically expedient. Hughes, more properly his family, is too important in the movement and, of course, the party to risk alienation."

"Best leave me to do it, and best leave me to reap the

consequences," I smiled wanly.

"And you say you're not a politician."

"I make enemies last night?"

"Probably," he chuckled, illustrated the point by stabbing a sausage with a satisfying squish, "but, hell, you won't be running for state's attorney for at least two years, shouldn't be a problem then."

"I could be killed."

"While convenient I don't think it's necessary," he stopped grazing for a moment, his eyes inherited an additional gleam, "the damage for you is not all that bad, you built a lot of goodwill at the railroad station," some part of his brain, or stomach, or both, reminded him that he not eaten in several seconds and he took revenge on several innocent, unborn offspring of rare water fowl. Done, the only evidence of his deprivations a thin, bright yellow glob of yoke on his mustache, he finished, "and, of course, your mother's great contributions."

I dropped my fork and a chunk of cheese filled omelet on my lap.

"Met her years ago. Great lady, beautiful," his napkin found the glob, wiped it, he looked at it, frowned and swore off eggs for the duration, "I knew she had a son at Wesleyan," oysters however, self-contained packages that they were, became his new preference, "not sure she ever mentioned you."

"She would not," I said evenly with great truthfulness.

"No?" He stopped mid-bite.

"Unlikely," I stared directly in the hopes of cutting off the next question.

"I know I'm being crass," he was oblivious, "but with your mother's connections and your . . . ah . . . background, you could raise your own regiment in Massachusetts."

"I have no wish to return to Boston right now and, with our committee I —"''

"We meet tonight at the Statehouse, Great Hall. I'm sure you'll be happy with none of our selections, Mr. Chairman," he laughed loudly.

"Anyway, with the committee," I continued despite his evident mirth, "I have more impact, more responsibility . . . Connecticut needs me a hell of lot more than Massachusetts," I answered, almost honestly, "and I have the added bonus of serving with you," he looked up speculatively, "my scapegoat for all military disasters - the amateur did it!" I finished with an exaggerated look of innocence.

"Well," he sputtered, "nice to know where we stand."

We ate in silence for a while, a silence that was not oppressive, an excellent omen for our future together.

Eventually Arnold pushed back from his plate, drained a large glass of juice, found my eyes and said, "You should feel free to talk to me anytime, about anything."

"Of course," I had no immediate idea of what he was talking about, saw something move behind his eyes, "have something specific in mind?"

"Now you insult me," he pouted.

Then I knew, "Damn," I muttered, "you're from Norwich . . . . there some relationship?"

"Great uncle," he answered with evident relief, "change your mind, William, serving with Benedict Arnold's great-nephew?"

"Not as long as you," I said carefully, the pain on his face made it abundantly clear he considered it a family stain, "aren't in this to atone for his sins."

"How eloquently biblical," he grinned self-consciously, "I can assure you I am not."

"Can you assure you?"

"Yes, yes," he shrugged, patted his mouth with his stained napkin, "I'm saddled with his name, not his sin."

"Not very Calvinistic," I observed.

"No, not very."

"Well," I considered, he looked as if awaiting some formal pronouncement, "if you're half the soldier he was we have no worries." Clearly it was not what he was expecting, he looked at me questioningly.

"In my opinion" I went on, "Benedict Arnold was possibly the finest soldier this country has ever produced, despite his failings as a man - which are pretty self-evident. We owe him a debt and without his actions at Valcour Island and Saratoga there'd no country.

"Nothing takes away from what he did before he turned, Seth, nothing."

"Thank you, William," he blinked away moisture, "that means a lot. Most people won't acknowledge any of that . . . it complicates matters."

"No one likes complications."

"Amen, my friend."

And so, I liked the man.

8

Enough food left on the table to feed a regiment, we moved through a bevy of fawning waiters and exited out to the cloudy, gusty day, a steady, wet-cold river breeze destroyed the lingering smells of breakfast. Five steps up the street Osgood magically appeared in step beside us.

"Colonel Arnold, may I present my friend, Osgood, "I said without a glance.

"Ah, Captain Osgood, how very glad I am to meet you," Arnold beamed, offered a meaty paw that Osgood eyed with justifiable suspicion.

"Osgood is fine . . . sir," he looked up at the looming Arnold.

"Osgood isn't used to the idea of being an officer yet," I explained, "although we do hope to have him somewhat inured to the idea of being a gentleman shortly." Arnold laughed; Osgood mouthed a two word rebuke.

They walked together chatting amiably, I trailed, content in the crispness of the day, engrossed in the problems before us: how to put the regiment together quickly, leave a legacy for the units to come, and get to Washington as soon as possible. We had no money or political hurdles to negotiate, all we needed was everything else.

We crossed the Park River into the incomplete park, joined a cadre of municipal workers meandering to finish the park in time for the planned July 4th unveiling.

"Seth," I broke into their bonding, "let's set July 4th for the regiment to be ready. We'll parade them here at the grand opening."

"Excellent!" Seth bellowed, startling the workmen nearby.

"That enough time?" Osgood asked.

"We'll make it so," Arnold assured us with such bravado

Osgood looked to me questioningly.

"You heard the Colonel, we'll make it so", I confirmed. We reached the crown of a rolling hill overlooking the Hartford Armory nestled below against the Park River. An immense, sandstone faux-castle edifice complete with its own moat, it was reputed to hold our state's military stores, although no one had had a reason to visit it since the British burned the White House.

What at first I took as a sapling by the front door turned out to be, in fact, a man. One who stood just over five feet tall and could not have weighed more than one hundred pounds. He sported wire rimmed glasses, the lenses so thick his eyes appeared pinpricks, and had a bowl shaped mop of long, light brown hair that flapped in the wind. He was clean shaven and looked like the kind of man who never aged. Simon Wycroft, of course, as Seth quickly introduced. He had a surprisingly deep voice, warm, friendly, not at all what one expected from a man of his stature and profession. He fell in with us naturally and we entered the sally port

It emptied into a spacious, windowless office lined with file cabinets, the desks laid out with military precision. A precision not shared by the young man in an unadorned solid blue uniform splayed back in a chair, feet on a desk, *Hartford Courant* in one hand, coffee in the other. As our visit was unannounced and he made no movement, no sound, to acknowledge our sudden presence, I could only deduce that he was a deaf mute.

Arnold tested my theory by clearing his throat and stomping his feet. When that produced a mere rippling of the newspaper, he tried the spoken word.

"We're here to inspect the arms and munitions," he pulled a paper out of his pocket, "our authorization from the Governor." The guard's eyes flicked away from the *Courant* for perhaps a full second, destroying half my thesis. A second later he murmured, "I-Immm," thereby neither confirming nor denying the second. He very carefully turned a page.

Arnold, finger still pointed, made a move to speak further. I grabbed his sleeve freezing him.

"Osgood, introduce yourself," I said simply.

Osgood was on him in less than a normal heartbeat.

Something the now terrified guardian of Connecticut's arms no longer enjoyed. Osgood kicked his feet off the desk, slapped the paper to oblivion, sent the coffee cup flying its former contents a dripping stain on our guard. Another second and Osgood had him by the neck of his blouse and pinned him on tip toe against the wall. Nose to nose said he said, quite conversationally, "The keys . . . please."

For the unfortunate guard, his entire universe consisted of Osgood's coal black eyes. The three of us did not exist, which was fortunate as we were each unsuccessfully waging a battle to hold back laughter.

"What's your name and rank?" I asked, aspiring to sound fearsome.

"Joseph Morris," he stuttered, eyes still fixed on his assailant, "corporal."

"What are you, Corporal?" I continued, dropping my fearsome voice for more of an educated sneer, "Judging by the way you're shivering, I'd have to go with State Militia…"

"Guard, mister — "

"It's Colonel, Morris. Lieutenant Colonel Hanlin, this is Colonel Arnold, Lieutenant Wycroft," Wycroft jumped at that, I shrugged back, "and the man holding you is Captain Osgood," Osgood dipped him by way of greeting, "we're from the Twenty-first Connecticut and we need in."

"We could have been anyone, Corporal," Arnold added, "maybe you've heard there's a war on?"

"Are you even armed?" I marveled. Osgood dropped the corporal back into his chair, expertly rifled through the desk and pulled out a pistol.

One shot," Osgood snickered, snapped it open, "empty and no caps or cartridges to be found. Effective defense, that," he dropped the harmless instrument on the desk with a clatter, the corporal grimaced.

"Corporal," I asked in an easy manner that seemed to capture his attention, "does anyone check in on you?"

"Yes sir," he answered, very pleased with himself for remembering the 'sir'.

"Who?" I rolled my eyes at a still amused Arnold.

"Oh, Captain Lenox ..... sir."

"Would that be Channing Lenox?" I asked with no small degree of incredulity.

"Yes, sir."

"You know him?" Arnold asked.

"Oh yes, " my turn to grimace, "Lord Nelson's clerk," as in my boss, Chief State's Attorney Walker Nelson, "the Guard's harder up than I imagined," I sighed with disgust, mostly at myself for saying it aloud in front of an enlisted man. There were some old habits I needed to reacquire, quickly, judging from the look that passed over the corporal's face.

"You're related to him, aren't you?" I asked in a moment of inspiration.

"He's my uncle," he said with a pride that only a relative of Lenox would have been capable of possessing.

"Of course he is," I whispered. Osgood walked by, close, whispered, "nice work."

"I'll bet he's due to check in on you at twelve fifteen or so, isn't he?" I went on, in for a pound.

"How'd you know that?"

"That's when Nelson goes out to lunch and they pry your uncle off his ass with a crowbar so they can go their separate ways for an hour or two," I answered amicably. Arnold lost the good fight to hold his mirth in, Osgood had no choice but to join him, Wycroft, lost, smiled "When he appears, Joseph," I added, for the hell of it, "you tell him he's ordered to see to it at least four men armed with rifles and side arms are posted here day and night. Two outside, two in. Can you remember that, Corporal?"

"Yes, sir," he answered in a tone that made it clear he would not forget anything said or done thus far.

"If the Captain has an issue with that order," Arnold produced a card from his coat pocket, "he may take it up with the Governor - that's his card, note on the back that we act in his authority. Now let us into the armory."

The corporal stumbled to a cabinet, I turned to Arnold, "What else have you got in that coat?"

"That's on a need to know basis."

"Can I have one of those cards?"

"Absolutely not. God knows what havoc you'll wreak."

"You know me so well yet we've only just met."

The corporal pulled a ring of keys off an overburdened peg and led us down a long, dank, high ceilinged hall to an ancient oak door, at least four feet taller than myself and wider than the three of us abreast. Morris fumbled with the ring before selecting a key last used to open the gates of Troy.

He fitted it with great effort and, straining, turned it gratingly until it reached fruition with a loud click. He pushed against the door, it yielded grudgingly with low moans of pain until it gapped just wide enough for a grown man to slide through sideways. Morris made a move to be that man only to be stopped dead by Osgood's grip on his arm.

"Whoa there, Corporal," Osgood, with great good humor, "I think you missed the point. You are here to guard the place, not give tours."

Osgood snatched the key ring from the corporal a second before he scurried down the hallway to sanctuary. We walked through a short, dark hallway permeated with the smells of ancient mildew. It opened into a cavernous interior, illuminated by dingy sky lights high above. Dingy sky lights, gray overcast day outside equaled a pall inside.

"Nice effect," the theatrically minded Osgood stated to immediate agreement from Arnold.

We were in front of a riding ring big enough to play a rugby match in. Easily. Cold enough to see our breaths, we walked across the hard packed, long unused surface kicking up small puffs of dust.

"I'll keep a look out for stray chariots," I announced, "while you three figure out where we're going."

"Straight across," Osgood replied, "there's a row of doors." He picked up our embarrassingly cautious pace.

"Well," Wycroft uttered his first words since our introduction, "this looks promising." The door closest in the gloaming read "ARTILLERY". It was thick, burnished oak, banded with studded iron, an iron ring hung above a lock big enough for a small child to stick a hand in.

To Osgood's credit, he was on his sixth key before he resorted to profanity. It worked on number seven and the key turned the lock with a definitive, Gothic clunk. I pushed my shoulder against it, the only thing that moved was something in my shoulder. Then again. Hard. The door did not budge, the something in my shoulder returned to place, painfully. I put my back and legs into it and, to the nasty comments of my cadre, it moved with high pitched protests.

"After you," I motioned to Osgood, "in case the Minotaur's waiting."

"Coward," he sneered, brushed by.

"Exercising my discretion by sending the most expendable member of our party in first," I explained to his back.

"That's what makes you a first rate officer," Seth agreed.

"Thank you, Colonel."

"You're welcome, Colonel."

Wycroft pushed past, "Whenever you're ready, gentlemen," he said with a rueful shake of his head. We followed into a large room, the roof lower, allowing a dirty sky light to let in enough dirty light to illuminate the almost empty space before us.

By my calculations the room was large enough to hold a division's worth of artillery and train. In their stead, in the furthest, dimmest corner, stood five lonely cannon. I trekked to the forlorn battery, ran my hand over the cool, dull green barrel of the first gun in line, traced a crest by the caked touch hole. I bent closer and strained to make it out through the murk.

"Brass, with, believe it or not, King George the *Second's* crest on it," I marveled, "it could have been at Quebec, for God's sake," I ran my hand all the way down the stout barrel, "fire this and they'll be picking pieces of metal out of your ass for days. Polish it and you've a nice museum piece."

"Melt it down," Arnold added, "and we have buttons for a division. Not exactly swords into plowshares, but close enough, eh?" He finished and all doubts as to who our pragmatist was were put to rest.

I moved to the other guns. Two were serviceable brass Napoleons. When cleaned they would glisten and, within short range, maim and kill as well as any. The last were obviously spoils of war - an iron spike had been driven through the touch hole to disable them. Done recently, one would have a chance to drill it out and use the gun. Eighty years after Yorktown it was hopeless. Even if possible, who would volunteer to be the first to fire it?

We left the chamber in silence and moved on to a door marked 'POWDER' in bold, optimistic print. After similar struggles with the lock and rusty hinges we entered a duplicate of the artillery room. Large enough to hold thousands of casks of powder, it held twenty. Along with tons of one of the most common substances found on Earth, dust. As far as the casks went, they held what appeared to be a fine black powder, packed away about the time the Alamo was being overrun. Still, it was a start and it would do for rifle drill.

With hopes rising, we burst into the room advertised as 'MISC.' To stand transfixed. Utterly.

"What are they?" Wycroft whispered, no one answered while we soundlessly stared at row after row of steel implements gleaming nastily even in the twice filtered light.

"Pikes and lances," I answered belatedly, walked slowly down an aisle flanked by upright stalks that bloomed fearsomely. All shapes and dimensions, the heads nasty, ugly things, razor sharp, designed to mangle horses in a multitude of inhuman ways.

There was a similar forest of cavalry lances with horrific points, some evilly barbed, all designed to do the same to humans should the pikes fail. I shuddered in primordial recognition of the thousands of years those instruments had been used to skewer men on foot.

Osgood spoke for our still rooted friends, "We are all set if Southern knights in armor appear on Avon Mountain."

That effectively broke the spell cast by the appalling weapons, we walked out chuckling nervously. I noticed that no one turned their back on them until we cleared the room.

We had no greater success exploring further. The small arms room, despite evidence that it had once been well stocked, was empty – it was of little matter with Colonel Colt's personal armory within walking distance.

One room held several hundred boxes of lead and many, many molds for musket balls of all sizes. The lead was helpful, the molds, curiosities. Another was full of cannonballs without number in row after row of head high pyramids. They were of all unmarked sizes, pitted and flaking. Properly cleaned up they may have been suitable for lawn bowling.

Our expectations plummeting with every step, we arrived at the room marked 'MUSKETS' with a complete lack of enthusiasm. Unlike the others, it opened easily and we walked into a room of muskets on wooden racks, their stocks rich wooden hues; barrels clean, burnished steel.

"Well now, here's something," Arnold exclaimed, I walked to the nearest rack, picked up a piece for inspection and began to laugh. Hard.

"That can't be good," Arnold snickered with irritation.

Controlling myself was no easy matter, but I managed to blurt out, "Grab one of these, Seth. God knows, one of them may have shot at your great uncle!" I handed him my piece, he took it nonchalantly, was surprised by its heft. He looked at me quizzically.

"It's a Brown Bess," I went on, regaining control, "standard British infantry issue from the War of Austrian Succession through Waterloo. A beauty, too." I pulled more off the rack, handed them to Osgood and Wycroft, who whistled in appreciation. I took one for myself and with it draped over my shoulder wandered through the rows of guns. Unfortunately it was, of necessity, with the eye of an historian.

I completed the circuit, found the others where I left them, handling the muskets, pulling out the ramrods, fooling with the hammers and pans.

"Here, these will help," I handed them a handful of flints, "there's a box of them in the back."

"Anything else?" Osgood asked, fitting the flint with an expertise I should not have found surprising.

"The latest model I could find were Springfields from the War of 1812, not a rifle in the lot."

"I'm afraid I've wasted your morning, gentlemen," Seth apologized.

"Not at all," I said with the good humor I felt, "I don't know about you, but I'm taking this beauty home to put over the mantle."

Brown Bess on shoulder I headed out the door and back across the arena. The others followed, similarly armed, none of us bothered to lock the doors behind us, We emerged in the guardroom to find the corporal wearing a sidearm, clearly confused by the sight of the four of us returning armed.

"Corporal," he jumped at once, bringing me great pleasure, "forget the orders to Lenox."

"Shit, son," Arnold added, "if you've got something else to do, go do it, you're wasting your time here."

Osgood tossed the keys on a desk with a clatter, "We left everything unlocked, nothing back there that locking up."

"Unless," Wycroft interjected with a grin, "you don't like spiders. Then I'd definitely lock it up."

"Big spiders," Arnold nodded sagely.

I patted my musket, "You go back there, bring one of these," I turned and headed out, "use the butt, you might have a chance."

We went back into the cold wind, the smell of freshly turned sod heavy around us. We walked briskly through the park, reveling in the looks from passersby at four well-dressed gentlemen sporting British muskets.

9

I made my excuses, left Osgood to Seth and Wycroft, and headed downtown to the courthouse. Halfway there I made a spur of the moment detour to Blake's to be fitted for my first uniform in ten years. They were doing a landslide business, at least ten self-appointed officers-to-be buzzed around the roomy shop confusing the staff in their ignorance of rank, uniforms and all things military. The Blakes - a father and four sons - owned and operated the store, each so ancient it was impossible to tell the generations apart.

The erstwhile officers were congregated around a jeweler's case bedazzled by Blake's impressive collection of polished, gleaming, expensive insignia including, in a remarkable burst of optimism, those of a Lieutenant General.

"George Washington leave those last time you waited on him?" I asked the Blake assigned to me.

"That is very funny, sir," he said in a ponderous monotone.

"You know the rank's retired, right?"

"One never knows, sir," he shrugged and led me through the crowd.

My card from Buckingham truncated the line, too much whispering and not very subtle pointing. Which intensified incrementally when I was overheard eschewing the baubles and opting to have my insignia sewn on the shoulder straps. In black thread.

"Black on blue?" My Blake wrinkled his already wrinkled brow at my parsimony, "no one five feet away will see your rank."

"Exactly."

"You want that?"

"I do."

"May I ask why, sir?"

"Sharpshooters, like ravens, are attracted to shiny objects, Mr. Blake."

As one the crowd looked down at their shiny, newly purchased insignia.

"No refunds," the crafty Blake at my elbow bellowed and gave me a shove toward the rear of the shop and the fitting rooms.

I finally arrived at the courthouse in mid-afternoon. A quiet, sedate courthouse where I heard my every footfall echo off the marble floors. Aside a sparsely attended hearing in a cavernous courtroom, the halls of justice appeared completely deserted.

A note posted on my office door directed me to go to the chief state's attorney's office upon arrival. That incited the usual emotions of irritation and annoyance of each and every directive from Lord Nelson. I was tempted to ignore it as I had numerous times in the past but this day took comfort merely in taking my time getting there.

The antechamber of Chief State's Attorney Walker Nelson's office was large by the standards of civil service but rather very much smaller than the throne room reception chamber he thought it to be. It was presided over as the latter, however, by Channing Lenox, Nelson's Lord Exchequer. He was the sole entry to Nelson and he was never not there. I knew that better than most, having tried everything to skirt him. Like death and taxes, he simply was.

On the few occasions he moved from behind the desk, Lenox stood 5 foot 10, weighed about one-seventy, all of it solid. He had dusty brown hair and a John Brown evangelistic 'I- don't- give- a-shit' overgrown beard that began under his turgid brown eyes and extended past his clavicles.

He was a lawyer, albeit one with a higher calling than the rest of us. He had one client only - Walker Nelson's public persona. A client he represented with a zeal that abutted fanaticism.

He was sitting ramrod straight when I meandered it into the room, only his nose twitched at my entry, like a rabbit getting the first whiff of a dangerous scent. "Captain Lenox, how are you today?" I asked with exaggerated jocularity.

"Hanlin," his eyes found every square inch of my face save my eyes. His look of disapproval of all things Hanlin was particularly well honed that afternoon.

"Met your nephew today," I went on, "doing a fine job guarding a worthless armory."

"From which you stole four rifles," no expression accompanied the words. If he were joking, indeed if he had a sense of humor at all, it was as dry as the Gobi.

"Muskets, Captain, there is there a rather large difference between the two. As I'd be happy to show you some time."

"Perhaps after I'm pried off Mr. Nelson's ass," he said without inflection.

"I meant that in the best possible way and metaphorically, of course," I lied, "so, who's going to take your place here when the guard is called up?" I may have detected a flinch at that, or perhaps a dust mite was repelled by his eyes.

"I'm not sure it will come to that," he replied atonally and without further explanation. Although I gave him plenty of time to do so.

"You have to go, Captain" he braced for what he knew was coming, "after all you started the damn war."

"Do not use profanity here," he snapped. I further irritated him by trying to make eye contact, a sport at which he always proved more adept at avoiding than I at catching.

"Look, just tell me how you escaped from Harpers Ferry and I'll let it go . . . for good."

"I do not," he drew out through a ten second sigh, "look like John Brown."

"You do that well, stick with it when they come for you."

"You're not amusing, Hanlin."

"You know, it just occurred to me you'll have to salute and call me sir soon. While it may be awkward, I hope it won't come between us," his reaction indicated it had never occurred to him. I went on happily, "tell you what, I'll get you promoted to lieutenant colonel if you just tell me who they hung your place. Who was your Sidney Carthon, Lenox?"

"I was right here when they hung Brown," he played the put upon bureaucrat to perfection – probably because he was, "we talked the day they hung Brown. And yet you bring it up every time I am unfortunate enough to have to deal with you. It's absurd." His eyes moved to the grandfather clock in the corner, "I suppose you can go in now."

"I could stay and we can get the bottom of this, clear your conscience, you'll feel better."

"Get... out," he hissed.

"Have it that way, Captain. God I look forward to serving with you," I said over my shoulder and let myself into the royal chamber.

Chief State's Attorney Walker Nelson stood with his back to me looking out his floor to ceiling, double window overlooking Main Street, hands clasped behind him. He did not turn with my entry.

"Envelope's on the desk, take it and have a seat, Hanlin," he said without moving, using his most official voice. I had no problem finding the envelope on his wide partner's desk, it being the only item on it. A sterile desk was one of Lord Nelson's peccadilloes. One among hosts.

I picked it up, recognized the handwriting immediately, felt the unease the notes from our killer always evoked. I took it to an uncomfortable wooden chair, purposely bypassing several comfortable cloth and leather chairs on the way. It offered the best view of the coming show.

"Read it," he commanded, as if I would not think to do so on my own.

I extracted the note card from the elegant envelope, read exactly what I expected to read:

Nelson,

I must apologize for the sloppiness and rank amateurism of this morning.

I failed to secure the scene properly; then compounded matters by, due to circumstances beyond my control, failing to send my usual communication.

Please apologize as well to Mssrs. Hanlin and Osgood, I certainly had no intention of disturbing them so early in the morning.

I shall endeavor to do better in the future.
Yours.

"If nothing else, he is unfailingly polite," I slipped the odious note back into the envelope, "and is certainly enjoying himself."

"That is not funny."

"I'm getting that a lot today," I admitted, waiting for the first motion.

It was not long coming, Nelson performed a nifty pirouette away from the window, gave me a look of wan resentment, settled into the well-worn track running north-south in his rug and did what he did best: pace.

In scant moments he was pacing seriously, as befitting his standing as a world-class pacer. He placed whenever he thought he needed to show he was thinking. Or angry. Or any emotion important enough to convey to the public at large and prove that he did indeed have emotions. Which, of course, he did not.

In short, he paced whenever he suspected that a man in his position should convey deep thought and moral commitment to whatever it was that triggered the pacing in the first place. As he utterly lacked the mental capacity to differentiate important from the trivial, he paced continuously.

He paced so much that back in the day when he was allowed to try cases, jurors strained their necks and shoulders trying to follow him; judges simply read the newspaper. Prolonged trials inevitably led to bouts of vertigo not unlike severe seasickness. As jurors are by nature predisposed to look unkindly upon the attorney who induces in them vomiting and headaches, Nelson no longer tried cases. Any cases.

That is why I and the three junior prosecutors I supervised tried all cases. That freed the "Chief" (as he so dearly wanted to be called and practically begged us to do so, though no one to my knowledge ever had) to pursue his raison d'être, the completion of paperwork and coddling of politicians higher up the food chain. In those skills he had no peer. Nelson was to bureaucracy and pandering what Genghis Khan was to world conquest.

Nelson was in full stride before he spoke, "I do not appreciate having to be informed by the Governor that you have accepted another position while already employed in one that occupies your full attention."

Leave it to Nelson to forgo the trivial matters of the girl's murder, a note from the killer, and a Civil War to go right to the truly important issue, him.

"I accepted this morning," I answered evenly, "after being offered it last night. I think the timing and circumstances speak for themselves," I ended without rancor. To resent Nelson for being an officious prick was to resent the moon for waning. Beside, my anger would only take away from another of my favorite pastimes, analyzing Nelson's gait.

After years of practice it was still no easy task. Part of the challenge was that at five foot three (he claimed 5'5") his stride was short and required intense concentration to ascertain. To do so - a positive side effect of the enterprise - one had to concentrate solely on the rhythms of his steps to the exclusion of his words and overall appearance.

One had to watch the stubby legs while ignoring the mostly bald head with strips of black hair streaked over a stark white skull; dark, reptilian eyes; clean shaven face crying out for hair; skinny body broken by a ponderous belly, like a python that had swallowed a piglet, silver watch chain stretched across his vest so tightly it threatened to snap at any second and fill the air with metal projectiles at lethal velocity. If one ignored all that, and it was easier the more one saw of the man, one could decipher the messages his pacing sent.

The stomp-like, unwavering stiff-legged almost jog indicated his fervent belief he was in the right (his base stride, it never varied, such it is so with the self-righteous). The hop every five steps was joy at having what he (and apparently Olga) perceived as his chief rival soon to be shot at on a regular basis; the heavy foot fall after the hop, his angst at the prospect of having to enter a courtroom again; the kick at the end of each round to turn and start over again was anger and the reason for our meeting. About what, I had several guesses.

"I am reluctant to let you go, Hanlin," he stamped while he spit.

"It's not your choice to make," I replied simply.

"But," his voice rose in a pitch, "but, Osgood? The two of you, it's too much! It is unacceptable. It leaves me an unacceptable position. It is," stride, skip, hop, kick, an impressive combination, "an unacceptable breach of the trust I have given you over the years. You get my meaning?"

"It's unacceptable?" I ventured.

"Keep that wit to yourself," he hissed as he tried, and failed, to execute the quadruple again, almost tripping. I felt better having my wit recognized, "it'll be weeks before this office recovers the semblance of order. Maybe a month."

"Guess this would be a good time to ask for a raise, eh?"

"Damn your eyes Hanlin, you can't do this! I cannot allow Osgood leave with you."

"That's Osgood's decision," I left off 'which I made for him', "and as he came here with me..." I let the conclusion dangle.

"You were a package deal, if I remember correctly," he snapped, wrong but uncorrected.

"And we're leaving together. Osgood, though, is seeking his replacement right now," I said to his back, just as he completed another circuit. In truth, the few people capable of the replacing Osgood would be recruited to the 21st, "he'll find someone satisfactory." I finished that without adding qualifications: over forty-five with some sort of physical impairment.

"What about your caseload?"

"I'm dispersing the few open matters evenly to my assistants. They'll follow-through more than capably," as they most surely were, as well as unfortunately unfit for duty and united in their hatred of Nelson. "Don't forget, until we are called up, I am available to help."

"I suppose it will have to do," he accepted with a grimace, "besides, it will be all over by Christmas."

"The war?"

"Of course," his pace showed he believed it, "how can it not?" The standard abolitionist line, i.e., the immorality and corruption of the South in the form of the peculiar institution made them too immoral and corrupt to stand long against the righteousness of the North.

When I did not answer the question on the floor, his pace slowed and, keeping well in character, he abruptly changed the subject, "You have anything on the murders?"

"We have a polite, neat, madman with immaculate penmanship killing very pretty young women, one every two or so months and leaving their bodies carefully posed in upscale locations all about town." I concisely summed up our total knowledge to date.

"In other words, you know nothing," he surprised me with an astuteness I had not previously encountered, "he's not going to stop, is he?"

"Why should he, he's having fun and is in no current danger of getting caught." It occurred to me then that we were probably boring the killer with our lethargic response.

Nelson stopped in front of the great window, looked out on the street below, hands re-clasped behind his back. His 'I am taking you into my confidence' stance.

"I have received some rather oblique inquiries from the *Courant* regarding several strange deaths. That is worrisome," he paused significantly, I knew what was next and was not disappointed, "I thought the whole point of assigning you and Osgood to the scene of sexual," he winced at his use of the word, "crimes was to keep this quiet."

"We can contain a scene, we can't control idle speculation among bored beat men or witnesses," I replied with the beginnings of heat. While it was true that he had taken that precaution, it was also true that he, I was sure intentionally, failed to specify murders only. As I was not copied the order, I did not catch on until I spent the better part of a week being called to the scene of every imaginable sex-related crime in Hartford County. From a man showing his privates to the unimpressed matrons of the Elizabeth Park Rose committee, to a very embarrassed farmer in Bloomfield with what looked to me like an equally embarrassed sheep. (The farmer asked Osgood, "Are you going to arrest me?" Osgood replied, "No, but I am going to warn the other sheep").

"Perhaps," said in a way that discounted the word.

"No perhaps about it. This is going to come out sooner or later in any event – that it hasn't you can probably thank on the war news. He kills again on a slow news day and it will hit the front pages... that might not be such a bad thing."

"How can you say that?" His voice echoed off the window.

"Make the city aware of it and it will be harder for him on every level."

"It will create panic."

"It will deputize thousands to keep an eye out and it will cause young women to take caution."

He ignored me, "It's admitting we're not doing our jobs . . . that we are losing."

"I was not aware this was either a contest or we had suddenly assumed the duties of the Hartford Police Department."

"Please, Hanlin," he either saw somebody on the street he knew or was dismissively waving me off, "we are the face of law enforcement when it comes to high-profile crimes."

"That from your platform speech?" I said flippantly

"Don't be flippant," he snarled. That time I knew the accompanying wave was certainly dismissive as I knew for a fact he did not have two friends in Hartford, "I am paid to think of the big picture."

"The Senate?" I ventured.

"Your new position has made you impertinent, I think," he sneered, "and blind to the fact you leave me in a morass."

"We're not the ones killing the girls."

"You're not the ones stopping it."

"Are you equating the two?" I asked with a nasty edge.

"Of course not," he backed off immediately, another thing he was good at, "just speculating aloud. I have decided that in your absence, however, I will head the investigation into the murders, particularly the last one, perhaps you missed something in your haste to enlist."

"We did not," I replied shortly, idly wondering when dueling had been outlawed in Connecticut.

"What do you make of Madam Petrovsky?" He asked suddenly and out of nowhere.

"Very impressive woman."

"Harlot," he corrected, harshly.

"Yet impressive."

"So you say. Perhaps she worked her wiles on you. Perhaps an older head should interview her," he prattled on, apparently without irony, "one immune to the charms of a woman like that."

"Well, you have me there," I quipped no reaction. It occurred to me that I should encourage his interest in Olga, he would be as a paca among piranha in her home.

"I'll want to go over your notes and Osgood's drawings, then I may have some questions for you. I want to be as prepared as possible before I venture into this. Could make all the difference,"

"You mean you'll find the overlooked clue and solve the riddle of the purloined letter?"

"Mock all you like, a fresh pair of eyes might help."

"Then good luck," I had lost his interest, the great window was showing him a future wherein he saved the day to great public acclaim and rode victory into the Senate.

"Perhaps this is a good thing," he mused aloud. I could or could not have been in the room, it mattered not a whit when he got like that, "you leaving and all that. I think I may have relied on you and Osgood a tad too much the last year or so."

"I'll leave you to ponder that," I sighed, rose, "want to talk about the murders, let me know," I headed for the door.

No reply, I had no idea if he had even heard me. I had the Dickensian thought he would talk the afternoon and evening away thinking I was sitting there hanging on his every word.

Lenox, immobile at his post, blinked up at my entrance.

"Fuck you too, Channing," I tossed off casually and strode out into the corridors of justice.

BOOK II: The Twenty-First

One thing as regards this matter, I regret, and only one thing I am glad of; the regrettable thing is I am too old enough to shoulder a musket myself; the joyful thing is that Julian is too young.

~ Nathaniel Hawthorne

1

Osgood, Arnold, and I strolled Colt's levee on a perfect, cloudless spring day. The Connecticut rushed by a few feet below, bloated and debris ridden with the last Vermont melt. In the glare off its surface were millions of pollens of every shape, size, and aroma; each and every one of them intent on killing Colonel Seth Arnold and, perhaps, depriving the newly declared Confederate States of America that singular honor.

Eyes red, watery and as lifeless as a losing prizefighter, Arnold looked as miserable as he sounded sniffling, wheezing, and gasping. I put myself between him and the river lest he attempt to end the torment by flinging himself off the levee to float to a pollen free Atlantic Ocean. At some point he noticed my kindness, inquired as to the reason for it, and expressed thanks in language surprising from one so normally erudite and good-natured.

Colt's Levee from East Hartford

We met by the river to hide, pure and simple - from a governor who could not resist tinkering with his new toy every two minutes and a steady stream of volunteers for everything from Mule Skinner (needed), to fortune teller (politely refused even after he predicted we would come to great grief without him. A grief he offered to detail for a modest fee, also refused), to mortician (yes, if he agreed to join us and serve on the line. I did not catch his reply as he hurried off to a previous engagement), to rainmaker (?).

The 21st Connecticut Volunteer Infantry had been widely and successfully – too successfully – publicized in every newspaper's every edition, as well as dozens of screaming, superfluous, broadsides glued to telegraph poles and fences

A position we did need and I had ignored from my somewhat Deist viewpoint was that of chaplain. That was brought home when a young, timid creature appeared before us battered hat in hand and volunteered to be our moral compass. Arnold requested a sample of a sermon upon which he turned, in an instant, from lipid epitome of the meek to salivating hellfire and brimstone preacher railing about man as a natural sinner and spouting eternal damnation. When I suggested that it might not be the type of thing men going into battle necessarily needed to hear, his still blazing eyes condemned me to a fiery pit of agony. While I struggled with the impulse to send him there first, Arnold politely took him aside and let him down easy outside the presence of the unfaithful. Returning, Arnold suggested that he spearhead the search for a real chaplain.

Our responsibilities had mounted in direct proportion to the requests put to us. Men were enlisting in droves and we were bombarded with telegrams and messages from the outlying towns angling to have their self-raised companies attached to the first formal regiment to organize. Aside the fact we had no uniforms with which to clothe, no shoes with which to shod, no food with which to feed, no rifles with which to arm, and no tents with which to house them, we were prepared.

"We certainly," I started after an orgy of sneezes from Arnold, now sporting the same expression of pure apology a dog does after vomiting on one's shoes, "have our pick of untrained, untested, naïve young men."

"I b'leeze summa t'aining already," Arnold wheezed.

"Not a comforting thought," I pointed to a large waddle of mucus stuck in his mustache, he shrugged in resignation, "we're going to have to untrain men who would have been better off left alone in first place."

"I agwhee, guess we'll see soon 'nuff."

"The Meadows all set?" A pollen free Arnold had met with Buckingham for breakfast to finalize our plans.

"Of coors," he choked, "I go..." Wracked by a series of coughs, hacks, and gasps, he pointed at Osgood.

"Going out there this afternoon, right after we get rid of you. It will be laid out by the time you return," Osgood finished for him.

"And here I thought the two of you would drink your way through the weekend without me," I was off to inspect the efforts of the, many, outlying towns offering their volunteer companies.

"Seth has an architect and someone from the railroad meeting us there," Osgood, unaccountably pleasant, "we'll get a hell of a lot done without you."

The reason for his pleasantness hit me, "Seth and I have already agreed to keep one or two base ball pitches," I informed him brusquely. Arnold either nodded in agreement or was contending with a closed off airway.

"Damn it. Why not set up for real sport like rugby? More warlike, that's for damn sure."

"Because we need enough men to survive training to make a full regiment."

"It will cull the week, make us stronger."

"We'll end up going into combat with ten heavily bandaged men."

"Ten worth a regiment."

"It would help solve our biggest problem right now, sort out the volunteers. What we up to two, three thousand?" An asthmatic Arnold hit my arm and held up four fingers.

"Four thousand?"

"Bill wants us to take," suddenly unplugged Arnold hurried through the temporary respite, "as many as possible from Hartford and companies from some select towns," he convulsed through the last.

"Is he suggesting we form a regiment the size of a division?" I sneered to his shrug, "Select towns?"

"West Hartford, Farmington, Simsbury," he wheezed.

"They officered by political hacks?"

"Yesssss."

"There'll be more regiments right behind us, what's the rush?" Osgood asked before I could.

"Everyone's afraid the war will be over before Christmas," Arnold spasmed, "makes the Twenty-first a political plum," he surprised himself and us by finishing unimpeded.

"There's no way the war will be over by Christmas," I said with vehemence, "and we're not going to rush just in case."

"I unners'and," Arnold huffed, "we go when 'ere 'eady."

"Unless you're intent on going as cannon fodder," when I saw the look on Arnold's face I made a mental note to persist from such casual references to our mortality, "we'll make the decisions next week and get the men into camp, I want to the bring the officers in first."

"Ossifers?" Arnold gurgled.

"Get them some training, know that they know their business to some degree, at least enough so that they don't have to be instructed in front of the men. Or corrected. Ideally we'd take the time to train the officers in full, but that's time we don't have."

"I'll gladlee join in," Seth snorted.

"Nice sentiment," I replied quickly, "but no. Nowhere does familiarity breed contempt more than when a commanding officer tries to be common. You command, you know—even if you don't."

Arnold was overwhelmed by a succession of sneezes and coughs, as if his body could not decide which allergic reaction was best and auditioned both. The contest firmly won by coughing, I added, "Just observe and act like you not only know what's going on, you ordered it."

"We're going to need a taskmaster, though, someone to train the officers, then oversee them with the enlisted men, all while teaching the non-commissioned officers their craft."

"What about you?"

"No," I laughed, "I haven't the patience and I don't need the officers and men united in their hatred of me so early in the game."

"You're talking about a sergeant major," Arnold said, to my surprise.

"You been reading," I smacked his back, both to acknowledge his admirable self-study and to set him breathing again, "a professional sergeant major would be ideal though . . ."

"I may be able to help," Osgood interjected.

"Really?" I said with interest.

"Perhaps," he sported a wary grin that did not invite further inquiry, "I can't promise anything, there are ... complications, but we'll see".

"Try," I requested, "you'll have news of Wycroft before I get back?" Wycroft had spent the better part of two days following me around notebook in hand peppering me with questions. He started out not knowing the first thing about outfitting a regiment, forty-eight hours later, by his own efforts, he knew enough to outfit an army. A prodigy. He had left for parts unknown with Arnold's checkbook the night before.

"Yes," Arnold exploded in a hybrid series of coughs and sneezes.

"Christ, Seth, we've got to get you indoors before this air kills you."

"I think it's too late," Osgood pointed out, "time to promote you to Colonel, William."

"Let's at least wait until the body's cold," I suggested kindly.

"Yes, Sir!" Oswald Osgood tossed off his first, and quite possibly last, salute.

A mucus laden Arnold glared sullenly at his two beaming tormentors, then fled the levee.

2

I was already a half hour late for my early morning meeting with Buckingham when the train pulled in . It took another twenty minutes to find a hansom and ride the six blocks to the state house through great gales of driving rain that perfectly matched my mood.

The driver charged twice the accepted rate, I threw it at him gladly and dashed through the monsoon into the State House. By the time I

bolted into the foyer I was sopping. I caught my reflection in a mirror and cringed at my two day old beard, plastered, matted hair, red eyes, and simply decided to embrace the veneer of one very put out Lieutenant Colonel.

My trip had everything to do with the look, that and the early edition of the *Courant*. While we strode the levee Friday, the Sixth Massachusetts laid over in Baltimore where they were attacked by a mob. 'Pug Uglies', the papers called them, pro-succession they added by way of explanation - unnecessary to anyone who had ever been to Baltimore.

The Sixth fired into the crowd, killed at least nine, wounded many others. They took four dead as well. It cast further doubt on

Maryland's teetering, tenuous association with the union. Worse, all contact with Washington was lost. No wire, mail, trains, nothing. Which allowed the newspaper to speculate freely and cite rumor as gospel with unfettered creativity in the absence of fact.

Such was my physical and mental state as I climbed the stairs to the Governor's office. Buckingham's assistant was waiting for me, was about to make the life altering mistake of remarking on my lateness when he took in the picture I made and meekly led me through to the inner sanctum without comment.

The fireplace was roaring, the heat smashed into my wet uniform, I welcomed and embraced it. Arnold and Osgood sat on the sofa sipping coffee, Buckingham was beside the mantel looking every bit the wartime chief executive. Between the fire, half burning oil lamps, and the murk outside, it had all the atmosphere of a clandestine midnight meeting scene in a bad play.

"Welcome Colonel," Buckingham called out without moving, "coffee's on the table, help yourself."

I poured a cup, resisted the urge to sample one of the overstuffed muffins artfully arranged around the urn and returned to the fireplace. Without asking anyone's leave I stripped off my sopping coat, left it in a heap, and sat in shirt sleeves in the chair closest to the flames.

"We were just discussing good news from Wycroft," Arnold eyed me worriedly as I sipped and stared into the fire, "he's procured rifles, ammunition, much, much more. He'll be here this afternoon with details."

"Great, Seth," I said wearily.

"Apparently your report is not quite as uplifting," Buckingham said an air of false good nature, "how do we look, Hanlin?"

"Would you like the long or the short answer, Governor?"

"I'd like both."

"The short answer is that with one exception I had to issue orders to cease all drilling."

"All?" Seth, eyebrows raised.

"Anything more involved than brewing coffee over an open fire and telling ghost stories."

"That bad?" Osgood mumbled.

"Worse."

"I'll take the long version now," Buckingham managed to sigh and command at the same time.

"Sure," I took a bracing sip, "West Hartford's company formed at seven sharp Saturday morning, great sign. They were led by an arthritic, fifty-seven-year-old Baptist minister who followed in a donkey cart issuing what I'm sure he thought were orders."

"Reverend Amos Littlefield," the governor grimaced.

"No," I corrected, "Captain Reverend Amos Littlefield. He was wearing a dyed black suit with bars the size of gold ingots on his shoulders," I took another sip, looked at Osgood, he promptly began a careful inspection of his shoe tops.

"He not so much barked out orders as sermonized while reading drills," I looked at Arnold, he found something fascinating at the bottom of his mug, "as in, 'with God's steely resolve to smite the wicked foe, double-time.'"

"Any hope there?" Buckingham, evincing little himself.

"As it happens, his men can tell their right from left."

"An excellent start," Arnold snickered into his mug, received a look from the Governor that was singularly lacking in amusement.

"We'll have doctors examine everybody and dismiss the physically and mentally unfit. That should cover the good Reverend on both counts," I added with hope.

"I suppose that's necessary," Buckingham muttered unhappily, recognizing votes lost with the incompetent.

"It is," Arnold and I said together.

"Go on... Hanlin," the Governor glared as if at co-conspirators in a palace coup.

"Simsbury was organized, they could march somewhat. They have a couple of militiamen who had training in one form or another from regulars and have a copy of Hardee's they follow religiously. I have hope for them. As I do Windsor they're in similar shape."

"Not bad," the governor brightened noticeably.

I shrugged without commitment, "Not so bad, but they're behind considering the amount of drill they've had . . . and, they've never fired a weapon, though they look pretty fearsome with sticks.

"Windsor has guns, a firing range, a few good shots, and no concept whatsoever on how or why a company moves or fits into a regiment. Their officers are under the impression they'll be operating independently raiding the South."

"They're good men, they'll learn," Buckingham said in a low, warning tone.

"I'm inclined to agree with you," I said to no evident relief from the governor, "they'll learn. As will Winsted. They're solid, trained by a factory foreman who lost a leg at Buena Vista. He knows what he's doing and they have Springfields from their own factory. They're joined by a group of gentlemen farmers from Norfolk, all armed to the teeth and proficient, up to a point, with rifles."

"Up to a point?"

"They could shoot, individually, not as a group . . . unfortunately they're used to shooting at just about the last animal left in this state... So their aim is, I would say, somewhat low."

"I'm not sure I understand," Buckingham replied.

"Let me put it this way, we're perfectly safe if attacked by an army of woodchucks," I answered in my exhaustion. Osgood and Arnold covered, barely, their laughs. I would like to think that Buckingham smiled. I went to the table for more coffee, maybe to give in to my hunger.

"You've omitted Farmington," Buckingham proved he was paying attention.

"Sure did," I poured then studied my cup.

"Enlighten me," He ordered after a long silence.

"I don't suppose Farmington can be assigned to another regiment?" I asked without hope.

"No." Said flat enough to require no further exposition.

"How about we take them and leave Huntingdon?"

"What do you think?"

"Let's see, he's obviously wealthy, spent a fortune on "Huntingdon's Legion" and I have the feeling you can't live without him," the governor chuckled at my wisdom, Arnold nodded, Osgood looked at us in some confusion.

I endeavored to enlighten, "Farmington was raised by Captain

Miles Huntingdon. He is an ass."

"No denying that," Seth confirmed, "but he's an important ass. Right, Bill?"

"His family owns Farmington, we need Farmington, and we need him," Bill replied with great good sense, "what happened out there?"

"We'll start with the fact that Huntingdon was wearing a uniform so ostentatious the Prince of Wales would be embarrassed in it; he led the company - a company of a hundred and sixty, by the way - while reading from a notebook.

"At one point he was so engrossed he almost led the company into the dregs of the Farmington Canal - would have, actually, if not for the alert actions of a young lieutenant who ran down the line halting everyone before they took the plunge.

"Huntingdon had already shown a short, nasty temper and he ripped into the lieutenant for issuing an unauthorized order, conduct detrimental, and a ton of other horseshit that proves only that he has read the Articles of War."

"He is a lawyer," Seth added with a meaty smile.

"Of course he is," I replied agreeably.

"His father lost a fortune investing in the Farmington Canal, he made a fortune investing in the railroad that took over for it," Arnold went on, "so he has more than one chip on his shoulder and more money than God."

"If I wasn't there he would've had the boy horsewhipped, or worse, for interfering with his war."

"No doubt of that," Buckingham, in the manner of one unhappy with a marriage of convenience, "surprised he didn't demote him on the spot, at least."

"He tried, I overruled him," I said simply.

"You overruled him?" Buckingham sounded incredulous, "how?"

"Very simply," I tried to smile but the image of the bully that was to be one of our company commanders popped into my head, "I told him not to report to the Twenty-first without one Lieutenant Edwin Fischer in tow."

"How'd he handle that?" Arnold, with genuine interest.

"He was not pleased, which made it that much more enjoyable.

He promised me you'd hear from him sometime today."

"What would a day without a complaint from Huntington be like?" Arnold asked with a nasty laugh.

"Indeed," Buckingham smiled thinly.

"You really want this man to command a company in this regiment?" I asked the room, "because I don't."

"You can control him, William," Arnold jumped to answer, cutting off the Governor, "I'm sure of that, he'll come into line."

"I'd rather reject him right here, right now," I answered Seth but held Buckingham's eye, "are you both asking me not to?

"We are," Arnold, with a nod to the Governor.

"I can give it a shot . . . . because, of course, I have final say over all company commanders."

"Of course you do," Arnold answered easily, directly.

Buckingham nodded after a long cold, uncomfortable moment, "Just try to work with him, Hanlin. He's difficult, I grant you. But as a favor to me, give it your best to get along with him. Or ignore him. I don't care, but try to keep him." He gave me a vote-winning earnest look.

"I'll try," I do not believe anyone beyond Osgood detected my complete lack of enthusiasm, "then I'll decide."

"That's all we ask," Buckingham, happy for the first time that morning, "you'll have the Twenty-first's roster ready soon?"

"This week," Arnold answered, "camp's laid out, siding will be finished by week's end, the station and warehouse any day. Wycroft will bring us up to date on supplies, I think we can start to bring the men in by next Monday."

"Excellent," the Governor, animated at last.

"We've agreed," Arnold continued, "that we'll bring in the officers first."

Buckingham shrugged, we learned early on that although he expected and commanded updates, he was uninterested in the ever boring details. Buckingham was that strictly American phenomena, the politician who thought armies formed themselves magically to meet any crisis, then went away in a flash to be resurrected for the next.

"We'll also," I added, "bring in a training officer from outside, if we can find one."

"Outside?" Buckingham asked while managing to hide all vestiges of curiosity.

"Outside. At West Point we were initially trained by regular Army hard cases, shell backs. All our enmity was directed at those bastards while the officers who oversaw them shook their heads in sympathy. It's going to be hard enough training a thousand men not used to discipline without having them hating us on top of it."

"You need a Hessian," the Governor, with surprising astuteness.

"Exactly," I agreed.

"Any candidates?"

"Several, Governor," Osgood spoke up, "we'll review them over the weekend," I look at him quizzically, he held up a hand discreetly conveying, 'I have this'.

"Fine," Buckingham's attention slipped away, "do I need to do anything?"

"I would like you to send the call out," my tone so respectful it caught Seth and Osgood's immediate attention, "You'll give the summons import."

"Certainly," he was pleased and that was as good a time as any to take our leave. We said our goodbyes and left him to the fire and a dozen honey muffins.

Back in the foyer, Seth touched my still wet shoulder, "Go home, get some rest, William, I'll handle what I can this afternoon."

"Thanks, I'll track you down later today."

"No... This is my first order to you," he smiled widely at the idea, "sleep, relax. God knows you need it."

It was no longer raining but the air and the dark promised an imminent resumption of the downpour. The wind picked up, something I would not have thought possible, threatening to blow our jackets over our heads.

After Arnold left for the Goodwin, Osgood yelled over the wind, "There's a surprise for you at home."

"I hate surprises," I yelled back, "what is it?"

"Nope, have to wait."

"I hate waiting."

"I know," he said with enjoyment.

"Several candidates for training officer?"

"One, I thought several would sound more impressive."

"Good thinking, who is he?"

"Later."

"When?"

"Maybe Saturday."

I stopped, "I have to wait to Saturday?"

"Going to be a long week for you," he finished with an evil laugh and picked up his pace.

3

I was two steps into the hallway when I caught a blur out of the corner my eye hurtling from the general direction of the parlor. Before I could react I was in a full embrace with a red haired bear.

"Brother!" The beast roared in my ear, "I'm free and come to join you!" A tree trunk sized, rock solid arm wrapped around my chest and cut off my air supply.

"Christian," I gasped, pushed against an iron chest to no effect, "let me go... Please."

He did, I breathed again, the relief of that mitigated by intense pain between my shoulder blades where my brother, thirteen years my junior, pounded me with paws the consistency of concrete.

"Christian," I groaned, "Great to see you, please stop hitting me," I turned Osgood for help, "nice surprise... help."

Osgood grinned back, "I got my beating yesterday, try to suffer yours gracefully."

I made an I- can't- believe- I- am- forced- to- do-this face, timed the next smash, pivoted as it arrived, grabbed a hand, found the thumb, and in one fluid motion, stepped to the side, turned the palm of his hand outward and enjoyed, immensely, his subsequent bellow of pain.

I led him to the study like that, softly said, "Now be a good bully and I won't have to break your arm."

"God dammit, I hate this!" He half groaned, half roared.

"Don't swear," I twisted his thumb just a tad to insure he was paying attention.

"Ow! God dammit," now he plain yelled, "I learned to swear from you, you bastard."

"That's just slanderous," I led him to a chair, "I don't swear," I pushed him down, "now stay there."

I left him rubbing his wrist, elbow, shoulder and went over to the sidebar where someone had thoughtfully left a fresh cup of coffee and a slab of what looked like fresh-baked cake. I took both and went to my chair.

"Hey, those are mine, Willie," Christian yelped but did not move.

"Thank you," I responded pleasantly.

"Bastard."

"You ready for round two already?"

"There's plenty in the kitchen?"

"Go grab some then, feel free, we don't stand on formality to be served here," I explained kindly.

"I'll get you something," Osgood, chuckling from the doorway, "you two catch up," he spun on his heels and disappeared.

I pushed into the cushions, took a moment to inspect the bear that was my brother. I had not seen him in six months although he was less than thirty miles downriver at Wesleyan College. Undoubtedly the largest senior in their annals; undoubtedly the largest anything in their annals, Christian stood a good two inches taller than me and was... vast. Neck, arms, legs, chest, vast. A circus strongman in an impeccably tailored suit, the fineness of the clothing the sure indicator that he was more his mother's child than I would ever be.

He had a wild mop of red hair, efficient, intelligent blue eyes, orange sideburns that faded halfway down his cheeks to reappear as a thin, downy mustache he had been fruitlessly cultivating for years.

"You look great," I said at last.

"Thank you," he seemed to take in my uniform for the first time, "my God you're in uniform already–shit, major?"

"Lieutenant Colonel, insignia's close," I corrected, feeling every bit the big brother.

"Christ, Lieutenant Colonel," he glowed, "when was the last time I saw you in uniform? Had to be, what, when I was ten?"

"Probably," I took my coat off and hung it by the fire, stayed to take the chill off.

"Where'd you get the medal?" He asked, laughing, "you buy it someplace?"

"It's nothing . . . just a service medal, states gave them out in spades," I answered, with a yawn.

"Service medal?" Confusion crinkled his stillborn mustache.

"Service, as in a war," I clarified.

He shook his massive head, searched the ceiling for an answer that was apparently there, "Oh, Christ, you were in Mexico!"

"Well . . . . yes," I let it hang.

"Mother..."

"Never told you," I finished, "she hated the war, her friends opposed it, and she was just so fucking mortified her oldest son was fighting it she told people I was in Europe serving as military attaché to some tiny state," I let out an overdue but purely unintentional sigh, "I could've messed it up pretty good if I had gotten myself killed and made the newspapers."

"I was seven when the war started," his great mane shook in wonderment, "she could have told me anything, I just thought your uniform was bully."

"So did I," I said to the fire. I did not have the decorations on my chest the last time he saw me in uniform for the simple reason our mother would not allow me in the house on Beacon Hill with them on. For what they represented. For what I did

"Well, you look great, what's your posting?"

"Chairman of the Governor's military advisory committee and executive officer of the Twenty-first Connecticut, don't you read the papers?"

The answer was in his embarrassed grin.

"How's school?" Afraid of where it was going, I changed the subject.

"Over," he said with glee.

"Over?"

"I graduated, Willie, two months early. The entire senior class and a few juniors who were close, it's..."

"The war," I finished needlessly, "you came to enlist, didn't you?" I added flatly, emotions mixed, mad at myself for not having anticipated it.

"I came here," he grinned wickedly, "to stay with my big brother. Who just happens to be a West Point graduate."

I looked at Christian and was almost overcome by the image of the little boy, tiny hand in mine, marching around West Point stopping every 10 feet to salute everybody and everything.

"I don't suppose," I gave it a shot, "you want to take some time out and, say, tour Europe?"

"Like you toured Mexico after you graduated?"

"I suppose telling you that was different would be a waste of breath?"

"Specious as well," he showed the benefit of a liberal arts education.

"Admitted. Short of shooting you - which would defeat the whole point - I can't stop you from joining up, can I?"

"Not a chance."

"Then I'd rather have you where I can watch over you . . . we'll have to get you a commission and assign you to a company."

"I've got a company, Willie," he smiled wildly.

"You what?" I stumbled in surprise I should not have felt.

"Eighty-seven men from Wesleyan," he thrilled to my surprise, "and they've elected me Captain," he added with total acceptance. He had been the captain of every athletic team he was ever on.

Osgood emerged just then toting a tray with coffee and the remnants of what was once a large cake. Christian having gotten there earlier.

"Congratulations, Christian," Osgood called out.

I sighed deeply, "Your company will be part of the Twenty-first," Osgood raised his eyebrows momentarily, nodded, "as long as you agree to be treated like everyone else, your company just one of ten, or twelve, hell the way we're going it will be a host by the time we're called up."

"It's a deal, Willie!" He shouted.

"One other thing, in front of the men and other officers, I am Colonel, or Sir, not brother or Willie or anything else, understood?"

He laughed his agreement, "Of course, brother, Willie . . . shit head."

I shook my head at my naïveté, "You'll move in here for a while?"

"Already have, teach you leave town for a couple of days."

"Osgood," I said wearily, my weekend catching up in blindsiding fashion, "take this big bear to Blake's and see if they can sew three or four normal uniforms together and make him one. I have to get some rest," I walked over to Christian's chair, pulled him up and gave him a proper hug, "great to have you, Christian."

"Thanks, Willie," he whispered.

"Get going you two," I commanded and pushed him on his way.

"Yes sir, Colonel," Osgood snapback with efficiency, "see that Christian, it's easy, probably sounded like I meant it, too."

"Certainly did, Osgood, but to the discerning ear it was clearly the insult it was intended to be. I think I can master this quickly."

Yawning, I waved them both away and headed for the staircase, "We'll finish this when I wake up," I said over my shoulder.

"Sleep well, old man," Christian booms, "you need your rest, that move won't work forever."

"I have others," I yelled from the top of the stairs.

I dragged myself to my room, struggled out of my clothes, toweled off, crawled under a plump comforter, and... remained wide awake for hours. I drifted, miserably, restlessly, frustratingly between sleep and total alertness. Images from the weekend watching amateurs play soldier blurred with indistinct tintypes from a half a dozen Mexican skirmishes and I warmed the comforter with continuous motion.

The recurring images that caused the most angst that morning, in that exhausted state, were of my West Point roommate and best friend, Zach. Pieces of us together at the Point, traveling through Texas, drinking in cantinas, chasing – unsuccessfully - senorittas, the fight at Molina Del Ray... everything except his messy death. For the re-creation of that scene my mind substituted the face of my favorite person in the world for poor, forever twenty-one, Zachary.

When Osgood and my brother returned home mid-afternoon they found me asleep in my chair, *Bleak House*, page eighteen, open on my lap.

4

Judge Crompton looked like a spry leprechaun behind his mammoth desk, bushy, snow white eyebrows knotted and approaching his hairline in the steepness of their arc.

"Nelson is an ass, of course," he had just endured my description of my last meeting with my boss, "and a buffoon, and a thousand other things, but," the judge held up a much needed restraining hand least I add a dozen more adjectives, "that does nothing to offset the political muscle he carries in this state."

"Which I'll never understand," I replied with a useless, unnecessary sneer.

"Which you better start understanding," he replied with the patience of the benevolent uncle he resembled, "if you're planning on returning home when this is finished."

"Right now, I hope to have the option," I answered truthfully, if not melodramatically.

"Don't be so melodramatic, you're a born survivor, you'll be back. And he'll still be here - you'll have to deal with him sometime," he leaned back, his ancient, much abused leather chair groaned menacingly, "and like an adult too. I know how difficult it can be keeping that wit to yourself."

"Not difficult, but a lot less fun."

"Despite his apparent thickness, having fun at his expense, especially now, could prove problematic in the immediate future."

"You don't seriously," I could not keep utter derision out of my voice, "think they'll give him the Senate seat?"

"Are you that disconnected from the political realities of this city?" Like the good attorney he was before his judgeship knew the answer.

"They impose some kind of rule assholes with no social graces or charisma in any form are destined for political advancement?"

"In this state, today, yes," my friend instructed me with firmness, "Nelson is a strict abolitionist —"

"There any other kind?"

He answered with a scowl, "He has money, connections, and the prerequisite killer instinct to make use of them to get what he wants."

"More power and better connections."

"Surprisingly, you can be taught."

"Then don't stop now," I chuckled as he considered it, "educate me."

"If you think he's insufferable now, try—"

"Dealing with him as a senator."

"You are a prodigy."

"I hate to sound selfish," my tone dripped selfishness, "but he goes to Washington he no longer concerns me, in fact, with luck, I would never see him again."

"I never took you for a shallow man," Crompton half grinned, "and, as you volunteered to lead troops in the coming war, you can't have such a narrow view of the public good."

"Look closer."

"Seriously, would you want that man representing you, this state, in Congress?"

"I would from Massachusetts."

"Laugh all you want," from long experience I knew that tone to strongly suggest all hilarity end, "it is an upsetting proposition."

"You have a startling low opinion of our legislature."

"Please," he waved that dismissively away, "as if they have anything to do with this election."

I nodded with a sagacity I did not feel, "it's preordained then."

"I never took you for a Calvinist, William," he snorted, "although there was so much I did not know about you."

"My apologies," I intoned with feeling, "may I ask, with me leaving why are we having this discussion?"

"You're not leaving for several months," he said with a certain amount of almost completely disguised insinuation.

"And?"

"Think you'll solve the killings before you leave?"

"Not likely," I felt some confusion at the sudden question,

"unless the bastard makes an enormous error and is caught in the act. Or gives himself up out of some sense of civic guilt."

"You leave, another girl dies, and your Nelson has a convenient, absent, scapegoat."

"If word gets out and someone puts all the deaths together."

"You that naïve?"

"Oh," I compounded it with the singular lack of eruditeness.

"He'll publicize them himself and he'll bury you in a heartbeat."

"I know that," I countered quickly, "I just don't know what it will matter while I'm getting shot at by Southern Democrats."

"It matters on several levels, at least to your friends," he said evenly.

"My friends being Nelson's enemies," I tersely summed up.

"I don't believe that a subset of people who like both you and Nelson would have any members," I nodded to his grin, "regardless, no one wants Nelson advancing himself at your expense."

"In my absence."

"In your absence."

"You're only saying that because I'm your favorite prosecutor."

"Purely because you are not entirely disagreeable and you are most certainly not Nelson."

"That's very flattering."

"Isn't it?" he maliciously agreed, "But the truth of it is that you were certain to be his successor, if done properly he would not be the threat he is to sully Connecticut's good name in the Senate. The war, unfortunately, has thrown a wrench into . . . everything."

"Maybe you can get a truce so this matter can take precedence," I said without rancor, without mentioning that there was no doubt I would have thrown that wrench myself.

"If only," he mused aloud as if considering it, "but in the absence of that improbability we must do something to, at the very least, keep Lord Nelson where he is today. Until you return safely."

"How do you accomplish that, wall him up like Fortunato?"

"That's a thought, but I really don't know at present. You have any ideas?" He sat forward, put his face in his hands, and gave me a long, searching look.

"None," I said after a palpable pause.

"Pity," he said in a voice that conveyed anything but pity, "did you know Nelson has targeted Olga Petoskey to begin his investigation?" His look never varied. I knew, probably had known since I had sat down in the office that he was telling me something that he could not tell me directly.

"That would be unfair," I said at length.

"It would. I imagine he's intent on making a morality statement," I knew Nelson had made many promises years before that he would rid the city of each and every vice. Perhaps, before my employment, he actually tried, I had never seen evidence of any such attempt.

"That and the fact that with the pressure only a chief law enforcement officer can exert, he can extort sufficient information from her to greatly assist his climb."

"That would be unfortunate," my turn to deadpan, "although I don't see Olga bowing to any pressure, on anything."

"The State's Attorney can bring a special brand of pressure on anyone, however innocent – done the right way, it's enough to be investigated."

"Olga knows she's not a suspect," I insisted.

"She thinks she knows."

"But, she's —"

"Helps to know where you stand for sure before an interrogation, don't you think?" His eyes never left mine. Only someone who knew him well would have caught the subtle inflection.

"Sure," I agreed.

"You are technically no longer an employee of the judicial department, are you?"

"Technically, no."

"And you are about to go off to war."

Belatedly, I got it, "And, who would begrudge a soldier some pleasure before he leaves."

"No one I know," Crompton may have smiled slightly, "even if someone did, it would surely be forgotten long before the war ends."

"I think I'll pay Olga a visit,"

"Your choice," he smiled.

"I can see a warning retarding the disease, but I don't see it curing it," I said with unintended irony.

"Why Doctor Hanlin," he laughed, "I'm sure you'll think of something."

"If I do, will that too be forgotten?"

"Does one ever remember the pain after it's gone?"

"They do not."

"I am very glad, William, we have been able to discuss this. I know a great many people who'll be pleased unpleasantness will be avoided."

"For Olga or themselves?"

"I believe their interests to be one in the same."

"You know," I nodded, smiled my best sardonic smile, "I like Olga, I would've gone to see her if you asked straight out."

"I know, William, but then it would not have been as much fun, would it?"

"I suppose not," I was forced to agree.

5

Charles pulled the reins with a jerk and we stopped a little too abruptly in front of the house in the lee of Asylum Hill, thereby announcing ourselves with skittering across the cobblestones and the clanging of metal fittings.

"So much for a stealthy entrance," I observed to Philip's deep scowl.

"Ya' look right dashing in ya' uniform," he muttered with a man of the world, knowing look.

"It's not that kind of visit, Charles, this is professional,"

"Of course, boss, they ain't free now, are they?"

"I'm not here for sex, that plain enough," I tried to snap but my heart was not in it.

"In that case," he grinned lasciviously, "I'd hate to think them unemployed for the morning . . . I'll take that bonus now,"

"I've never promised a bonus, indeed your continued employment is somewhat doubtful," I alighted the rig, "I won't be long. Wait. Quietly." I started up the walkway.

"Ya' better not be coming back with a smile on your face," he muttered under his breath.

I suppressed a smile and meandered up to the porch. I was visiting unannounced and, mindful of their niche market, I had waited to noon. I knocked on the door, so lightly I had trouble hearing it, berated myself for gross timidity, tapped the portfolio containing Osgood's drawings against my leg, tried to organize my approach to the meeting.

No answer, of course, my knock would not have gotten a twitch from a ravenous weasel. I knocked again, far too loud unless announcing a raid. I cringed and waited. And waited. Long enough to begin to wonder if I had underestimated the sexual avarice of my fellow Hartfordians. I almost knocked again - just

106

right this time, I presumed - when the door swung open and I was leveled by a pair of deep, incisive hazel eyes.

"Colonel," a clear, sweet voice with an underlying hint of throatiness, "I'm sorry you had to wait - our clients let themselves in. Come in, welcome," she pulled open the door and may have made a motion, I cannot say, I was loath to take my eyes off her eyes.

"Rather like a doctor's office then?" I mumbled the single most inane sentence of my life to date.

"Rather," she obviously shared my appraisal, led me down the hallway nevertheless. At my chest height with reddish-brown hair, perfect face, full lips, she was magnificent.

We moved into a small parlor, "Please have a seat Colonel."

"Thank you, Miss?"

"Call me Bridget, Colonel," she smiled her name.

"William . . . Hanlin . . . call me William . . . please," I was pleased it came out somewhat intelligible.

"Of course you are," she agreed. With great effort I tore my eyes off her and looked around the room. Expensively and tastefully decorated, I was relieved to see that the art was all landscapes. I took a plush chair by a window, was absorbed into softness. Bridget sat directly across, a look on her face that did not match the demureness of her conservative dress. I judged her to be her late twenties and, upon further reflection, deemed her simply stunning.

As if summoned telepathically an attractive, diminutive in all measures save cleavage, black woman appeared to the doorway. I knew at once she was no servant, it was obvious by her walk and manner that there was not a subservient bone in her body. Her pretty face broke out in a wide smile when she saw my uniform.

"Colonel Hanlin, Maria," Bridget sang out.

"A pleasure, Colonel," Maria's voice had a deep alluring timbre, "or it certainly could be," she oozed suggestion so genuinely sincere part of my body horrifyingly stirred.

"Maria," Bridget, in a good-natured schoolmarm voice, "don't be so forward, William hasn't announced his intentions. Leave him be."

"But that uniform," she protested in a voice now a sweat

107

inducing purr.

"It does have allure," Bridget replied, hoarseness more apparent in her speech. I crossed my legs, "we'll be seeing a lot more of them now, so try to control yourself."

"It's hard, Bridget," she stepped closer to my chair, "he's tall too, why the combinations we. . ."

"Maria!" Bridget yelled with a smirk.

"Sorry, Bridget . . . Colonel," Maria gave me a slow, obvious once over that would have buckled my knees had I been standing, "so, why are you here, Colonel?"

"You're being rude, Maria," Bridget pretended to snap.

"Sorry again," she said in a tone that was anything but apologetic.

"Quite all right," I managed to get out, "I'm here to see Madame Petrovsky on business," and yes, it sounded lame to me as well.

"Everybody's here on business," Maria chortled.

"Maria, you're embarrassing Colonel Hanlin," Bridget, with a motion indicating it did not embarrass her a whit.

"My apologies, sir," Maria, suddenly demur, "I'll fetch Olga and have cook bring some refreshments," she headed for the door in an exaggerated, hip stressing walk, "last chance, Colonel," she said with a wink that would've resulted in exile not all that long ago.

"I apologize for Maria," Bridget said without a hint of apology, "she tends to be too forward for Connecticut Yankees," her smile took a decidedly different tactic and she completed her thought, "never mind a Boston Brahmin."

"That news traveled fast," I tried without success to remember the last time so simple a conversation had made me so complexly discombobulated.

"I assure you it was heard here first, Colonel," she continued with a knowing look, "and relayed no further."

"Of course," I agreed, "please call me William."

"Well, William," she started promisingly only to be cut off when Olga walked into the room.

"William, what a pleasant surprise," Olga floated across the floor, I met her halfway, Bridget watched with an unreadable expression.

Olga took my hand in a warm, solid clasp, "Sit down, my dear, Cook will be along with some refreshments," she held my eyes, "delighted to see you again."

"And I you," I replied automatically feeling vaguely idiotic. Olga arranged herself in a chair to my left, directly opposite Bridget. Together, they leveled their incandescent eyes at me. It was intoxicating at the moment, I was realistic enough to suspect they could just as easily be wielded in deadly combination. It only took a few seconds to realize not a word would be spoken until I started.

"I came by for several reasons."

"That's a relief, most of our visitors come for only one," Bridget interjected, ably taking over for departed Maria.

"Depends on how you count," Olga countered, "but I fear we are being unfair to William, making him needlessly uncomfortable," while I could not be absolutely sure, I swear she winked.

"Perhaps he likes being made uncomfortable," Bridget said with a suddenly predatory smile.

"Later, Bridget," Olga laughed, "we're being quite wicked and poor William looks like he has important business."

"You know, "I admitted, "I might like this game."

"We've others," Bridget broke, perhaps permanently, my chain of thought. Olga tittered and shook her head.

"I'm sure you do," I collected myself, not for nothing had I led men into musket fire, although that seemed child's play now, "as does our chief state's attorney, that's why I'm here." Quite intentionally I sucked the banter out of the air.

"I thought, Colonel," Olga's tone changed immediately, though I could not say to what, "you are no longer in that profession. Or is one always a member, like some Masonic Temple?"

"Oh, I left, Olga," I replied hastily, "but Lord Nelson remains."

"A shame that."

"Indeed," I said to her cool appraisal. Bridget stared at her intently, "what's worse is that I'm leaving him unsupervised and he's assuming my caseload."

"Is he?" Olga's eyes began to calculate.

"He is," I confirmed, "all my outstanding cases . . . as soon as I give him this," I patted the portfolio case next to me.

"What is that, William?" She asked quite pleasantly.

"My files on the murders."

"What a curious thing to carry with you on a social visit. A habit of yours?"

"No," I smirked in wane response. With Olga to my left – attractive, intelligent, crafty – and Bridget to my right – radiant, sly, attending to every nuance of Olga's responses – I was having great difficulty concentrating. All the while, I felt my own reactions, statements somehow artificial, somehow not me. A feeling I had had but very rarely in my life to date, and then only when I was out of my element. As I most surely was.

"So, a singular honor then, sir," Olga grinned at her sarcasm, "why?"

"I wanted to impose on you to help me once again."

"I was not aware of having helped you previously."

"You're too modest, Olga," I said with a deliberate edge, "you made very helpful observations when we viewed the body upstairs."

"You were able to identify the girl?"

"Received word yesterday, Elizabeth Holt, first-generation German, daughter of Henreich and Gertrude Hollenzoeller. South End."

She nodded slowly, "I'm glad my guess helped."

"It was more than a guess, Olga," I said with open admiration, "with your analysis and Osgood's sketch we had a Hartford cop named Jonas Smith, nee Schmidt I'm sure, walk through Colt's factory in mufti. He found her parents." And I found a master sergeant.

"Good."

"The other bodies are still unidentified and unclaimed."

"You want me to look at their sketches," she said without inflection.

"The murder scenes," I stressed to insure she fully understood.

"Give me the pictures," she replied with no hesitation. I

opened the portfolio, removed Osgood's sketches and handed them to her. She inspected them without expression, "pretty girls," her only comment.

She took her time and she concentrated. I had seen enough witnesses of every description flick over a sketch if it were an incredible inconvenience, an annoyance of life altering portions, to appreciate her attention. Still without expression Olga neatly lined up the sketches, stood in a quick, flowing motion and, to my appall, handed them to Bridget. I was about to voice my objection when I noticed Bridget looking at the sketches without obvious emotion. Perhaps a slight widening of the eyes, nothing more.

"Bridget", I whispered, she looked up with curiosity, "you saw the body upstairs, didn't you?"

"Yes, William," she said simply and went back to her inspection.

"Did you find it?"

"I did," annoyed with the interruptions.

I flicked from her perfect face to Olga's, "Olga, you..."

"Lied to you, yes," she finished without outward signs of regret, "how did you know?"

"Please," I waved her off, "all the bodies are the same, Bridget didn't so much as hesitate to take the sketches from you, and she didn't blink when she saw the body. She saw the real thing."

"Of course," Olga without inflection, never mind apology.

"Notice anything?" I asked somewhat testily.

"None of them," she stopped when an older, matronly woman entered the room carrying a tray of coffee and cakes. She put them on the table next to Olga and shuffled out without a spare motion. Olga waited for her to clear the door before finishing, "are professionals, but then you know that yourself. Now."

I nodded thanks for the earlier lesson.

"I would guess the first is Irish, perhaps Scottish, the second Portuguese. Your killer has eclectic tastes," she observed grimly.

"Does indeed," I nodded, held her eyes, "you have any clients that have any proclivities in that regard?"

"Which regard, dear?" She blinked as if registering the fact I had assumed the moral advantage in our now hours old relationship.

"We'll start with exotic tastes for foreign flesh."

"No one," she answered at length.

"Would you tell me if you did?"

"Yes," she nodded, "the most adventurous the average Yankee gets is Maria," she shook her head at the timidity of New England Victorian manhood.

"She's been very popular ever since *Uncle Tom's Cabin*," Bridget pointed out, smile rigidly affixed.

"Any of your clients," I asked without mirth, "particularly suited to the role of Simon Legree?"

Olga chuckled, "Well asked, William . . . we have had few clients partake in anything rougher than spanking."

It was Bridget's turn to laugh, "Of themselves or their monkey, mostly." Olga joined her laughter.

I smiled briefly, "What about those few?"

"William?" Olga responded with measure.

"The few who wanted more than a smack on the ass," that quickly I saw her irises widen and the calculations begin. A long involved mathematical calculation whereof parts of the proof could be found on her shoes, my shoulder straps, the window, the seascape above the untouched coffee urn, and, finally, Bridget's immeasurably deep eyes. I swear there was an audible click when she made her decision.

"Before we go on my dear," she said breezily, "I would love a cup of coffee, black," she managed a girlish smile.

"As would I," I rose, went to the table. Bridget was soon by my side, her shoulder and hip pressed against me. She set about preparing two cups, all the while finding innumerable ways to accidentally touch my hand as we vied for the urn, sugar, cakes, butter. Rather than break the, for me electric, connection, I put ten times the normal amount of sugar in my cup of sludge. She smelled of rose water and eroticism.

Bridget broke contact with a knee buckling smile and an impish glint and left me standing there, undrinkable cup in my hand, silently thanking my Blake for leaving my working uniform pants with plenty of room for riding and emergencies such as the one I then experienced.

I pretended to have a cramp that caused a sudden limp and

returned to my chair without further embarrassing myself. I even managed to sit without spilling cake crumbs all over the affected area. The coffee was no threat, it having already congealed into some previously undiscovered adhesive.

Somehow I managed to find that part of my brain that still operated in an intellectual manner and I settled down and remained silent for Olga to resume. She calmly, almost ceremoniously, took a dainty bite of the cake followed by a sip of coffee.

"Two, William," she resumed slowly, "the first, banished from here perhaps two years ago, is an odious man from Farmington, Huntingdon," I kept my gaze level despite the surge of what, happiness, elation, excitement? "He beat one of my associates quite badly, using fists and a belt, he has not been back since," she took a long slow strong sip and stared intently at her curtains.

"I've met him," I said evenly.

"I should think you would have as he is to be one of your officers."

"No longer, I think," I spit out.

"He is. I think," she smiled knowingly, "he is not your man, William. He was at that fundraiser in the early morning hours, then he was abusing some poor girl at a rather less . . . ostentatious competitor until finally banished from that establishment about the time you and Osgood arrived here. I'm guessing," her eyes took on the narrow gleam of sharpshooters I had known in Mexico, "he will have to content himself with fucking in alleyways from here on."

"You're sure?"

"I am."

"You could've told me this earlier."

"No, I could not have," she said with complete certainty.

"When did you find out about his alibi?"

"Shortly after you left here."

"And if you had not been able to verify his whereabouts?"

"You would have received a nice postcard, anonymously, of course."

"I would've known you sent it."

"That's of no account. I can't help it if your powers of

113

observation are so acute."

A thought struggled through the thickening haze in my head, "Would you recognize Huntington's handwriting?"

"Oh, yes," she chortled, "he sent me a number of delightfully obscene hate letters for months after his exile."

I reached into the portfolio and handed her one of the killer's notes. She read it, leaned over and handed it to Bridget with no visible reaction except to flash a quick smile my direction.

"It's not his handwriting, I'm sorry to say," she apologized, "your killer is quite polite."

"Very," Bridget echoed.

"And that is not our Huntingdon," Olga with a nasty smirk.

"I noticed that in our brief acquaintance," I understated, considerably, "I still think it best that he not serve under me."

"Because he's banned from a brothel?" Olga laughed, followed rapidly by Bridget, "that's absurd, William."

I nodded dumbly. She was, of course, correct.

There was a brief silence while we contented ourselves with coffee and cake. Bridget and I exchanged glances at varying intervals.

Eventually, I broke the silence with the obvious question, "Do you have a similar alibi for the other . . . I assume you must, else I would've had a different postcard." I spoke lightly, surprised to see Olga's face darken. She exchanged a long look with Bridget, one that had me feeling the interloper.

"There was no need to check his alibi," Olga offered, flatly.

"Why not?" I came close to demanding, backed off at the last moment while a myriad of possibilities coursed through me

"Because he is your boss."

Stunned, I look stupidly to Bridget for confirmation. She nodded gravely.

"Walker Nelson?" I mumbled.

"Made the girls call him Chief," Olga supplied all the confirmation I needed.

"Holy fuck," I sighed, the first and last time in my life I used that phrase.

"Yes," Olga agreed.

"Well," I mused aloud in my shock, "I know his writing,

there's no resemblance. And, he's not physically capable of these murders."

"In several ways," Olga added to my arch look, "I understand he has problems performing, hence the roughness."

"Definitely not our man," I said with regret.

"No," Olga's sentiment matched my own.

"And yet he wishes to interview you about the murders."

"Does he? She smiled, "In what regard?"

"To implicate you somehow, anyhow, after all a nude young woman found dead here gives him justification to visit again."

"That gets them in the door," her turn to muse aloud, "but implicate me? He cannot justify me as a suspect, semen alone rules that out."

"Olga," I said conversationally, "that sick, twisted fuck can postulate that the girl worked for you, you had a falling out, and you had her killed and mimicked the other murders, which of course you knew about due to the indiscretions of the police commissioner," I looked hard for reaction. I received none.

"Nice try, William," she said with grudging respect and no hint of confirmation.

"In any event," I went on, happy to be leading the witness for once, "it matters little how he wraps you in, he'll do it and will magnanimously let you out of it –"

"With a few tidbits about certain of my clientele. My contribution to the Senate run," Olga intoned.

Once again I regarded her with deep respect, watched while she calmly finished her coffee and took a bite out of her carefully buttered cake.

"I suppose," I traded a look with the softly smiling Bridget, "it's a moot point now."

"I don't suppose it is, completely, dear," Olga's voice was severe, "as long as he accuses first, counter accusations – especially from someone of my gender and profession - are worthless."

"But you could always . . ."

"*I* could always nothing," she said calmly, "*my* word, *alone*, is worthless," she and Bridget stared pointedly at me, "but a representative . . ." she trailed off.

"An attorney, say," I began to catch up

"Indeed."

"Someone who knows him well," Bridget added.

"That puts the fear of God into him," Olga emended.

"Someone tall, big," Bridget, with a lovely lift of an eyebrow.

"A large attorney who puts the fear of God into Nelson, then," Olga mimicked Bridget's eyebrow to a thoroughly different although equally enticing result.

"Any prospects?" I asked in total innocence.

"What, exactly, is your status with that office, William?" Bridget asked.

"None beyond handing this file over and remaining available for questions that are sure to never be asked," I turned toward Bridget, "Though I suppose I can have my position back - if," I stared fully into her eyes, "I come back from the war." Bridget giggled at the oldest of all soldier ploys.

"Shameless," Olga groaned, eyes upward, "I assume you retain your ability to practice law."

"Why yes, Olga, I do," I was enjoying myself.

"Then I propose that if you are still here and not," she glanced at Bridget, shook her head, "lying lamented on some distant field, would you consent to act as my attorney?"

"Delighted to."

"Thank you, William, I will very much look forward to that day, then, and the look on that sick twisted fuck's face when you sit next to me," she beamed.

"As do I," I agreed, rose, put my dish and cemented coffee cup on the table, "I have to go ladies, I'm afraid, I'm late for the Meadows." Indeed, the magnificent Seth Thomas clock on the far wall showed me already very late.

"I'm sorry to hear that," Olga rose and walked to me. I put my hand out, she ignored it, put her hands on my shoulders, kissed me fleetingly across the mouth, leaned into me and whispered, "thank you."

She broke contact as swiftly as she had achieved it and moved to the door, "Bridget will be delighted to see you out." With that she disappeared down the hallway.

"I certainly will," Bridget was up, nearing. She hooked her

right arm through mine and walked me into the hallway. We strode down in an edgy silence. At the front door, we stopped and turned toward each other. Her left hand found my right hip, her right hand slipped into mine, held it in an interlocking grip. I was rendered mute by the surprising intimacy of the moment.

"You'll come see me," She said softly, not a question.

"God, yes," emerged from somewhere. I, curiously involuntarily, stepped closer.

"Soon?"

"Soon," I moved closer still, put my hand on her hip, slowly slipped it up her back. She moved lightly into me, my hand in the small of her back, pulling.

"Good," she said lowly, her hoarseness more pronounced. One, or both of us, I have no idea, closed the remaining space and we kissed. Slowly, lips parting, tongues just touching.

It was over that quickly, so quickly in fact it left me to wonder if it had occurred at all.

"I'll be back soon," I mumbled and fumbled for the doorknob.

"I'll be here," she smiled widely and pushed me through the doorway, laughing as she shut the door behind me.

I wandered down the stairs and up the walk still smelling her, thinking of the last time I left a beautiful woman to go off to do harm to my fellow man. That must have shown in my face because Phelps looked at me quizzically as I mounted the rig. More so, he had no witticisms of any kind as we drove off.

6

Dawn, Saturday morning, Osgood and I stood on a windswept platform awaiting the, late, train to New Haven.

"Tell me again," I tugged at my collar, "Why I am in dress uniform and you are comfortably civilian?"

"You require the moral authority the uniform lends, whereas I require no such accoutrement".

"You're a shit."

"You make the point for me," he smiled mercilessly, "where we're going you require the uniform for . . . deflection, while I will be accepted at face value."

"Where exactly are we going, again?"

"New London is sufficient for now," said the exact moment our train came around the bend a hundred yards up the line, "relax, enjoy the ride," he yelled above steam and screaming brakes.

I did just that, spent the leg to New Haven reading newspapers – each and every one utterly unhindered by the fact there was still no news from Washington. This left them carte blanche to speculate on what the news might be if Washington were actually in contact with the outside world. Exclusives abounded and though no newspaperman myself I had to believe it was a glorious time for the industry, unencumbered as it were by troublesome facts.

By Meriden I eschewed the papers for Dr. Holmes' *Elsie Veneer*, did not look up until we slowed for the long, torturous, smoky approach to New Haven Station. When we crashed to a stop I snapped the book shut, was immediately aware of a dull roar outside. I looked down out the window and into a boiling mass of blue-clad humanity. Pure bedlam across the platform, spilling out of the station, several thousand, at least, newly minted

Federal troops mashed together in something approaching a riot without the overt violence.

We were required to cross the platform, enter the station and exit on the far side to make our Shoreline train, due to leave in twenty minutes. We were, therefore, left with no choice but to detrain into a milling mass of men going in all directions save the same, willfully oblivious to the threats and conflicting orders hoarsely screamed by low ranking officers standing on trunks, holding onto lamp posts, looking for all the world like flood victims balancing on flotsam.

A few steps – and several bumps and subtle shoves – into the solid blue surf, I recognized we were amid at least three regiments attempting to move south to New York. Bad enough to have 3,000 men bottle-necked, worse when they were from three different states. Rhode Island, Massachusetts, New Hampshire – the accented oaths were that evident – troops thrown together with no one pleased with the resulting mix.

My maple leafs caught attention, the very utterance "Sorry, Twenty-first Connecticut," was enough to clear our way. They were no more – probably much less, in fact – inclined to accept orders from a Connecticut officer than any state not their own. The state above all regardless, exactly what the men in blue were headed south to fight against.

"Not the best trained lot, are they?" Osgood yelled above the roar.

"This is why we're going to New London – we will not bring a mob south," I averred, "this is insane."

"I've seen better organized riots," Osgood agreed with disgust.

"You've been in better organized riots,' I corrected.

"Hell, I've started better organized riots."

An hour later, New Haven fading behind, we were comfortable in an almost deserted car staring out at the coastline and a sail studded Sound. Just past Madison, Osgood handed me a thick dossier, "Read it," he commanded.

"Well, yes, sir," I weighed it in my hand, "Jesus, Osgood, Gibbon's *Decline and Fall* too short for the ride?"

"This is more interesting," he shook his head, went back to the scenery.

The file on the man Osgood felt worthy of a day's trip. I did not really need it, the mere fact Osgood felt he was worth the trouble was recommendation enough. Out of a sense of duty and avid curiosity, I flipped it open and dove in. It was in English, French, and German – which I could not read, but got the gist nevertheless – and it was thorough, detailed, and fascinating. Where or how Osgood had put it together I could not begin to guess, nor did I contemplate asking. Osgood had his methods and contacts and was not disposed to divulge them to anyone, even me. Simply put, though, what he needed to know about someone or something, he found.

I did not put it down until we crossed the Connecticut and slipped through Waterford, "That all you got?" I asked with facetious nonchalance.

"That's only the important stuff."

"And it's all true?" I tweaked him, "Not the first draft of a novel?" I received a withering glare, went on gleefully, "It's *Barry Lyndon* without the sex, for Christ's sake."

"I left that out . . . it would only have distracted you to no end."

I acknowledged the basic truth of that with a shrug, "And this mythic hero is willing to see us?"

"No," he replied with ersatz derision, "he is willing to see me."

"Does he know I'm with you?"

"Of course and it does not matter. He had reservations about even meeting you, but I assured him that to know you is to despise you somewhat less."

"Reservations?"

"With what you represent," said in the off-hand manner that never failed to annoy the hell out of me – as he well knew.

"Represent? The United States Army? That could prove a sticking point considering where we're going."

"He is obviously hardly averse to any army," Osgood sighed, took the file back, carefully reinserted it into his portfolio case, "but you . . . you represent so much of what he abhors. Aristocracy – his word, not mine – college educated officer, all bad enough. Made so much worse by your intimate service to a state ill disposed, if not hostile, to the likes of him."

I nodded understanding, "He does know I'm not a Connecticut native, doesn't he?"

"Oh, sure, William," he exclaimed, "makes all the difference in the world. He feels so much better you're from Beacon Hill rather than a native born Yankee. That's like asking a lobster if he would rather be split in half or dropped in boiling water. Nice choice of oppression."

"I'm not sure your metaphor works," I pointed out helpfully.

"Fuck off," his ungrateful reply.

"Well now you're just hurting my feelings with all this."

"Good," he sympathized, "you have to admit he has cause to feel cautious."

"So admitted. I'll try to keep the Mayflower descendent, Protestant- work- ethic-obsessed, predestined- for – paradise- and – knows- it, abolitionist, anti-immigrant, sexually-repressed, class conscious, blue-blooded -holier -than -thouism out of my personality today."

"There's a good bigot."

I smiled, looked out to the Atlantic, then thought to ask the obvious, "Wait a minute, he has these preconceived notions about me because . . . . ?

"I may have, completely unintentional, mind you, reinforced a few of his 'preconceived notions' based on your name and profession when we met last week," he finished with a very satisfied smirk.

I considered for a moment before, "Am I to assume that while I was slogging through the backwaters of the county all weekend, performing my duty, subjecting myself to all manner of buffoonery, you were slandering me in New London?"

"No," he smiled happily, "I was slandering you in New Haven."

I eyed Osgood with suspicion and no small dose of hatred, "But for me to meet him —"

"We go to his turf, yes."

"To make me uncomfortable."

"Very much so."

"Great," I exhaled, "he have a clue I'm not what he thinks?"

"None . . . I have left it to you to disavow his notions – within reason, of course."

"Of course," I rose, tottered down the aisle as the train slowed, lurched around a wide bend and approached Ft. Trumbull at the mouth of the Thames. I stepped out onto the observation deck, breathed deep the tangy salt air, gripped a rail, and watched the old fort slip by, enormous national flag straight out in a strong breeze.

"You and castles and forts," Osgood, from across the deck, "I think the reason you went to West Point is that it's the only institution in the country with forts scattered about."

"I went to West Point to piss off my mother and escape her crowd. Harvard proved too close and I was somewhat ill suited for the Divinity School in any event."

"I'll say."

"That was less than generous," I smiled at his reaction and the mental picture of myself sitting through a theology lesson, "I confess, though, that climbing up to Ft. Putnam in the snow was worth it alone."

The train lurched to a stop a few hundred yards from the fort, feet from the docks lining the West bank of the Thames. We dropped to a cobblestoned street, assailed immediately by a

Ft. Trumbull. 1861

deadly mixture of salt air, tar, fish, and what had to be ancient whale oil.

"We're right on time," Osgood announced to the seagulls.

We walked toward the now distant fort, docks to the left, a motley collection of frame and brick buildings to the right. They were universally decrepit and looked older than they possibly could have been, New London having been burned to the ground almost exactly eighty years earlier by the British general Benedict Arnold.

We stopped in front of a once-white frame house, worn steps leading to a battered porch. I stared at opaque with grime windows and peeling paint held in place by dirt and thought Arnold had not been nearly as thorough as I had been informed. We were decidedly beyond the fashionable mercantile district of New London. A sign that had seen countless Nor'easters creaked in the breeze on rusty hinges. Mentally filling in the missing letters I took it to read 'Flanagan's Tavern & Inn'.

"An Irish bar?" I snapped as soon as it sunk in, "You're taking me to a fucking Irish bar?"

"You are amazingly perceptive, Counselor," he threw off my anger with ease, "It's a Saturday afternoon in a port town, you are meeting an Irishman, and the yacht club was unavailable."

"Wonderful," I snarled at his sarcasm and my idiocy, "he better be as impressive in person as he is on paper, Captain, or some lucky ship is going to have a new tar."

Up the stairs, across the protesting porch, I moved to grab the green brass handle of the oft coated black door, stopped when I noticed a sign tucked into a curtained window: '**Irish May Most Certainly Apply**'. I opened the door, stepped into the usual crowded barroom din assaulted by the ubiquitous combinations of stale beer, spilled spirits, seafood, unwashed bodies, and tobacco smoke. It hit hard and evoked a cadre of memories, some pleasant.

That was all on my first step in. I heard my second footfall quite clearly as complete, utter silence descended over the room like a sopping wet curtain. I was aware I was the object of obvious scrutiny when every head in the room swiveled toward the door and all movement ceased.

Osgood stepped in beside me, shut the door and cast the room into a cave like haze. I stood stock still while my eyes adjusted. Once they did I saw exactly what I could have described from the street, sight unseen: long, polished mahogany bar, brass railed; scattered stools in various stages of decomposition occupied by the brave who held on to the bar with one hand for much needed stability; eight taps for brews; a tiered selection of what had to be every whiskey on the market (and then some) backed by a bar-length mirror festooned with postcards, photographs, and other keepsakes; green flags adorned with harps, shamrocks, and/or sunbursts in gold hung thickly, interspersed by portraits of middle-aged men, some with dusty black crepe draped over equally dusty frames.

In the center of one wall, dead center, the place of honor, draped in green, white, and orange, the colors of lost hope and eternal grief, hung two portraits I recognized, Theobald Wolfe Tone and Robert Emmet. Fitting, between the two they covered the Irish gamut: rebel, dreamer, mystic, poet, warrior, martyr. I willed myself to an open space, leaned against the bar, the men on either side moved their stools without rising, the screeching and rasping reverberated like artillery through the silence.

To my amazement the barkeep, an overweight, balding, handle-bar mustachioed, mutton-chopped, elf of a man, ambled over at once. He made a show of starring at the uniform, to the poorly hidden smiles of those nearby. He frowned at my maple leafs, whistled, and shook his head.

Inspection complete, he boomed in a perfect tenor, "What'll ya have, Gen'rl?"

"It's Lieutenant Colonel," I corrected lightly, "and I'll thank you for a stout and a Bushmills," that brought arched looks from my recently relocated neighbors.

"The same," Osgood materialized next to me, back to the bar watching those watching us, "I was going to announce I'm not with you," he whispered, "but it seemed rude,"

"You expect thanks?"

"Under the circumstances, absolutely."

"They still staring?" My turn to whisper.

"Look in the mirror, for Christ's sake," he hissed.

I did, they were, "I was hoping they were just startled by the light when the door opened."

"Hope away."

We fell silent as well, the only sounds in the place the barkeep filling our order and the distant clinks of dishes from the kitchen out back. Eventually, the barkeep shuffled over and gently put our drinks down. I reached for my breast pocket but he shook his head and with mirth-filled eyes danced away.

I handed Osgood his shot glass, took mine, turned and faced the room. I took a deep, prayerful breath, raised my glass, said, loudly, "God save all here!' and knocked back the smooth as ice, much needed, whiskey.

Surprised, automatic 'here, here's' passed through the taproom, subsumed by sounds of drained glasses thumped down. Low whispering replaced the deafening silence.

"You brought me to a Republican bar?" I whispered with some heat.

"I think you would agree that the alternative could prove problematic," he smiled nastily, "and it was his choice."

"Fuck, Osgood, the only portrait missing over there . . . ." I was cut off by Osgood's iron grip on my forearm. For a second I thought it a warning, then followed his gaze, and watched with him as an older, handsome, square built man strode through the room toward us.

I had plenty of time to watch and assess, he stopped at every table shaking hands, patting backs, exchanging greetings. He could have been forty, he could have been fifty, age would not show on him until the end. He stood about five-nine, had a stocky, compact build that radiated several forms of strength. Dark auburn hair, fairly closed cropped, strong blue eyes set deep in a weathered, clean shaven, perfectly scarred face. His appearance screamed professional soldier.

By the time he reached us he sported an unreadable smile, looked intently into Osgood's face, ignored me completely, "Osgood, c'mon with me." His voice was light, airy, with the suggestion of a brogue, but not one of the bogs.

Osgood hit my arm to make sure I knew I was invited, we weaved through the taproom toting our pints, occasionally catching the eye of a patron, unfailingly received a glass salute in return. Past Tone and Emmet, into a smaller, dingier back room with a dozen high backed booths. Osgood's friend selected the last one on the far wall, the two closest were premeditatedly empty. I slid opposite him, Osgood sat next to me, uncharacteristically with his back to the doorway.

"Grand to see you again, Sean," Osgood started, "this is William Hanlin."

"Ah, sure it 'tis," he smiled without a hint of warmth, "pleasure, Colonel, Mr. State's Attorney Hanlin," he reached across the table, engulfed my hand in his. His grip was firm. My grip was firm. We locked eyes. His grip tightened, mine followed. I affixed a 'I'm a good sport' smile across my face while grinding my teeth, he widened his.

"That's . . . . assistant state's . . . attorney . . . . and . . . I've retired," I ended with a grimace.

"Wha'tever helps you sleep at night," he grunted. As if by mutual consent we broke contact, eyed each other for signs of pain, surreptitiously flexed our hands checking for broken metacarpals.

I ignored his jibe (what choice had I?), "It's William . . . . please."

He considered for very long seconds, reached a decision, "Sean O'Shea, Sean will do," his hostility belied the invitation to familiarity. Before I had an opportunity to react an astonishingly attractive woman materialized out of the smoky gloaming and stood, beaming, by our table. Jet black hair, impossibly deep blue eyes, perfect lips, unblemished white skin slightly blushing high on dimpled cheeks. I was mesmerized, could only think that I had fulfilled a year's quota of meeting beautiful women that week . . . and I should have spent more time at Olga's when I had the chance.

"Tooley, lass," O'Shea instantly became the happy host, "be a dearie and bring us a pitcher of ale - and make sure tha' cheap son o' a miser Flanagan uses tha' spigot he keeps hidden. An' bring us a coupla' plates of seafood, too."

"Sure, Sean," she answered in a voice that, well, it was a great voice. I watched her until she was consumed by the room's gloom.

"You've taste, William," O'Shea chuckled, "Black Irish, she. Ta' my mind tha' most beautiful women in tha' world. Fiery devils, too, if ya' like that. No one can hold a candle to 'em . . . . except, I suppose, tha' Greeks . . . . French, too. Then there's tha' Spanish. An' a Turks," he laughed hardily. It was a very good laugh, "ah, fook it, William, they're all beautiful! Thank God!" He put a knuckle to his forehead, I tipped my pint in agreement.

I took a great gulp of stout, O'Shea watched unblinkingly. I took that, probably childishly, as a challenge of some sort. Making the kind of split second decision prosecutors and infantry officers are paid to make, I met the challenge, stared back, and drained my pint. Done, I thumped it on the table and sat to full height without breaking contact. O'Shea never moved a muscle.

After an indeterminate time, Osgood interrupted, "I hope this is not going to degenerate into arm wrestling, or maybe something really, manly, like darts."

Sean laughed, broke contact, I wondered where my beer had gone, "So, William, ya've come ta' recruit me to a Yankee regiment, have ya?"

"I have indeed."

"Now ya' know," he sat back, addressed Osgood, "tha' last time I was recruited - back in the mists of time - you'll understand tha' sergeant told me I'd see tha' world and lay all kinda girls . . . if I'd jus' take tha' gold guinea off the drum head . . . . tha' bastard."

"You didn't see the world and get laid?" I asked.

"Course I did, he jus' left out the parts about floggin', bad food, marchin' in the pourin' rain, an' of course, gettin' shot at . . . . frequently. "

"Good recruiter," I observed.

"Right up until the Sepoys got 'im, I'm sure."

"So," I surmised, "I guess it wouldn't do any good to promise you'll see Virginia and get laid by exotic American women of all persuasions?"

"Can you promise I'll not get muddy, bored, shot at?" He grinned.

"Certainly," I promised immediately.

"You'll not be insulted if I donna' believe ya', will ya'?"

"Not at all "

"What can ya' promise me?" He smiled winningly

I hesitated not a whit, "The chance to treat a bunch of blue blooded Connecticut Yankees like shit for a month or so."

"Ah, now," he laughed, "that has a certain appeal. You included tha' group?"

"God, no!" I yelped, aghast at the thought, "I've already been properly abased. My tormentor was Sergeant Major Lawrence Chilten. Of the red necked and proud of it, North Carolinian Chiltens. Hated, and I do not overstate this in any way, everyone born north of the Mason-Dixon Line."

"Sounds like a sergeant major."

"A sadistic piece of shit," I summed him up with great economy, "but effective."

"Of course," O'Shea snickered, "He down south train' ya new enemies?"

"Coyote food," I said with some satisfaction, received a puzzled look from O'Shea, "The Apaches were not nearly as cowered by him."

"You in the Apache wars?" He asked, eyebrows raised.

"No, I resigned my commission in '51."

"Why?"

"Personal reasons. Family," I said, tersely.

"An' you're not about to share wi' me," he surmised.

"No."

"Fine," he said in a tone that indeed conveyed acceptance of my privacy, "when did ya' graduate this Wes' Point of yours?"

"Forty-six."

"So," he weighed his words, looked hard at Osgood, "What were ya' doin' between forty-six and ya' family problem? If that's not too personal," he chuckled lightly, "I'm assumin' ya' dinna' buy those trinkets at a pawn shop," he motioned at my chest.

"Why does everybody think that?' I asked no one in particular, "I was in Mexico, Sean."

"Were ya' now?" He nodded, "How long?"

"All the way through to Chapultepec."

"Ah, now, that was a smartly done action," he smiled at Osgood, happy to have someone to expound to, "two hundred foot fortified hill, outnumbered two to one, even the British commented well on tha' one."

"Gave me a healthy respect for artillery," I interrupted their bonding.

O'Shea gave me a reappraising look as Tooley emerged from the gloom with a pair of foaming pitchers. I stared, could only hope my mouth was closed. I received a quick smile in return before she once again became one with the smoke and dusk.

"Rank?" O'Shea went on.

"Started out an ensign, promoted lieutenant, brevet Captain by Chapultepec, mostly attributable to attrition," I internally grimaced, "and one stupid, impetuous, crazy act I still shudder about late at night.'

"Well," O'Shea's expression may have changed, but remained unreadable, "we all have those."

With impeccable timing, Tooley reemerged, prettily balancing three steaming plates of scallops, shrimp, and fried oysters. Without a word or an extraneous motion she placed them soundlessly before melting away, leaving only a lingering smile where her face had been. The Flying Dutchman of barmaids.

"You've the experience," he smiled with a hint of warmth, "why don't you train 'em?"

"You know that answer."

"Aye, but I'd like to hear it from you."

"My job is to lead. I'm not a twenty year old ensign anymore - up to me to find professionals to do what's needed and make sure they're allowed to do so without interference."

"Well said, but do ya mean it? Or are ya' goin' to hover to make sure tha' jobs done . . . or nursemaid your fellow Yankees, or worse, do both? Jus' ta' let 'em know you're really one of them?"

"Think I want for a second to be any way associated with you when you're dressing down somebody who's important in the real world? God forbid someone I'll have to see at the club?" I replied in mock horror, "For Christ's sakes, Sean, I need the best man available to train my regiment or I might as well take a gun to my own head and be done with it. If these men are not trained properly I'll end up standing with a few close friends alone in front of a rebel battle line while my former friends sprint for the rear.

"I need them trained and I need you to do it," I said succinctly, pouring an ale, I had no idea where the others had gone. To prevent further theft, I drained half of it immediately. Sean leaned back and stretched against the high backed pine booth, "Ya've jus' met me."

"You make a hell of a first impression," I grinned, "and I've read your paperwork, Colonel O'Shea," if any part of me expected surprise, it was disappointed. Only his left eyebrow twitched, and that could have been from the whiff of a particularly obnoxious pipe tobacco cloud that chose that moment to enter the booth.

"Well, whaddaya' know?" He mused, looked ruefully at

Osgood. An Osgood who had suddenly found his cuticles fascinating.

"A lot," I answered, "Sean P. O'Shea . . . . I'll go out on a limb here and guess that the 'P' stands for Patrick. Sergeant Major, Royal Irish Brigade, until kicked out for suspected Republican leanings. Nothing overt, or —"

"I'd be dead or in Australia," he grinned widely, "tho' I'm not sure tha's much of a distinction."

"Quick visit," I went on, "as a Lieutenant in the Prussian Army. You know, Sean," I smiled at him, "I may not read German but I could pretty well sense the anger in the court martial papers."

"Ach! The Prussian bastards sound pissed off sayin' good mornin'".

"Never mind when an Irish sergeant strikes an aristocratic major?"

"Thought ya' couldna' read German?"

"Told you I got the gist, and 'von' was all over the place."

"Von Shithead," he said absently, "Papers tell ya' how I got outta' the cell they tossed me in?"

"Could have, I wouldn't know."

"His men," Osgood startled both of us, it was his first sounds since we sat, "took the jail and escorted him out."

"I didn't know you knew German," I said to a smug Osgood.
"You never asked."

"Your men broke you out?" I said in wonder.

"Aye, Forty-eight was a fine year for rebellion."

"Prussian soldiers rescuing an Irishman from a court martial," I was moving toward awe, "that's . . . . different."

"Sentimental people," O'Shea patiently explained, "tha' Germans are. Ya' stop one Junkers asshole from usin' his ridin' crop on the head of one a ya' best sergeants an' they make a big deal of it," he sported a faraway look of complete satisfaction.

"And so to France," one more long, satisfying pull of ale, "captain in an émigré brigade at the outset of Crimea, a handful of decorations later it's Colonel —"

"Brevet colonel," he corrected, as if there were some vast gulf between them.

"Full colonel by Solferino, where you led your brigade after

General Berthiaume was killed —"

"Good man, that."

"And took the center of the Austrian line. Awarded the Legionne d' Honnore, offered a star and . . . poof! Next thing we know you're a man of leisure in the thriving metropolis of New London, Connecticut." Finished, I drained my glass, looked for a reaction and waited for some form of exposition.

"Quite a town," he said with a straight face.

"You're not bored out of your mind?"

"I'm very much enjoyin' my life o'leisure, thank you."

"Permanent retirement, is it?"

"We all have to some time, for me maybe as good a time as ever."

We drank in silence, I tossed down a few oysters, more scallops, addictively so, and contemplated my dilemma while avoiding eye contact – easy to do as my companions were doing the same. I had become so used to great enthusiasm from everybody I met for the war I was completely at a loss at how to handle a reluctant recruit. My immediate response seemed imminently sensible: drink deeper, pop a few shrimp, and wait for inspiration.

A good deal of drinking by all concerned followed, Sean started to regale with stories of Crimea, plates of seafood evaporated, my head got lighter, hazy . . . pleasant. Tooley made more appearances, refilling pitchers, replenishing food, growing more ravishing while basking in the light of my increasing devotion.

At some point, the room just beginning to tilt ever so slightly, Sean looking fuzzy across the steaming table, the din from the taproom roaring and then fading away, the germ of an idea took hold. It seemed ridiculous at first, grew in intensity and probability with every Tooley visit. Finally, I waited for O'Shea to take a drought, blurted it out in ale-enhanced confidence.

"You would be of immense service to your country, you know" the shrimp he was about to eat had a reprieve - he stopped dead and regarded me with cool eyes

"Well," he drew out, "I've only been here a few years, an' while I'm getting' attached to it, I donna' know if appealing to my patriotism is tha' way ta' go here."

"I meant Ireland," it came out casually, but that did not stop him from going rock still, eyes narrowed. I drank my ale without a care in the world.

"What," he matched my casualness - hell, he outdid it, "do ya' know of Ireland'?"

Osgood turned to gape at me with a 'what are you doing' look. I meet his eyes for a heartbeat, he followed, as I knew he would, with a 'you're on your own' sigh.

I got yet more ale into me before going all in, "Look . . . Sean, I'm making an educated guess . . . pure conjecture from someone no longer affiliated with law enforcement," he nodded his approval, "but, I see an Irishman with your military background sitting in a busy port city - but not nearly the biggest or busiest - in a state that produces weapons and munitions on an immense scale, and I meet him in a tavern with Wolfe Tone's," my invocation of the saint finally brought the satisfaction of seeing him surprised, "portrait in a place of honor, I can only think of one thing."

"Tha' is?"

"You're running guns home."

"An' wha' if I am?" He affected amusement, did not quite bring it off.

"Then, this war will impede that, what with guns being needed for our war, naval blockades, commerce raiders, God knows what else."

"You could be right . . . if I was engaged in such activity, I'd be right worried."

"But you would be intrigued by the possibilities once the war ends."

"Would I?"

"Sure," I warmed to my theory even while he was proving it, "the war over, arms, ammunition everywhere. A grateful commanding officer, not much for paperwork, particularly where surplus equipment is concerned. Just think, America would become the land of opportunity once again."

"How big a surplus?" He asked with a smile of previously unseen brilliance.

"All."

"All as in?"

"A regiment's worth of arms . . . at least."

O'Shea's chuckle warmed his eyes, "Ya' were right, Osgood, he is . . . interesting."

"And a duplicitous bastard," Osgood said with pride.

"That, then, and I still get ta' beat up 'onna bunch of blue bloods?"

"Oh, yes."

"Sergeant Major, I take it?"

"You want a commission?"

"God, no," He yelped in disgust, "I don't need ta' be joinin' no gentleman's club. I assume I'd only report ta' ya'?"

"Yes."

"You'll not subject me ta' any amateurs?"

"I'll deal with them . . . solely."

"I can resign if I find otherwise."

"Yes."

He looked at Osgood, rueful grin in place, studied a half-eaten shrimp as if it were the Rosetta Stone, made his decision, "Then ya' got ya'self a sergeant major," he reached across the table and we shook, solidly, quickly, like normal human beings, "we'll have a lot ta' talk about when the war ends."

"We will," I agreed readily. We refilled our glasses, clinked in the center of the table, drained off a good half or more, thus sealing the deal in good Irish ale. I felt tension I did not know I had drain out of me.

We spent hours destroying plates of seafood and pitchers of ale without count. Perhaps the others were hungry, but I ate and drank to see Tooley as often as possible before my evening train home. At that I succeeded admirably. I saw her often, though at the cost of a bloated stomach and addled equilibrium. I imagined that our attraction grew with each encounter, incrementally so when we began to exchange words.

Eventually I had to rise and start my goodbyes – not easy, I was rather more unstable than normal sliding out of the booth. Upright on not quite steady legs, I turned to my companions, "Gentlemen, I have to leave lest I wake up on a ship bound for the Orient. Sean, I look forward to serving with you."

"As do I, William," we shook for the third time, hard, our rubber match, "you know," he started a deep, soulful laugh, "I wasn't gonna miss this one for anything, an' Osgood had spoken so highly of ya', I wouldda' signed without ya' kind offer.'

"Had to put me through my paces, eh?" The alcohol deadened the surprise and any negative response I may have normally felt or expressed.

"It was fun," he roared, "just like Osgood said it would be."

"Really?" I asked the walls, Osgood confirmed his part by avoiding my gaze, "You're both under my command now, so . . . ample opportunity to come up with a proper response."

"Aw, it was in fun." O'Shea protested.

"I'll try to keep that in mind . . . in camp."

"Fook," he laughed, I waved, turned and lurched toward the taproom, almost walked into the ethereal Tooley, stopped inches short of her.

"You'll be leavin' us now, Colonel?" Her voice was a song, her right hand rested on my forearm.

"Yes," I eked out in a rasp, held her eyes for a long moment.

"Pity," she sighed, my knees jellied.

"It is," on pure impulse I squeezed her hand and sadly pressed by. One, two, three steps, I turned to give her a last look, was surprised and ridiculously elated to see she was watching. She smiled, I lurched off.

I stepped into the taproom and began to weave around the tables, cutting through the gloaming like a man wading into the incoming tide, with the same result. This time the room was buzzing and seemingly indifferent to the slightly reeling, besotted gentleman bobbing among them. I caught many an eye on the way, accompanied by smiles and nods.

I washed up against the front door after what seemed like an hour. Just as I reached for the doorknob a loud, brogued baritone yelled, "Stop!"

I whirled, almost too fast to retain whatever dignity I still had, instinctively felt for the door the better to put my back against. I managed to steady myself although the room stayed a little off kilter. From my precarious vantage point I watched uncomprehendingly as everyone in the room rose. The barkeep was standing on something behind the bar, held a mug of black stout in his maw of a fist, tipped it in my direction.

"Three cheers for Colonel Hanlin and the Twenty-first Connecticut!" His voice rang through the room. I was rooted, transfixed, cheers echoed around the room, yelled with abandon. Tooley, Osgood, and O'Shea stood together in the back of the room, yelling along.

The cheers faded, I was left standing without a mug with which to acknowledge the kindness. Using the last of my cognitive functions, I touched the brim of my black sugar loaf hat and yelled, "Eire go brách!"

I had enough timbre in my voice for all to hear - I knew that for a fact because every mouth in the room dropped in utter shock. With that, I walked out into a cool night sea breeze, the stink of the room instantly replaced by the sharp clear smells of a port city on a windy night. Alone, I walked the deserted street to the station, my eyes tearing.

7

Six mouths gaped in a medley of shock, suspicion, disgust, opprobrium, and outright anger. The Governor chose another means to show his unhappiness - his lips were so pursed they looked like a knife scar. A good return, all in all, on my waiting to drop the news of the Irishness of our new sergeant major on the members of the Advisory Committee mid-meal. A perfectly timed thrust indicative of both my ability as a trial attorney and the reason I would never attain high political office.

The Connecticut Military Advisory Committee. Impressive sounding off the page, but one would be hard pressed to find a less martial looking group of men in all New England. Take, for example, my immediate neighbor to the left, Malcolm Russett. So heavily whiskered as to lack any other facial features, owner of more factories than Osgood had suits, he stood five foot eight. None of that, of course, precluded him from a military career... except for the hardly unnoticeable fact he was also 5'8" wide.

He was, however, the one member the committee I would invite to join us in battle - after all he was a waddling, perfectly mobile, rolling breast work. A close second would be Hughes, resplendent that night in an orange tweed coat that assaulted the senses. He was fitter and more suitable to service but for the fact his constant, fawning prattle would result in the shooting of one of us. By me.

Those two were Spartans compared to the other four civilian members. It should be noted here, that if I err in my assessment I do so on the side of understatement.

"You want an Irishman to train our Regiment?" Buckingham unpursed his lips just barely enough to speak, "I assume he's Catholic to boot?"

"I did not inquire as to his religion," I answered with patience,

136

"but he is Irish, and he's eminently qualified – if not overly so," I looked around the mammoth roundtable stacked high with foods of every description – plates Russet's small brown eyes coveted with blindingly quick darts that conveyed nothing if not naked avarice, "God damn it, he could command a brigade, never mind train this regiment."

I intentionally threw the profanity out just to watch the comic workings of the long, clean shaven, elastic face of Reverend Horace Pennyfarther when he reacted to God's name taken in vain. I may have been cruel in that regard, but I was not disappointed.

The Reverend gave a solemn, respectful invocation before each meeting and had, to date, yet to utter a single syllabled word thereafter. His face, however, expressed his every thought as clearly as if a Greek chorus followed chanting behind him. As his family was wealthy, I imagined he had dozens of offers to sit in on any number of high-stake card games.

It was less than 24 hours since my meeting with the indomitable O'Shea and I was not in a charitable mood toward my fellow committee members. I was in fact still feeling the effects of alcohol from Flannigan's which I either greatly enhanced or exacerbated - depending on one's viewpoint - by the two, possibly three (off-chance, four) brandies I consumed over the long, lonely ride home. It was pique, reluctance, or the lingering effects of a world-class hangover that caused me to wait to mid-meal to drop the news about my new sergeant major. Whatever, I thoroughly enjoyed the response.

"I don't see it working," a myopic, densely bearded, emaciated gargoyle of a man solemnly intoned over a plate of turkey that weighed more than he did. Aaron Colson. Speaker the house, Connecticut legislature, the comment constituted his mantra for life in general. Colson made John Calvin seem a bubbly, uplifting optimist.

I ignored him without expression, as I always did when the voice of doom spoke. I picked at the uninspiring food on my plate, looked across the table at Buckingham – he dove into his Beef Wellington, a dish he found not only endlessly enjoyable, but extraordinarily apt.

"I'm inclined to agree," Buckingham said with distaste that did not extend to his food, "it'll be an unnecessary hardship for our volunteers."

"They'll have to deal with far worse than a trainer with a slight brogue in short order. If this upsets them they can go home," I spit out to no discernible reaction from anyone save Christian, Arnold's invitee, who nodded sagely, "it'll work fine, the officers get in and start getting some training from O'Shea, by the time the men get there it'll seem perfectly normal."

That received noticeable reaction from several quarters. Buckingham moved uncomfortably in his chair, Hughes, hovering over his plate like a patient vulture, stared at him with intensity waiting for a cue, a look replicated by Russett and Colson. Of the three remaining members, aged Jonas Withington was asleep; Silas Deane Wickham was deeply, happily immersed in his umpteenth glass of wine, as his glassed-over eyes attested; and, George Washington Stafford was engrossed in something outside the floor-to-ceiling window behind his seat. No one would look in my direction.

"What is it?" I asked, sickening feeling in stomach.

In reply Buckingham shoved two large chunk of meat into his mouth and with a marvelously innocent shrug motioned to Hughes.

"The governor," Hughes started, Buckingham chewed loudly, "considered your suggestion to bring the officers in first, and was on his way to do it, but" he paused, had the decency to look at me, "but after input from several . . . individuals, the order was rescinded and the call went out to all the members of the Twenty-first. Tuesday, noon." He purposely flicked his eyes at Buckingham, ensuring I knew it was his idea alone.

"You're telling me that instead of a handful of men we'll have twelve hundred from day one?" I asked with astounding measure.

"Yes," Hughes answered promptly.

"May I inquire as to why?" I politely asked of the still chewing Governor. As the Hartford Club's reputation was hardly built on tough meat, I could only assume he was planning to avoid the subject for the duration. Again he deferred to Hughes with a wave of the hand. I resisted the urge to assist the governor's chewing.

"I don't know... Governor?" Hughes said, exhibiting backbone previously undetected.

"Governor?" I nodded thanks to Hughes, took the time to smile at Arnold and Christian to assure them I was fine and up to handling the matter like an adult. Christian looked confused, Arnold dubious.

We all waited, watched Buckingham swallow, pat his lips with deliberation and gaze longingly at the morsels remaining on his plate, before deigning to say, "It was felt that the officers were being treated apart from the men and that could cause resentment before we even started. Everybody wants in, why should officers start first, that sort of thing." He shrugged it off, began to carve another piece of beef.

I stopped his knife mid-slice when I said, "And you agreed to that horseshit?"

"Hanlin!" He snapped.

"Despite our agreement?" I persisted.

"You were unavailable," he pointed his knife in my direction, "I thought it made sense. You know, you're regular army, Hanlin, you have no experience with volunteers. It's not the same – discipline, formalities, everything. Especially," on the stump now he visibly relaxed, confident his argument was persuasive, "where the officers and men are concerned – it is a fine line. After all, they all have to live together after the war," finished he smiled to let me know I agreed with him.

"First," I fought to keep a snarl out of my voice, "we had volunteers in Mexico, if we hadn't Santa Anna would be better thought of by history. Second, this is funny because my job is to give the men a chance to come home again. Solid officers, discipline, and an unshakable command structure, are the key to that. You just truncated that." I smiled to indicate he was a horse's ass for thinking differently.

"Please, Hanlin," a forkful of beef waved in my direction, "you over dramatize," his voice was all manful good cheer, "I have enormous faith in you, Seth, and all the fine young man like your brother, you'll be fine."

I resisted the urge to tell him Christian was registered to vote in Boston. I looked at the objects of Buckingham's stump speech:

Arnold was smiling and nodding – at me not in agreement with our Governor; Christian, the very embodiment of youthful military bearing, rolled his eyes.

"Do you realize," I persisted, "you've set a terrible precedent?"

"How so?" He asked and answered.

"If one does not like an order, one appeals to the Governor."

"This was a special case," he waved my concerns, and me, away.

"It's the first fucking order they ever received, and you rescinded it at the drop of a hat, how the fuck do you think that was perceived?" I ripped out furiously.

Mouths sagged, eyebrows raised, Pennyfather dropped his fork onto his plate, the clang was like a cannon shot in the deafening silence. Even Wickham tore his eyes off the window and whatever demons awaited him out there. Buckingham stared with a curiously blank expression, pushed back in his chair, (the furthest he had been from his food since we sat) picked up his wine glass with great precision, took a short sip, and regarded me over the rim.

"I applaud your ardor, Hanlin," he said affably, "I really do. But the thing is done, I'm told you are most competent in many ways, deal with it."

I motioned my brother to close his mouth, "What of the precedent of allowing men to go directly to you?"

"It will not happen again," he said flatly, employing the exact inflections of his earlier promise to me, "you really need the Mick, eh?"

"We do," Arnold replied, "More than ever."

"Fine," Buckingham ignored the implicit jibe and cracked a laugh that almost sounded genuine, "all this fuss and the war will be over by Christmas." Everybody but Hughes, Arnold, and my brother fell over themselves muttering agreement.

"That old saw," I surprised myself saying it aloud.

"I've heard you feel differently," Buckingham said in a tone indicating we were best friends again, "but I haven't heard your reasoning."

"It's a Civil War," I explained carefully, then tried the beef. It was amazingly tender.

"That's enlightening," Buckingham noted, the bigger sycophants in the room laughed lightly.

"Actually," Hughes stepped into the breach, serious, earnest, "concisely said and explanation enough. If one can compare evils, civil wars are the worse wars. Too much history, too much pride, I'd venture."

"Too much intimacy," I added to his dramatic nod.

"Pompeii thought he'd triumph in a few weeks," Hughes was in his element, face animated, his thin, long hands weaving his thoughts, "as did Cromwell, our Tories, and countless others. I very much agree with William, it'll be a long war."

I tilted my wine glass at him, "I've traveled through the South, Governor, it's vast, rural and will not be conquered easily – and that's what it will take to win this. I served with many Southerners, they're more than capable and they are having the same conversation under the same circumstances we are right now."

"They'll fold house after the first battle," Buckingham said through his wine.

"Amen," the Reverend stunned everybody by speaking mid-meeting.

"What if they win the first battle?" I blasphemed.

"Then we defeat them in the next," Russet stirred his great bulk to support his reply, "then it's over."

"We don't quit if we lose the first battle?" I asked maliciously.

"Of course not!" Buckingham snapped, tiny red-tinged droplets covered the white linen tablecloth in front of him.

"Then why would they be any different?" I asked, "I'll bet the governors of the new Confederate states are paraphrasing that prominent Republican governor who said that this war should be so terrible that future generations shall not dare repeat the crime. That, Sir," I pointed my empty fork at Buckingham, "is not the sentiment short wars are founded on."

"Strong words, great words," Colson beamed and turned toward their author.

"Thank you," Buckingham said considerably less emphatically than when he shouted them into national headlines a week earlier, "but, no, they are not the words short wars are founded on."

"Going to be a long war Governor," Hughes volunteered.

"It is," Arnold readily agreed.

"Your Irish Hessian is needed," Buckingham stated with nary a raised eyebrow.

"We'll be the best trained regiment in New England," I promised.

"And you think the men will listen to a Mick?"

"I defy anyone to ignore O'Shea," I had a certain degree of wry bemusement at the thought, "and any that do will be sent home." With that threat, Buckingham's eyes scanned the portraits lining the walls looking for the spot they would hang his. The wartime Governor.

"Meaning exactly what?" He asked absentmindedly, narrowing his search between two expendable early century shipping magnates.

"Meaning I will personally escort any man – regardless of rank – who challenges O'Shea out of camp. Provided, course," I smiled and malicious anticipation, "he can still walk by the time I get to him."

"No, William, you'll do no such thing," Arnold interjected, receiving a wide smile from Buckingham. A smile that faded and dried up when Seth added, "that's my job."

Buckingham resumed his inspection of the art with a heartfelt sigh, Seth went on unabated, "I raised the Regiment, I get to have some fun."

"I stand corrected, Colonel," I apologized.

"Understandable mistake, Colonel."

Buckingham pulled his eyes off General Israel Putnam – an unassailable goal unless the good Governor led the final charge against Richmond himself - waved in our general direction, "well, it's your head if this experiment implodes, I trust you understand that."

"Yes," Seth and I replied together.

Buckingham's head showed surprising dexterity pivoting toward Arnold, "I was addressing Hanlin."

"In terms of the Twenty-first, Bill," Seth replied slowly, solemnly, "you addresses us both."

"So," Buckingham considered, "that's how it is, is it?"

"How it has to be," Seth answered with a wag of a finger.

Buckingham considered the turn of events for a long moment, "just promise me," he finally offered in a properly contrite voice, "you'll review all dismissals of officers above lieutenant with me."

"Of course," Seth answered, looking hard my way. I calculated that the approved group was comprised of the twelve company commanders and nodded in return.

The rest of the meal was spent in virtual silence, the rest of the meeting was short and perfunctory, all decisions were left to Seth and me.

8

O'Shea stepped off the train resplendent in a new uniform, hastily tailored at Blake's hours earlier. His chevrons seemed to glow off the deep blue coat, the medals I insisted he wear glittered in the sunlight. The overall effect screamed authority, the very picture of a professional soldier come to survey his new posting.

Osgood detrained behind him clad in uniform for the first time, looking lethal. He gave me a mocking salute that I chose to ignore.

"Welcome", I said with warmth, "to a full camp," that raised eyebrows, "officers and NCOs will be assembled in the main parade ground in a half hour."

They nodded, said not a word as I led them on a tour of the grounds, filling them in on the details of the meeting with Buckingham et. al. They registered little surprise and dismissed both the revised order and the governor as inconsequential. Much more important to them was the camp. They were impressed walking through the freshly hewn station, the smell of sawn wood still in the air; the attached warehouse nicely filling due solely to the Herculean efforts of Wycroft; and, out down the deeply green grassed, gently sloping cow path to a plain that spread out for almost three quarters of a mile before ending as the West bank of the Connecticut River.

To our right were hundreds of brilliant white, canvas tents standing as further testament to Wycroft's genius. They were laid out as a town, a wide avenue splitting the Regiment neatly in two, headquarter tents at the top under a copse of elderly oaks. Twelve companies (the regular Army officer in me still objected to the extra two) were divided by streets, many of which already sported street signs.

We followed the tree lined path past the Avenue, angled away from the tents. To our left, on the flats hard by the riverbank, a few hundred men in shirt sleeves were observing a base ball game on a well groomed pitch.

"You could pitch another thousand tents there," Osgood helpfully observed, "I'll be happy to take care of it."

"I make this easy for you, Osgood," I growled, "you go within fifty yards of that field, I'll have you escorted off – by bayonet, I may add."

"You're breaking my heart."

"And leave the players alone in camp."

"You expect me to have no fun at all?"

"You're not an admirer of the game?" O'Shea asked.

"Only for real sports, like rugby or football," Osgood answered with feeling.

"Now you're talking, playing fields of Eton and all that," O'Shea smiled.

"Oh, Christ," I lamented, "you've got an ally."

"Just another man," Osgood, with evident self-satisfaction, "opposed to your bastardization of cricket."

"Now there's a dynamic sport," I replied no one in particular.

"Exactly my point," Osgood started as we emerge into a stone wall enclosed pasture, the former resident bovines recently replaced by similarly randomly meandering uniformed commissioned and noncommissioned officers. Three flagpoles were in the center, national flag centered, Connecticut flag to its right. The left poll was reserved for our regimental flag - when finally awarded.

Arnold and Wycroft stood under the center pole, Seth talking, Wycroft nodding furiously and jotting in his ever present notebook. Arnold made a huge but dashing figure in an immaculately tailored uniform; Wycroft's uniform was several sizes too large and made him seem smaller than ever. Seth touched Wycroft's elbow, together they started across the pasture toward us, Wycroft, for the moment at least, pocketed the book.

Seth ignored Osgood and me and strolled straight to O'Shea, "Colonel O'Shea," he said warmly, extending a quickly taken hand, "Seth Arnold, welcome."

"Please, Colonel," O'Shea beamed, "but it be Sergeant Major

O'Shea, reporting, suh!" He snapped with deadly precision, stomped his feet in the British fashion, and sliced a salute that crackled the air.

Seth laughed, introduced Wycroft and led us to the flag poles through a small herd of men – each of whom looked up from the grass to study the newcomers.

"The rest will be filtering down in a few minutes," Seth said, "be interesting to see how close to being on time they'll be. As you can see, a good many men are observing William's favorite pastime. The rest of the enlisted men were given passes to Hartford for the next two days, so we won't have an audience."

"No need for enlisted men to see what dolts their officers are at the outset," I replied.

O'Shea laughed, "Yeah, better to let them figure it out later," he made a point of looking at each of us in turn, "present company excepted of course."

"Of course," I answered for us, "my, how quickly you dropped the pretentiousness of a commission and joined the masses."

"Aye, once a sergeant major, always a sergeant major, suhs!" That last boomed off the river while he snapped off another regular British Army salute.

"Christ sakes, will you stop that," Osgood chuckled, "it sends chills down my spine."

"Sorry! Suh!" the screamed response. Osgood shook his head sadly, the rest of us laughed, drawing strange looks from the strays closest to us.

"Sean," a suddenly somber Arnold began, "I've a request from the Governor," I groaned loudly, Arnold nodded in response, "it's not from any of us, but I promised to relay it," he stopped, apparently waiting for O'Shea's permission to go on.

"Please, Colonel, just get it out," he said in great good humor.

"Governor Buckingham would like you, for his own reasons, to assuage his own fears, to be known, at least for now, as John Shay," he got it out with only a hint of embarrassment.

"That's insulting," I blurted.

"Fucking ridiculous," Osgood added.

"Awful," Wycroft looked personally offended.

"I apologize," Seth added hastily, "I hope I –"

"It's fine," O'Shea smiled, the object of our commiseration seemed anything but put out, "John Shay 'tis. That a proper Yankee name or does the governor jus' object to the rhyme that is my name?"

A surprise Arnold struggled to respond, "Shay's a respected name in Connecticut, prominent Revolutionary family."

"As long as it's a proper rebel name," Shay laughed, "though I hate to lose my 'O' - royalty as it 'tis."

"Like every Irishman I've ever met," I added.

"Aye, 'tis a bit redundant, I admit."

"I must say Sean, I didn't expect you to take this so, well... well," Seth intoned, still in doubt.

O'Shea burst out laughing, "Colonel, I appreciate your concerns and humanity, I really do but I've been a traveling soldier for some time now... Christ, I was Juergen Schuster or some such shit in Prussia, not even sure anymore. And tha' name that goes with this beauty," he touched the Legion of Honor glowing on his chest, "well, tha's mine but it could jus' as easily been Jacque something or other," He shook his head, amused at the fuss.

"Well," Arnold, not sure what to make of it or him, "thank you, Sean, John Shay it is then."

"Fine, perhaps the governor would like me to do the training in French, n'est pas?"

"That'll be fine, Sean," Arnold, proving he was a quick study, "we'll go with your peculiar blend of English for now... unless it proves too much of an impediment."

"Oh, Colonel," Shay chuckled, "we're going to get along just fine, you and I. You don't by chance speak Gaelic, do you?"

"No."

"Good," Seth gave him a questioning look, got a raised eyebrow back in lieu of an answer.

The bantering continued, men walked down the avenue and out into the parade ground, promptly began to clump together in small groups. I noticed, and noticed Shay noticing as well, there was no interplay between groups. The companies had segregated themselves. I waited until the path cleared and the last groups clustered before I strode as purposely as possible to the flagpoles, Seth and Shay close behind.

"Form by companies in a square around the flags, men," I said almost conversationally. Out of the corner of my mouth I whispered, "let's see if they can figure this one out on their own."

The answer to that came in short order – they could not. At all. It was equally apparent that the previous occupants of the field would have had a better chance completing the task.

A nod from Seth sent Wycroft wading into the blue mob and, within minutes, he began to sort it out assigning specific companies to specific areas. Slowly the throng became a loose, irregular circle, then an octagon, soon a rectangle and, finally, a square with Wycroft striding about its edges dressing the lines.

"Oh, boy'o," Sean hissed over my shoulder, "we have work to do."

I nodded agreement, cued Arnold to move to the center of the square. This he did with style and military bearing noticed by precious few. He stood motionless under the limp flags while conversation buzzed through the ranks, men craned their necks and stepped in and out of line to get a better view. Wycroft moved toward the breaches like a Dutch boy leaks in a dyke. With much less success.

I moved next to Arnold, thinking it might help. I even held a hand up. We continued to be completely and obviously ignored. "Gentlemen," I said in a normal tone in the thin hope they would quiet down out of curiosity. In that, I was spectacularly wrong. Not for nothing, however, had I gone to West Point to learn the subtleties of command.

"Attention!" I screamed, exercising vocal muscles last used yelling above the artillery in Mexico City. Seth jumped about a foot in the air, the men froze in their ragged lines.

"Gentlemen," I spoke loudly but without strain, "it is traditional that you come to attention when your commanding officer, or officer on parade appears. You will do so from here on end, understood?"

My only answer, the sounds from the distant base ball game.

"It is also traditional to respond 'yes sir' to direct questions as well. Understood?"

Scattered, uncoordinated 'yeses' floated past, with a few 'yes sir's faint in the background.

"That's pathetic," I observed with generosity, "look, on the count of three, every damn one of you yell 'yes sir' at the top of your lungs. One, two, three..."

I was greeted with a moderately loud, somewhat coordinated, 'yes sir' that would've earned the lash in the old Army.

"Thank you," I turned to Seth, "Colonel," and left him alone in the center.

"Welcome, all of you," Arnold started in a pleasant yet commanding voice that bode well, "I am Seth Arnold, your Colonel. I raised this Regiment and it is an honor to have you join us. All I expect of any of you," he pivoted to include every side of the square, "is to learn all you can in the upcoming days. Ask questions, study, do whatever you can, do whatever you need to do to bring knowledge to your men. Good luck and God bless all of you."

He moved away in almost total silence, when he passed me on my way to the center he whispered, "Tough crowd," and kept going.

I walked slowly around the square, looked above their heads and avoided eye contact and the chance of a spark of familiarity that would have been counterproductive at that point. Two complete circuits before I stopped where I had started, the ranks still silent.

"I am Lieutenant Colonel William Hanlin," I started, voice loud but not so loud as to preclude a conversational tone, "some of you know me as assistant state's attorney for Harford County," I smiled briefly at the frumpy, smiling, grotesquely mustachioed walrus of a man I stood next to, well known as Harford's leading odds-maker, "a few of you like Joseph Knowlton here, are present today only because I failed to convict," laughter swept the square, no one laughed harder than Knowlton.

"Tell me, Joseph," I resumed after allowing a Lieutenant Colonel's worth of mirth, "any relationship to Colonel Knowlton?"

"Direct descendent," he beamed.

"Hard shoes to fill, the Connecticut Rangers were Washington's best troops."

"They sure as hell were, William."

149

"Sir or Colonel out here, Lieutenant," I said with good cheer.

"Sorry, Colonel," he said through his perpetual grin.

"Well, Joseph, try to avoid the good Colonel's fate, eh?" I began to walk away ready to give my much rehearsed speech.

"Likely," Knowlton however was not done, "doubt I'll run afoul of any Hessian bayonets, unless you know different, Colonel?" I waved a hand to indicate touché, laughed with the rest.

I waited for the ranks to get as quiet as they were going to get at this stage of our development, winked when I passed Christian, "So, gentlemen, before embarking on a career fruitlessly pursuing Knowlton I attended West Point," a rustling flittered through the ranks, "I do not tell you this to curry favor or respect, for while I hope to earn your favor over the next weeks, I seek no respect for I have earned a lifetime's worth from men I loved and served with at Buena Vista, Cerro Gordo, Churubrisco, Molina Del Ray, and Chalpatetec.

"I have seen what artillery and bullets do firsthand, I've seen what good order and discipline do in return. In Mexico we were outnumbered more than two to one in every engagement. We won every engagement. That's what discipline and training do. This regiment will be well-trained and that begins with obeying orders and obeying them quickly. My orders and Colonel Arnold orders are never to be questioned. You have a problem with an order, you may always bring it up in private, no problem, no stigma, no anything, we'll be happy to discuss it. But when an order is given in front of the men ... never. Is that understood?"

A solid volley of 'yes sirs' echoed across the pasture while I walked over to my erstwhile companions, "these are Captain Osgood and Lieutenant Wycroft," I announced, hands on their shoulders, "Captain Osgood is aide de camp to Colonel Arnold and myself. Lieutenant Wycroft is our quartermaster and resident genius. An order from either of them is an order from us. They most emphatically do not accept orders from any of you."

I moved next to Shay, he stiffened in anticipation, "This is Sergeant Major Shay. He is to be addressed as Sergeant Major. Know this one unshakable fact, you, none of you, out rank this man," I pointed to his chest, "unless you have two of these at home in a drawer somewhere. The Legion of Honor, the highest award for valor given by the French Army.

"Mr. Shay earned his first leading a regiment in Crimea, the second a brigade at Solferino – one of the brigades that broke the Austrian center," that caused significant ripples through the ranks.

"This man is qualified to command at least a brigade, he has instead chosen to assist us in our most important task - he is going to train you to train your men. Then he is going to watch you do it and make sure it's done correctly. He's the sole authority in the regiment on all training matters, on those issues his decisions are final. He will make us the best trained regiment in New England and we will set the bar high for the Connecticut regiments to follow. We are to leave that kind of legacy, gentlemen," I had their attention, that much was certain. Time to yield the floor, "Mr. Shay, the officers of the 21st Connecticut."

Shay silently walked the perimeter, stopping here and there to adjust a hat, tsk over a dirty button, flick lint – real or imagined – off a shoulder. He did the same for the second row, not a man moved, no one in the front row turned around to look raising my hopes that we had a group of fast learners.

Back in the center, he started in a deep, attention-getting voice, "Well, ya' not the worst troops I ever inspected, an' seein' as ya' mostly officers, that will certainly do as a complement."

A nervous chuckle ran through the assembly. His brogue was not as noticeable as it was in New London and did not seem to register on anyone. I imagined most took it for a more socially acceptable British Isle accent while the rest had the good sense to be scared shitless.

"I will teach ya' all I know," he went on amicably in the manner of a big brother imparting wisdom and experience, "as quick as ya' can learn it. I'll teach ya' everything except what ya' must learn ya'selves under fire."

He began to walk the perimeter again nodding, smiling, gesturing to the men as if old friends, a politician running for an office that was already wrapped up.

"We'll treat each other as the gentlemen we are, but disobey me, question me in front of your men – or, worse, ignore me – and I'll knock ya' on your arse in front of everybody," the last was relayed with a brilliant 'who would do such a thing' smile, "talk ta' me privately about anything under the sun, we have no problem ever. How's tha' suit ya?"

A solid chorus agreed, he acknowledged it as an indulgent parents does a precocious five-year-old, "Tis true," he took up when the choir quieted, "I was in Crimea, bloody stupid waste o'time it was too. I saw the Light Brigade go off, lads," there was an audible snap of heads coming to attention, "I'm sure it's a stirring poem for most of you, for all I know some of you signed up because of it... in which case I suggest a more thorough reading," he received a few laughs from the more literary men.

"Reads real nice, but I saw them slaughtered and I saw the field afta' - unless you enjoy the sight of well-dressed flesh lyin' about in a sea of blood and horse entrails, there was nothing fooking poetic about it."

"That," his friendly veneer never changed for a moment, "is what happens when officers fook up anna' that will never happen here. Any questions?"

As far as I could tell no one was breathing, never mind curious. We dismissed.

Thus began the education of the Twenty-first Connecticut Volunteer Infantry.

9

Two weeks later I was splayed out on my chair at home, legs thrown over the ottoman, alone and relaxed for the first time since New London. It was late, a moderate fire burned bright, warming the room chilled by a sudden spring cold snap. The room was deeply shadowed, the only lights the embered fireplace and my low-wicked table light.

Too comfortable, too relaxed, I fought the good fight to stay awake while I leafed through the reports Osgood and Arnold  compiled on the regiment to date. At home and at peace, I was finally away from curious eyes after fourteen days of total immersion in every area of our men's lives. Total immersion, everything from how to dress properly to cleanliness, camp sanitation, admonitions not to play with the new Springfield rifles, and the avoidance of diseases of the sins of the flesh – to the extent that they already had.

Eighteen to twenty hours a day devoted to twelve hundred idiosyncratic men and officers suddenly in close proximity and expected to live together in harmony and uniformity. Officers, by the way, who put the prima in prima donna.

The most notable and vexing deficiency of those first days was a total lack of military protocol. Arnold and I became inured to being stopped midstride and mid-comment by the lowliest private and asked the most mundane of questions. Military order and proper channels were unknown and no one seemed anxious to adapt them despite (or because of?) the constant corrections.

Truth be told, a few days in it was plain Seth and I had time for diversions because Wycroft and Shay were running everything with effortless efficiency. Wycroft had a steady stream of materials flowing into camp even while breaking in his new staff, all prior employees of Seth's mills. Shay was simply everywhere, checking the men, teaching, drilling, entertaining during breaks. He adapted his style of address and instruction to his audience, dressed down those who demanded it, praised all for completing the most mundane of tasks.

The officers and NCOs endured three days of intense drilling during which I observed not a hint of animosity toward our loud, funny, driving, patient, profane sergeant major – not that he left them any time to dwell on personal issues, they were lucky to get four hours sleep a night.

The fourth day we let the camp sleep in – except for headquarters, we spent the early morning hours planning and organizing over an ocean of very strong coffee. At noon we assembled for the first time as a full regiment. Twelve hundred men in ordered ranks forming an almost perfect square around two thirds of our colors. Captains a few paces to the front, lieutenants, sergeants slightly behind, all radiating in their new found professionalism. It almost seemed real.

We reprised our earlier talks, this time to loud creative catcalls, laughter, and ragged huzzahs. Formalities over, Seth, Shay, and I wandered about greeting, meeting our companies. We arbitrarily started with Company F, Windsor. They were comprised of factory workers and tobacco farmers, standing as militarily as currently possible, wearing uniforms so new they still had folds in them. In the time-honored Army tradition it appeared that none fit.

Shay roamed freely through their ranks with jibes, insults, small talk, obviously enjoying himself, obviously entertaining the men. A block of pure energy until he stopped dead before a peach fuzzed, rail thin, blond haired boy with wire rimmed glasses. A smile of pure benevolence lighted Shay's face and eyes as he stood unmoving, the boy eying him with obvious apprehension.

Shay looked away from his prey for the second it took to catch my eye and motion me to join him. Practicing nonchalance I strolled to the unfortunate boy, now sweating profusely in the face of a cool, steady breeze off the Connecticut.

"What's your name, son?" Shay asked quite kindly, the boy gulped audibly.

"Nathanael Greene Tecumseh Crane... Sir," under the circumstances he managed significant pride.

"Good God," I announced to the Regiment, "we can't lose with a name like that on our side." I felt bad immediately as I brought a symphony of catcalls down on the now red-faced namesake of two warriors. I inadvertently made it worse by adding, "at least the joker that named you didn't go with Ichabod."

That struck the assembly as hilarious and our proceedings were put on hold while the men hooted and hollered. Shay gave me a look of utter reproach for stepping on his lines.

"How old are you, boy'o?" Shay asked when the noise abated.

"I am over eighteen, sergeant major," he answered with remarkable confidence, all things considered.

"You'd swear to that, wouldn't you? Take an oath?"

"Already did, when I joined up, sergeant major," the youth beamed back at him.

"Of course you did, and right handsomely too, I'd wager," Shay patted him on the arm, vigorously enough to make him rock, "now be a good lad and take off your shoes."

"Sir?" He was suddenly ashen.

"Take off your shoes, private," Shay maintained his smile but it no longer touched his eyes, "don't make me make it in order."

With a soulful sigh the boy bent over, unlaced his battered brogans, and stepped out of them, losing an inch in the process. Quick as a cat Shay snatched them off the ground, brought them to eye level, peered into their dark recesses, nodded sagely, reached in and pulled out a slip of moist, sagging, torn piece of paper.

He gingerly waved it in my direction, I was three feet away and still not far enough to avoid the reek, "See it, Colonel?"

"Ah . . . sure . . . "I said without conviction. He took a step closer, I resisted the urge to step back, held my breath, and did what he apparently needed me to do – I inspected the limp paper. With some squinting I could dimly make out an '18' printed in a bold hand.

"Eighteen," Shay laughed a confirmation, slapped Nathaniel on the back hard enough to rock him off the line, "so he won't be lyin' when asked if he's over eighteen," he gave his victim a proud look, "so, how old are you without your shoes on, son?"

"Seventeen . . . eighteen in August . . . sergeant major," he said sadly.

"August," I echoed, 'do your parents know you're here?"

"They do indeed, Colonel," an older gentleman a few men down answered loudly.

"You know that how?" I asked.

"Because I'm the joker that didn't name him Ichabod," he said with a nice, sardonic edge that was immediately and raucously appreciated by the regiment as one. He was of average height, clean-shaven with intelligent brown eyes that appraised me frankly as I neared him.

"Your name?"

"Thomas Crane, Colonel, we've come as a family."

"Don't tell me your father is here as well?" I cracked.

"No sir," he grinned, "just my five brothers, the boy's uncles and me."

"I see," I pretended to mull that over, "you're all obviously fine with his being under age."

"Yes, sir! He'll be of age soon enough and, besides," he turned toward his son and wagged a finger, "this way here we can keep our eyes on him," he brought a chorus of abuse down on his son from the rest of a regiment now more than willing to help keep an eye out for the unfortunate Nathanael Greene Tecumseh Crane.

I grinned and threw a shrug at Shay, he handed the slip of paper back to the boy saying, "Well, Private Crane, put yer' age back in your shoes and stay awhile," the private did just that to the applause of the assembly.

Six or seven companies into our tour brought us to the first of the Hartford companies – the paleness of the soldiers was starkly noticeable after the farmers of the outlying towns, hell, even the factory workers had color compared to our city denizens.

I recognized more than a few faces, though, of course, names were in no danger of popping out. Second row center was a familiar, readily identifiable face and I stopped and gazed into the bug eyes of Robert Hughes. The late professor of military history, logic, and rhetoric stood at shabby attention in a sagging uniform.

"Private Hughes," I said after a long moment, "come to check up on me, have you?"

"Just taking your advice, Colonel," he smiled with a sincerity I had never suspected.

"Here alone?" I smiled back, had to, I was in awe of his gesture.

"No, sir!" He proudly proclaimed, "there's forty-three of us late of Trinity, professors and students alike – and," he smiled widely, somehow managing to stifle his usual grotesqueness, "I think you'll recognize the men behind us, we managed to recruit most of the Blues, Colonel."

"Your doing, Robert?"

"With some help, Colonel."

I nodded, then asked the most important question, "We have enough for a full side?"

"And then some."

"Excellent," I was inordinately pleased and sounded it. I turned to Shay, who was examining Hughes with interest, "Sergeant Major Shay, this is Robert Hughes, he is to be made sergeant."

"Sir."

I returned to a very pleased Hughes, "Sergeant Hughes, you will immediately, when not engaged in training, organize base ball games between companies for Saturday afternoons. From those games you will select a team to represent the regiment at a later date, understood?"

"Yes, sir! Thank you, sir!" he shouted, not unprofessionally.

"Good to have you, Robert," I said and moved away, a very

tangible sense of having just done something very wise settled over me.

I stopped again three feet away where stood another face I could definitely place. He stood five foot three, was twig thin, and mutton chopped so heavily it looked like his face was pressed between the asses of two yaks.

"Fellson," I said.

"Counselor," he answered in a low baritone that always held a hint of irony.

"It's Colonial here, Jeremiah," I replied, matching his good humor, "I thought you were in Newgate," I generously left out 'where I put you', "tell me you didn't escape."

"Escape to come straight to the army?" His eyes gleamed, "Nah, colonel, I left a few weeks ago on the up and up and now I can't think of a better place to enhance my return to society than to stand right behind you in battle . . . . sir," Shay let out a too-late-restrained snort, the men in hearing distance laughed riotously.

"Very well, private, mind you, though, no safes to crack where we're going."

"Well sir," Hartford's leading yegg responded quickly, "I'm sure there'll be other opportunities."

"Undoubtedly," I agreed, "Just save them for Virginia," I gave him a smile and moved down the line, nodding to men doomed by my memory of faces to remain familiarly anonymous.

And so it went, those few moments standing out with clarity in the otherwise unending kaleidoscope of faces and foggy conversations of that first day as they blended into the next and the next and became a bottomless pit of fractured memories that reached into fitful nights complete with bizarre, shapeless dreams.

We went two solid weeks of drills, parades, dawn to midnight, rain or shine, before I called a break and gave everyone a weekend furlough guaranteed only to fill the coffers of Hartford's merchants, gambling houses, and brothels. Through some miraculous alignment of the planets I found myself alone at home, Osgood, sporting a mysteriously guilty look, took off for parts unexplained, Seth was off to Norwich, Wycroft to the road for more supplies, Sean to New London for 'time with proper speakin' folk', Christian to Middletown and the attentions of its worshipful female population.

I sat in silence and comfort, sipping a subtle port, scanning through officer fitness reports. Incomplete, of course, but interesting enough in their infancy. My personal, also too early, impression was positive even while I harbored the fear I was overcompensating for my understandable bias toward the regular army in my inordinately polite conduct with my nescient officers. I knew I was expecting and accepting less from men who were certainly no product of a rigid course of study, drill, or promotion through the ranks by virtue of death or obvious competence. My officers were commissioned by virtue of birth, wealth, connections, abolitionist leanings or some combination thereof. The worse by far, a combination of all four.

My officers expected to be obeyed by, at the least, their men while demonstratively unhappy at having to follow any orders they did not understand and/or agree with. They chafed at the repetitive nature of drilling, especially when they failed to master it after a dozen or so attempts – particularly if the error was, in their new found professional opinions, imperceptible.

In such circumstances Shay's smiling, paternal presence would walk them through it, taking care not to assign blame while leaving them ample opportunity to assume it themselves. He inevitably turned each such exercise into an us against the world scenario. If they still failed (rarely) and his standard line of 'if ya' cannaught do it right here, ya' cannaught do it under fire and you'll fookin' kill us all,' had a similar lack of success (rarer still), he would resort to a string or two of incomprehensible Gaelic oaths. If especially upset he would mix in colorful, descriptive French and German phases of dubious origin in rapid succession before shaking his head ruefully, smiling painfully, and returning to the perfect teacher once more. It worked wonders.

My biggest concerns revolved around the company commanders from the smaller towns. They seemed to me far more autocratic than the captains from the city. Big dogs from small yards had many social inferiors (everyone?) and did not gracefully suffer instruction, never mind criticism regardless of the good grace from which it was offered or from whom (everyone?).

Not that they ever overtly expressed — or even hinted at — such pique. Theirs was the occasional hard look, raised eyebrow, one syllable answer, subtle dragging of feet — literally and metaphorically.

These were never offered to Shay, who enjoyed a honeymoon of prodigious length, but rather at Arnold and me. Perhaps for inflicting Shay upon them, perhaps because they felt entitled to command, perhaps simply because they could. None of this was remotely troubling to anyone who had ever commanded men. (The best advice I had ever received on the subject was also the earliest, imparted by an older, far wiser, heavily bearded Virginian West Point graduate in Mexico moments after I assumed command of my regiment — "Just keep the men who like you and the men that hate you away from the one's that don't give a shit either way, and you'll be just fine".)

What was troubling was the fact that those so covertly put out tended to gravitate to one another whenever the regiment was at rest. What was worse, they almost always gathered around Huntingdon — a Huntingdon who from afar appeared to be holding court. And relishing it. As Huntingdon never spoke to Arnold or me beyond a 'yes' or 'no sir', unfailingly polite on both counts, I had no further insight into the matter, itself worrisome in the extreme.

At some point the files in my hand slid to the floor and I fell into a long, deep, dreamless sleep. I awoke to a cool room and the smell of eggs frying. I rubbed my eyes, worked the kinks out of my neck, stood, staggered to the kitchen where stood Phelps, back to me working several pans at once.

"Coffee's ready," he said without turning, "grab a mug."

"What time is it?" I mumbled, went to the stove, blinking in the strong sunlight streaming through the windows.

"There's a clock in yer' study."

"Forgot to look."

"It's about ten-thirty, that'd be a new record for you sleepin' in. Try yer' bed sometime an' you might not look like a train run over ya'"

"Hmmm," I agreed, poured a cup of very black, very hot, very needed, coffee. I sat, sipped carefully, threw my arm over the chair next to mine, wondered idly who had left a sergeant's tunic draped over it.

Phelps appeared at that very moment and placed an oversized plate of eggs, bacon, home fries, and toast in front of me. I noticed for the first time he was wearing blue pants, white shirt with startling red suspenders instead of his usual tweeds.

"What the hell you dressed for?" I politely inquired.

"Ah, ya' like it?" He asked as he unceremoniously snatched the jacket from under my arm and in a rather graceful, fluid motion put it on, "I rather fancy it," he turned sideways to show off the chevrons.

"Who the hell enlisted you and who the hell made you a sergeant?" I demanded wearily, "I suddenly despair for our cause."

"That's a lovely sentiment," he sat next to me with his own plate, one I could not help noticing was heaped twice mine, "Don't worry," he noticed me noticing, "there's more on the stove," he took an enormous forkful and shoved it into his mouth and began to chew merrily.

When it seemed he would have to eventually swallow I asked again, "Who?"

"Osgood," he replied, cleaned his palate with an impossibly long pull of steaming coffee, in the process still managing to convey the stupidity of my question, "he says I'm assigned to you and need ta' have a proper rank to serve one as exulted as yerself. Wouldn't do for you to have a civilian manservant and it'd not do to have a batman of lessa' rank."

"Good God, you unleashed on the army," I sighed before a thought brightened my mood, "does this mean your salary is now paid by the United States government?"

"Alas, no, Boss," he laughed at the ridiculousness of my question, "I couldn't take that kinda' cut in pay, now could I?"

"To keep up with your extravagant life style."

"'Xactly, Colonel William."

"Well," I said with feigned resignation, "you do make a good breakfast and your salary will be radically reduced if you ever get close enough to the front line to get shot at. So, I suppose it works for me."

Phelps laughed, "Near the front lines," he shook his head and plunged back into his food.

10

It was a simple drill. Simple, but essential. It sounded far more complicated than it was in practice: 'Change front forward on the twelfth company'. A command to the regiment in battle line, it meant 'swing the regiment around without falling to pieces to meet a flanking threat with a solid front.' A maneuver that had been a standard regimental movement from Blenheim to the Plains of Abraham to Monmouth Courthouse to Jena to being a complete, utter mystery to the men and officers of the Twenty-first.

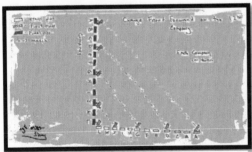

Shay's Sketch

In theory, upon command the company furthest left was to execute a ninety degree wheel and stop. Each company down the line would, in turn, wheel forty-five degrees, march straight ahead until it's left reached the first's right. Then stop, wheel the remaining forty-five degrees and, amazingly, two companies now faced the same direction with a solid face. Joined in short order by the rest. In theory.

Like bricks falling into a wall (as no few of the masons among us irritatingly noted every time we butchered the drill) and essential in combat. When suddenly threatened on another front the movement allowed us to bring the regiment's full fire power to bear on attackers. The alternative was being rolled up by the flank and leaving someone with a lot of letters to write home. It was a drill we could only forgo if we had it in writing the Confederates would attack head on.

That it was only important - vital, really - and an easy concept to grasp had been acknowledged by all after it had been carefully explained and copies of Shay's sketch handed out to all company commanders. And yet, for a variety of inexplicable reasons, we may just as well have asked the regiment, men and officers alike, to solve problems in Euclidian geometry - something at least the Trinity and Wesleyan companies might have had a fair chance of accomplishing.

We were consistently inconsistent in our bungling, at times brilliantly innovative. After a full afternoon of repetition, what should have resembled the movements of a German figurine clock instead looked more like a mob of village idiots scanning the skies for rain on a cloudless day.

We came close on occasion, each near miss inevitably followed by utter disaster. Several, in fact, before we again approached competence. Then the cycle repeated. Endlessly. At the end of each cycle I announced that we were not stopping until we got it right. And by right I did not mean West Point cadet parade perfect, nor regular army precision, nor even well trained militia competence. Just correct and preferably before the Confederate army appeared in Hartford.

That edict firmly affixed in their minds the Twenty-first spent hours without success, each failure attributed to a different miscue - although miscue may be somewhat misleading, for unless stopped at the first hint of an error, the mistakes would accumulate at astounding rates until the regiment resembled an out of control locomotive.

Shay's attitude changed little over the course of the afternoon as he continued to show remarkable restraint that at times approached compassion. He tried over-preening praise at one point, but realized quickly that it rang hollow considering the circumstances. Later it was sarcasm, lost on most of the men and resented by the officers smart enough to get it. Anger flashed very briefly, then he stopped in mid-Gaelic oath when he realized that not only were the men trying, they had no idea he was mad, the melody of the Erse served only to make them smile stupidly in incomprehension. He eventually settled on bemusement.

Arnold had it the worst for his one and only function was to give the order and move forward alone. Once he set the impending catastrophe in motion he had no more authority or control over subsequent events than one who kicks loose a stone from a mountain top has over the ensuing avalanche. He had the look of a man who knew it well, too.

I passed frustration long before evening fell, moved through anger and regret quickly and settled into a punch drunk state in which I found every error, misstep, fall, trip, wrong turn, dropped rifle, and ensuing looks on the faces of Shay and Arnold the absolutely most hysterically funny thing I had ever seen.

That, of course, was problematic on many fronts, not the least of which was failure to complete the drill on a dry, serene, non-lethal cow pasture turned parade ground did not bode well for my future wellbeing standing in front of that mess under fire. So, as the sun began to set behind me I rode to the river, biting my cheek hard enough to draw blood and trying to keep my shoulders from shaking until I was out of sight.

By the river bank my horse, Clio, happily nuzzled lush grass and I watched the darkened currents rip by. Legend had they were so strong there no one had ever swum the few hundred yards to the other side – so further escape in that direction was not possible. I clearly heard Arnold's still deep, still hopeful voice yell out the command yet again over the rippling Connecticut. Just as a moment later I heard Shay yell, "Right, let's do it again."

With back and tail to the parade ground Clio and I heard the last command of the day echo across the fields and into the void of the river. It faded and was replaced by the careful tread of twelve hundred feet tromping through the dusk. A sound I found comforting in some indefinable way and Clio ignored in her pursuit of the perfect grass shoot. I relaxed on her, she noticed immediately and took it as an opportunity to explore closer to the bank of the unswimable river, finding a juicy morsel at the very limit of the extension of her neck and head a good five feet down the steep bank. A morsel so tempting she was willing to sacrifice me for it.

I leaned back, realized that the steady marching had been

replaced with the thud of running men. Followed closely by a dull roar and the sound of flesh striking flesh. Even in my stupor I knew immediately that the 21st Connecticut Volunteer Infantry was engaged in its first fight of the War of Rebellion. I pulled Clio's reins, annoying her but saving myself from a trip downriver, and we trotted up the hill to investigate.

When I reconstructed events later it went like this: Arnold called 'change front on the first company', the exact opposite of the 'twelfth company' command and one we had been doing every four or five attempts in the vain attempt to defuse the boredom; the drill started perfectly; Companies C and H, as tired and frustrated as any other, heard what they heard eighty percent of the time and had expected to hear yet again. They wheeled to the left; much to the consternation of certain other companies who had quite professionally wheeled in the correct direction and therefore right into the wayward men; a discussion ensued whereby the aggrieved men at least four companies expressed their dissatisfaction with C and H; C and H offered their opinions of the others' military competence and deviant sexual habits; fists flew (like their forefathers at Lexington, no one knew who threw the punch heard round the Meadows); the other companies joined in, out of frustration, for fun, to redress unheard grievances, and a host of other reasons. Regardless, in moments the entire regiment was at it.

Which is what Clio and I rode into - a uniformed riot of every known form of brawling. Men on the ground wrestling; others half-standing, half-slipping flaying about or hugging ineffectually; a few boxers sparring happily; experienced alley brawlers who had pulled the jackets of their adversaries over their witless heads and were pummeling away unabated with glee.

A scattered handful of officers littered the periphery of the riot, some clearly amused, some irate (helplessly so), some at a loss of how to appear. It was apparent that the remaining officers were in the melee with their men - and I detected no peacemakers plying their trade in the mass of heaving humanity. I made a mental note to find out which officers dove in, they had promise.

On the far side of the tumult Company L, the boys from Wesleyan, stood in perfect battle line, Christian out front, smile firmly affixed.

I rode over to my little brother, "Nicely done, Captain, my compliments to you and your men."

"Thank you sir," he beamed back.

"Very impressive display of discipline," I said, looking over the chaos, "Tell me, Captain, is it possible that your men have no grudge with any other company? No grievances?"

Christian looked at me, over at the battle raging in front of us, glanced at his company then peered back at me through slit eyes. The sudden, nasty grin he sported showed he got my meaning. "To tell you the truth, sir, we're not all that fond of the men from Winsted."

"Really, why?"

"They condescend to us because we go to college rather than work honestly . . . and they stole a sheep from us last week. At least we're almost certain they did it."

A number of his men smiled widely and nudged each other. I leaned off Clio, "Know where they are in that mess, little brother?" Laughter broke out behind him.

"We'll find them, Willie."

"Then go get them, Christian."

That was all it took, he turned to his men and yelled, "Company L, advance to the melee, charge!" They smashed into the fray, energizing it to new heights.

I spied Seth and Sean together sitting on the stone wall talking animatedly, looking all the world like two men betting on a horse race. Clio picked up her pace when she saw Shay, she had taken to him in a big way, accounted for in large measure by the ready supply of sugar cubes Shay carried in his pockets.

Clio nuzzled Shay's chest, he produced a treat, stroked her nose. "I take a five minute break," I started while Clio munched, "and you two let everything go to hell."

"Ya' surely tha' glue that holds this unit together," Shay replied, poked Arnold in the ribs, "nice job wi' Company L by tha' way, they're already resented because ya' brother commands an' they're the best drilled. Sittin' this out would have been tha' last straw."

I nodded, "They're not all that enamored with everybody else as well, so here's a chance to work it out in a less theoretical environment."

"How long do we give them?" Seth jumped when Clio nudged him, hard. I looked at him in admiration. One would have thought that with his background, upbringing, manners, he would be appalled at the feral activities of his command instead of recognizing it for its restorative possibilities.

"Well, they've got to be tiring," a group of officers were striding toward us with purpose, "but let it go while we deal with this."

They were spearheaded by Huntingdon, resplendent in a ridiculously ostentatious uniform as heavily braided as a British admiral at the end of the Napoleonic Wars. A very successful admiral.

Huntingdon stood five feet nine inches, was fit but somewhat slight, had dark brown hair, a sharp patrician nose, and close cropped brown beard. None of that was particularly memorable except that it was accompanied by a pair of dead blue eyes that had last expressed emotion when he stopped weaning.

He was trailed by four captains, three of whom looked to him with intensity. The fourth, Stephenson from Windsor, seemed to have tagged along out of curiosity. As if reading my mind he smiled and nodded.

Huntingdon was five feet away when he started, making a point to stare over his shoulder at the noticeably weakening melee, "Colonel, I saw the men who instigated this . . . embarrassment and stand ready to assist in bringing charges."

"I've no doubt you do, Captain," I said lightly, left out 'and happily'.

"I am addressing the commanding officer, Hanlin," Huntingdon snapped.

"Watch your tone, Captain," I bit off with malice, instantly heated. I did not like the way the man addressed his troops, the way he handled himself and his subordinates in drill, his aristocratic bearing and, well, his uniform and it all came out at once, "You will address me properly."

He turned, glared, blinked furiously, mouth working without words.

"Captain," Arnold saved him for the moment, "Colonel Hanlin is in charge of this situation, you will deal with him and," he found something in his pocket for Clio, presented it to her, his nonchalance obviously irritated Huntingdon, "you will certainly address him with respect."

"Yes .... sir," he whispered with petulance, made no move to address me.

I was about to chime in and most likely make things incrementally worse when we were interrupted by a low roar from the center of the riot. The men had stopped their personal eye gouging, ear pulling, and, by now ineffectual punching to stagger together to watch something or someone in the center of the mass

Without a word to Huntingdon and his posse I spurred Clio forward, and we gently pushed our way through the men, most of whom - I could tell up close – were more dirtied than bloodied. They had drawn up in a rough circle in the center of which two of the larger specimens in the regiment had squared off and were sparring like professionals.

The closer I neared the center, the more grudgingly men moved aside. I clearly heard a regular army mutter - 'goddamn officer gonna' ruin a goddamn good fight'. When I finally pushed through to the front I found Osgood and Wycroft in deep consultation.

"I thought you two were doing inventory in the warehouse?" I dismounted, handed Clio's reins to Wycroft - who instantly gave her a treat from his pocket. I had a quick image of riding a hideously obese horse into battle.

"And miss this?" Osgood grinned, "We ran down the hill and got here just as it started."

"We would have invited you over," Wycroft deadpanned, "but you seemed busy with your friends."

"So, who's who?" I asked to the surprise and evident approval of the men around me, one of whom turned out to be Fellson.

"The one with the red beard, dark hair is Wright, Counselor," he answered quickly, "late of Frog Hollow. He's something like forty-one and one, the one being attributable to the clean shaven gent, Gilbride, North-end, who as far as I know has never lost – oooh!" He grunted as Gilbride landed a vicious right to the side of Wright's head, leaving an ear reddened and putting a wobble in his gait.

"Much action?" I asked, Wright recovered and hit Gilbride twice with a lightening quick jab combination. Wright was clearly the better boxer. Gilbride merely looked like a killer.

Fellson did me the honor of not pretending to not know what I was talking about, "A sizable piece of change," the two fighters warily circled each other. Gilbride did not look like a man who liked taking short hard jabs to the face while Wright looked like a man who had no further interest in taking shots to the side of his head.

"You'll give up the vig today, Fellson," I said amicably.

"If you say so, Counselor," he replied without enthusiasm.

"I do indeed. And I'll check, you don't make money off of your fellow soldiers tonight."

"You do me a disservice, sir," he chuckled. The fighters settled into a punchless dance.

I waited good thirty seconds for some pugilistic effort on either's part. None forthcoming, I moved toward them, "Put me down for a draw," I said over my shoulder to Fellson's groan, "and remember what I said."

I strode between them, "Gilbride, Wright!" I yelled to their evident relief, "thank you for an admirable exhibition," the men quieted but otherwise seemed confused

"You're both sergeants," I announced to huzzahs that crescendoed when they shook hands. I waited for the noise to abate before adding, "Gentlemen," I used a voice that would cost me in the morning, "I trust you enjoyed your recreation period."

The intensity and creativity of the oaths that invoked indicated that they had indeed. Again, I waited for the yelling to die away, "Good, so did I!" I was interrupted by more hoots, catcalls and invitations to join in next time. I held up a hand and received moderate silence, "And while a good time was had by all, this will not occur again. Or there will be twelve hundred men pulling extra duty from now until the end of the century. Is that understood?"

A resounding, coordinated, "Yes, Sir!" rang back, the best to date.

"Except, if they are willing, I for one would like to see Wright versus Gilbride part two." That to rollicking cheers and nods of agreement by both pugilists.

"It's been a long day for all of you, I know, but," moans and a flurry of rather pedestrian oaths broke out - they had been soldiers just long enough to know where I was going, "we need to finish this in style," the groans grew into yells that subsided into the low hiss of disappointment, "so that when you sleep in tomorrow you can do so without guilt"

That got them and they cheered wildly, the few who retained their hats threw them into the air. A day of rest mid-week was unprecedented and most of them guessed it would never happen again.

"So, here's what we're going to do," I had their rapt attention, "when Sergeant Major Shay gives the command, you are going to pick up your property - Clio here," I pointed to my always hungry mount, currently not so gently nuzzling a private's pocket, "would appreciate you picking up all the rifles before she stomps on one and shoots someone.

"Get your equipment and fall into line of battle by company as usual." I walked around the packed, irregular circle, nodding, smiling at the men, stopping to check a particularly brilliant black eye. I received huge smiles in return, only a few of which had newly formed gaps in them.

Christian sported a smile I had last seen when I came home to find he had cut all the buttons off my dress uniform. "Captain," I said sternly, "I am deeply disturbed to see you involved. What kind of an example did you set for your men, sir?"

"Well, Colonel," the smile widened just as it had when I chased him through our mother's house with the buttonless coat, "I think I showed them a few things, as Captain Sykes will attest," He threw an arm around the dirty, bleeding from the mouth captain next to him. The great bulk of his limb almost buckled the poor man.

"Yesss, ssir," Captain Sykes lisped through swollen lips, "I thing he ssset a fine 'xamble, ssir." He tried to smile, but as it hurt me to see him try it must have been excruciating for him.

"I'm appalled," I made a show of shaking my head, "two officers roughhousing like common soldiers."

"Yes sir!" Christian beamed.

"Yesss, ssssir!" Sykes echoed.

"Well done, both of you," I stage whispered as I walked by, noting the many nods and grins of the men around them. I moved back to the shrinking center, the men crowding closer.

"Also on Mr. Shay's command, all company officers will form on Colonel Arnold and Captain Osgood over by the flags."

Puzzled looks were thrown my way. "For the purposes of this drill," I went on unconcerned, "the senior sergeant of each company will act as captain. If you doubt who the senior sergeant of your company is request Sergeant Major Shay's assistance. Nicely boys, remember he was itching to get in there with you, I don't know how long I can hold him back."

More cheers, I was enjoying myself immensely, "All yours Sergeant Major," I ordered, walked to the flag pole and a gloomy gathering of suddenly superfluous officers. "Cheer up, we needed it and no one's to blame. Relax," I repeated to the group as necessary. One or two of my officers visibly relaxed, most managed to look only less uncomfortable.

We watched while Shay gave the command to reform, setting off a mad scramble for guns, hats, teeth (?), that quickly took on all the solemnity of an Easter egg hunt. Huntingdon and his small command were still by the stone wall deep in animated conversation. I stored the image away for future reference.

I chatted with Arnold, Osgood and Wycroft as the men dragged their bedraggled selves to reform the battle line, coats, hats askew, rifles shouldered.

"Companies formed in battle line, sergeants squared and ready to go," reported a smiling Shay.

"Then take them through the drill, Sean," Arnold bellowed. With British army precision, Shay stomped, pivoted and trod back to the line.

"Twenty-first Connecticut," he roared in perfect baritone, "change front forward on the twelfth company!" That echoed through the almost dark grounds before he added, "That's you, Company L, ya' fightin' fooks from Wesleyan!"

Laughing, the companies set off at once and fell in perfectly. I held my breath when companies A and B approached the perfectly formed line. They fit seamlessly. The drill completed at long last, the men remained silent.

"Change front forward on the first company," Shay yelled without acknowledging their accomplishment, "that's you, ya' Fancy Dan fooks from West Hartford!"

Again they set off in laughter, again I held my breath as companies K and L approached the perfectly reset line. Christian grimaced concern with every step his company took until they finished in perfect order.

It was finished in a silence that stayed unbroken while Arnold and I walked to the center of the reformed line. Shay faced us with a face suffused in professional pride.

"My compliments, Mr. Shay," Arnold announced, "well done."

Shay pivoted, surveyed the men and intoned with gravis, "Twenty-first Connecticut, give yourself three cheers!"

The huzzahs rang out, Arnold beaconed the officers to rejoin their units.

I stood by his shoulder and whispered, "Band."

The prodigy that was Colonel Seth Arnold understood immediately, "Men, I think it will make drilling more enjoyable if we raise a regimental band. I'll supply the instruments if you supply the talent." The men cheered yet again, hoarser perhaps, but with the same enthusiasm and loud enough that Arnold had to yell over them, "Tomorrow, after supper, I expect any man with musical talent to appear here and we'll see what we have."

"Captain Wycroft."

"Sir?" Wycroft yelled back in the spirit of things.

"How are we supplied with whiskey?"

"I've a few excellent barrels just in," Wycroft replied with wolfish grin.

"Well then, break 'em out and distribute them evenly. The regiment is dismissed, good night men!"

A last, hoarse, raspy cheer, the men dispersed and shuffled up the gentle hill to their tents, mess, and tobacco to await the promised whiskey. They mingled freely, companies were social barriers no longer.

I turned from observing that happy sight to find Huntingdon

and an officer I dimly recognized as Bryce from West Hartford standing in front of me.

"You've both been dismissed," I said, not unkindly. Neither moved.

"That was disgraceful behavior," Huntingdon went on as if I had not spoken, "and you are condoning, encouraging ..."

"It served its purpose and is over with," I interrupted, "The matter of the fight is closed, Captain . . . as is the matter of your earlier insubordination. I suggest you retire, sir, and consider that good news."

They hesitated only for the time it took to look at one another before they slouched off into the darkness.

"You are going to have trouble with those two," Osgood relayed when they faded into the lane.

"We are," Arnold stepped in, "and they have a few friends, not to mention the fact that they are on the governor's safe list as well." He punched me on the arm for emphasis.

"I can hope they're not on the Confederate safe list," I quipped, "but it's been too good an evening to ruin with this horseshit."

We ambled up the hill, the sounds and smells of a regiment settling down reached us well before we arrived at our tents. A silvery half mood emerged above the trees at water's edge illuminating the white tents.

Arnold touched my sleeve, "What was that with the sergeants finishing the drill?"

"So many reasons, Seth," Shay answered for me, "Firs' at least some o' these sergeants will be commandin' a company, an'..."

"Like you ended up with a brigade?" Arnold interrupted.

"Yeah," Shay nodded, "second, they need ta' know we trust 'em. Or am I wrong, William?"

"You're never wrong, Sean," I replied without hesitation. Phelps had fires burning, chairs out, the air was saturated with the smell of steak. I stripped off my tunic and took a seat by the fire, a chess board was already set up and ready for the resumption of my perpetual series with Osgood.

Shirt sleeves rolled up, brandy snifter in one hand, lemonade in the other, Osgood took his seat and handed me the latter. I had a very tangible superstition about never drinking alcohol in the field. I did not begrudge it for others, but I would not, could not. It was acquired in Mexico in the midst of a hard drinking officer corps that provided first hand evidence of the effects of heat on hard drinkers.

"Fantastic, William," Shay said as he sat, "smartly done." He tipped his glass at me, I tipped mine back before taking a sip of cold, sweet liquid and moved my king's pawn to e-4.

"I'll never understand what you two see in that game," Arnold said, as he said every night to our steely silence on the subject, "it just seems so.... so needlessly complicated."

"Well," Osgood surprised me by deigning to answer on that occasion, "you can learn a lot about war, strategy and your opponent. Especially your opponent. That makes it interesting."

"Really?" Arnold sat forward, stared intently at the board, swirling his brandy, "well, then, tell me what it says about our Colonel Hanlin."

Osgood looked at me with malevolent intent, I shot him a warning look that had all the effect of a mosquito on a rhinoceros' buttocks. "I am glad you asked me that, Seth," Osgood emoted, "we would all do well to note that Hanlin plays quietly and logically from the start. He builds and builds without threatening, pure strategy. It's a pleasure and an enjoyable game over brandy and a cigar. Enjoyable, that is," he beamed hatred, "until you either make a mistake or he springs a long dormant trap. Then, well, then it is like having a pit viper in your bedroom. He's vicious, unrelenting and goes for the throat. He will sacrifice his pieces - any piece - to do so. He won't let go until you resign or he checkmates you – no gentleman's draw for him."

Silence around the fire for a moment until Wycroft's voice cut through the gloaming. "Is it too late to transfer?"

I answered through their laughs with a grunt and made a move.

"Good to know, Osgood," Arnold said lightly, "about what I've suspected all along. Our friend here is not as stoic or proper as he would have us believe. Indeed, his civility—"

"Don't force me to dissect your mercantile personality, Arnold," I growled, primarily in the hopes of distracting Osgood long enough to overlook the queen trap I was two moves from springing. It worked, he made the move I wanted.

"I was complimenting you, William," Arnold quickly replied in mock fear, "just meaning —"

"You bastard," Arnold was interrupted by Osgood's belated realization my move insured his queen's demise, "see what he's done?" He appealed to the assembly, "He used the conversation to distract me from another fucking trap."

"On the other hand," I offered in turn, "by careful study of the way he plays chess it's obvious Osgood is an exceptionally poor sport." Osgood was too busy seeking divine intervention for a hopeless situation to respond.

Arnold, chuckling, continued, "I was saying, William, that I agree with Osgood's assessment, except perhaps, for sacrificing men."

I thought about putting on professional airs and professing the ancient credo of the good of the many outweighing those of the few, but his complete earnestness stopped me cold. That and the fact I did not really believe in it myself. Necessarily.

"Wouldn't happen," I said blithely, more dismissively than I intended, I think, "I can't see it happening. I think the days of Leonardis at Thermopylae and Horatius at the bridge are pretty much over with in the age of the rifle."

"Glad to hear," Arnold replied with enthusiasm, "it's just that I like these men and sometimes, perhaps you'll find this morbid, but sometimes I look over the companies and I —"

"Wonder who's going to die," I completed.

"You too?" He asked with hope.

"Yes," I answered with utter sincerity, "But I catch myself and I make myself stop. It made me sick in Mexico and I was responsible for a hundred men there, not a thousand."

"It's funny," he sounded relieved that his was not a singular emotion, "and maybe you feel this too, but I look at men like your friend Fellson and — "

"Ya' bloody well know he's comin' outta it without a fookin' scratch," Shay interrupted, "an' I feel tha' way 'bout Huntingdon and Byrce."

"Pricks like that do not attract bullets," Osgood interjected, "but they are carriers." He casually flipped his king and glared ineffectually at me.

"Biggest threat against them," Shay added, "would be from their own men, I'd wager."

"That's a cold, unchristian thing to say," Seth responded, "as is the sentiment you are all undoubtedly thinking - no one would grieve," he glanced at Osgood who affirmed the assumption, "well, Osgood, what the fuck, who would grieve 'em, eh?"

Delighted laughter erupted around the fire once again.

"Mr. Arnold," Osgood yelled across the flames, "I believe you have been too long with the wrong element."

11

Within the fortnight we had a reputable band outfitted with new instruments, courtesy of Arnold and the people of Norwich. More importantly, we found a bugler - a very good bugler. Harry Biggs, five-foot seven inches tall, two feet broad, an inch or two thick, auburn hair, open, bright brown eyes set on a clean shaven face with more sharp edges than a picket fence.

A day after Biggs reported that he could 'manage a few notes' Wycroft magically appeared with a gleaming new bugle and a ream of military sheet music. Biggs matched Wycroft's genius by mastering, over the course of a few days, the calls we needed: 'Peas on a trencher' (breakfast); "Roast Beef" (dinner); 'Assembly" (squads form into companies); 'Colors" (companies form regimental front, flags unfurl); 'Tommy Totten' (advance on enemy); and so on.

Arnold also made good on his earlier promise and brought in Reverend Thomas Ashford from the tiny community of, well, Ashford. It seemed that among the multitude of protestant churches and sects in a Protestant state, finding a minister who had an opinion of the impending conflict as anything less than apocalyptic was rather difficult.

Arnold's search for someone who could look South and not see the horned armies of the Anti-Christ finally settled on an Episcopalian. A most imposing Episcopalian.

Reverend Ashford stood at least an inch or two taller than me and was a good fifty pounds heavier, not fatter - I do not believe he had an ounce of fat on him. He had dirty blond hair, pale eyes that probably hid a sense of humor, and thin wisps of blond beard confined to his jaw line. Osgood took one look at him and said, "Now there's a man who can beat the word of God into you!"

I was invited to sit in the front row at his first service the

Sunday after his appointment. I debated begging off, citing a crushing work load, an excuse that had the added benefit of being true, then re-thought it and decided it prudent to make an appearance.

Which describes my participation perfectly. I sat in the front row with Osgood, Arnold, Wycroft, Christian and special guests, Sergeants Gilbride and Wright. I sat doing my best to look pious and familiar with the proceedings. I had not been to services since West Point and found it, if not enjoyable, certainly more bearable than I had anticipated. I was relieved to find that Ashford was positive, dynamic, and delivered on the humor his eyes promised.

Services over, I enthusiastically shook Ashford's hand, thanked him profusely, left and promptly began a week long game of cat and mouse with him, lest he corner me alone and attempt to engage in serious soul saving. Admittedly, the game may have been entirely one-sided, but I was not taking chances. Particularly when I missed services the following week and had no plans to make up the deficit any time soon.

While this occupied some of my time, the rest was consumed by real issues, foremost among them our first mass movement of the regiment, across the Connecticut River no less. It took a full week to organize, we would be fortunate indeed to have more than twenty-four hours in action.

Under the auspices of Wycroft - his most energetic assistant now seemed to be Osgood - we were ready on schedule and what I had initially feared to be an impossible task for our still very green men began without a hitch.

We crossed the mirror that was the Connecticut River as the sun rose. Our borrowed long boats left on time and we debarked at East Windsor on schedule and without the loss of man, beast or wagon, nor did we have to engage in any mid-stream rescues. Completely unexpected by all, especially me as I had three near drownings and the loss of a wagon in the headquarters' pool.

We formed beautifully on the far bank and marched in perfect order, in column, through the tiny town. The townspeople spilled out onto their walkways and quickly filled the town green, some produced small American Flags which they waved with vigor. We marched out of town as the sun rose higher in a stark, cloudless sky and the day turned hot for early June. I cursed, not for the first nor the last time, the moron who had decided, undoubtedly from a cool, subterranean office, that the U.S. Army looked best in dark blue wool. I paused frequently to watch the column pass by, each time Clio looked over her shoulder, wondering what moron had burdened her with a hundred and eighty pound dark blue perspiration machine.

Our enthusiasm waning rapidly, we marched past the scattered farmhouses and long, narrow barns of the tobacco fields of South Windsor. At the town center we broke from column and, to the amusement and awe of the gathering crowd, began to drill. The men were invigorated by the yelling onlookers, the drills were crisp, impressive, and ended with a regimental blank volley. The men sat down to their first meal in the field, one quickly supplemented with food brought out by proud townsfolk. The officers ate at a nearby tavern, hosted by Arnold who had pre-arranged a feast.

All and all a great day to that point. Unfortunately we had to return as well. Once out of South Windsor reality returned in the form of roads dusty after a day's baking, the sun directly in our sweating eyes. No cheering, no refreshments, no flags waving.

The sun was dripping behind the western hills when we trudged down to the boats and a collective groan rose to a still cloudless sky when the men realized we still needed to row. We were miraculously intact except for a dozen stragglers overcome by the heat, now lying in our ambulances. Along with six very red, very drunk, very about to be extra duty-laden privates who could not keep out of the taverns when we got too close to the Boston Turnpike. They had been rooted out by a dutiful Sergeant Phelps who took time off from his temporary duty as ambulance driver to cleverly disguise himself as a fellow duty-shirking alcoholic. He was quite put out when informed there was no decoration for so meritorious an action.

We shuffled up the hill to camp in total darkness. I was proud to see that the overwhelming majority of men took the time, despite their exhaustion, to start fires and go about their normal nighttime routines. They had done relatively well in a task veteran troops could do with relative ease. Their true test, and the reason for the march, would be their reaction to the hard drills scheduled for the next day, starting at dawn. That would give me a good gauge of the relative fitness of our men and officers.

I was proud again, and relieved, when the morning went without a hitch or a complaint beyond a good natured jibe. The regiment shrugged off the march as if routine and went about its new business. I was so pleased, in fact, that I left the rest of the day's drill to Shay and joined Wycroft, Arnold and Osgood in the warehouse where we went about the preparations for an additional five regiments. We worked among the mountains of crates we had accumulated, the towering, rolling doors open to allow a cool, gentle breeze in off the river. The murmuring sound of training in the distance was serenely reassuring.

My companions jumped aboard a Hartford bound train for dinner at the Goodwin and an inspection of a very different Armory than the one we had last visited. The train chugged down the line, went around the wide bend to Union Station, silence descended over me and I enjoyed a moment of solitude.

Enjoyed, that is, until it occurred to me silence was problematic. That realization was accompanied almost simultaneously by the sound of footsteps pounding up the cow path. I peered down the darkening path, made out a shape that could only be my brother sprinting up the hill.

I resisted the urge to run and hide in the warehouse and started, slowly, toward him into the cold shade. He pulled up, panting deeply, "Quick, Willie, before you have a dead captain on your hands!"

"Wha—", was as far as I got before Christian turned and headed down the trail.

I sprinted after him, drew even when he looked over his shoulder, "What?" I gasped.

"Shay," he paused for a deep breath, neither of us broke stride, "and Huntingdon," all I needed to increase the pace.

We cleared the tree line and had a clear view of the parade ground where the regiment stood in battle line minus a company - as ugly a sight as a wide smile missing a front tooth. The incisor in question was in column across the grounds a good fifty yards away, Huntingdon prominent in front, legs shoulder wide, hands behind his back. I wondered briefly if there was a single volunteer officer in the Union army who did not affect one or more Napoleonic mannerism.

Shay stood a few feet away, at ease, somehow insolent, facing Huntingdon with malevolence. There being no mayhem at that moment I settled into a brisk walk, more in keeping with casual decorum than my outright sprint. Christian matched my pace and together we advanced on the tableau.

"Christian," I whispered, "you take the regiment. Dismiss them, see that they get to camp and stay there."

"Of course, Willie, thank you," Christian whispered back, "that'll be a lot easier if I can issue a dram of whiskey."

"Excellent, do it."

"Good luck," he said aloud and peeled off before I could ask him to send a whiskey back to me.

I watched him saunter to the center of the line like he was born to command. He spoke briefly, decisively with coercion. He was clever enough to put a time limit on receipt of the whiskey in question, thus clearing the parade ground of the uninvolved in a heartbeat.

That done, I walked as calmly as possible toward one obviously irate Irishman and one very stupid Yankee.

"Sergeant Major, Captain," I greeted them as if we had run into one another on Main Street. Shay nodded, Huntingdon said nothing, just continued to stare with intent at Shay. I surveyed the column, more than a few of his men met my eyes, many smiled, some shrugged subtly. That told me volumes.

"Captain Huntingdon, does this matter involve the company at large?" I asked curtly.

"I want them to witness this . . . sir."

"You did not answer the question, Captain," I struggled to maintain an air of cordiality, maybe overdid it while mindful of my predisposition toward him, "does this involve the company?"

"Not directly," he answered sullenly.

"Then dismiss them," I disregarded the insubordination, I had the feeling it was going to be fairly insignificant compared to what was coming. That feeling was reinforced when he made no motion to comply.

"You men are dismissed," I yelled over Huntingdon's head to his company, "if you double time it to camp there may still be whiskey left - tell my brother to fill yours to the brim!"

That sent them off in a flash. I was struck by the fact that not a single officer so much as glanced back to see how his commanding officer was doing. In no time, as if they had never been there, they disappeared into the gloaming.

I turned to Seth, "So?"

"Sir!" Huntingdon interjected with heat, "I am the aggrieved party here! I have first satisfaction."

"This isn't a fucking duel, Huntingdon," just that quickly I lost any regard for a balanced approach to the matter, "if it was, you'd already be lying in a pool of blood and I could get on with my evening." He recoiled as if struck.

"Shay?" I started over.

"Jus' a misunderstandin', Colonel."

"Oh for Christ's sake, Sean, just tell me what happened."

"Tha' an order?"

"Yes, that's an order."

"Captain Huntingdon questioned a parade drill order," Shay answered without inflection, "an' tha' wisdom and necessity for repeatin' it again. I believe tha' exact phrase was, 'we've been doing this damn fucking drill all fucking day for no fucking reason,' Colonel, tho' I could be misquotin'," I bit the inside of my cheek so hard I drew blood - Shay had done a pitch perfect, dead on impersonation of Huntingdon. So dead on even Huntingdon could not have failed to notice.

"And your response, Sergeant Major?"

"I tole him to move his bloody arse an' get the fookin' drill right so we could all go home."

"That's right," Huntingdon growled, "he —"

"You took your company out of regimental drill?" I interrupted him with such vehemence he stopped and stared at me with mouth agape, "No need to answer, it's rhetorical."

He did anyway, "He made me look like an incompetent in front of the entire regiment, and him, a —"

"Officer on parade?" I interrupted once again, probably saving him, completely inadvertently, from a fatal mistake, "and in command by the fact he is the training officer of this regiment. You, sir, choose to ignore a legally binding order."

"What?" He stuttered.

"What, sir," I corrected him, "Your insolence is about to lead to another insult to your honor, Captain." When he made no immediate attempt to correct me I really loosened up, "You disobeyed a direct order and in doing so you left a gap in our battle line that -"

"For Christ's sakes, Hanlin," a frustrated Huntingdon erupted, "it's just a fucking drill, it doesn't mean -"

"It means everything, you dumb fuck!" I yelled loud enough to visibly rock him, "Everything! You do this here so you'll do it when it counts." A gross simplification but my temper had snapped with the sheer arrogance of the man, "You do not question, never mind disobey or refuse to carry out an order, period. And you sure as fuck do not –ever - make it obvious to your men that you disagree with that order. That's mutiny, Captain. Do you understand any of that?"

"You put this Irish son of a whore over me and —"

"Shut the fuck up!" I snapped flatly and surprisingly calmly. Shay stepped forward, eyes hard, fists balled. I stepped within a foot of Huntingdon, shielding him, though my heart was not in it. "Stop right there, Huntingdon," my voice was completely calm. Calm and level, "or I will leave you and Mr. Shay here, in the dark, to work things out on your own. Without the worry of legal consequences. Do you know what that means, Captain?"

"Yes," he rasped out, eyes focused over my shoulder at the looming Shay.

"Do you wish to retract your last statement?" I asked conversationally.

He did not hesitate, "I spoke in haste .... sir."

"I thought so. Sergeant Major?"

"Forgotten, Colonel," Shay replied, voice hard, grudging.

"Thank you," I said lightly without taking my eyes off Huntingdon, "listen to me very carefully, Captain Huntingdon... Miles," the use of his first name confused him, 'I am going to say this to you once, as a courtesy."

He looked at me expectantly, as if he thought I was about to unburden myself of some loathsome secret.

"If you disobey or refuse an order, or insult this man further - a man who should command a regiment, at the least - I will see to it, I will make it my mission, that you are cashiered from the service after we are called up to federal service."

He stiffened, reddened, and said nothing.

"I know you have wealth and political power here in Connecticut, but I assure you it will not help you once we are called up - you'll be in my arena then. You'll go and not be missed."

"And," I continued, deadly earnest, "should you wait to do any of this shit under fire, or anywhere near the enemy, I'll put a bullet in your back and write a wonderful letter to your next of kin telling them you died with your face to the enemy."

I never took my eyes off the bastard. He avoided them and stood shaking with either rage, fear, humiliation or all three.

"This is over, Captain, unless you wish it otherwise. Do you wish it otherwise, Captain?"

"No ... Sir," almost a whisper.

"Then you are dismissed, good night." I said, resisting the urge to have him repeat himself, louder. He pivoted and slouched away.

"Well ya' scared tha' piss right outta' me," Shay laughed after Huntingdon disappeared, "I, fo'one, believed ya'."

I nodded and began to walk to camp, wondering what Phelps had prepared for supper.

"William?" Shay called from behind, I stopped, "Tha' was no idle threat, was it?"

"I meant it, once we're federalized I'll cashier him."

"Nah, ya' daft shit, tha's not what I meant," he chuckled, "tha' whole thing 'bout shootin' him in tha' back."

"You know, Sean," I said with a short grunt, "answering that could make you a conspirator. I wouldn't want to get you in trouble with the law.'

"Christ, no, William, I'd naught want tha'," he laughed, "but I think ya' jus' answered me.

12

Despite or because of her forty-something years Olga Petrovsky looked better than good in the soft light of her second floor sitting room. It had been an abnormally hot, humid June day and now, well after dark, thunder rumbled somewhere in the starless, pitch black night. A strong breeze blew through the open windows, billowing the lace curtains and Olga's diaphanous shift.

She floated from window to window peering out into the night while clad only in an unlaced corset and said flowing undergarment. She was more comfortable than I in both the warmth of the night and the state of her undress. I sat sweating, shirt sleeves rolled up, top buttons undone, stocking feet on an ottoman of such ornateness it inspired guilt at the very thought of soiling it. I concentrated as intently as humanly possible on my glass of excellent wine and tried to stop noticing the fact that every time Olga walked between a light and myself the shift disappeared. Completely.

I was tired from an exceedingly long day at camp and the wine had immediate effect - though I did not need it to enhance Olga's allure. She had sent for me the day before, I received the invitation from a smirking Phelps while watching rifle drill, three days into our intensified drilling in preparation of an extended march. We had been pushing ourselves and the men, sleeping little, covering much, staggering around in mutual exhaustion when not fully engaged at work.

Which is why I did not hesitate to accept Olga's invitation and came to be sitting in the lap of luxury, sipping expensive wine, trying to avert my eyes from the half nude woman gliding around my chair.

As hospitality demanded, the reason for my summons remained unsaid while I was made comfortable, offered refreshments and chatted up with comments on the weather and items of local gossip.

All before Olga started, although, of course, I was unaware of when, precisely, she did, "I'm curious, William," her voice was suffused with seduction and strength, "what do you think about Lincoln's suspension of habeas corpus?"

I liked and respected Olga and would never have denigrated her or her profession, but I could not help but think I never expected to be quizzed on Lincoln's fiat by the proprietress of a brothel.

"I don't see where he had a choice," I answered, "except watch Maryland join the Confederacy and have Washington surrounded in less than a week."

"You don't?"

"I don't," I answered her endless legs.

"But the law ——" she started.

"He got an opinion from Attorney General Bates, it's not like he issued some kind of dictatorial proclamation," I rudely interrupted.

"I'm surprised at you,"

"Sorry I interrupted."

"Not that," she sighed, "I'm surprised you agree with the President."

"You expected different?"

"Yes."

"It's war, it's draconian, but the country is at risk," I shrugged and took a long sip of wine.

"No," she said slowly, "Washington is at risk, and if the rebels want it for the summer, I say give it to them."

"Unfortunately they'd keep it the rest of the year . . . and Great Britain would probably notice."

"You don't find it," she walked to the far window, her shift billowed and merged with the curtains. She leaned out into the face of the wind, leaving me with a view, when I chose to accept it, of a beautifully proportioned ass, "a somewhat underhanded approach to the problem?"

"As opposed to surrounding the statehouse with cavalry and shooting the secessionists who vote aye?"

"Now that's direct," she replied, laughing lightly, "and what I'd expect from you."

"Well, I do command an infantry regiment," I tried to sound fierce.

"I believe you are second in command, William," she smiled back.

"You know what I mean."

"No, I do not," her smile stayed in place, "you assume I do." I replied with a shrug and a deeper pull of wine.

Silence while she peered out the window and the wind picked up, flashes of lightening lit her outline, peals of thunder punctured the air, the smell of ozone filled the room. I was concerned only with the falling level of the wine bottle next to me.

The spell was broken seconds later when rain cascaded down in sheets and instantly turned the breeze refreshingly cool. Olga fled her post by the window and found refuge on the sofa diagonally across from me where she arranged herself quite primly despite the outfit. She began a deep contemplation of her crystal wine glass.

"Why the invitation, Olga?" I asked while I was still almost sober.

"Now that is direct," she smiled, "how refreshing," she may have meant the particularly brisk breeze that blew in just then or my question, I was unsure, "I invited you, my dear, because Osgood, Seth and I thought it best that I speak with you."

"Speak to me?" I did not mask my surprise.

She stretched with the languid ease of a cat, "Seth is an old friend - an old, non-professional friend - and Osgood, well," she held my eyes steadily, "he and I have developed a relationship of sorts."

"Osgood?"

"And I, yes," she smiled deliciously, "for some weeks now."

"The things one misses when one works eighteen hour days," I shook my clouded head.

"I'd be explaining it if you had been on holiday the past month," she replied without delay, "as Osgood says, you have blinders on to most of what goes on around you."

"Uh-huh," I was well aware of what Osgood said, "why'd they

suggest we talk?"

"Because they care for and are concerned for you."

"And they asked you to do the honors because?"

"On the theory that because of my sex you will politely listen to me and not dash off to solve the problem in your own fashion."

"So," I chuckled the chuckle of the slightly more than slightly inebriated, "I have a problem. Imagine that, trying to get twelve hundred strangers to meld together as a unit, and me running into problems trying to do it."

"There are problems, William, and then there is *a problem,*" she frowned back, "and your success thus far with the regiment -and it's far more than anyone expected this soon - has bred a major one."

"No one expected?" Curiosity compelled the question.

"Everyone thought that you would get the men marching a little, look presentable, then go off to Washington to be trained. No one thought these men would actually become *soldiers.*"

"We're doing what needs to be done, that's all."

"Listen to me, dear, it's more than anybody expected. I hope you know that," she smiled sweetly, "nothing breeds antipathy more than success, especially in those who cannot take the credit and are used to doing so."

"We're a long way from success," I laughed.

"You are far too self-depreciating."

"I'm realistic," I shook my head, it did not work, there was no way to clear away my exhaustion, the wine, and the fact I was having this conversation with a half nude woman almost my mother's age with the body of a twenty-five year old, "and anything less than what we've done so far would be unfair to everyone. Selfish, too, I don't like the idea of walking into enemy fire and finding out no one is behind me."

"Understandable," she sighed.

"Osgood, eh?"

"A most amazing man," she said slyly, "most informed and loquacious on so, so, many subjects, and yet," she laughed and leveled me with a challengingly direct gaze, "aside from his current concerns for you, remarkably silent on the subject of one William Hanlin."

"How odd," I tried my increasingly drunken best to level a gaze back.

"Indeed," it left her unimpressed, "but concerned he is, as is Seth, who admires you even as you intimidate him in so many ways," I started to ask how, she waved me off with an imperious hand, "they're concerned that you are so focused on your tasks you are unaware of certain realities."

"The problem?"

"Oh yes, one that you greatly exacerbated recently."

"I've made an enemy."

"Rather more than one, dear."

"Enemies with the ear of certain authorities?"

"Without doubt."

"All right," I smiled ruefully, "how many?"

"You certainly have a casual attitude toward the sudden existence of enemies."

"Impressed?"

"I expected it."

"Comes from having been shot at by a few thousand very pissed off Mexicans and threatened on a daily basis in court," I shrugged, "how many?"

"Seven," she said with certainty.

"And they've gone to Buckingham."

"And they've gone to the Governor," she echoed, "with whom they curry a great deal of political favor – certainly more than a Boston Brahmin —"

"God, I'm sick of that term, Holmes is one himself, and —"

"Boston Brahmin, Assistant State's Attorney," she ignored me, "with no political ambitions and no roots here."

"I account for no votes."

"None."

"That's a crushing thing for a man to have to face in his thirties."

"This is not funny."

"Perhaps not, what are they demanding?"

"I'm surprised you have not asked their names," she said, no such surprise evident.

"Huntingdon's the leader," I reeled off tiredly, "Bryce right behind him - the bastard's so far up his ass he'll have to be mined out - McPherson, nodding so furiously in response to Huntingdon's every word he's likely to throw up on the Governor," Olga smiled furiously, "that'd be it for company commanders, I can think of four lieutenants who would join them. I doubt I could name four lieutenants in the entire regiment, but I'd recognize them, they're the only ones that pay the slightest attention to the fucker."

She smiled absently, "I'm impressed. Completely accurate, although you might want to learn a few more names."

"What are they demanding?"

"Your dismissal."

"That all?"

"They have the pull to do it - not now, but soon if they persist with reason."

"Fine."

"Are you being willfully obtuse with me, William?"

"No, Olga, I'm being willfully realistic. So what? Remove me and I'd have my own regiment in a week or two, on the outside."

"You don't really feel that way," she said without any visible trace of emotion.

"I could."

"But?"

"Well, shit," I laughed, "I've grown attached to this regiment."

"That's reassuring because the men adore you and the rest of the officers would walk through brick walls for you," she said with passion, a blush spread above her breasts up to her lower neck, "but those seven, William, can fuck it all up. And they are motivated, you cut the balls off Huntingdon, and you did it here instead of in Washington. That was stupid, really stupid. And you, my dear, are not a stupid man."

"I thought -"

"You did not, that's the point. No man in this state, from Bill Buckingham down, does what you did to him twice. Ten years ago he would have challenged you to a duel."

"Then he would have ceased to an irritant," I answered happily, envisioning the result of that meeting.

"I've no doubt," she smiled with an evil intensity that made her even more attractive, "a lot of people, myself included, would have enjoyed it greatly. A bully's comeuppance is always fun. You know why I would enjoy it more than most."

"Shame he had an alibi."

"Osgood double checked it just to be certain."

"Of course he did."

"He didn't say anything because he did not want to bring it up and further color your issues with Huntingdon."

"How is you raising it now going to help?"

"As if it could be made worse."

"You underestimate me, Olga."

"After promising to shoot him in the back, I think there's little room for your relationship to deteriorate further."

"To be fair, I did offer to write his family a nice note," I pointed out in my defense.

She laughed - a singularly pleasing sound - repositioned herself on the sofa with feline precision, "The problem here is that you do not see the whole picture. You tear Huntingdon apart and for you it's over, no hard feelings, let's get back to work."

"Being dressed down by a superior officer is an occupational hazard," I shrugged.

"Don't you understand, William?" She gritted her teeth in frustration, "this is politics, not just the army. The two have combined and you're only aware of half, or you're only concerning yourself with half.

"And while in some ways that is quite admirable, it's certainly naive. Men like Huntingdon do not take their lumps and move on. They bitch and moan first so that everyone knows they are the injured party, then they plot. Plot and bide time. And when they strike there is no mercy, particularly after you've undoubtedly extended mercy to them. That's just cause for more resentment.

"These are people who are not satisfied winning, that's secondary to the total ruin of their adversary." She finished her speech and took a long pull of wine.

"You just described half a dozen Shakespearean plots, Olga," I said with a grin and a snort.

"Laugh all you want," she glared, "it doesn't make it go away."

"I'm not laughing, Olga," I sighed, "I'm feeling ridiculous to be the object of this . . . whatever this is."

"A coup, I think," her smile returned.

"What exactly occurred when the seven saw Buckingham?"

"Huntingdon outlined a long list of grievances, most of them obviously slight and petty, the major ones being you allowed the fight to continue, and, of course, you threatened him while backing 'your Irishman'."

"And then they demanded my removal?"

"Your removal or Huntingdon's promotion to Lieutenant Colonel," she arched her eyebrows.

"They are the same thing."

"Of course."

"And the Governor?"

"Bill's in a tight spot," it could have been the wine, it could have been many, many things, but I thought it no accident she used Buckingham's first name for the second time, "Huntingdon's important to him, but does he outweigh the rest of the officers, all of whom support you? If he acts he risks looking like a political hack backing a backer's whim."

"Seth?"

"Will do what he can, I'm sure, if asked. He certainly doesn't feel like he can function without you. Nor would he care to try, he's enjoying himself too much."

"I get the feeling, then, that no decision is imminent."

"I do not believe so, it will wait until there is another incident."

"Which Huntingdon will try to instigate."

"You're learning."

"That, Olga," I poured another glass, "is a problem, if I am to maintain discipline in the unit I can't do so while excusing his behavior."

"He'll never be that overt."

"Of course not," I replied with resignation.

"You need to maintain discipline over yourself if you —"

"Lose my temper with him -"

"He'll react in a heartbeat to spur you on."

"I understand." I saw it all clearly.

"I know you understand, William," she half sighed, half laughed, "the question is, can you deal with this maturely and can you take care of the issue over the next months?"

"I can," I confirmed, "If only for my brother and Seth."

"On both fronts?" She dripped innuendo.

"Oh yes," I muttered, the wheels already spinning. As was my head.

"I am sure you'll take care of this .... properly."

"I will."

"I'm relieved."

"Thank you."

"It is truly my pleasure," she purred, "as it is to inform you that you are my guest tonight – it being the informed opinion of your friends that you need rest and diversion."

"Olga, I . . .", she cut me off. Thankfully as I had no idea what I was about to say.

"Don't," she laughed, rose from the sofa and walked toward me, "there is someone here who very much wants to get to know you better."

She extended a hand to help me up. I took it, pushed halfway out of now damp cushions and slipped back into the spinning chair, taking Madam Petrovsky with me.

In a flash, I was supine in the down, Olga on top of me, her hands astride my head, my hands on her nearly naked hips, her face inches from mine.

"Osgood's a lucky man," I said, in what may have been a normal voice. Without a word she bent into me and kissed me, hard, open mouthed, her tongue flicking across mine.

It lasted perhaps ten full seconds before she pushed herself up and, smiling widely, said, "I'd kill you, William."

I laughed, cursed Osgood aloud and struggled to my feet. That I accomplished alone, although the room did not quite cooperate.

"Come on, William," she sang out, having mysteriously transported to the doorway. I joined her, unsteady, but in something approaching a walk. Olga took pity and put her arm through mine and steered me into the hallway.

"You know," I said thickly, "I didn't come here for sex."

"It's included with the drinks," she said gaily, "besides, that is entirely up to your friend."

She veered to the right, almost too quickly for my equilibrium, pulled me in front of a door. She knocked lightly, quickly, before softly opening it and stepping in with me in tow.

Bridget sat in the corner of the bedroom reading a book. She greeted me with a smile, closed it with a thud.

"William, how nice to see you again," she sang out.

"Bridget," a look at her loose, unlaced night dress stopped further discourse. Not as sheer as Olga's, thin enough, though, for a man of my imagination.

Bridget rose and walked to me, I had no choice but to notice she was nude under the nightdress. She took my arm from Olga and gently pulled me away. Olga kissed my cheek and patted me on the ass before she sailed away. My arm was around Bridget, I could feel her heat through the thin fabric. Our eyes locked, finally.

"Ah, am I glad to see you."

"You're exhausted, William," she declared.

"Drunk, too," I added, helpfully.

"Yes," she laughed, led me to the bed, helped me sit. She stood between my legs and began to unbutton my shirt, "I think you need a good rest."

"Yes," I agreed, put my hands on her hips. She took off my shirt to my great relief just as a gust of wind drove in her curtains, bringing cold air and small droplets of rain across my steaming back.

I was eye level with Bridget's nipples, watched with fascination while they responded through the fabric. I kissed one through the cloth before she gently pushed me away.

She moved her hands down to my belt and deftly began to unbuckle it, her eyes focused on mine. My hands found the creases of her buttocks, kneading lightly. My belt and pants loosened, she pulled slightly away, bent and pulled my uniform pants off, ignoring the erection straining to escape my shorts.

The pants gone, Bridget returned to her former position, put her arms around my neck and leaned in and kissed me. At first lightly, almost chastely, considering, then, as I responded in kind, hard, open mouthed, tongues locking. She moved against me, I drew her in further, wrapped my arms around her back. She pushed her pelvis into my erection, and, gently, slowly, rocked.

After what seemed like an eternity, she broke off the kiss and whispered in my ear, "Plenty of time for all that later, you need to sleep." She pushed me back into the exquisite plushness of her bed, helped get my leaden legs up.

I crawled to a pillow, hit it hard face down. I felt the bed move slightly as she climbed in beside me. She talked softly of our first meeting, her breath and gusts of wind from the ionized air outside flowed across my naked back. Her voice was soft and sensual, lightening flashed, crackled, thunder roared and shook the house.

I dreamed of Mexico.

13

"You and Olga Petrovsky, eh?" I asked with as much innuendo as I could summon with such a badly swollen head.

If it hit the mark, it was unacknowledged, Osgood spurred his mount forward and left me alone with Seth by the side of the bayonet drill field. Shay had stations set up in a dozen spots over a mile and a half of the grounds, rotating the companies every hour to a new station at a double quick pace. The day was heavily overcast, the breeze strong and cool, keeping it from becoming oppressive and leaving the men in a light, bantering mood.

Shay, as usual, was everywhere. He was a superb rider and flew from drill station to drill station overseeing his proxies, insuring that his teachings were properly conveyed. That he had found worthies to delegate to relatively quickly was a very real surprise to me. I had observed him long enough to know that beneath the hail fellow well met veneer was a demanding perfectionist.

As it turned out, however, one of the camp boxers, Sergeant Wright, was quite simply a genius with the bayonet and rifle butt, coming close – close only – to surpassing Shay. Marksmanship was the jaw dropping, world shaking, stereotype smashing surprise. Professor Robert Hughes, late of Trinity College, was a living, breathing Hawkeye. All his years spent reading Clausewitz, studying Thucydides, memorizing Hardee had somehow created an uber-sharpshooter. For his part, Hughes was having the time of his life, respected by his peers (and me), having discovered a skill he would never known he possessed had he been an officer.

Seth and I rode to Osgood, I gave it another try, "You've excellent taste, Osgood," I went on, "if she were twenty years younger —"

"She'd kill you," Arnold guffawed, punched Osgood in the shoulder.

"Et tu, Colonel?" I snarled, neither was moved by my filthy look.

"Have a nice time at Olga's, Colonel?" Seth archly inquired.

"For a bastion of Republicanism," I answered, "you're a lecherous bastard."

"I'll take that as a compliment," he laughed.

"It was not offered as one."

"That's of no bearing, sir."

"I do need, however," I ignored him, "to convey my thanks to you both for your concern. I appreciate it, can't begin to tell you how pleased I am you chose a so much more attractive vehicle for the message than either of you ugly bastards."

"You really know how to express gratitude," Osgood sneered.

"Makes me want glad I could help," Arnold agreed.

We quietly rode up the tobacco roads of Bloomfield, Clio and I brought up the rear. While I day dreamed about Bridget, Clio kept looking over her shoulder wondering why we had left the company of so many blue clad treat dispensers. Clio could not get the thought of endless sugar cubes and apples out of her roan head, I could not let go of the image of a disheveled bed and a spectacularly nude Bridget.

"Ho! William!" I was dragged back from lingering thoughts of Bridget's rosy aureole by the dim awareness that Seth was speaking. I stared in his direction until my eyes refocused, wiped my suddenly salivating mouth on my sleeve, "I was saying, if I'm not interrupting, that the regiment is running very efficiently these days, like a fine tuned timepiece."

"I agree," Osgood took up immediately, "it's a joy to watch them."

I pulled Clio to a dead halt, eyed my two suddenly banal companions with hangover sharpened suspicion, "That sounded rehearsed," I said slowly, "I know we're doing well, I just don't know where this sudden wellspring of optimism comes from. Especially considering the issues we have."

"Issues?" Arnold asked.

"Issues?" Osgood echoed.

"The cabal," I said with perhaps rather more frustration than intended, "Huntingdon, Bryce, the rest?"

"Cabal?" Arnold inquired, eyebrow uplifted.

"The cabal," I stressed, to no obvious reaction from either of them, "the move against me?"

Osgood shook his head, "You are rather full of yourself to think you are the target of a cabal."

"I'd have to agree with that, Osgood," Arnold snickered, "if indeed there was a cabal. As there is none, I think our friend has become depraved, thinking people are out to get him."

"I have always despaired of his sanity," Osgood chirped in, almost keeping a straight face.

"Are we going to play games all morning," I did my best to sound grumpily perturbed, "or are you going to let me in on whatever the fuck it is that is fucking going on?"

"Christ," Arnold laughed, "you'd think a guy that just got laid would be in a better mood."

"Not this one," Osgood offered, "ornery and distracted as usual."

"You left out," I grunted, "ornery, distracted, about to lose my temper, and, oh, yes, armed too."

"I stand corrected," Osgood muttered, "and will, therefore, relay the fact that there is no current issue with anyone officially associated with the Twenty-first, Sir," he finished grandly, Seth nodded in the background.

"None?" I asked, surprised.

"None," Arnold replied, kindly.

"What did you do to Huntingdon?" I demanded of Osgood, a host of possibilities flooding through my aching head.

"There you go, jumping to conclusions," Osgood mocked a hurt tone, "it is not, unfortunately, what I did to Huntingdon, but what your friend Mr. Arnold did for you."

"Seth?" I nudged Clio sideways toward him.

"It's been handled, William, that's all," he said with a hand up.

"Uh-huh," I grabbed his horse's halter. Clio looked up at me, unhappy at the forced intimacy with Arnold's gelding, "What did he do, Osgood?"

"Colonel Arnold, yours truly in tow, along with Shay, Fischer, Wycroft and Reverend Ashford —"

"Ashford?"

"Yes, Reverend Ashford, you heathen, he is quite the student of human nature and despite his concern for your soul he has no doubt you are good for the souls he has hopes for," he shrugged as if such concern was beyond his comprehension.

"'In any event," he continued, still irritated with the interruption, "we met with Buckingham yesterday and made a case for Huntingdon and Bryce's' dismissals - the others could not decide what to have for dinner without them."

"Yesterday?"

"Yes."

"While I was at Olga's?"

"You complaining?"

"Outside the duplicity of getting me out of the way, of course not."

"Good, because your presence would have ruined everything . . . shit, your knowledge of what was going on would have ruined everything."

"Ruined what? It couldn't have worked well, I saw Huntingdon and Bryce at drill."

"It worked fine," Osgood said lowly, "for you were in camp this morning to see them at work."

"It was that bad?" I muttered abashedly.

"Almost, not quite," Arnold answered, "just headed in that direction."

Osgood nodded, "Buckingham would not budge, repeating that he could not endure dropping Huntingdon and Bryce politically. He thought it easier to drop you, next incident, as I am sure Olga told you in her own, gentle way. He also intimated that the closer the regiment is to readiness, the more expendable you become."

"There's motivation to keep working."

"Moot, regardless," Osgood resumed, "because at that point Colonel Arnold and Captain Wycroft employed their trump cards, with brilliant timing, I may add," high praise from a man whose life was defined by perfect timing.

"Mr. Shay was carrying a portfolio, from which he, with a flourish, produced several documents. The first was Colonel Arnold's resignation. The second, Captain Wycroft's. The third, just about as thick as that *Bleak House* you tote around, was a ledger. Mr. Arnold's bill to the state for the regiment no longer his . . . It was not a small number."

"You did not," I said to a reddening Seth.

"He did," Osgood went on. I may have detected admiration in his voice, "I thought we would have to revive the Governor, he blinked and sputtered that much. A sloppily drunk glass of water later he announced that as far as he was concerned the matter was closed with the status quo intact and his promise to speak to Huntingdon about the consequences of any further interference with the regiment.

"And that was that, I would say it was most likely the most uncomfortable fifty minutes of his administration."

"Thank you, Seth," I said sincerely and earnestly, genuinely touched.

"It was nothing," he answered in a shaking voice, "I have no plans on getting shot at without you right beside me."

"That's somehow less reassuring than it should be," I retorted and let go of the halter.

"Good," he yelled as he half galloped off. Clio looked up to see if we were chasing, moving expectantly while I held her back for a moment looking at Osgood.

"Thank you," I said as he came closer.

"All Seth."

"Thanks anyway."

"Welcome."

"We're going to have to take care of Huntingdon sometime soon ourselves, aren't we?"

"Of course," he answered quickly, "any ideas?"

"Of course," I replied and spurred away to catch up with Colonel Arnold.

14

It was hot, humid, miserable weather and therefore perfect for my purposes. We left camp at dawn, crossed the river, and set off through Eastern Connecticut on a route and to a destination only I knew. Just like the real thing and I could not have ordered better conditions in which to see how ready we were.

We were in East Hartford an hour and a half after dawn, the blinding, rising sun directly in our eyes as it smashed over the hills we would be tramping over soon enough. By the time we moved out the beginnings of real heat were shimmering off the road. Despite the hour, the town turned out for us, Main Street was thronged with flag waving civilians of all ages. Our band – quite good, actually – had the van, playing our soon to be abandoned favorite 'Dixie' along with standards 'Yankee Doodle', "The Bonnie Blue Flag', and others, all equally uplifting. We were sharp in crisp, neat uniforms, knapsacks perfectly aligned, rifle barrels glinting on unbent shoulders.

The column was endless and mighty, a long line of men flanked by officers on horseback, trailed by wagon after wagon of supplies (including some ammunition) and two new ambulances, bought for and fitted out by the people of Simsbury and Avon and presided over by our new surgeon, the reclusive Dr. Leonard Smith.

A perfect parade of men, arms and the accoutrements of war, marching on a macadamized road through the center of a good sized town to the cheers of its citizenry served to invigorate us even as each man knew it would be a scorcher of a day. That holiday feeling stayed with us a solid hour after we left town, encased the flags, stowed the bands' equipment in the ambulances and settled into a fixed pace on narrow, dusty country lanes, raising a dust cloud that had to be seen for miles.

The excitement and momentum evaporated along with our sweat when the sun cleared the hills and became incrementally more unforgiving with every subsequent inch it rose and heat began to radiate through our shoes. I walked beside Clio for long periods, giving her respite and to better gauge what the men were feeling – though I was thankfully unburdened with a backpack. I was pleased to note that every officer was doing the same.

The sleepy community of Glastonbury gave us a brief jolt of energy, but once we passed through its brief downtown and began our assault on the rolling hills of Eastern Connecticut all vestiges of an outing were gone for good. Long climbs up increasingly steeper hills, knee-buckling descents into sweltering, airless dales and back up again sucked the energy from everybody. Occasionally a hilltop would yield a slight eddy of moving air and bring a moment of apathetic relief - a moment eviscerated by the sight of wave after wave of successive hills stretching to the horizon.

We started to experience straggling about an hour outside Glastonbury. Men short of breath, sweat soaked, bloodily blistered, muscles uncontrollably cramped, or all of the above, dropped to the side of the road to either rest and resume in time or to curl into a ball and give up. On my orders they were checked, given whatever nourishment they required and left where they lie. The ambulances would be sent back for them after we stopped for the evening. It was up to them to catch up or give up - as it would when things were for real.

I had no fears stragglers would get lost as, ala Hansel and Gretel, a regiment on a long march, particularly a raw regiment, left a wide trail.

The men had been told only that they were going on a training exercise that would include three nights of camping. They were each issued one half of a pup tent, blanket, cold rations - beans, hardtack, salt pork - and a canteen (with the strong suggestion it be used for water). New to it all and fully imbued with romantic notions of camaraderie and singing around campfires under the stars, the men packed accordingly. By the time we reached tiny Marlborough a trail of objects from the expected to the surreal littered the sides of the road as man after man found that in the heat he could suddenly live without his poncho, extra straw hat, complete china and dinnerware kit, guitar, and/or dress coat.

I rode up and down the column, astounded by the general store's worth of items by the side of the road. I stayed by a brook while the column moved up its steepest hill yet and watched the wagons pass by, entranced by the blue line snaking up the hill.

Clio helped herself to the slow, swirling water she stood in to her relief, while around her it appeared as if a sutler's wagon had exploded, so heavily strewn the equipment. Five little boys were walking agog among the riches before them, so intent in their inspection of the riches before them they did not see me sitting there until Clio snorted a snootful of water in their direction.

They froze, stared at the two of us with enormous eyes. Clio sauntered over and nuzzled each of them in turn. They took it as a hello and stroked her nose, I knew it for what it was, a search for a snack.

"You can help yourselves," I answered their unasked question, "take whatever you like and tell your friends, the men aren't coming back this way – and even if they were they'd hardly want to tote any of this . . . stuff back with them."

Not a boy moved a muscle.

"You afraid, boys?"

The oldest, reddish brown haired, blue eyed, maybe ten, slightly built, smiled shyly, nodded slightly, the only movement in the group.

"What's your name?" I asked gently.

"William," he answered with timidity tinged pride.

"Willie," the younger boy behind him tittered.

"Hello, Willie, I'm Willie, too," He lit up in a dazzling smile, "you and your men," they grinned at that, "are to take as much of the equipment you can carry - get a cart if you want. If anyone says a word to you, you tell them Colonel Hanlin ordered you to get this mess cleaned up. And if someone from the Twenty-first comes along, you tell them to get a move on or we'll eat supper without them."

The boys laughed, hit and pushed each other, "That's an order, boys," I yelled over their antics, "you're part of the Twenty-first now, understand!"

"Yes," Willie yelled back.

"Uh-huh", the boy behind him mumbled, the others nodded.

"You can do better than that," I snapped with a grin, "you're soldiers now, give me a 'yes, sir!'".

"Yes, sir," they screamed.

"Yes, Sir, Colonel Hanlin!"

"Yes, Sir, Colonel Hanlin!"

"Excellent," I smiled widely, "Willie, you have the command, carry on."

I reined Clio around, tipped my hat, rode off and left the boys to pummel Willie in recognition of his honor.

I easily caught up with my huffing, shuffling column and the march continued over more hills, down fetid valleys, across tepid streams, at some indefinable point it became a forced march. I allowed no stopping save fifteen minute water breaks every two hours. Not long enough to recover, not long enough to stiffen like boards, not long enough to really wonder why they should head back out.

The sun was just dropping behind us when we came to the top of the largest hill of the day, on its crest the tidy village of Hebron. Spread before us was a long, wide green, our home for the night, announced with little fanfare and less acknowledgement by the dust caked, weary men.

Small clumps of locals watched in something approaching awe when tents magically sprang up across the common by company, quickly followed by the smell of coffee, tobacco, and frying salt pork. Arnold and I wandered through the settling camp, visiting every company, trading hellos, jokes, insults with the enlisted men and most of the officers - with several notable exceptions.

The sun well down, the heat abated, a breeze popped up and the sounds and smells of a contented camp settled over us. It was all quite pleasant and got only better when groups began to sing in the dark, songs rotated through the camp well into the night.

We listened from canvas chairs arranged in a half circle in front of the headquarters tents. At some point Phelps brought me a canteen and a plate. One whiff of his breath was enough to indicate that not all canteens contained water. I sighed and decided to ignore it as he was shortly to regret it. Deeply.

15

I slept for three hours that felt like three minutes. It was an exhausting sleep, a half awake, half dream state through which repeated scenes of the day's events intermingled freely with the past, wistful fantasy, and the bizarre. I was destined to wake more tired than when I had staggered to my cot.

I awoke in utter darkness two minutes before Shay stepped into my tent at the agreed upon time of 3:45. I saw his profile clearly outlined in the tent flap, a half-moon almost directly behind him. He saw me sit up, turned, and went out. I quickly tugged on my boots, eschewed a coat and walked out into a cool, breezy, perfect night, wispy clouds floated in the starry sky.

Biggs stood with Shay in the moonlight, "Morning, Corporal, morning Shay," I whispered.

"Colonel, sir," Biggs whispered back. A reed of a man - a reed playing a brass as Arnold had remarked to Biggs' amusement. Of which he had much, the man found joy in everything without much provocation.

"Let's go," I whispered. We walked, carefully, toward the center of the green. Halfway there I felt, then heard, a set of footsteps and Osgood emerged into our sight line.

"My God, you people make a lot of noise for clandestine work," he wheezed to Biggs' muffled laughter.

"You been up all night, or did you just guess?" I asked a little peevishly. Surprising Osgood was the small detail that would have made the scheme so much more enjoyable.

"Got up about a half hour ago, thought you might have something planned."

"Damn," we reached what looked like the open area at the center of the camp. I motioned to Biggs to hold off for a moment while I enjoyed the stillness and vast array of stars on what could have been my private hilltop. I silently asked any deities up and about to forgive me for breaking the predawn tranquility in such barbarous fashion.

With a sigh, I said, "You may sound assembly, Mr. Biggs."

Almost immediately the night was shattered by his mournful rendition of what was normally a stirring call. It went on for an inordinate time until it mercifully petering out. I braced myself for the onslaught of a thousand footsore men called awake too early.

I was instead greeted by the same sounds I had heard since rising, vague rustles, the leaves in the steady breeze, a bullfrog like cacophony of snores, grunts, farts and – far fewer - scattered, unimaginative oaths.

A boot thrown with extremely poor aim sailed well past us and off into the darkness, "I'm assuming he does not play for the Blues," I stared off in the direction of the missile.

"I should hope na'", Shay replied.

"Stupid game," added the ever dependable Osgood. We stood around like five men waiting for a long overdue express with nothing left to say about the matter. We stared at one another as best we could in the moonlight, completely, utterly, stymied.

"I believe the men are somewhat tired, William," Sean observed as footsteps approached.

"Planning an early breakfast, Brother?" Christian's voice cut through the dark while it finally occurred to me that our whispering was counterproductive. Christian was accompanied as usual by his Wesleyan roommate, the always silent, James Benjamin.

"Captain Hanlin, Lieutenant Benjamin, you managed to rouse yourselves. Good morning."

"Pretty much expected this, William, both of us. Maybe not quite this early, but, well, something," Christian said with great good nature.

"I'm that predictable?" That was met by a chorus of agreement, joined in by a hastily moving, breathless Seth Arnold.

"You could have given me advance warning," he shouted.

"I know how much you like your sleep," I replied, "look at what a great mood it puts you in."

"More handsome, too," Osgood added.

"At leas' ten years younger," Shay laughed and smacked him on the back.

"You're all goddamn bastards," Arnold yelled. Perhaps in jest.

"Shut the fuck up, you fuckin' ignorant cocksuckin' shits," a voice somewhere nearby rang through the night.

"You're going to get *that* out of bed?" Christian asked, not unreasonably.

"With your help," I said louder than necessary, just to give the fucking complainer something to really fucking complain about, "this time Biggs will wait for my signal to blow assembly. When I do the rest of you run through the camp and collapse the tents of the non-responsive. Don't be shy about using your boots and swords."

"Fucking right I will," a still grumpy Arnold immediately agreed.

"Sounds like fun," Christian pronounced, I could hear Benjamin's nod behind him.

I walked to a stand of rifles, picked up a comfortably heavy Springfield and removed a cartridge and percussion cap from my pocket.

"Shall I count out the manual of arms for you?" Shay helpfully offered to my automatic suggestion that he perform an impossible biological function.

"I was afraid it would come to this," I managed to load the piece without Shay's proffered advice and hefted the now lethal weapon, "Mr. Biggs, wait for me to fire, everybody else take off and create mayhem. Biggs, blow until I tell you to stop."

"Cry havoc —" Christian started.

"And let slip —" Shay tried to finish.

"Let's wake the bastards up," I interrupted the classical oratory, aimed at the Belt of Orion and fired. The sound was devastating in the night, its echo consumed by the yells and screams of my small cadre of dream stealers. After a few seconds Biggs joined the shattering of the night with a particularly stirring rendition of Assembly.

In ones, twos, threes, in various stages of undress, men tripped, lurched and tumbled into the clearing to form ragged lines. The only thing uniform about them was the look of utter contempt they threw my way.

I called Biggs off after a good ten minutes, nine minutes too long, to my mind, for that particular tune. It appeared that most of our twelve hundred men had managed to find the clearing. With that many men on a darkened, unfamiliar space we resembled nothing less than an ant colony stomped on by a five year old.

The men were just starting to settle into something resembling order when their officers arrived. Most had taken the time to dress completely and they waded into the soldier ants with all the moral and legal authority they thought their shoulder straps conveyed. Within moments they managed to turn a disordered group of men standing around with no purpose into a mob.

I watched them attempt the amusing but hopeless task of deploying properly for five minutes before I began to reload the rifle. The men nearest me, either because they had great interest in an officer wrestling with a Springfield or feared capital repercussions, calmed down and watched.

This time I aimed at Cassiopeia, even while telling myself that perhaps, just in case, the Greek Gods were better left out of it. I fired nevertheless, the rifle's retort stopped the din dead, I could feel the regiment crowd closer, silently.

"Good Morning, Gentlemen," I yelled, a sentiment neither returned nor shared, "Break camp, be prepared to move out in thirty minutes! No fires, no coffee, strike tents, form by company. We will be on the march in thirty minutes, no less! Dismissed!"

If it was possible for twelve hundred men to move sullenly, that is precisely what they did as they shuffled and moped off to their tents. More than a few were doomed to find theirs stomped flat – Christian had always believed in thoroughness when performing acts of wanton destruction.

Osgood materialized beside me, "Judging by the conversations I just overheard, I would have to say that you are fortunate to be the only armed man on the grounds. I highly recommend you keep it that way."

"As usual, your support is noted and appreciated."

"Charles is almost done packing you up —"

"You too."

"Us up, if you want to continue target practice, you're probably going to need it."

"Only if you want to provide a target," I snapped, the few hours of restless sleep bubbling to the surface. Osgood wandered off in search of someone to appreciate his wit.

I walked through camp, cloaked in the darkness, observing as it was struck. I had the delightful experience of hearing myself frequently, and at times quite creatively, damned. I was not unmindful of Henry V's walk the night before Agincourt, but with less eloquence and sense of impending doom and a lot more profanity.

It took just under an hour for the regiment to form. The first halo of light bled over the hills to the east when we shuffled away from Hebron. I made no public comment concerning the time taken in forming the, realistically, slovenly lines, having no wish to further ingratiate myself with the men.

We had marched less than two hundred yards when I rode up to Arnold, my sense of order offended by our zig-zagging lines, "I suggest you endeavor to dress the lines, Seth."

"Good God, William," he greeted the suggestion with a face awash in astonishment and dread, "they already hate you, no sense ruining their good will for me as well. By Christ, I shouldn't even be seen near you," the last said over his shoulder as he spurred away.

I rode back through the length of our column, issued the proper orders to dress the columns, endured slitted looks from the ranks. The sky became a clear, radiant dark blue without the slightest hint of cloud cover. By seven o'clock it promised to be another hot day, by nine the promise had been delivered on.

About then we leisurely descended a hill that seemingly sloped gently for miles. A pleasant walk assisted greatly by gravity. Under normal circumstances it would have elicited good cheer and joking from the men. The lack of sleep, coffee and breakfast were the minor reasons for the lack of enthusiasm, the major one stared the men in the face every step down that gentle slope for every sweat soaked, hungry man was exposed to a full, brutal view of the roadway up - a humpbacked hill rising at least three times higher than our descent and steeper than any we had yet come across.

I rode to Shay at the head of the column, splashed through a creek, motioned him aside out of earshot. He rode to me making a show of reluctance, continually looking over his shoulder at the distinctly unhappy faces grimly filing by.

"There's surely no way the men could mistake ya' maple leafs wi' my stripes, is there?" He asked, keeping a good distance from Clio.

"Talk of mutiny is getting somewhat stale, Sergeant Major," I grumbled, "please pass the word to the officers, everyone walks up this hill."

"Hill? It looks like tha' fookin' Alps, Hanlin."

"Spare me the dramatics, Sean, I've seen the Alps."

"As have I, mon Colonele," he grinned widely, gave me an exaggerated, Continental salute, "great strategy, by the way, unitin' the men and officers in their hatred of ya'," with that he rode off. Quickly.

We walked up the long, redundant hill, the sun blasted down, sweat poured and soaked into the heavy wool of our uniforms. We had no choice but to bend into the hill, our view comprised of the ten square feet in front of our noses. Just when it seemed that another step would be one too many the never ending hill flattened out and we were in Lebanon. A village for which the sobriquet 'sleepy hamlet' was by several measures too exciting.

A handsome, white colonial with enormous porch dominated the crest of the hill overlooking the valley behind us. A well-kept lawn was enclosed by a wrought iron fence, a small sign on it read 'Home of Jonathan Trumbull, Governor of Connecticut during the Revolution, father of John Trumbull the painter'.

Thirty yards on was a long, wide, tree lined, immaculate green, much larger than one would associate with towns many sizes larger. Colonial homes were scattered around the outside of the one-lane road that surrounded the green. Here and there small groups of locals congregated to gawk at the dusty horde before them.

I remounted Clio and rode onto the plush, freshly mown grass of the green, joined by Seth and Osgood. I beaconed Shay to have the regiment form around us.

"Beautiful spot," Arnold said, "looks big enough for the regiment, too."

I nodded absently, spurred forward to watch the men drag in. Those not blinded by the increasingly vicious sun, or by the sweat congealed in their eyes took the time to stare daggers my way.

I passed the word that the men could strip down to shirts and ordered the ambulances down the hill to gather up the distressed.

I sat and watched, Clio enjoyed the freshly clipped grass, over the next forty minutes the regiment plopped down company by dust covered company, most men staring vacantly at the grass. The ambulances arrived shortly after and disgorged their cargo, a heap of men who had just enough energy left to bemoan their particular maladies to whoever would listen.

I dismounted carefully and slowly walked to the center of the assembly, Seth and Shay a good ten yards behind me. Not a man stirred or met my eye while I surveyed my used up men.

"Bring them to attention, Sergeant Major.," I said as officiously as possible.

"Right," he shouted before screaming, "Attention!" The men slowly made their way to their feet, reeled into lines, a few automatically brushed their shirts in a vain attempt to resemble something military. They were still shifting and settling in when I took pity on them and yelled, "At ease."

That command stopped the shifting and they visibly relaxed. I had a speech to give, one that I had rehearsed in my head over and over on the march up, but now hesitated. It is one thing to know what one is going to say and how one is going to say it, quite another to actually perform it in front of twelve hundred men each with his own notion on how the speaker could best be killed. Slowly.

I would like to say that I was confident, as I had been trained to be, but that would be a lie. I was afraid I had pushed them too far, too soon. I was treating them like regulars, not men who just weeks ago had been my neighbors, my community. They were, to be sure, about to take the same risks as regulars, God knew they would die as easily. That was a dichotomy I am not sure I ever solved in those early days. Perhaps never did any time before the Wheat Field.

It was, then, with much trepidation that I began. "Gentlemen," my voice at least did not betray my emotions, "welcome to Lebanon. If you can find a tavern here, feel free to imbibe," that said to the whistles of birds and the chirping of squirrels.

"We are going to camp here for the next two days and nights, during which there will be no drills." A smattering of politely appreciative ripples ran through some men before stern whispers reminded those misguided few I was the spawn of Satan. "I've brought you out here because it's important to have a realistic march - this will never get easier, and Virginia is a lot hotter than New England." Clearly not welcome news.

"I chose Lebanon because I wanted us all to understand what you now represent to yourselves and your nation," any number of eyes rolled at that. It did have the whiff of horseshit, and even men new to the army could sniff out officer horseshit at great distance, but I was sincere.

"Look around," a suggestion studiously ignored, "almost eighty years ago General Washington slept in the Trumbull house and inspected Rochambeau's cavalry camped on this very green," that caught their attention as only the invocation of Washington' name could. Our American saint.

I pointed to a small, indistinct building nestled across the road in a copse of trees. It had the appearance of a one room schoolhouse. Unused.

"That small house is the 'War Office'; Washington, Rochambeau, Knox, Putnam, Governor Trumbull, and Lafayette were all there at one time or another."

Now they were interested, "You saw Trumbull's home when we marched in, a family of great patriots. Two signers of the Declaration of Independence had homes nearby . . . And now we're here, American soldiers on our way to war again. I hope you all see this. I hope you are all as proud of yourselves as we are of you."

That brought cheers from the suddenly no longer quite so exhausted men. I was not then naive enough, nor am I now in my dotage, to think they were cheering anything besides Washington and their fore-fathers-in-arms. Still, I basked in it.

"So gentlemen, set up your tents, brew your coffee, settle in. The War Office is open for your inspection and I happen to know that several homes will be serving refreshments."

That was interrupted by guffaws and wisecracks, so much so that I hastened to add, "Behave yourselves, a provost will be posted and will accost the rowdy." Much discussion erupted revolving around, I gathered from my central point, who the rowdiest were.

I talked over the murmuring, "Tonight, the owner of a large dairy and beef farm, one Alan Lamb - his farm, by the way, is out of bounds, not that it's close enough for those with sore, blistered feet —".

Invective cascaded over me, pointedly directed at the bastard who put those sores there in the first place, "- is driving our dinner in on the hoof, black angus steak for all!" Huzzahs took over.

"Tomorrow will be a day of leisure. The Hartford Blues, myself included, will take on all comers up at the north end of the field. See Sergeant Hughes if you have a team and so little pride as to wish to be routed by us," I was bracketed by less than polite rebuttals.

"Finally, a sutler's wagon with beer and spirits will be here this evening, you may imbibe at your pleasure. However!" I cut off the cheering as it started, "Drunkenness will be dealt with harshly - so if you get drunk," I let that hang in the air for a long moment, "you better quietly sleep it off in your tent and not draped over the bushes in someone's front yard. Dismissed!"

I walked away to cheers, and good natured insults that felt even better. They lasted until it finally dawned on them they had missed their coffee and breakfast. Their voices ebbed and extinguished altogether as they set about rectifying the situation.

I started to walk away, Seth grabbed my arm, "That was

outstanding, William," he gushed, "great planning, inspired, although I wished you had let me in on it."

"Wanted to surprise everyone," I answered, simply.

"Well done, Colonel," Osgood slapped me on the back, "but right now I could use a cup of coffee."

I nodded my agreement, scanned the common for Charles, finally spied him busying about under two large oaks. A perfect, shady spot for a well-deserved rest. He had fires going and that was all I needed to quicken my pace.

Almost at sanctuary Shay sidled up and, with no hint of humor save for the Irishness of his deep blue eyes, said, "So who is this Washington you people speak of so highly?"

16

I did not sleep with the men on the grounds of Rochambeau, breaking a long standing, if seldom applicable these past twelve years, rule. Shay, Osgood, Wycroft and I instead accepted an invitation to stay in the Trumbull house. The current owners, distant relatives of the originals, offered to vacate and leave the premises to us, an offer I was constitutionally unable to resist. Washington had enjoyed the same hospitality and that was enough for me.

I suffered no guilt whatever eschewing the campground for comfort, not with the men in the midst of an orgy of beef, whiskey, and beer - to the extent that few would feel or remember much in the morning. Certainly no one would be in any condition to care a whit about their officers' whereabouts.

The chessboard was set up, Osgood already either ignoring or failing to recognize the first onslaught of a Ruey Lopez opening he always either ignored or failed to recognize. Tired, happy, contently sipping coffee, I coolly watched Osgood self-destruct in a vain attempt to salvage his defense. Shay, as was his wont, watched in a way that indicated he knew the game beyond a casual understanding, although he remained adamant in his protestations of incomprehension.

We had been quiet for some time when Seth broke the contented silence, "I can't tell you how much I've enjoyed the trek thus far. And, I'm grateful to you, William, for bringing us to this place."

I nodded acknowledgement, put Osgood in the first of what was surely going to be a series of checks, sat back to enjoy the expressions on his face as he blundered deeper and deeper into an inextricable position. I looked over Osgood's head for at least the tenth time that evening, and stared at Trumbull the son's *The Sortie Made by the Garrison of Gibraltar*. I would like to say I was such an art expert I knew immediately it was somewhat too small, somewhat too rough, truth be told I had seen the final, famous version dozens of times at the Boston Athenaeum.

Art appreciation hour was interrupted by a guttural throat clearing somewhere behind Osgood.

"Oh, for Christ's sake, Arnold," Osgood snapped, "just yell and throw something at him when he's in one of these states."

I grimaced in Seth's direction, I had quite forgotten that he had spoken earlier and I was oblivious to the fact he was patiently waiting to engage in conversation.

What?" I asked eloquently.

"My only real fear," Arnold addressed Osgood, "is that we'll be advancing on the Confederates and he'll see some plant he's read about —"

"Or some unknown species of woodchuck," Charles offered as he entered the room from the kitchen, brandy in hand.

"And we wait," Shay picked up, "under rifle and artillery fire while he inspects it, having forgotten all about those annoying Confederates."

"And thinks about where he read about it," Osgood again, thrilled to have allies.

"Or some lecture he went to twenty years ago," Shay enjoying himself as well, "jus' so he can tell us tha' time, place and substance of it, as we get shot to bloody pieces."

"I am not anywhere near that bad," I protested vehemently, "although I acknowledge I get somewhat preoccupied at times. . . you know, that reminds me of this essay I read in —"

"Oh bloody hell," Shay threw a napkin past me, "somewhat

bloody pre-occupied? Do ya' have even tha' slightest fookin' clue how many times today we rode up ta' ya' ta' gab tha' time away only ta' find you starrin' off o'er tha' hills sportin' one of ya' damn silly grins?"

"You ever notice how your polish erodes and your brogue asserts itself when you're drunk?" I replied conversationally.

"Oh, you doth slay me sir," he replied in perfect Elizabethan English.

"See how he lashes out under pressure?" Osgood pointed out and flipped over his king in a well-practiced motion.

"That's disturbing," Arnold snickered, "I have to depend on him. My God, what if he snaps? Completely?"

"It'll infect tha' whole regiment," Shay said with a sad shaking of his head.

"Just think," Osgood shuddered in exaggeration, "the entire regiment employing sarcasm."

"It'll destroy us if directed at each other," Arnold took up, "but —"

"It's a helluva weapon if used against the South," Wycroft spoke up, an act of betrayal that earned my wrathful glance, a glance Simon threw off with ease, "we could end the war in a week."

"Imagine the Twenty-first cutting through Confederate lines armed only with Colonel Hanlin's twin senses of irony and sarcasm," Seth was turning red with mirth, "the rout would be awful; men fleeing —"

"I imagine many would choose to take the easy way out," Wycroft again, to my widening shock.

"I contemplate that myself at times," Osgood intoned solemnly.

"As do we all," Seth agreed, "the rebels wouldn't stop running until they got home."

"To spread the news of the North's horrible new weapon," Wycroft finished, trying to hide a smug smile behind his brandy snifter.

"Almost makes you feel sorry for the poor bastards," Osgood summed up.

"They'd never forgive us for unleashing such a cruel weapon,"

Arnold shook his head in sympathy.

"But could we forgive ourselves?" Wycroft applied the coup de grace.

"You know, of course," I yelled over their self-congratulatory laughs and shouts of mutual admiration, "that none of you are nearly as witty drunk as you think you are?"

"Whoa! I'm sorry," Seth threw up his hands in surrender, "For God's sake, please don't skewer me with your wit."

"God," I snapped in exasperation, "it'll be a relief to get shot at."

"Will it?" Arnold unsuccessfully tried to take a sip of brandy, "that refreshing is it?"

"It is after this."

"Funny you should say that," Arnold's laugh subsided to labored breathing, "that's something I've been wanting to discuss."

"Me getting shot at?"

"No, me getting shot at," he roared, "it's the only thing we can't practice."

"Don't bet on it," I sneered.

He laughed, deep, long, his brandy sloshed out of his snifter and onto his lap, "Well, I know you don't mean it that way, but I'd do it, just to get it over with and see how I'll do."

"Bloody soon enough for all of us," Shay, still smiling, said with ease, "ya' worrying too much about it, ya know tha'?"

"Ah, Sean, that's horseshit and you know it, you and William have been through it, and, to tell you the absolute truth," he grimaced then smiled abashedly, "it scares me to death that you two never talk about it - God knows you talk about everything else."

"Don't worry, Colonel," Shay assumed the demeanor of a professor, a somewhat drunk professor, but a professor nevertheless, "ya've become a fine officer, you'll not disappoint anyone."

"Thank you, Sean," Arnold replied with warmth, recognizing a platitude from a respected source, "I don't want to sound full of myself," he stared at me, "but I know I've become a passable officer in many ways - maybe every way I can right now. But I don't think it really matters until I get through the test."

He held my eyes with such a sincere gaze that, despite my best intentions, I found myself nodding.

"I thought so!" He yelped, pointed accusingly at Shay, "So don't tell me being a good officer at this point means anything as far as being a good officer in combat.'

"Aye, but —" Shay started.

"And don't tell me," the finger leveled again, Seth cut him off abruptly, "that you can tell, I know that's horseshit as well."

"Ah, you think too fookin' much," Shay dismissed him with a wave and a smile.

"You are right there," Arnold sat back, took a sip from his turbulent snifter, "you know I've been reading everything I can - secretly, of course, knowing all of you - on the military arts, starting with Caesar's Commentaries and —"

"I prefer Thucydides," I interjected, somewhat seriously, not solely motivated by a wish to avoid the subject at hand, "he had empathy for the average soldier, having been one."

"Gotta' agree wi' ya' there," Shay responded, "everything about Caesar is his fookin' havin' ta' grab a sword, step into the breach an' show his legionnaires how ta' do the job he should have bloody well have trained 'em ta' do in the first place." Pleased with his critique he drained off his snifter and in one fluid motion held it out to Charles for an immediate refill.

"None of them, like you two, helped me understand - never mind prepare for - what I'll be walking into."

"That leaves you in the same boat as the rest of the regiment," I observed off-handedly.

"You, Shay, Sergeants Mallory, Nash, Ricketts," Osgood reeled off while nodding to Arnold, "are the only veterans in the regiment, as far as I know." The rest of us looked at him briefly, as if there were anything about the members of our regiment Osgood did know.

"Not being unique is hardly comforting," Arnold's voice affected the precise manner of the nearly inebriated, "I'm asking you two combat veterans to share some experiences. I'm sure Mallory, Nash and Ricketts are likewise solicited."

His request was met with sounds from outside. Shay stared at his swirling brandy; I played absently with Osgood's fallen king.

"I don't require much," Arnold sported a sly, beguiling smile, knowing well he was wheedling, probably well aware he was being successful, "just the overall experience, sounds, sights, smells, for Christ's sake —"

"It fookin' reeks," Shay surprised at least two of us by interrupting, "somethin' they don't write in any o' them fookin' books," a long sip temporarily interrupted his evident disgust, "smoke, gunpowder, blood, gutted horses, fook, gutted men, leave a foul stench that stays wi' ya' for days, fookin' coats ya' in it."

"That's what it was like fighting the Saracens, Shay?" I tried to break the mood, my heart not much in it.

"Funny, ya' shit," Shay snapped, not without a glint of humor, "tell me the smells don't get ya'."

I nodded, "But the sounds —"

"Aye, the sounds," he took up, "ya' don't hear 'em, ya feel them."

"To your marrow," I agreed.

"It's like this, Seth," Shay took a deep sip, sighed and launched into it, "it's fast, noisy beyond anything you can imagine, an' that includes your factories. On top o' tha' shells burst right o'er ya' and sometimes a piece of spent shell hits ya' jus' to let ya' know how fookin' lucky you've been and how fookin' quick that can end.

"Then ya' get the cannon balls bouncin' through the lines cuttin' men in two. Aye, Seth," he slouched, "get through that and ya' only have ta' worry about the bullets."

"Lots of bullets," I repeated for no reason whatever.

"Lots of bullets," Shay repeated as if at prayer.

"Comforting," Arnold laughed nervously, looked up to see if that was a proper response.

"Believe it or not," Shay sensed something in Arnold that made him return to a benevolent, professor demeanor, "the first seconds everybody - almost everybody - goes through pure, abject terror . . . it's how ya' handle tha' terror tha' decides everthin'. Some run, most get o'er it - an' once ya' do, ya' don't give a fuck any more. You wade into it an' ya' get it over with, and every once n' a while ya' get pissed and ya' do somethin' stupid. If ya' do and ya' live, you're a hero, otherwise ya' jus' fookin' dead."

"You know, Seth," Arnold sat forward, consuming every word, "I donna talk about it 'cause it disturbs me, lots of things disturb me n' I talk about them. I donna talk about it because I can't do it justice."

"I think you did a fine job," Arnold answered immediately, "and I'm grateful."

"Thank ya', but with all due respect, Seth, only William here can judge tha' n' he doesn't seem ta' have much to say," he turned to me, "do you, Colonel?"

"I agree with everything you said, Sean, and the manner in which it was said, well done."

"But?" His eyebrows arched.

"But what?" Petulance dripped off my words.

"But," his eyes reached and held mine, "not quite the same with ya'. There's sometin' about it tha's different for ya', isn't there?"

I reappraised my friend, instantly, while his eyes continued to bore into me. An observant bastard, my first thought, hiding behind a lilting brogue he could turn on and off when he was not speaking guttural German, diplomatic French, or poetic Gaelic.

"Is there?" I replied cleverly after a significant pause during which all eyes had swung to me.

"Oh, yes, Willie, my boy, you're different, you are."

"You know for sure, Shay, or you just making a brandy fueled wild guess?" I asked in that special voice reserved for those who inspire both vanity and fear when talking about you.

"For sure," said with utter confidence that was further unnerving.

"You know something of me that I do not?" I inquired as smugly as circumstances allowed.

"Ya' know it yourself, it's why you never talk of it - not that ya' bloody well talk about anything that has to do with you, anyways."

"I hate to bore people."

"Anybody here," Shay motioned to the room, "think they'd be bored by anythin' Willie boy would have ta' say 'bout himself?"

The nays carried the room while I shook my head and raised my eyes, "In that case, Sergeant Major," I said with formality, "enlighten me . . . us."

"In front of everyone?"

"Sure."

"If I'm right —"

"Thought you knew for sure?"

"Yeah, I do, ya' shit, jus' a turn of phrase, literal bastard. When I'm right, you'll talk about it an' not stare off into tha' painting hopin' we go away?"

"Yes," I answered with some trepidation, standing as I was on the threshold of changing, perhaps, my relationship with the men that were fast becoming my first real friends in a long time, "if you're right I'll talk a bit."

"There you go, Shay, well done," Osgood gloated, "break the cipher for us."

"Sure ya' don't wannta' do this yourself, boy'o?" Shay asked me.

I shook my head, "I don't know what you mean but I find this fascinating," I chuckled, sure he was backing out. A thought I apparently shared with Osgood.

"For God's sake, Shay, out with it while you can!" He shouted.

"Please," I seconded him, spread my hands in invitation.

"Well then, everyone, William, and there'd be no judgment in this wha'ever. None. It's how it is . . ." he paused, readjusted himself in his chair, sipped brandy and surveyed his audience, "it's like this my friends . . . our always in control, shaper of regiments . . . likes it."

The others sat forward, craning. I felt a curious hollow in the pit of my stomach, gripped my armrests, experienced a wave of dizziness.

"Not like the rest of us, our friend here," he went on, his diagnosis confirmed by my glassy eyes and red face, "cowerin,' wincin', worryin', doing whatever the fook's needed ta survive. Willie thrived in it. Bloody fookin' rock he is ..." he trailed off.

"Whatever," I spoke evenly to keep the tremor out of my voice, "makes you say that, Sean, without us having been in a fight?"

"True, though, isn't it?"

"You didn't answer the question," I prodded.

"Been in enough armies an' enough actions to know the type afta' a piece. An' you're tha' article," he looked at me for a long moment, noted my lack of a smile and the red blotches rising up my neck, "Ah, hell no, William, I dinna mean any of this as an insult," he added in haste, "no, no, you're no vainglorious fook or any of that. It's jus' in ya' blood. When ya' in it, ya' in your element."

He took a long gulp, "An' it scares the shite outta' me, tho' I'd follow ya anywhere, 'cus it'd be my best chance of makin' it." He blinked, strange smile affixed, continued sipping and looked around the room. The others stared at me awaiting explanation.

A dozen smart replies sped through my head, none of them remotely appropriate. So, I answered sincerely, "Truth of the matter is when I was in Mexico I never felt more alive or in control as I did under fire. Never. So aware, so . . . engaged. Calm, controlled. Shit, I'm not sure what verbs to use . . ."

"You liked being in charge an' ya' were good at it," Seth intoned from the safety of his arm chair, "'there bein' no one ta' tell you what to do once it started."

"Exactly," I agreed with ardor, "and everything I did meant something. No words, no horseshit, just doing, showing, leading . . . no regular life to interfere."

"No regular life," Arnold said with an air of disturbing wistfulness.

"Doesn't mean it's not terrible, Seth," I said quietly, "because it is as Sean says it is – this is something I could have lived just fine without ever having discovered.

"It's not as if it doesn't affect me, you know, it just gets me after the fact . . . and it gets me hard. After everything calms down I'm a mess, in a daze, out of it for days. Then there are the dreams . . . Still, it served me well."

"Give us one instance," Shay with a glint, "an' you're off the hook for tha' night."

"Chapultepec," I answered without hesitation, "it looked impregnable. Long causeway directly under a two hundred foot citadel, outnumbered two to one. a nut-squeezing sprint . . .

artillery pounding overhead, that causeway, three, four men wide and who knew how deep the water was on either side. Except for some of Cortes' long dead conquistadors – and I've always understood a bunch of them drowned.

"Somehow, we got across, seemed like a miracle even while we were doing it . . . up the hill. I was in front of my men when we hit their battle line. Firing at them would only have slowed us down so we just went at them. I slashed and stabbed wih my sword, the men used their bayonets and musket butts. The Mexicans were packed in so tight they could barely move to get out of the way.

"I remember chunks of it as if it was yesterday, the street, smells, yells, everything as they tried to get away from us ... me. They broke and we chased them up and into the citadel. All they seemed to care about by then was getting out of our way.

"Anyways, at some point we ran into the last of the resistance, bashed into them the way the lines do in a scrum. I was slashing away, pushing, elbowing. At some point I raised my sword to cut down on someone's skull and I realized, somehow, that I was about to take the top off a little boy's head – ha was maybe twelve or so. One of the 'Los Ninos', cadets from the Mexican Military College.

"My sword stopped dead about an inch from his hair. I remember thinking 'thank God, I saw him in time.' A little boy barely holding a bayoneted musket that was a foot taller than him.

"I know I smiled at him, he looked ridiculous, I'm pretty sure he smiled back. I don't know how long we stood like that. Long enough for the Mexicans to melt away. For weeks, hell, years probably, I was unable to shake that image or fail to shudder over how close it was. I was never going to sleep again if I hadn't stopped my swing, that I know. Shit, I still fucking shudder at it.

"It's the reason why I'll have no drummer boys in the ranks . . ." somewhere along the line I had shut my eyes, I opened them, blinked, and smiled to the room. They were rapt.

"Great story," Arnold spoke first, "thank you William."

"All this time," Osgood croaked, "you've never told me," Charles nodded furiously, shaking the brandy bottle.

Shay eyed me, intently, nodding. "What happened to tha' little boy?" He asked at long last.

"The boy?" I asked in mock surprise.

"The boy," a chorus came back.

"Well, that little boy, cute as a fucking button, took the moment we were smiling at each other to stick that bayonet through my left buttock," I finished to peals of laughter.

"Laugh away," I yelled at my former friends, "God knows it's what my men did. They laughed hysterically while they took the gun away from him and gave the little bastard a well-deserved spanking.

"I spent a day in the hospital only to limp back and have him serve me breakfast. I was informed that he had been adopted into the company. Every time the little shit saw me limping he'd laugh his head off. Really came to hate that kid."

Over all the gibes, Shay roared, "That's war! Now, let's see the scar."

17

Two days of rest, good food, drink, and easy camaraderie complete with the Hartford Blues, Colonel Hanlin at third base, whipping all comers; two perfect, clear, mild, breezy days were eviscerated and forgotten not three miles out from Lebanon on the return march.

The always fickle New England weather had turned abruptly and descended over us with all the subtlety of a Biblical plague. The crystal clear sky gave way to thick, black-gray clouds that threatened a spirit drenching downpour any moment. It was warm, might have been hot, it was impossible to gauge because of the suffocating humidity that wrapped around us. It was like walking in a pungent broth.

Four miles of easy, flat road before we reached a high ridge, grumbled our way up, descended to the Willimantic River and the flourishing, namesake mill town straddling its banks. There were few people out to watch, though we could see dense shadows in the factory windows. Our footfalls echoed off stone and brick, three-four story buildings, we merged into the Boston Turnpike, threaded through streets thudding and thumping with the echoes of hidden machinery, and moved out of town. Into a long, flat stretch of empty fields and lonely farmhouses, the air too close and restrictive to subject the horses to carrying anything beside their own bulk as we walked through fields Nathan Hale had tended.

The column was bleeding away at a rate that would be alarming within fifty miles of the front. Stragglers littered the road with the same frequency personal property had on the way to Lebanon. The ambulances plied down the road behind us dispensing water, salve and advice; none but those who passed out were taken in. Past noon, the head of the column - Christian and the boys from

Middletown - were at least an hour behind the schedule I had in my head.

I was soaked with sweat to the point my boots were filling and I walked as a man underwater. Arnold and I were together in proximity only, both lost in thought, our horses trailing behind us quietly. Every time I looked at Clio she snorted and eyed me suspiciously.

Somewhere along the line our solitude was interrupted by an incongruously cheerful voice, "Colonels, how be you?"

I looked up at Reverend Ashford. He smiled widely through the soup. "Reverend," I said without enthusiasm.

"Why the long faces, gentlemen?" He asked with what could have been genuine curiosity.

"Hot," Arnold answered.

"Humid," I added.

"You're not enjoying the walk?" Ashford asked.

"Well," he resumed when we did not answer, "it is somewhat warm, I admit, but that hardly takes away from the camaraderie and exercise, does it?"

"You can take that camaraderie —" I started.

"It is good exercise," Arnold unartfully cut me off, saving me from a unique blasphemy, "but I think you're one of the few enjoying it in this weather."

"You're definitely the only one enjoying it," I hissed. Arnold elbowed me, hard, in the ribs, "Ow, what the —"

"I'm glad you're enjoying it, Thomas," Seth saved me again, "but you're not going to get much agreement from the others."

"That's for —" as far as I got before Arnold's elbow caught my kidney, "Jesus Chr—"

"Like William," he went on loudly, "the weather affects his personality quite aversely," he held up a warning hand that forced me to swallow a most non-Episcopalian reply.

"I apologize, Colonel," Ashford said, apparently to me.

"If you can apologize for the weather, Reverend," I observed, "you can change it as well."

"Well said, Colonel," Ashford laughed, Arnold paused mid-strike. It looked like he had targeted my sternum that time, "very good."

"You know, Reverend," I gave Seth a watch-this-I'm-going-to-be- nice look, "William is fine in this company."

"Why thank you, William," I arched my eyebrows at Arnold, "as long as you call me Thomas."

"But, a man of the cloth," I said stumbled.

"Not like you attend services, William," he blithefully replied, "so it's unlikely you'll confuse me with the message."

"Alright, Thomas," I stuttered, "I've been busy, you know, but I'll —"

"It's fine, William," he held up a restraining hand, "I did not mean it as a rebuke. I'm sure you have your reasons."

"Yes," I said without further explanation- my only option, as I had no reason – good or bad - whatever.

"But," he smiled down at me, "anytime you want to escape the burning fires of the hell you're headed to, you're welcome to attend."

"What?" I startled.

"Just fooling," he laughed, Arnold joined in a little too hesitantly to please me, "loosen up, William, you're too serious on this whole religion thing, the days of Cotton Mather are long gone."

"Remind me again, Arnold," I sneered, "why we have a regimental chaplain?"

"To comfort the men and make you uneasy," he answered without hesitation, "I find Reverend Ashford most satisfactory on both accounts."

"Tell me, Reverend, Thomas," I asked with sincerity, "are heaven's doors open to a man as cruel as Colonel Arnold?"

"Of course, William — he attends services."

"That's not hypercritical, Reverend?"

"It's the Episcopalian deal with the Lord, Colonel"

"That's fairly flippant," I observed, "don't you think?"

"I am allowed to be flippant with those so clearly destined for eternal damnation."

"Unless I attend services, then ..."

"You're saved. But," he managed the nasty smile of a confirmed saint, "don't let that color your decision to attend."

"You're leaving me with little choice but to attend services this Sunday, should we survive this march."

"Very good, William, but don't feel pressured."

"Oh, I won't," I chuckled and turned to Seth, "we should go see how bad this is getting," I motioned toward Ashford before adding, "and preferably before he convinces me to join the clergy."

I mounted Clio, she whinnied in derision, "Reverend, I leave you to tend to your flock," I tipped my cap and spurred off.

Seth was beside me in a moment, we slowly moved down our ragged columns while our horses exchanged mutinous looks. "You thinking of calling a halt?" Seth asked with hope.

"No, they had two days of rest that they'll never get on a campaign, it's more than enough... they'll just have to work through it."

"But the heat..."

"We're not training to invade Canada, Colonel."

"There any other point to this torture?"

"To prove we can do it of course," I answered simply.

"I think you have the makings of one of those German philosophers I've been reading lately."

I pulled Clio's reins, hard, "German philosophy?"

"I can't have intellectual pursuits?"

"No, fine, of course you can," I said and we moved on, Clio shook her head at her companion, "just surprised. I don't really get them . . . besides, I'm more of the warrior poet type I think," I ended, modestly. Seth's horse snorted loudly, "I see your horse agrees with me."

"Augustus is the world's foremost authority of every imaginable category of horseshit."

"He's going to be overwhelmed, then, when we join the regular Army."

"He'll adapt."

"As will, hopefully, our woefully out of shape comrades," we rode up on at least ten men sitting, leaning on a wood fence, several massaging bootless feet.

"You know, boys," I shouted, "if your feet swell up, you're gonna' be finishing this barefoot... right?"

That was acknowledged with waves, nods, and not a few

comments concerning Clio's shoes. I questioned their parentage in turn before riding away to their laughs.

"Now that," I said proudly, "bodes well."

"They're good boys," Seth replied in kind, "I never doubted that, I just question the wisdom of killing off the entire regiment before they ever get to a fight."

We continued down the long, dusty, snaking column. Most of the man looked up briefly, acknowledged our passing without malice, the rest were intent on putting one foot in front of the other successfully.

I was relieved to see they were still somewhat in companies, recognizable though stretched out. We reached the end of the column, reined up and watched them slowly, ever so slowly ebb up the road toward a hazy horizon.

"We seem short to you?" I asked at length.

"Two companies," he replied at once.

"You've been counting."

"I thought one of us should."

"Thanks. Which two?"

"I believe that answer is right in front of you," he pointed at a small, heavily bearded, bespeckled man walking with his head nestled well within his shoulders, as close to a turtle as any human I had ever seen.

"Lieutenant Stokes," Seth yelled, "aren't you missing something?"

"Sir?" Stokes replied, face reddening above the beard, his head, amazingly, drew in deeper.

"Your company, Mr. Stokes, do you happen to know where they could be?"

"With Company B, Sir," he answered warily.

"Very good Lieutenant," Arnold coolly acknowledged his avoidance of the question, "and where is Company B? Before you answer that," he held his hand up, "please understand that if you answer with Company C you will wake up tomorrow a private."

Mr. Stokes head rose out of his shoulders as he surprised me in failing to cower before the non-idle threat, "Company B, Colonels, is with Captains Huntington and Bryce . . . Sirs".

Seth smiled at Stokes with paternal goodwill, then turned to me, "it appears, Colonel Hanlin, that the Lieutenant is attempting to relate the fact that while he is well aware of the whereabouts of the companies in question, he is loath to answer as that may lead to some misfortune falling on his superiors and he does not wish to be taken for an informer. That sound correct to you, Sir?"

"It does indeed," I answered in awe, Arnold, as in all things military, was a prodigy, "A practice that started with Achilles."

"Undoubtedly," Arnold replied a great good humor, "well Lieutenant, while it would be wonderfully diverting to play this game longer, I believe, sir, that you have adequately discharged your duty. We'll figure it out, dismissed!"

The relieved, amused, sweat soaked officer pulled his head back in and staggered away.

"I note," Seth said when Stokes was out of earshot, "that whatever Huntingdon and Bryce are doing does not have the approval of Mr. Stokes."

"I'm starting to think you don't need me anymore," I said with complete sincerity.

"Thank you, but I've much to learn."

"I begin to doubt that."

"Don't for a moment, for instance what do we do now?"

"I have a feeling that they —"

"Are about a mile back by that pleasant—"

"Little creek under the weeping willows," I finished to our laughs.

"You want me to go and roust them?" He asked with enthusiasm.

I looked off at the ridge immediately to our left, remembered maps I had read weeks ago in planning. Something clicked, "I have a better idea," I said, inspired.

I turned Clio, trotted slowly to the front of the column, a quiet Arnold by my side. We rode past my brother and out into the open ground. A few hundred yards from Christian's company we found an overgrown, hard-baked, disused, dirt road angling off toward the ridge.

We took it, rode in companionable silence under a cathedral of trees up a long, gently sloping hill. We emerged into a wide clearing to find exactly what the map had shown – an overgrown green bordered by half a dozen rundown, abandoned buildings.

"Welcome to Gay City," I announced.

"Of course!" Arnold yelled in recognition, "I should have realized."

"I needed a map to remind me it was here," I admitted, "I heard about it at the time, I was just a kid but it was big news in Boston."

"Same here, of course . . . " he gazed around the green, "funny thing is, it never occurred to me they left everything," he motioned the broken houses, "so . . . complete."

"Like the Mayan ruins."

"Exactly."

We rode to the far end of the green, a weedy avenue led off into the forest, a few buildings visible in the tree canopy gloom, a large pile of charred timbers was heaped beside a gentle brook, the burned out sawmill that was once the centerpiece of Gay City. Gay City was a planned community of a Millennium Utopian cult – and therefore unremarkable for the Northeast in the early 1800s. What distinguished Gay City, and brought it so briefly to national attention, was the fact that it was thriving and populated one day and abandoned the next. Unseen. Unreported. A ghost town in every sense of the word. That it was still, almost thirty years later, untouched was testament to the thriving superstitions of our eastern Connecticut brethren – a very different type of cult.

"We'll stop here for a rest, water – there were wells marked on the map – and some fun."

"Excellent, William,' the prodigy that was Arnold got my meaning immediately, "I'll have the ammunition wagon brought up."

I nodded, "I'll scout out the wells if you don't mind riding down to the column and bringing them up."

"I'm off," he yelled, "stay away from the ghosts!" He yelled over his shoulder and was gone. Clio lingered a moment to watch Augustus disappear before we rode around the weed choked former lawns of the dilapidated houses. The heat, humidity, and eeriness of the surroundings reminded me of another hot summer day when I was the only person tramping around the Waterloo battlefield.

I found a well with crystal clear water a few feet from the green, took the saddle off Clio, and watered her – for which she loudly forgave me my earlier trespasses. I stripped off my jacket, poured several canteens worth of utopian water over my head then drank my fill. I sat, rested my sore, soaked back against an ancient maple, ignored by Clio rhythmically munching foot high grass. I was uneasily dozing when the first of the men filed, in the unmistakable tromp of the terminally exhausted, into the clearing.

Over the next half hour undermanned companies reeled into the green and fell raggedly to the ground where they stayed. The hardy collected canteens, laboriously filled them (and themselves), and lugged them back to their crumpled mates. Stragglers began to wander in and abashedly found their companies under a canopy of insults. The ambulances rolled in and disgorged their living baggage onto the green grass where volunteers not so gently shoved canteens at them.

We rebounded well, with humor, and without a trace of the sullenness on arrival at Lebanon. I walked through the ad hoc camp collecting officers to meet by a teetering wood frame building that must have been the general store. Clio tip-toed through the lounging men, successfully sating her never sated hunger.

I had most of the officers collected together when Seth and Osgood rode up, Seth fluidly dismounted before Augustus completely stopped – to cheers from the men, deep grins from the officers, and a pantomime bravo from Osgood.

"Our lost companies," Arnold panted, "are still by the brook."

"Excellent," I said with a glee that drew puzzled looks, "Gentlemen, take your companies in order to the ammunition wagon, each man is to draw ten rounds . . . Go! There are targets aplenty!"

They were off before I finished, "They going to be at the brook long?"

"Just starting to brew coffee," Osgood answered for a still winded Arnold.

"They within earshot of a volley?" I asked.

"Most definitely," he grinned viciously.

"Very good."

There was a healthy pandemonium in the green while the men armed themselves, Shay in their midst weaving a whirlwind of insults, jokes, and earthy advice. The scene was decidedly unmilitary, at once human, the officers very much a part of it, very much enjoying themselves.

"This unit is going to do fine," I said to no one in particular.

"You just realizing that now, Colonel?" Osgood laughed.

"We've known for weeks, William," Seth added with a hard punch to my shoulder, "you get too caught up in things, my friend."

"Could you possibly stop hitting me?" I snarled at Arnold.

"I was just thinking I like it."

My response died mid-throat when Biggs appeared, bugle in hand. I took a moment to glare at Seth before giving Biggs leave to blow assembly. Despite their exhaustion, the men never formed so quickly, so precisely, so avidly. Shay took great pains to redress the lines and leave a gap where our missing companies should have been.

"Gentlemen," I yelled to our armed horde, "we are going to decimate those menacing buildings – volley fire by company . . . go to it."

The lines cheered, caps were thrown, "Nothing like the prospect of destroying property not one's own to inspire men," I remarked to my colleagues. Neither made a move to acknowledge, though Osgood may have grunted slowly through his scowl.

"Upset you weren't issued a rifle, Osgood?" I asked.

"Damn right I am."

"Then you're dismissed, there's extra in the wagon, try not to shoot anything living," he ran off, Seth's eyes plaintively followed him.

"For Christ's sake, Arnold," I yelled, "you bought the damn rifles, you don't need permission to use one."

"The men won't think it beneath me?"

"Not as long as you don't shoot any of them." That was all he needed to go loping off after Osgood.

The gap toothed regiment, Shay in command, began to move, Osgood and Seth took the place of Company B, a second or two behind them came Wycroft and Ashford, now our Company C.

235

Shay wielded the regiment like a synchronized machine, the companies moved in tandem as they had rarely to date, wheeled in front of the houses, and fired as one. The roar of each volley trembled the ground and rattled what was left of the windows around the green. The targeted houses shook to the basements, the .577 caliber minie balls smacked hard into decrepit wood, left gaping, ragged holes. Chards of wood, glass, masonry, plaster, dust, dirt and curtain fabric exploded in plumes around the unfortunate edifices while black powder smoke enveloped us.

Shay the maestro moved, pivoted, and hand directed his units as one by one they blasted apart the abandoned houses with such pounding ferocity I was surprised they did not collapse and erupt in flames. With two rounds left, Shay conducted them in an intricate pattern of drill that would serve the regiment well if ever surrounded by a Mongol horde.

I tore myself away from the spectacle with great reluctance for one of our wayward companies had started to emerge onto our hillside. I was almost to the prodigal troops when a disheveled Huntingdon, admiral's uniform buttoned comically wrong ran up the hill and began to frantically attempt to organize his mob into something resembling military order – at that he was singularly unsuccessful.

"General Desaix, I presume," I said amicably to what could only be described as a malevolent blank stare.

"Desaix? March to the guns? The Battle of Marengo?" I amplified in my friendliest voice, a voice he received with obvious and warranted suspicion, "no, eh? Well never mind, he died anyway. You will hold your company here, Captain – and Bryce's as well if he decides to join us – until we're done with rifle drill. I would offer your men use of the very refreshing well we've discovered but I gather you're already well rested and watered . . . coffeed too, Correct?"

There being no coherent and correct reply possible Huntingdon stared, his cold blue eyes wishing me dismemberment, at best. Buoyed by the fact Huntingdon so openly despised my good humor, I endeavored to continue it, "When we're done here, you have command of both delinquent companies – you're first independent command, congratulations.

"Your companies will police the green while the regiment takes a brief rest – I'm sure they'll have many helpful suggestions for your men. When we resume the march you will be in the van. Any man from your command who fails by the wayside," I stopped to watch the regiment wheel in front of the general store and unleash a thunderous volley, "will be assigned extra duty and you, Captain, will personally supervise that duty, understood?"

"Yes," he grunted through pursed lips.

"Yes, Colonel," I corrected with a smile.

"Yes, sir," he hissed.

"Close enough," I agreed and left him to his men.

18

Samuel Colt

The Hartford Club was close, hot, smoky, and close to unbearable despite the wide open floor-to-ceiling windows liberally spaced around the third floor ballroom. It was the worse Southern New England in July had to offer and it was the night the officers and NCOs crammed together to be feted by Colonel Samuel Colt, Hartford's mad-genius, philanthropist, utopian, salesman. Should one of more of the above appear contradictory, such was Colonel Colt.

I sat at the head table with my friends and Governor Buckingham, pretending to sip a glass of wine. Our host was ostensibly seated with us but occupied his seat for mere seconds at a time before he bounced up to bustle about and oversee every detail of the banquet, the better to see that 'his boys' had the best of everything.

Every thirty seconds or so my head nodded to my chest without warning, I glimpsed some far away land, realized I dozing, and snapped to with rocking clarity. I would then resist the urge to glance around the room to see if anyone noticed, give in and look, furtively at first, then overtly when I realized that, in that crowd, had anyone observed my less than rapt attentiveness I would already be the brunt of a dozen barbs.

I took pains to keep my hand on my wine glass and take a sip every few minutes in case our host walked by. Colt took every culinary pause as a personal affront that required immediate atonement – attonement which involved penetrating questioning about the real or perceived deficiency, profuse apology, and instant personal follow-up. One with a need for solitude need not come within a mile of Colt's hospitality. Nice man, but a pest.

When I was awake, I stared three tables to my left at the unmistakable profile of Captain Miles Huntingdon. He was obviously enjoying the highly recommended and eagerly proffered wine, an outstanding vintage, I was told uncounted times, from a particularly happy year.

Huntingdon's red face, glassy eyes, slight drool (I may embellish somewhat – his face was not all that red) did nothing to remove or even diminish his look of condescending smugness, a look he would take to the grave with him. The sooner the better.

He was as oblivious to my inspection as he was dismissive of my authority. I remained fixated on him until Shay's arm wrapped around my shoulders and his slightly bleary voice asked, "Are ya' going to survive this?"

"It'll be close," I admitted.

"No doubt, dare I ask wha' ya' thinking?"

"Dare away."

"What ya' thinkin'"

"If I should invite Huntingdon to the balcony for a brief conversation, or do I wait to shoot him in our first action?"

"Same result in either case, I tink, William."

"I can talk with him and not be violent," I said with a small measure of hurt.

"Not alone," he shook his head vigorously, "an' certainly not on a balcony," he laughed at the image.

"I have yet to practice defenestration," I said sanctimoniously and with pride.

"There's a first time for everythin' – ya' bring tha' captain up there, he'll piss ya' off and you'll defenestrate at ya' leisure."

"That a word, defenestrate?"

"Good question," he threw himself mightily into the abandoned chair next to me, "defenestration is death by fallin' –"

"Or being thrown out," I added, motioning toward the still oblivious Huntingdon.

"Or bein' thrown out," he corrected, "a window – but, tha's what, a noun? Referring ta' a specific type of death?"

"I would guess," I shrugged.

"But I got to believe, it's one o'those nouns tha's also a verb, quick way o'saying I threw the motherfucker outta' tha' window."

"I defenestrated the motherfucker," I said with elegance.

"Tha's it, short an' sweet. Does it work in all tenses, do ya' think?"

"I defenestrate, I have defenestrated, I will have defenestrated?" I postulated.

"Sounds grand," Shay agreed.

"It does, doesn't it? I promise if I talk to Huntingdon I won't defenestrate the fuck."

"Ya' remarkably consistent in ya' opinion of 'im."

"I pride myself on consistency," I said modestly.

"Despite Emerson's admonishment?"

I looked at my Irish sergeant-major with new found wonder, a look I sported at least ten times a week, before I answered, "He meant foolish consistency, not good old fashion tenacity."

"I somewha' doubt your interpretation – on both counts."

"I know Emerson, I'll run it by him next time I see him – in the meantime . . ." I starred hard at Huntingdon, now holding court at his table.

Shay followed my stare, "Ya' know humiliatin' him is na' tha' same as disciplinin' him, don'tcha'?"

"Perhaps," I pretended to mull it over, "but 'tis a hell o' a lot more fun, don'tcha know?" I finished in a dead-on imitation of our sergeant-major.

"Ah, bloody hell," he groaned, "I agree, but it's not very effective, an' you'll still have tha' problem when ya' done."

"That's why I'm contemplating tackling it head on," I said at the exact moment Osgood managed to tear himself away from a Buckingham anecdote and join us. In his honor I added, "in a controlled, rational, adult manner, of course."

"You talking about Huntingdon?" Osgood asked.

"Of course," Shay and I answered together.

"You planning on talking to him man to rodent?" Osgood sneered.

"Can't do much else," I deigned to answer, "I can't remove him or cashier him when we're still stuck in Hartford and not even part of the army yet. Beside," I nodded toward the intensely occupied Buckingham, "I promised him I wouldn't interfere with his voting base, which apparently consists of self-righteous, faux-wealthy, assholes."

"And you think," Osgood started, stopped for a moment when Christian sidled up and handed him one of the two enormous whiskeys he toted, "that with your attitude toward him you are capable of discussing the weather with the man?"

"You underestimate me," I replied defensively.

"No, you underestimate how accurate your opinion of the man is – if anything the bastard is worse than you give him credit for. You need to wait until he's federalized and then nail the prick on your turf."

"I merely seek to employ my best efforts to solve it now and forgo future unpleasantness," I said with sanctimony.

"God, I hate it when you turn idealistic," Osgood, with exasperation.

"Idealism has nothing to do with it, I'm sorry to admit, I'm just giving it one more chance, to save future efforts."

"Talkin' ta' him will do no good, not from you," Shay offered, eying Christian's oversized whiskey.

"The regiment's fine," Osgood added quickly, "Sometimes trying to make something that's good perfect ruins it."

"Advice from a drunken Irishman and Poor Richard," I observed with a shake of the head, "though you make some sense – amazingly enough."

"Aye, an' best heed it," Shay returned with conviction.

"Let it go, brother," Christian chimed in, "his men hate him, despise him to the core. It'll catch up with him, you can bet on it."

"You know that how?" I asked.

"By not being so far above the rank and file by virtue of an exalted figurehead of a position to have retained the ability to speak to the average man," he finished with a straight face.

I stared at my brother for a long moment before, "You are aware that you were adopted, right?"

"Thankfully so," he answered without missing a beat,

"seriously, though, Fischer tells me story after story – the men hate him, he treats them abysmally and they can't do a thing about it because he'd ruin them in Farmington."

"Wish we could ruin him in Farmington," I muttered into my wine before capturing Osgood's interested eye.

"If I've learned anything from Shay's stories," a very inebriated Arnold had lurched behind me while I was muttering, now he leaned over my shoulder to offer his take on the subject of the day, "it's that these kind of regimental problems tend to take care of themselves in action," he laughed with a maliciousness that was newly found and somewhat unsettling.

"Mr. Shay shouldn't be putting those kind of thoughts in your impressionable head," I said at an unrepentant Shay, "our men aren't Shay's scum of the earth, they're not soldiers, they're a bunch of men who are new to all this and have no reference points – they don't know a good officer from a shit, never mind even thinking of taking corrective steps."

"I don't know, William," Shay, undeterred, "from what I've seen New Englanders learn fast, 'specially where their lives and pocketbooks are concerned."

"Shit," Arnold, leaning hard on my shoulder, "if it was their pocketbooks he was threatenin' Huntingdon would have been floating face down in the river weeks ago."

"In the meantime," I went on, conspicuously unconvinced, "in the meantime, the bastard is already a regular army lawyer and knows exactly how much he can and can't get away with – and he always will."

"Well," Shay sat back hard, took a long pull of wine, "he didna' manage to fook up the parade today, tha's something."

"No, he didna'," I parodied our inebriated Sergeant Major, reflected briefly on the fact the men from Farmington were every bit as polished, professional, and flawless as the rest of our shiny new regiment. I stared hard at Huntingdon, pondering his day long cooperation.

"Forget him for tonight, for fook's sake," Shay whispered in my ear.

"I need to clear the air," I decided, fully aware of my own obstinacy.

"You'll fook it up more," he said aloud to the table, drawing concerned looks from all.

I stood to audible sighs, "Into the breach," I whispered, left my island of relative sanity, and sailed off into an ocean of drunks obscured by banks of tobacco smoke toward the hostile shore of Huntingdon's table.

When I was about a foot away Huntingdon leaned over and whispered something to the lieutenant next to him who started to smile until he saw my stare and deadened his face. I made an effort to remember his face - there was an officer with a solid career path in front of him.

Not fazed, Huntingdon turned to the officer on his other side, an already snickering Bryce, repeated the same and produced a braying laugh that could be heard above the din of the room. Perturbed but undeterred, I pressed home, my eyes leveling Bryce – who showed he had not a whit of sense or self-preservation about him as him as he continued to bray.

I nodded to the rest of the sun-burned, smoke-shrouded faces floating above brass buttoned blue jackets. A few nodded back, most looked at Huntingdon with some type of expectation.

"Captain Huntingdon, I wonder if I might have a word with you?" I asked in a strong voice that belied the fact I had already realized what a god-awful idea it was and should be back at my table drinking wine out of the bottle.

Instead of responding, Huntingdon leaned over and whispered again to Bryce, who grinned viciously, an idiot sealing his fate. Still without a word, Huntingdon took a sip of wine, slowly dabbed his mouth with stained napkin. With infinite slowness he stood and adjusted his jacket.

I motioned he follow me, spun on my heels and headed toward the back of the room, pausing only to see if he was in tow. He was, without further glance I pushed through the door, stomped up the stairs to the fourth floor and a landing with a small table and two chairs. When I turned, Huntingdon was standing opposite, no more than three feet away, stone faced and glaring.

I took the chair closest to the stairs, nodded to Huntingdon to take the other.

"I prefer to stand," he said flatly, fully employing his self-satisfied smugness. Well-earned this time, in fact, as he had clearly won round one and we both knew it – if I continued to sit he would loom over me, if I rose to face him I acceded to his parameters, if I ordered him to sit I abused my authority.

I made a mental note to never ignore Shay's advice again before deciding the better part of valor was to stay seated. Decision made, I pretended to relax.

"I thought, perhaps, we should talk."

"Why?" He replied, staring in perfect ignorance.

"Because our relationship is one of discipliner and disciplined and that is not healthy for the regiment," I said it quickly and reasonably. If I had sprouted wings and flown away right then and there his expression would not, could not, have been more incredulous.

It hit me with all the subtlety of a rifle butt to the gut that in the eyes of a man like Huntingdon, the very act of attempting to communicate with him at any level beyond commander and commanded was a sign of abject weakness, if not complete surrender. The human equivalent of a dog presenting its belly.

Huntingdon let his expression and silence speak volumes. I considered my tactical error, roughly equivalent to the Romans at Cannae. I finally, however, recognized Huntington for what he really was, a bully. And bullies, since David met Goliath, can only be handled with the expert wielding of that medium they respect solely, bullying. No talk was, in any way, going to accomplish anything with him, at any time.

"Look, Miles," I went on despite my certainty that I should have stood and left him with his smirk, "none of this will stand when we are in federal service. The Articles of War will apply, your state contacts will be superseded by the Army's and the closer we are to the enemy the quicker and more severe the consequences."

He smirked a smirk that rendered all his previous smirks utterly inconsequential.

"That a threat, Hanlin?" He hissed.

"No," I elongated the vowel to maintain my temper, "it's the way things are in the Army, your current behavior will not be tolerated and you'll be a long way from your state political ties –

and, just to be clear – you will not be allowed to harm this Regiment."

"My God, you're the prosecutor for this County and you're this naïve?" Open derision in every syllable, "You think that I have what I have without friends in Washington? Christ, this is going to be easier than I thought."

He started to turn away, I jumped from my chair, grabbed his shoulder, pulled him around to face me.

"I don't much care what you think," my voice rose, "you fuck up camp again and I will put you under house arrest, you fuck up under fire, you'll be buried on the spot, please doubt me on that because I'd like nothing better -unless you'd like to settle this man to man right now, loser resigns?"

I yelled the last, prayed he would raise a fist. Instead, he did much worse. He smiled. And shook his head.

"You really are amusing at times," was his final assessment before he bounded down the stairs, back to his alcohol and allies.

I waited to allow the flush in my face to recede, the tremor in hands that dearly wanted to bash the smug-faced prick's face to ease, and my anger at my stupidity to fade.

Near calm, I returned to our table, ignored curious looks from the others, picked up my goblet and took a long drought of mildly metallic liquid. I took another long slip – it was an excellent vintage – and stared a hole through an otherwise completely unoffending dinner roll.

"Went that well, eh?" Shay inquired. I snorted acknowledgment.

"Great . . . ya' know duelin's illegal?"

"Shouldn't be," I answered with feeling, "how'd you know I offered to settle it man to man?"

"Please," he laughed, "how else was tha' conversation goin' ta' come out."

"Well, he said no."

"Ah, hell, he would've just cheated anyway."

"And that's what you would've gotten to shoot him."

"Now that would've been a pleasure."

"Next time it appears I am about to ignore your sage advice, you have my permission – make that an order – to hit me, hard."

"An order I'll obey gladly," his voice left no doubt he looked forward to the duty.

My brother, never one to not torment me when opportunity arose, leaned in, "It amazes me that you get along so well with the rank and file, and yet have no skill with your peers."

"Another drunken philosopher," I noted, took another long pull on wine too expensive to be guzzling in my doomed attempt to catch up, "I get along fine with Arnold by the way, you little pissant."

"He's older than you, it's not the same and –"

"Wait a minute," I interrupted in a shout, "Huntingdon's no peer of mine, you shit."

"Close enough for the point to be made."

"There is no point," I said with petulance.

"There is," Shay joined in, "ya' no idea how ta' deal with Huntingdon and if he was a private or a general you'd not a problem at all."

"You know I get along fine with my base ball team and we range from store clerks or factory owners."

"Means nothin'," Shay answered without hesitation.

"Stupid game," Osgood yelled across the table.

"How does it not count? We've been together for years."

"Prowess in the field transcends social standing and rank," Shay said, staring off into space, "it doesn't mean friendship or even camaraderie off the field."

Dead silence descended our side of the table and we all stared at our Sergeant Major. "Where the hell did you come up with that?" I finally asked.

"You're na' the only ones tha' read books, arseholes," he snapped to laughter around the table.

"You're an expert on sports as well, Sergeant Major?" I asked imperiously.

He sighed the sigh of one indulging a simple child, "I played bloody rugby for years, ya' heathen, bloody British Army tradition, playin' fields of Eton, an' all that."

"Now you were at Waterloo?" I snorted.

"My Da was an' ya' startin' to sound like a blithering idiot."

"It's a myth, you know," I went on undeterred.

"What's a myth?"

"Playing fields of Eton – had nothing to do with readying anyone for Waterloo – they didn't even play sports in 1814."

"You're an insufferable boor," Shay answered to smiles of agreement from Christian and Osgood.

"Doesn't make it any less true."

"My Da could'na have found Eton on a bloody map," Shay went on with a smile, "he was jus' one a' the scum of the earth and damn proud of it. To be a sergeant in the Queen's Own Irish Rifles, that was as good as it got."

"Queen's Own Irish Rifles" I asked, interested.

"Aye."

"He was at Hugomont before enduring the cavalry recovery attacks in the center?" I asked, ready to fly off to a new direction.

"Utterly, fookin' amazing," Shay shook his head, "ya' a bloody freak, tell me 'xactly where my Da was over forty years ago."

"Forty-seven last month," I corrected with great malice.

"Forty-seven years ago," he shook his head again, "ya' can probably tell me where he shat that day as well. An' yet what to do with the likes of Huntington throw ya' like calculus to an eight year old."

Christian nodded so furiously I worried for his remaining conscious, "You don't bloody well recognize rats, brother."

"Turning Limey, Christian?" I asked, staring at Shay.

"Limey?" Shay growled.

"Sorry", I said with no undercurrent of regret, "I meant that Christian is starting to sound like an Irishman whose idioms have been affected by an elongated stay in the British Army – that better, Sergeant Major?"

"Some", he tilted his wine glass at me, "tho', if you like, I could swear at you fluently in French for a while, *vous grande merde a tete.*"

"*Je ne comprends pas.*"

"I said you're an insufferable asshole."

"You called me a shithead, shithead," I took yet another great gulp of wine.

"None of this is helping to solve the Huntingdon problem," Christian is slurred into the conversation, exhibiting the narrow focused thought patterns of a drunk, "not at all."

"Go away you evil little gnome, the grown-ups are talking now," I shot back.

"You're getting drunk," he pointed out, "and you're just jealous I got all the good looks, charm, and the ability to get along with everybody."

"Well, mother likes me best," I said without thinking.

My brother erupted in great guffaws as he sputtered to get the words out, "She emphatically does not, as you well know," I had no choice but to nod as he choked it out, "if she ever did – which I sincerely doubt – West Point clinched it."

"I'm sure," I agreed, quietly.

"She says hello, by the way, she's thrilled you're putting your education to good use going south."

"I went south when I graduated."

"Too far south," he roared.

"Well, I'm glad I'll be killing the right people this time around," I sulked.

"At long last, to quote mother."

"Indeed," I sighed.

"You know, Willie," Christian looked around the ballroom, "I think I may use my skills of persuasion and go and chat with Mr. Hunt –"

"No!" Osgood, on the sidelines listening quietly, exploded seconds before Shay and I joined in. Together, we were loud enough to draw a brief, ire filled glance from Buckingham.

Christian seemed more than taken aback by the simultaneous admonishments, "Well, I –."

"Ya' will do nothing," Shay hissed at him while throwing a glance warming me to stay out of it, "ya' will worry about ya' men, ya' company and ya'self – and that is all!" Shay was intense, Christian accepted without comment, "Go near tha' human piece of flotsam an' I'll flay ya' myself. Ya' understand, Hanlin?"

"Yes," he conceded, "but I'll need whiskey," he smiled and rose.

"Bring a round, boy'o," Shay commanded.

"Yes, Sir!" He threw off a salute and was gone.

Shay looked at me, shook his head and let out a long exhalation as if a burden - yet another – had been lifted from his already bowed shoulders. I tipped my glass at him and was about to take some more wine when Christian arrived with much more potent whiskeys for all.

"Drink up, lads," Shay held up his glass, "it'd be bad form to leave a party thrown by Mr. Colt while still retainin' the ability to walk."

We settled in, took our seats while food was borne in on elaborate trays like so many sacrifices to the gods of war. Countless courses later we left our table and waddled the room to drink and talk, congregating among our comrades under the portraits of past prominent Hartfordians, insulting them as we saw fit.

I was standing with Wycroft and Ashford, both gleefully reliving their destruction – single-handedly – of Gay City when a loud thumping noise caught our attention. It appeared to emanate from the head table. I blinked through the never moving smoke, Shay lurched over and together we tried to make sense of the scene: ahead in the murk Samuel Colt banged something hard on the table in front of him; Arnold, Buckingham and a half a dozen waiters scooted away in half crouches.

"What the hell is tha' in his hand?" Shay shouted.

"My Lord," Ashford gasped, "is that a gun?"

I focused my somewhat inebriated faculties on Colt and answered with virtual certainty, "It's a revolver."

"Bet it's a Colt," Wycroft cracked to our riotous laughs.

Colt finished using his product as a gavel, laid it on the table, the waiters came back under his gesticulating arms to perform their duties with noticeable efficiency and haste and frequent glances at the gun.

We were transfixed by our Hartford born guru of social welfare as he orchestrated his army of waiters – alas for his military ambitions, lately laid aside by Buckingham himself, the only army Colonel Colt would ever command. Additional waiters materialized carrying dozens of handsome walnut boxes, piling them by on the table in front of him..

Waiters gone we gathered, as beaconed, around the table and Colt spoke. It was a brief speech, heart-felt, and therefore perfect. He spoke well despite the smoke and wine. In my befuddled state

I found him eloquent as he expressed deep, sincere regret the banquet was necessary. Yet, being necessary, he expressed his adoration for 'his boys', and wished us the greatest, quickest success possible to return home.

With his soliloquy ringing in our ears he presented each of us  with a wooden case containing a 1860 Colt Army revolver. He imposed a sole condition on the generous gift – the condition he always imposed.

"Boys, just make sure you tell everyone where you got the revolvers. Tell them they can have a discount – but, hell, they've got to buy theirs!"

Cheers – for Colt, his business acumen, the Union, Lincoln and ourselves rang out through the hall, probably through half of Hartford. The rest of the night faded away in dreamlike good cheer.

19

Two days later we still had no orders from Washington; the newspapers, while urging 'On to Richmond' in ever more demanding headlines, had little to report in the way fo actual news beyond Lincoln's July 7th address to Congress – a speech bemoaned in New England for the absence of slavery from his otherwise well expressed war aims – we gave the 21st a well-deserved and happily received week off. The war was on holiday.

I was singularly, contentedly unencumbered, having only to attend a Bar function where I was given an exquisite presentation sword as a 'token of esteem in leaving one brotherhood for another.' Nelson gave the key note address noting that he fervently hoped the sword would soon – in all its righteousness – be bathed in the blood of the slave-owning enemies of the Union.

I accepted the instrument of vengeance with a squeamishness and a tinge of disgust that I hoped I hid well lest it serve as blood to sharks attracting barbs in a room full of lawyers. Even as I held it in my hand I remained dubious I would ever strap it on, never mind wield it in anger, with its Nelsonian connections.

Beside that much appreciated, if not hideously presented, honor I had nothing else to do and reveled in my nothingness. My energies were engaged only to the extent needed to turn the pages of the latest must read British novel, *The Cloister and the Hearth.*

Calm, relaxed, recuperating, I was prepared to continue my suddenly enjoyable existence as a ne'er-do-well and did . . . right up until four o'clock in the morning on July 14th.

I woke then to a creaking floorboard and, presumably, a hand trying hard to not rattle the ancient brass knob on my bedroom door. Despite my grogginess, my first thought was how strange it was that people sent to wake one up in the middle of the night are so damn careful to be quiet about it.

251

I sat up at the exact moment the door creaked open and revealed a profile that could only be Charles thereby dashing my brief, flimsy, ridiculous hope it was Bridget.

The specter of my sitting up rather than prone and snoring away completely froze Charles. I imagined him as a tall, tweed covered frightened rabbit, not a muscle moving while only his mustache laden nose flared and unflared.

"I'm up, Phelps," God knows why I whispered.

"What the hell you doin' up, Boss?" His voice startled while he remained stock still.

"What the hell you doing sneaking around the house?"

"Come to getcha."

"And I got you."

"Normal people sleep. You ain't normal."

"That from your extensive experience creeping around people's homes in the middle of the night?"

"Get plenty of practice sneakin' inta' bed past my woman afta' a long night's drink."

"You need more practice."

"My point to her exactly."

I rose, began to dress, "I need a uniform or can I go as a normal human being?"

"Mufti's fine," he snorted, leaned against the doorpost.

"Want to tell me why you're here watching me dress?"

"Not because I wanna, believe me,"

"Care to tell me why?"

"Osgood sent me, Mr. Randle needs you . . . now."

"For?"

"Just that, he needs you, s'all I know."

I nodded in the dark. Elias Randle was the general manager of the Goodwin and a good friend. I had lived in the hotel in a permanent suite for almost a year after I came to Hartford and into Nelson's employ. A small, fussy, detail obsessed man – exactly what one would expect to find running a first class hotel in a capitol city – with a first rate sense of humor based on an original, deeply skewered view of the cosmos. He had to be sixty, looked fifty, acted twenty.

"I take it there's a problem at the Goodwin?" Osgood and I

252

had assisted Elias on more than a few occasions, cleaning up hotel related indiscretions; a category in that industry that extended from squabbles over call girl fees to the apocalypse.

"I will tell you everything I know," Phelps announced, "they want you at the hotel."

"Illuminating, thank you."

Apparently I was keeping Charles from other appointments for he added, "It's four o'clock in the morning, Boss, nobody cares what you look like an' there's nobody about to impress."

"You have plans, Charles?"

"Night's young."

We walked out into a perfect night-morning, stiff breeze off the Connecticut, stars gleaming in a moonless sky. Charles's rig stood waiting in the silence.

"I'll walk," I said as the night pressed in on me.

"I think it's a rush, Boss."

"It's all of six blocks, I'll walk."

"I'll come with you," he offered, quite the act of gallantry for the exercise averse Phelps.

"That's too great a sacrifice to ask, Charles."

"I wuz kidding, anyway, never walk when you can ride."

"That's remarkably obvious," I retorted, "then take the rig and let them know I'm on my way."

"Gotcha, Boss, have a good walk," he said dubiously.

Charles meandered to his rig and clip-clopped off into the night. I walked in peace, the only sound my shoes on the brick sidewalk echoing off the flat faced buildings of the sleeping city. Whatever or whoever we were supposed to be fighting might as well have been on another planet.

When I turned into Asylum Street my eyes were blinded by the bright lights of the Goodwin. Charles and the rig were just pulling in front – leave it to Charles to take the long way around to respect my solitude.

I walked into the Goodwin under the hiss of gas lights and almost into – over, really – Elias Randle. Before I could react he had a death grip on my forearm.

"William, thank God you're here," he whispered without breath, his face unnaturally pale, his normally darting, snapping brown eyes dull and still.

"You alright, Elias?" I asked reflexively.

"What? Oh, God save you, William, I'm fine . . . but it's awful, awful!" He turned abruptly, my following a forgone conclusion.

I knew then, before I was dragged another step through the deeply carpeted lobby, the gas lights there low and ghostly, I knew.

"Where?" I asked.

"Your old apartments," he replied without affect while my heart froze, "Osgood's there now," he grunted as we climbed to grand staircase on our way to the fourth floor.

Once on the landing our pace increased and we strode purposely through opulence. No words were spoken even as we reached the door of my old rooms. Elias looked furtively from side to side, lightly rapped on the solid oak, cracked it open with an excess of caution, and slipped in like a wrath. He looked over his shoulder eyes pleading I follow.

I swallowed my dread, consigned it to the pit of my stomach and stepped into the familiar sitting room. Without pause Elias moved into the master bedroom, stopped dead, I stepped around him . . .

. . . my first sight was Osgood, arms crossed, back against the wall-papered flowered wall, head at an odd angle, staring at the bed. I followed his gaze, saw what I already knew I would see: a nude woman, raven black hair, spread-eagled on almost bloodless sheets. I looked back to Osgood, watched as he finished his mental inventory.

At long last our gazes met and he shrugged with awful resignation.

"Fuck," I sighed my first word since the lobby.

"Amen," Elias seconded.

"I take it the rooms were vacant?" I asked absently and rhetorically.

"Yes," Elias answered hoarsely, unable to tear his gaze off the bed.

"Police?" I asked.

"Elias sent a runner to the desk," Osgood answered, "turns out the desk has standing orders in the event of a murder like—"

"To rouse Nelson," I needlessly finished.

"I assume he will be here soon."

"Well, it's his case now," I muttered to the walls.

"You know it's not," Osgood snapped. He was right, of course, we both knew it was ours until we arrested or killed the sick bastard or he quit out of boredom or lack of available victims. No intervening war and duties elsewhere would diminish our responsibility – not as long as Nelson was the best Hartford could throw at him.

"Nelson couldn't figure this out if he walked in on the fucker stabbing her," I agreed with a grimacing Osgood.

"He know we were called first?" I asked the room in general.

"Not unless you told him," Osgood replied without humor, "he will not be barging in, though, I have Phelps watching the street."

"Good," I had expected nothing less, "anything different with . . . her? Anything stand out?"

"As beautiful as the others," he mused aloud, "darker features, I think she's – "

"French," I interrupted as something clicked, "it's Bastille Day, Osgood."

"Shit."

"Yeah," I agreed, "he's working his way through Europe."

He nodded, "Other than that, same shit – I could just take one of my drawings, change the head, same story."

"The man has a way of knowing what exclusive surroundings are empty when he needs them, doesn't he?" Osgood saw no need to respond, Elias looked at the two of us while shock cleared the grief off his face,

"Are you two intimating this has happened before?" He asked at length.

"It has," I answered my friend directly – his profession and who he was defined confidentiality and discretion.

"How many?" He asked the logical follow-up.

"This makes five," I said.

"My God."

"Who found her?" I asked, aware that Nelson's arrival was imminent.

"I did," Elias answered weakly, "we have an important

function this morning and I couldn't sleep," A happy bachelor of long confirmation, he had a plush suite near the ballroom, "I heard something upstairs and it being so late, I ran up to investigate. The door was open, I came in to . . . her. I could only think to get Osgood first."

"That's understandable," I replied.

"I've created a problem for you with Nelson, haven't I?" He asked with concern.

"I don't work for him."

"That's not what I mean," he answered at once.

"Am I the only man in this state who doesn't think he'll be our next senator?" I asked.

"Yes," Osgood and Elias answered together.

"Well he won't," I averred with heat before returning to present circumstances, "you two want to get out of here before Lord Nelson arrives?"

"Yes," they answered as one again.

"Can I tell him you'll do a quick report?" I asked Osgood who nodded with resignation, "Good, maybe that will placate him for the time being."

"Sure it will," Osgood sighed.

"Now get," I commanded. Osgood headed toward the door, Elias grabbed his arm.

"I'll take you out the back way," Elias said and they hustled out of the room leaving me alone with the body. I involuntarily shuddered and walked into the sitting room, almost colliding with Charles.

"I got maybe five minutes on that bastard Nelson," He forwent all preamble, "if you'd like to get out of here."

"Thank you, but I better stay," I replied with regret.

"He's got about five coppers with 'em."

"I think I'll be fine regardless of who's with him," to this remark I received two looks from Charles. The first - complete disbelief that anyone would trust the police; the second, that anyone who could trust them was a class not of his.

"You go Charles."

"No, boss, you'll need a friendly face about," he replied quickly, once again justifying his long-standing employment.

We waited wordlessly, two companions in a predawn vigil over a dead body. After good a five minutes or so, four Hartford policemen rushed into the room to stand menacingly around us. After enough appropriate seconds had elapsed Nelson strutted in – right past me, Charles, the coppers and straight into the bedroom.

I had never known Nelson to go to a crime scene, I learned why then and there when he almost immediately stumbled out of the bedroom, his face a lovely shade of ash, hands over his mouth. Instead of taking a right toward the water closet he took a left and after a remarkable parity of a tap dancer he regrouped and ran into the hallway. A moment later, the sounds of violent, voluminous vomiting reached us.

"That was a big supper," I observed.

"It's going to leave a stain," Charles pointed out.

The six of us struggled to maintain composure while I traded glances with two cops closest to me.

"Morning, Anderson, morning Shaw," I miraculously remembered their names.

"Mr. Hanlin howbeit?" The taller, older of the two, the one with the single largest mustache ever seen in our environs, the envy of walruses everywhere, answered amicably.

"Eh, idiot, it ain't mister no more, it's Colonel," the shorter, younger one corrected in a high nasal, "how are you, sir," he smiled widely, "my brother Sam's in company K, sir."

"And doing a fine job," I answered automatically and, probably, truthfully. I looked at the other two cops, nodded to one who looked somewhat familiar. He raised a bushy black eyebrow, grunted.

"Morning Simmons," I said. The grunt did it, I remembered him immediately. He was not being rude or standoffish, it was his manner, his entire mode of communication. He could convey virtually any emotion with a combination of eyebrow flexing and finely pitched grunts. He was to the raised eyebrow and grunt what Nelson was to pacing.

My musing was interrupted as a somewhat restored, very much angered Nelson strode into the room.

"What the hell you doing here?" He skipped the pleasantries. I was almost knocked over by the stench of his breath.

"I –."

"And who the hell is this?" He pointed, somehow accusingly, at Phelps, who smiled back disarmingly.

"My friend, Charles Phelps, Master Sergeant Charles Phelps," I said pleasantly. Charles bowed slightly in acknowledgement.

"Play soldier on your own time," Nelson snapped and five pairs of eyes flicked to me in unison. I knew myself well enough to know my eyes had hardened almost as fast as my checks had reddened.

Straining to sound casual, I turned to Charles, "Thank you for keeping me company, I'll see you later today."

Charles began to move toward the door mouthing 'sure?' as he passed by. I nodded.

"Where you going?" Nelson snapped nastily, "I haven't dismissed you."

"He's leaving," I answered for him, matching Nelson's tone precisely. I shot a warning glance at Charles for he was, of course, evidently capable of giving Nelson the answer he deserved.

I stared levelly at Nelson who for once stood stock still. I could sense him running through the permutations, searching to see how he could best assert authority over either of us.

That answer obvious, reluctance evident in his posture and voice, he said, "You may go" and waved his hand dismissively toward the door.

"What do you want me to do, Colonel?" Phelps asked, making a show of ignoring Nelson.

"Go, Charles, get some rest," I answered decisively.

"Why are you here, Hanlin?" Nelson started as Charles disappeared out the door, thereby displaying his politician's knack for turning the page without regret.

"Elias Randall called for me."

"And you didn't think to contact me at once?"

"You're here aren't you?" I pointed out.

"That did not answer the question."

"Hell Nelson," I thought I saw him flinch, "I didn't know why I was summoned here until I saw her," at that he definitely did

258

flinch, "then I was told you were on your way – does that answer your ridiculous question?" Warning voices assailed me as I, dimly, realized I was on the verge of losing my temper.

"Always with everything figured out, eh, Hanlin?" He slurred and began to pace. At least two of the cops grinned – they had seen the act before, "always so fucking glib."

"You're drunk off your ass," came out of my mouth, much to my astonishment.

"And you have no right to be here, no right to ..." for a moment I thought he was going to vomit again, but he somehow managed to regain control of his stomach – if nothing else, "Abusing your former position, , still usurping my authority . . . need I remind you, you're not a law enforcement officer, any longer."

"You know what, Nelson," I ripped back, knowing my internal editor had just quit entirely, "I am sorry the ownership of this establishment continues to turn to me in times of crisis; I'm sorry I dragged myself out of bed to get here before you could be found in whatever after hours dive you were holed up in," I spit in a steady staccato. Nelson stopped dead and stared with saucer sized pupils, mouth agape, "I am sure as fuck sorry that I had to view another dead girl,' I pointed at him with as much menace as I could summon, "And I am so very fucking sorry that you don't have the balls to so much as look at that poor girl and do the fucking job you were elected to do."

He gaped like a good sized trout out of water, mouth working wordlessly.

"I'll have a report for you this afternoon, though I doubt you'll be able to do anything with it," I went on, freely now, "perhaps by then you'll be sober and will find the courage to at least face her on paper."

Finished, I walked out of my former rooms, disgusted with Nelson, disgusted I had ever worked for him, disgusted I could not control my temper, disgusted at not being solely disgusted with the killer.

I walked home barely registering that the night was still gorgeous.

20

I crawled back to bed with predictable results. I tossed, turned, stretched, scrunched, stared while wide awake, squinted when half asleep while images of the girl floated by and I replayed my rant with Nelson. Christ, even Mexico made an appearance. Briefly.

I gave it a good effort, quit after almost an hour of torture, rose and plodded wearily to the kitchen where Charles sat, leaning back, feet on the table, sipping coffee made stronger by more than coffee beans.

I sat with an uncharacteristically quiet Charles, an unattended cup in front of me, watching rays from the climbing sun filter through the transom and race toward us.

Before they could reach us, I stood, stretched, and said, "let's get the hell out of here."

"Sweet Jesus, yes," his immediate, gleeful response, "I'll get the rig."

Eschewing my uniform, I dressed casually and stepped outside into blinding sunlight and a glorious July day. Warm, not hot, high wispy clouds promising some occasional relief from the sun, light breeze flowing north, I reflected that one never got a rainy day when one needed it. I climbed up into the rig, and sat next to Charles.

"Where to, Boss?"

"How about a nice, long drive to Wethersfield?" I asked, "I know an inn on the cove where we can get some solid food and they won't look askew at us ordering alcohol with breakfast."

"I know the place," he replied with enthusiasm.

"Of course you do," I agreed to his radiant smile.

We headed out of the slowly stirring, city, past rumbling incoming traffic bringing in all that was necessary to allow the city to survive yet another day. Neither of us spoke, we cleared

Hartford proper, rode past Colt's state-of-the-art, onion topped factory, followed the glistening, already sailed filled river south. We moved into flat fields, the traffic cleared out, I began to feel human again.

We reached Wethersfield an hour later, both of us slouching at ease, still silent. The Cove is an inlet, well back from the great width of the Connecticut, fed by a long mouth barely two boat widths wide. A sea of masts rode unmoving on the glassy water.

"Well, Boss," Charles broke the silence, "look, there's a tavern right there on the shore and they're tables outside."

"They look empty."

"They do indeed."

"Shame to waste them," I pointed out.

"Shame," he responded, increased our pace.

We corrected the perceived wrong by taking the table closest to the unmoving water and ordered a prodigious breakfast with matching drinks. We thoroughly enjoyed the hospitality of Connecticut's oldest town in a manner that the strict Protestants who originally found their way to the peaceful cove would have found most objectionable.

Hours later, a fact confirmed when the nearby clock tower struck eleven, I stirred out of my comfortable fog.

"We need to get Osgood," I said, or at least intimated something approaching that sentimentality, my speech may have been slurred.

"You alright, Boss?" Charles asked. He showed no effect whatever from the liquid portions of our long breakfast while maintaining the expert's nose for the effects of alcohol on the less experienced and dedicated.

"I'm fine," I lied, "but we have to move out," I got to my feet and did a passable imitation of a slightly inebriated man walking. Back on the rig, headed north, I was thankful beyond words that it was an almost unnaturally cool July day.

The bucking, swaying, swinging, jarring, banging of the rig on what at best could have been described as a heavily used road, combined with the noxious gases that regularly passed from a member of Phelps' team (surely indicating the need for a change of diet) should have combined to send me reeling into the high weeds and refuse on the side of the road. Instead, everything mixed perfectly with the steady breeze, serene landscape, occasional cloud over the sun, and my alcohol level and I simply dozed without reference to the intensities of the morning's discoveries.

I made no comment when we passed by Osgood's apartments and continued to Olga's house, where we stopped, to my momentary confusion.

"I said we should get Osgood."

"And we have," Charles replied at once, as if to a child.

"He has either moved here," I observed, "or you have more details about his sexual habits than is healthy."

"Your education has not been wasted, you going in?"

I answered by carefully climbing down and starting up the walkway in something approximating a straight line. Halfway up the walk the front door opened and Osgood appeared in the doorway.

"Heard you coming. Not much traffic here in the daylight," he called out.

"Nice place to have an office," I observed. He nodded enthusiastically and led me into the house, down a long hallway and into a study, curtains blowing almost straight in on the breeze.

"You've been drinking," he pointed out as I gracelessly fell into an unexpectedly soft chair.

"You've been fucking," I guessed back, he selected an austere high backed chair across the room thereby causing me uneasiness at the metaphysical positioning.

"That just makes me happier than you."

"Don't bet on it."

"How bad did you lose your temper with Nelson," he asked knowingly.

"He was still standing when I left," I answered honestly. I knew better than waste my breath asking whereby he came by that nugget.

"Pity that," he surprised me, "you really remarked on his lack of balls?"

"Sure did."

"Outstanding."

"Long overdue," I replied suspiciously, "Do I detect the absence of your usual 'don't burn bridges' message? Why is that?"

"A messenger from our ex-boss just left here, he's asked Olga to come in for questioning tomorrow afternoon or he'll have her subpoenaed."

"Under what law?" I sneered, "Connecticut adopt the grand jury system since I resigned?"

"You never miss a thing, sober," he deadpanned, I shook my head at the barb, "it is a blatant scare tactic, and, thankfully, Olga knows better –".

"Having more balls than Nelson," I interrupted.

"I can attest that she is, thankfully, ball-less, but I appreciate the sentiment and that is certainly true. Will you go with her tomorrow?"

"Of course, as promised," I answered without hesitation.

"He'll not be pleased."

"Especially when I raise the specter of another anti-vice, upstanding servant of the people paying to dip his wick with frequency away from the loving confines of his home."

"I think that's a good start."

"He might even get a slogan out of it," I said wearily, "vote for Lord Nelson, Family Man, Abolitionist, Fornicator."

"That will appeal across a wide range of voters," Osgood agreed.

"He touches us all in his own special way, doesn't he?"

He nodded, "Reports are ready by the way, you headed straight there?"

"Going home to change first."

"Good idea," he said with superiority, "you smell of whiskey and stale sweat."

"Don't forget ale and horse," I pointed out.

"You drank ale at dawn?"

"Nah, just whiskey and coffee – but one of Phelps's horses farts barley."

"That is not surprising," he chuckled, "you might want to sober up before you go see Nelson."

"Good God, why?" I asked, horrified at the thought.

"Point taken," he said as I rose and headed for the hall.

"Don't hit him," he yelled behind me.

"Ah, you ruin everything," I yelled back, "I'll be back tonight!"

"I'll warn Bridget."

21

I went home, put on my dress uniform, strapped on the odious presentation sword (in the fervent hope I would indeed baptize it in blood that very afternoon); insisted that Charles don his dress uniform, and walked to the courthouse a few short blocks away. Charles and I were made stronger every step we took, accompanied as we were by our companion, moral superiority.

We entered the marbled halls of justice, Charles, white Chevron's against a dark blue background, positively glowing, carrying Osgood's report as if it were the recovered Holy Grail. The light sparkled off my maple leafs and Mexican medals, attracting the attention of assorted ex-colleagues who followed us as we strode forward, heels clicking on the marble floor.

In the purity of our virgin blue wool, we approached Nelson's chambers spiritually, physically, in every way, ready to do battle with – indeed, to prevail over – the forces of mindless bureaucracy. Modern Day St. Georges walking into the red taped cave of a government dragon.

To be immediately outflanked and defeated, for the fire breathing administrator was out for the day. Or so a carefully printed note informed us, along with a request to slide the report in question under the door. With no outward indication of my utter deflation I dropped the package on the floor and kicked it into the creature's lair.

I pivoted, and followed by my master sergeant, marched back down the long hall looking neither right nor left, still trailed by our followers.

"On me, gentlemen," I shouted when we reached the front doors, and pushed out into the sunlight. My announcement put a noticeable bounce in Phelps step as we descended the granite front steps, crossed Main Street. I unbuttoned my dress coat, loosened my sash without losing a step, all the while sensing Phelps' increasing hopefulness. I barged unwaveringly into the Municipal Café, not stopping until I assumed a stool at the bar.

I ordered a much needed beer while my newly recruited army filed in behind and flowed around me occupying the other barstools to thus maximize my generosity by proximity to the spigots.

The day called for alcohol induced stupor and I was intent on achieving it. I drank, watched the blinding sun trace an arc through the extravagant plate-glass window behind the bar, the first such in Hartford. Eventually it blinked out and was replaced by gas lights. Dinner fare was set out, free, salty indulgences designed, as we all knew but were helpless before, to make us thirstier.

Despite the setting sun and the coolness of the evening, the room became a cauldron. I was no longer pleased with my choice of attire, most unhappy about the impotent instrument hanging by my side. The haft dug into my hip and the shaft chafed my left leg. None of which was nearly as irritating as the constant need to slap, elbow, punch and otherwise fight off my brethren at the Bar as they attempted with annoying frequency to draw the sword. I knew better than I knew any other fact in life that attorneys as a rule should not be trusted, drunk or sober, with sharp instruments, so I defended it with adroit, consummate skill. It was testament to my diligence under extreme conditions that no one was impaled or beheaded during the course of the evening.

The crowd grew, the conversation was eclectic and multifaceted. The odds of the 21st, or any Connecticut troops for that matter, seeing combat before an early end of the conflict were set long. Those taking that action believed that the 21st would be called up for an enormous massing of federal troops for a Waterloo style winner-take-all battle that, of course, would lead to the South's capitulation.

I said nothing during those discussions despite near constant baiting, I just drank cool beer and thought their optimism naïve and dangerous, an opinion I kept to myself. Until, that is, an old acquaintance – in both senses of the word – left his seat at the end of the bar, waddled through the crowd, snuck up behind me and threw a grizzled arm around my shoulders.

"Hello, Henry," I said.

"My dear, dear William, my you have been a busy lad," Henry Ratchings responded in his famously melodious tenor. With his arm still heavy on my shoulder, he made some motion to the noisy rabble of barristers. They immediately cease their cackles. Henry, by virtue of so many, well, virtues was without doubt their leader in all things.

"So, Willie," he went on, the only Hartfordian to call me that and stand uncorrected. He used his powers to command the room, "what's your expert opinion on all of the Armageddon speculation floating around this room of cutthroats?"

"I think," I shifted my stool, his arm dropped away and I endeavored to make eye contact with the masses, "it's going to be so glorious and fun, the rest of the Bar should take a week or so off from suing one another and join us. I'll make room for them in the Twenty-first. Except for you, Henry," I yelled above the fray, "you head south, get ready to represent Jeff Davis in his treason trial . . . that'll seal his fate."

The room roared, my ale was topped off, a shot of, I soon found, fine whiskey, was thrust in my hand, Henry patted the back of my head in applause.

"I take it," he resumed when the noise ebbed, "you do not foresee a one- battle- takes- all, then? All humor aside."

"It's never one battle," I answered firmly, the alcohol assuring me I was dead right.

"The Hundred Days was settled by Waterloo, Willie," Henry offered as if submitting evidence.

"Ligny and Quatres Bras came first, and they were bloody and nasty in their own rights. And," I took a long pull of ale, smacked my lips with satisfaction, "Waterloo, to quote Wellington, was a near thing - the Hundred Days could've easily been the Hundred Weeks . . . or Months."

"I see your point, and you've almost swayed me - but I can't quite get there, Colonel," Henry answered good-naturedly, him at his most dangerous.

"You know, Henry," I cut in hurriedly as I knew from past, bitter experience he was rearming, "you could make this all go away in an instant."

"Could I?" He asked warily.

"Sure, just go down and orate to Beauregard's army, they'd throw down their arms in minutes – and you'd just be warming up."

"That would do it!"

"Send him to Richmond, Davis would deliver the government to him if only he'd stop! "

"No hanging just more of Henry."

"That's cruel and unusual."

"Just like Henry!"

That and more echoed through the room, another shot glass appeared in my hand and my depleted ale miraculously grew a new head. With a "Well done, Willie" whispered directly in my ear, Henry hit me on the back and tottered off to bother others, leaving me alone with my two new friends, the pint and shot glass. I thought 'another six hours or so of this and I just might be able to forget the dead, naked French girl'.

I sat in deep consultation with my two friends, listened to the conversation swirling around, though, and over, and slapped the occasional hand trying to grab the sword. Eventually, it seeped into my numbing senses that the conversation had moved from wild conjecture concerning Great Britain's interference in our family squabble to wild conjecture concerning the murders of several young women of Hartford.

The murders had been buried under the war news and had not been connected by any of our newspapers – busy as they were creating war news for a war in which almost no one was currently shooting at anyone. The members at the Bar, however, were very much more clever than prose creating newsmen and had been able to put together a few accurate details with some highly reasonable assumptions and small pieces of almost fact from various sources in varying levels of government and find a pattern.

To whit: the lawyers now drinking themselves to oblivion had interacted with cops, whores, pimps, thieves, reporters, doctors, coroners, bereaved next of kin, and comparing notes in a dozen different bars on a dozen different nights managed to, with the aid of high levels of alcohol, put together something close to the truth.

The truth being:

There was a madman/lunatic/monster
loose in
Hartford/Western Connecticut/the Valley;
Killing/dissecting/butchering/vivisecting/stabbing;
Women/girls/anyone;

And had thus far

accumulated/racked up/scored/gruesomely amassed;
Four/Five/Ten/Twenty/countless victims;
To date/so far/known but certain to climb.

The permutations were deliciously incalculable and they circled around the room at a dizzying rate. Eventually it came around to me, as did Henry, his vaguely bovine face more flushed, the only evidence he had continued to share the same bar since our last repartee.

Again he wrapped his arm around my shoulders, the room's roar noticeably dimmed - apparently the act of Henry tossing his arm over me had become the agreed-upon sign entertainment was in the offering.

With a grin that could keel small animals over dead, he announced to the room, "So, you're representing Madam Petrovsky, eh?"

I was proud of the fact I managed to stay seated on the suddenly not so steady stool; so total was my shock. I stared blankly at Henry while he gave me one of his famous 'of course I know' looks, oblivious to the murmur that ran through the room. My addled mind made a snap decision to handle the matter by ignoring it.

I succeeded for thirty blissful seconds. "Willie," he shamelessly asked in a louder voice, "what's Nelson want with the good Madam?"

"I can't discuss that," I blurted out, the answer of desperation for any attorney, "and how the fuck did you know?"

He grinned, showed his open palms as a magician before a trick, thrilled to have moved me to profanity, "I never reveal my sources."

I shook my head, it never ceased to amaze me how circumspect people became when they asked another to break a confidence.

"Well, Henry," I regrouped heroically – at least in my head, "it's not quite true, represent's too strong a word. Nelson invited her in for discussion, she asked me to escort her, for moral support. Hardly earth shaking."

A chorus of 'horseshit' and worse erupted. Henry stood on the lower rung of his stool, arms out, exhorting the crowd to new heights. He made a slashing motion, they went silent and he turned to me with a cocky grin.

"Oh, no," he mocked, his mouth forming an elongated 'O', "our best prosecutor representing our notorious, albeit charming and successful madam in a hearing before his former boss is hardly an everyday occurrence even in the Sodom that is Hartford."

The room exploded in laughter, absent the murders, our Puritanically inspired city juxtaposed with Sodom was too much for Hartford's bored citizens.

"Come on, Willie, my boy," Henry persisted, "she some kind of suspect? Wait a minute," he eyed me warily, gauging my intoxication before plunging in, "was a body found in her place?"

I ignored the second question, "Utterly ridiculous, Henry, impossible for her to be a suspect. If you knew the details, you'd know that," I put a hand in front of his face to stop him from interrupting, "they just need to discuss some . . . matters, that's all," I felt divine inspiration descend over me.

"They need to talk?" Henry bit, discounting his many losses to me.

"That's all", I gave him a little slack.

"What possible," Henry addressed the jury that was the bar, publicly taking the hook firmly, "matters could the Madam have in common with our chief state's attorney?"

The room echoed the question in many forms, some astoundingly, creatively profane. I patiently waited for it to subside.

"Her bill for one," I timed it perfectly at a lull. A lull that became a dead silence save some light tittering from those unsure if I was joking. I took full advantage of that uncertainty by going on.

"You see," I said conversationally, "we have a contractual dispute in its early stages, still, I think, reconcilable with a modicum of negotiation."

"A contract?" Henry asked, "What kind of contract?"

"Just a normal, everyday contract," I replied, "one that started with an offer, gratefully accepted I am told, followed by long, long bouts of climatic consideration," I smiled treacherously.

"Our chief state's attorney and our chief state's madam," Henry announced, "and sex and money – fantastic!"

"I never said anything about sex, Henry," I protested loudly.

"William!" Henry screeched, "What the hell else could have been going on?" His peers yelled agreement.

"You got it all wrong!" I yelled back, "I'll tell you exactly what services were provided if you'll quiet down."

That got them where they lived in their dirty little hearts, "The woman in question – the exquisite woman in question – has, indeed, made a living in the extensive study of the carnality of others – "

Hoots and hollers of agreement filled the confines of the Municipal.

"But!" I had to scream over them, "But! As a result of her years of study she is an acknowledged expert in a field of human endeavor little spoken of in polite company – knowledge that Nelson desperately desired, being a professional of sorts himself. Madam Petrovsky has, in fact, been providing lessons."

The room was a riot of noise, Henry yelled over it, "Lessons in what, Willie?"

"Why, Nelson's raison d'être, Henry," I shouted to rapt attention from all, "how best to fuck his fellow man."

22

I awoke in luxury. Unexpected luxury with a very much unexpected warmth pressed against my left side. I would have opened my eyes and surveyed my surroundings except I had temporarily forgotten how to do so. Besides, it would have taken far too much effort.

I suspected where I was but had no memory or empirical proof of it. I was on my back, nude, in a deep bed, under silk sheets and downy comforter. My head hurt, my mouth was a desert, but I was as comfortable as I was going to get with a head that hurt as much as mine and made no immediate plans to move. Breathing slowly seemed aspiration enough.

All that went by the board when the warm form moved in a way that begged for response of some kind.

"You're awake," a soft voice whispered in my ear. An equally soft hand found the erection I did know I had. Or had the soft hand caused it? I decided then and there it was a philosophical question for later.

Indeed, further contemplation as to what came first, the erection or the hand, was truncated when about 120 pounds of soft flesh slithered on top of me and a warm, wet sensation descended over the phallus in question and began slow, steady gyrations.

I had yet to open my eyes, decided not to, it would only ruin the effect. That decision was further reinforced when a warm wet tongue broke the drought that was my mouth. The long kiss finally broke off, two arms clasped under my neck, hair fanned over my face. The slow gyrations quickened and soft, short, pants filled my ear. My hands found a pair of silk-smooth hips and held on.

"This sure as hell better be you, Bridget," I groaned lowly. The reply was a giggle and rolling of hips and a faster, more grinding rhythm. A nipple was pressed into my mouth, hands grasped my shoulders.

"Good... Morning... William," her breathless answer, precisely at the moment I pushed down on her hips, she held me like a vise, released, held again, and I spasmed into her. A few gentle thrusts later, her hair over my face again, she released me and lay atop.

"Feel better?" She breathed into my ear.

"God, yes," I managed gasped back, "although I don't recall having felt much of anything."

She pulled her head up, "You don't remember last night at all, do you?"

"Oh," I answered cleverly, opened my eyes, stared directly her astoundingly beautiful eyes while they appraised me. I was so taken with the sight it took minutes before I became aware of the stabbing pain in my head and groaned.

"What is it?" She purred.

"You're so beautiful it hurts," I dug out of somewhere.

"Please," she rolled her eyes, "from what I saw last night you're lucky your head's still attached," she rolled off and nestled against my chest.

"That bad?" I groaned rhetorically.

"If you call the inability to walk or speak with anything approaching coherence bad, then yes."

"Shit."

"Exactly."

"How'd I get here?"

"Charles brought you. Apparently he felt that the sight of a fully uniformed lieutenant colonel in the Union Army arm in arm with a short, fat, civil attorney arm singing songs of rebellion – especially in present circumstances – was too much."

"It was a revolutionary war song, for Christ's sakes," I muttered as a glimmer returned to me.

"Fine," her eyes flicked up again, "anyway, he exercised his discretion and extracted you before further embarrassment could be suffered."

"Charlie exercised discretion?"

"I understand there's a first time for everything."

"Were we singing well?"

"That is currently unreported."

"Charlie was sober enough to drag me in here?"

"He had help," she may have tsked.

"Who?"

"Your friend," she said, as if I had only one and it was self-explanatory, "he half carried you up the walk last night while Charlie gave instructions. Tall, good-looking, strong enough to move a drunk you easily enough. Very charming, actually."

"Christ, I'm surprised you didn't have me thrown in the rosebushes while you jumped into bed with him."

"It was a consideration."

"Sure. You get his name?"

"No, and I remember names," she stared at me accusingly, "so I suppose it wasn't offered."

We lay together in silence for what could have been five minutes or five hours. I had no way of knowing. I was in and out of a series of half-sleeps and almost dreams. I awoke, finally and perhaps permanently, to Bridget's fingers gently stroking the underside of my penis, not without some result.

Her fingertips increased the pressure in direct proportion to my now readily evident response. I could feel her smile against my chest.

"You know, William," she said in a sleepy–hoarse voice that added to my response, "those were wonderful things you said to your friend about me."

"Hmmm-mmm," I answered, my penis reaching the point where it would respond to the merest stimulus, "what?"

"He told me some of lovely things you told him about us," she stopped stroking and gripped me gently – as what she had just said sunk through my lust sodden hangover. My penis retreated from her hand like a frightened turtle into its shell and I sat bolt upright, practically knocking Bridget aside, sending stabbing pain through the back of my skull.

"What was that?" I unintentionally yelled.

"William!" She snapped back.

"I'm sorry," I said absently, realizing she had most likely never encountered such actions under similar circumstances, "this man who never introduced himself said he knew about you . . . us?"

Bridget sat up on her knees and leveled me with a cool gaze. I briefly forgot my anxiety while I took in the vision that was she: reddish blond hair cascading over shoulders ending just above perfect round curved pink-tipped breasts; demure bellybutton; slim milky white waist flaring out to those amazing hips; reddish tinged vee between her legs just visible. The epitome of eroticism, she knew it well and wielded it better.

"Yes, William," she held my eyes while I tried to let her by not roaming all over her perfect form, "he knew all about us," she shook her head slowly, got it immediately, "you've never mentioned me to anybody have you?"

"Not a soul, Bridget," I answered, struck by her supple intelligence and encouraged by the tone of her voice, lacking as it did recrimination or disappointment.

"That's disconcerting," she summarized, tersely.

"Yes," I agreed, proud to be staring into her wise eyes, "extraordinarily disconcerting."

"I'm sure there's probably some rational explanation," she announced, unmoving.

"Undoubtedly," I agreed.

"You don't believe that for a moment. Do you?" Her eyes sparkled as they bored through me.

"Not really, no," I admitted.

"Why is that, I wonder?"

"It's . . . too curious, that's all," that sounded lame even to me.

"I think it would be curious for most people, at worst," she straightened her shoulders, her breasts swayed, "but to get the reaction you just had, well," her legs parted ever so slightly, "that's the reaction of someone with a reason to fear something," she finished with a dazzling smile, and waited for me to come apart.

"Who taught you how to interrogate?" I asked without humor.

"I don't know what you mean," she lied with an even more dazzling smile, moved her knees apart another inch, noticed me noticing and gave a look of 'oh-my-I-am-an-immodest-one-aren't-I?' that almost killed me on the spot.

"That," I somehow found the strength to speak, "is unfair."

"Isn't it?" She smiled and moved her upper body forward, left nipple brushing my arm, "You have anything you want to tell me?"

I decided to be almost honest, "I can't talk about it, Bridget, not yet."

"I didn't take you for one to speak in empty clichés."

"That doesn't change the fact I can't talk about this now – shit, I don't even know if there's really a problem," I replied, tired and feeling it.

"It's serious, else you wouldn't be reacting like this," she pointed out with something akin to real concern – enough to touch me.

"Perhaps," I admitted, "I'm probably overreacting – but I need to talk to Charles and Osgood," sincerely regretting uttering that statement under those circumstances.

Bridget pivoted off the bed, a flash of white-pink flesh covered in an instant by a clinging robe, "You're clothes are being cleaned," she answered, no discernible change in her voice, "I'll have a bath drawn for you, I'm sure Osgood will find you at breakfast."

"Thank you," I said to her back, having already been dismissed. She walked across the room, doing things to the robe that were illegal in my hometown, reached into a closet, threw me a cotton robe destined to do nothing for my image.

She stood across the room, arms crossed, watching me with curiosity as I donned the robe, "I understand, William," she said evenly, sporting a lopsided smile, "your reticence, your . . .evasiveness . . . But I dearly hope you're smart enough to share with someone, soon, you'll feel better," she opened the door, the robe slipped open revealing a perfect leg, "I'm available anytime, know that . . . and I'm an excellent listener."

She slipped through the door and was gone. I believe, even now, that had she waited another moment, I would have told her everything.

23

I walked down the hallway in something resembling a straight line, got to the bathroom without stumbling or knocking over any of the lamps or equally ornate objects littering the many tables along the way. My second accomplishment of the day.

Soon, I was lowering myself into a scalding hot tub. I welcomed it initially as self-immolating atonement for my gross stupidities over the past twenty-four hours, later for its relaxing, soothing qualities.

I settled into the caldron immersed to my neck, dozed, and was at the point where breathing no longer brought pain when the door opened and Olga strode in, softly closing the door behind her.

Without a word she perched on a chest next to me, high enough to have a probably not flattering view of the male anatomy.

"William, William, William," she sighed to my instant chagrin – in my almost thirty-five years of experience with women of every ilk the one (and only) thing I knew with certainty was that when they said your name more than once you were not going to enjoy what followed.

"Olga," I answered warily after briefly considering intoning her name three times – that, however would have been playing a game in which I was not only ill equipped to play, I did not even know its objectives.

"You, dear, had quite a night."

"Morning, too."

She cringed, frowned, and pursed her lips, a hideously effective facial combination that dripped disappointment.

"There a problem?" I asked with certainty, wondering in sudden pique if it were ever allowable for a man to get drunk, have sex, and not be forced to confront a problem upon rising.

She answered both questions by making an obvious show of looking from my face down the length of my half and not enough submerged body and back with no discernable change of expression – which surely said enough.

"What the hell did you do, William?"

"I have no idea, Olga," I went with honesty, "why do you ask?" Anticipating a recitation of horrific drunken acts, I sunk deeper into the tub.

"All I know, William, is that my confidences to you have been somehow betrayed as – well, damn it, look!" She commanded and threw a slightly soggy newspaper at me. I was amazed I had the reflexes to snatch it before it hit water.

I opened it where it had been folded, the *Courant*'s early edition, the source of Olga's irritation was boxed off in the lower left hand corner.

LT. COL. HANLIN AND THE MADAM

HARTFORD (Staff) A source close to this paper reports that the 21st's Lt. Col. Hanlin, late of the Chief's State's Attorney's Office, has agreed to represent our charming, albeit notorious Madam Olga Petrovsky in a hearing before Chief State's Attorney Lord Nelson at 2 o'clock this afternoon, subject matter unknown.

We are reminded, however, of Lord Nelson's campaign promises of long standing to root out our many houses of ill-repute, even those reserved for the elite, and clean our city of this blight on our morality.

Look in this space in this evening's edition for details on this interesting development.

In the few seconds it took to read the column a hundred thoughts hurried through my already sore head. To hide whatever the hell it was I was feeling, I perused another fold of the paper – it was my bath, after all – was momentarily riveted by:

MCCLELLAND ROUTS REBEL HORDE
'The Young Napoleon' reports "Our success is
complete, succession is killed in this county."

RICH MOUNTAIN, VIRGINIA July 13 Major
Gen'l G. McClelland's forces continued the
energetic movements and battlefield successes that
have elicited great enthusiasm from those who care
about our great cause in capturing a rebel army
under Col. John Pegram, CSA, before Rich
Mountain this morning. Our young, ever gallant
Maj —

"William!" Olga's voice," I am speaking to you."

"Sorry, Olga, I was just wondering if this McClelland is –"

The paper was torn from my hand and dispersed to the corners
of the room, "Damn it, William, pay attention," said in a voice
that did not invite me to finish my thought.

"How," she went on when I made eye contact, "did this get
out? Anything to do with your blatherings and singing last night?"

"I take it you don't covet publicity," I said facetiously.

"Don't be an ass," her delicate response, "what happened?"

"Damn if I know, it was out by the time I got to the Municipal
last night – if Henry Ratchings knew about it, everybody soon
knew about it as well. Fucking town crier of the Bar."

"Would you say it is a puzzle, then?"

"Sure," I was happy to agree.

"Then I am at a loss," she reached into the folds of her dress,
her fine, white, blue-veined hand stretched over the tub and she
attempted to hand over an envelope addressed to her in flowing
penmanship – Nelson's penmanship.

I was clean, therefore I made no effort to take it from her lest
I require another bath. Beside, in a flash of intuition I knew its
contents.

"He cancelled the meeting," I said decisively.

"He, cancelled our meeting," she echoed with a sidelong look,
"with regrets, no reschedule, sorry for the inconvenience."

By the time she finished I was chuckling hard enough to churn the water.

"I do not really see the humor in all this, William," she said in a tone that was solid proof of said lack of mirth, "I think he will just wait for you to be called up and start this all over again."

"Never, Olga," still chuckling, searching for a way out of the tepid tub, now with a thin scum across the surface. The towel, however, was unhelpfully hung a good five feet directly behind Olga. I was nude, clean, amused and trapped.

"How can you say that?" she demanded, annoyed with being left out of the joke.

"Olga, he will never meet with you. Never – war, peace, feast, famine . . . never."

"Again," she was fast losing patience, "why?"

"At some point last night I may have told the bar – small and capital b – that you were meeting with my former boss to resolve some kind of contractual matter."

Her face brightened considerably, "You may have?"

"Did," I admitted, "with the proviso there was some kind of issue of compensation for services rendered."

Her turn to chuckle – she did it far better than me, "He can never be seen with me again."

"I would think not."

"Excellent," she stood, bent over the tub and kissed me gently on the lips, "thank you, William, Cook is up and ready to get you something – try to eat, Dear, you look like death."

24

A short while later I was sitting in Olga's kitchen attempting to sip coffee that was still aboil, staring at an untouched plate of eggs garnished with virgin toast when the door exploded open and Charles fell in the room, eyes wildly looking about.

"Oh, sweet Jaysus, thank the motherfuckin' Almighty," he blasphemed grotesquely upon spying me in the corner. His body sagged in obvious relief as he slouched toward me. He pulled out a chair, dropped the dead weight of his body into it, groaned a groan that rattled my teeth.

He was a mess, eyes crimson and set deep in cardinal-red rimmed sockets. He had started to shave, took off one side of his upper lip and two zig-zagging rows down his left cheek before he wandered away from the mirror. Worry was etched in every crevice of his face. I had known him long enough to know that that look of worry was for himself.

"I thought I'da lost you," he explained breathlessly, "I been lookin' for you everywhere. Turned the whole house upside down, even checked the stables – "

"I find that a little insulting," I interjected with feeling.

"Sorry, I was desperate, hadn't no idea where I left you."

"Here, Charles, you left me here," I explained with gentleness.

"Yeah, I know tha' now – afta' I checked the Municipal and …"

"And what, you thought I was still there frozen petrified on the barstool?"

"Somethin' like that," he said in complete seriousness, "I just plain forgot where I left you and I was worried, Boss, you don't never get drunk like that . . . never," he suddenly noticed my plate, raised an eyebrow, I pushed it over to him with a 'you're-a-better-drunk-than-I-if-you-can-eat-that' look.

I knew the answer, but asked nevertheless, "you don't remember a damn thing about last night, do you?"

He took an enormous bite of egg, topped it with half a slice of toast, chewed loudly and ineffectively, and looked at me in misery.

"Relax, Charles," I took pity on the human-like creature, "I'm fine and I have you to thank for getting me here."

"Sorry I forgot, boss."

"You recall dropping me off here at all?"

"Not 'xactly.".

"Anything at all, anything you can remember, might be important."

"The girl," he brightened, "God, what a looker, real concerned about you too, my God was she a pretty 'un. I tell you, Boss, I –"

"That was Bridget, Charles, can you manage to get past her looks and remember small details, like the man who helped carry me in?"

"Who?"

"That answers that."

He shook his head until he looked like he might get seasick, "Couldn't tell you, may 'ave been someone with us, might've not."

"Fine, Charles have some coffee," I poured him a cup, he eyed it warily, eventually reached across the table, pulled the sugar bowl close to him and shoveled spoonful after spoonful into the fast congealing black liquid.

"If you had asked I would've just poured some coffee into the sugar bowl," I offered, "what's the last thing you remember from last night not named Bridget?"

"From the bar?" He asked, sipping the coffee tinged sugar.

"Christ, Charles," I snapped, "I thought you were a professional in these matters, doesn't this happen to you all the time?"

"Shit, boss, I drink at night, I don't normally start at breakfast, go all day and all night. Never," he looked at me, smiled wickedly, "never occurred to me to try, but then I didn't go to law school," he laughed himself silly.

"Nicely done," I sighed, "but, if you don't mind, could you try to concentrate one moment – one moment – and help me. I dearly need to know what your last memory is."

"You and Henry, arm in arm singing some loopy song."

"That's it?"

"Yeah."

"Know what song?"

"Nah, everybody be talking about Nelson and the Madam – helluva shot by the way," I waved thanks. He paused, fingers to lips.

"Except?" I asked cautiously.

"Well," he considered carefully, "I seem ta' remember a tall gent, very well-dressed, leanin' against the bar, drinking something real slow, kinda' just smiling. I think you was amusin' him to no end - you sure as shit was amusin' me," he mistook my serious look for opprobrium and added, "beggin' your pardon."

"Don't," I waived him off again.

"You think he's the same that helped me drag you in here?"

"No idea," I lied, "just trying to piece the night together."

"Well you're looking the wrong way for help here, that's what I know."

"Not like I was any more observant."

"I'll say amen to that, if you had to rely on me getting you home. Didn't tha' lovely lass notice anything?"

"Too concerned with me and I'm guessing he never came out of the shadows, and with her being under the gaslight . . ." I finished with a shrug.

"Guess he didn't want to be seen," Charles said with the utter lack of guile only the truly innocent could summon.

"Yes."

"Oh," light dawned in those red orifices, "that may be a problem," I nodded as more came to him, "you want to be talking to Osgood, then."

"I do, I admitted, "the whole evening was so . . . careless of me," I said with a grin that was eagerly returned.

"Understandable, that was a sight, not anyone wants to think about sober for too long, Boss, poor girl."

I was about to answer when the door swung open, hard, and Osgood, half dressed, fired into the room. He acknowledged Charles with a perfunctory nod while his coal-black eyes sought to destroy me.

"Rebel songs, why don't you just paint a goddamn bull's-eye on your back?" He bit off and spit out each syllable in a level but biting tone that really did not invite reply.

"Good morning, Osgood," I said anyway, trying to sound cheerful. The look that clouded his face said I was singularly unsuccessful, "they were Revolutionary War songs, for Christ's sakes, nothing to worry about."

A minute measure of relief manifested itself, briefly, before he replied, "I did not mean to imply you are a child incapable of control. Although early returns on your evening clearly support that hypothesis."

"Wasn't all that bad," I dramatically underemphasized.

"Course it was, had to be," he snapped back without delay, "because you are, and always have been, a bad drunk."

"I can hold my liquor well, just not after sixteen hours or so," I answered defensively.

"No, that does not matter. You can drink forever and manage to not be ugly, sloppy, dangerous, stupid or disgusting – you are none of that," he let that hang in the air, I was smart enough to take no comfort in any of it, especially as he exchanged nasty grins with Phelps, "but when you drink, you think everyone is your friend. Worse yet, you need everyone to be your friend."

"Wait a –"

"Not that you are all that different sober, most of the time. 'Need to be liked', it will be on your fucking tombstone."

"You would think you'd wake up in a better mood in these surroundings," I observed dryly, accurately.

"I'll admit you are a funny drunk, there's your compliment of the week."

"And you were that, Boss, highly entertainin'," Charles hurried to add.

"Thank you," I said out of reflex, "what about our mystery man?"

"I would guess," Osgood replied immediately in a manner indicating he had thought much about the answer already, "by your presence among us this morning, considering your helplessness last night, and the fact that you were safely delivered here to get laid, there was obviously no threat."

"It's not one of our friends."

"'Course not."

"Else, I'd —"

"Your fool drunk ass would be in a ditch with a second mouth with your neck is," he said with a chilling lack of emotion.

"That's what I thought, plus it's been so long —"

"Never too long for them."

"You sound somewhat wistful saying that," I observed.

"It would relieve me of my one remaining burden in life," he said with a grin, "of course, you have managed to bind me up in this Union Army thing, but I could probably find a way out."

"And onto a pirate ship where you belong," I added, "you'd miss me."

"I would dearly like to have the chance to discover that on my own."

"Funny," I commented without mirth, "you know I'd write it off to a Good Samaritan if it wasn't for his remarks to Bridget."

"I know you well enough to know you have not mentioned her to anyone not in this room."

"Precisely," I announced, "and Bridget and Olga would never —"

"Their profession requires a level of discretion not seen in many others, and even less utilized," as if an afterthought he went on, "and Bridget is far too intelligent to be tricked to disclosure."

"I know that."

"You know she is far smarter than you as well, right?"

"I've gathered."

"Best to remember that," he looked up toward the ceiling, sighed and continued, "so, it was not a Samaritan nor was it anyone who wished you harm."

"Who went out of his way to let me know he knows something about me."

"Obviously."

"Well," I stretched, ostensibly to indicate my nonchalance while I disposed of my tension, "none of this is at all reassuring."

"You want reassurance, try not getting blind fucking drunk."

"Noted," I said absently, began to run permutations through

my still sluggish mind.

"Maybe it's just someone wants to be your friend, Boss?" Charles said, chewing his coffee.

"Charlie," Osgood seemed to startle at his sudden participation, "that's –"

"Not entirely crazy," I finished, softly, "not ridiculous at all," I repeated, dwelling on the placement of the French girl. The ideas that were coming could probably only have been formed as a result of my hung over, post coital state. But come they did, weaving a bizarre logic.

I became aware Osgood and Phelps were both staring, grinned in return.

"You just put something together," Osgood stated flatly.

"Perhaps."

"You going to share or you just going to sit there smiling like the insufferable prick you are?"

"Personal insults are the last refuge of the unimaginative," I replied insufferably.

"And your insults?"

"I think of them more as bon mots."

"Who's unimaginative now?" He asked with the look he would have sported had he ever won a chess game, "What do you have, William?"

"I think it's our man."

"What man?" He snapped.

"Our killer, perhaps, is moving beyond notes."

Silence descended the kitchen while they considered my theory.

"Your old apartment was no coincidence," Osgood stated rather than asked.

"You believe in coincidence?"

"You know I do not."

"Then what were the odds at that being a random event?"

"Large."

"And when combined with this morning's events?"

"Astronomical."

"Exactly, I think our killer desires a relationship of some sort with us," I stated carefully for it still sounded ridiculous.

"Not us, William," Osgood's black eyes sparkled, "you. He knows who you are sleeping with and where you drink – hell, he probably knew your schedule yesterday."

"You're embracing this theory of mine rather enthusiastically, Osgood."

"I'm enthusiastic about my lack of involvement in it," he chuckled, "and my relief that our killer has fixated upon you rather than myself."

"There were two of us there last night," I pointed out, "maybe he's fixated on Charles."

"What!" Charles started, almost spilling his coffeed sludge.

"Relax, Charlie," Osgood intervened, "if he was tailing you he'd be an incurable alcoholic by now incapable of thought, never mind the ability to commit murder."

"Thank God for that," a relieved Charles sighed

25

I returned to Bridget's rooms happy that I had no duties that day, planning, with her cooperation, to find things to do on her soft, wide bed. The first sign my spirits were going to be crushed in that regard was in front of me when I opened the door: my boots were polished and sitting in front of an overstuffed chair.

The second was the muffled, melodious voice that crept out from under the comforter, "I hope you're here for the boots because I'm about to get up and I've things to do."

"I had thoughts –"

"Erase them."

"That has a nasty edge of finality about it."

"You're very perceptive man," she responded. The comforter began to move, I sat heavily into a chair so plush it threatened to consume me.

I leaned over with effort to pick up a gleaming boot, when I straightened, I saw Bridget sit up, her legs dangling over the side of the bed, feet not quite touching the floor, breasts to me in saliva inducing profile.

I forgot the boot in my hand and watched her while she stood and walked to the dresser. I was mesmerized by the movements of her flesh, soft jiggle of her upright breasts, clearly defined muscles of her upper legs leading to the tight yet soft curves of her buttocks, even the back of her knees. She strolled through the light streaming through the curtains, her pubic hair reflecting it in a dazzling display of red hues that brought to mind all manner of trite and therefore completely inadequate metaphors.

When she reached her dresser she glanced at me as if just noticing my presence. I continued to sit, mouth agape, frozen with pathetic boot in hand. She registered my gape and gave me the look that only a woman can give a man of short acquaintance, the

'I know you so much better than you know yourself' glance that was as unnerving as it was correct.

"I'm getting dressed, William," she finally acknowledged my attentions.

"So there's no chance of coming over here to help me with my boots?" I thought I owed it to myself and mankind to give it a try. In response, to a flip of my heart, she turned and faced me in overpowering nude glory.

"You mean," a mischievous lilt was in her voice, I'm sure it was echoed in her eyes, but I would not have noticed, "walk over, slide the boot out of your hand, turn around, straddle your leg and begin working the boot over your foot, my box and ass accidentally rubbing against your leg, my tits swaying with each tug and thrust as I struggle to pull the booth on.

"I find it's too hard, so I ask you," she dropped her voice an octave, "to hold my hips. Of course, I have to widen my legs a bit further for better balance, and I'll have to move more vigorously . . . up and down, side to side. Is that what you meant, William?"

"Yes," barely escaped my throat past a gulp and sudden dryness of mouth, "'tas 'boud id."

"Sorry, I really have to get dressed now, you'll just have to think about that all day – at least."

"That's just cruel."

"No, cruelty would be extra."

"But I don't pay all," I pointed out.

"My oversight," she retorted, reached into a drawer, pulled out a dazzling white pair of drawers and, with what could only be described as exquisite grace, put them on. They covered her to the bellybutton.

"I, ah, don't know how these, ah, things go," I started, recognizing that I was fumbling and well out of my depth, "I have certain feelings –"

"You think I fuck like that for money?" She asked, amused, "I suppose the real question, for you, is do I fuck for money period?"

"I don't know what your relationship with Olga or this house is," I defended myself, poorly. She smiled in return, reached into a drawer and withdrew a pair of silk stockings, sat on the edge of the bed and began to roll one up her calf, silk on silk.

"Olga and I are partners, dear William," she finished one stocking, started the other, "she's the managing partner, to be sure, but partners we are, dear friends as well. And we both care for our lost boy of a Colonel . . . and, my dear, you are lost."

"Bridget –"

"Don't, William," she caught and held my eyes, "we don't need to discuss that now," a dazzlingly unreadable smile broke across her face, "tell you what, as soon as I get some clothes on I'll show you what I do for money, aside from keeping the books."

"Bridget –"

"It's fine, William, I'm with you because I care for you and I suppose living here has stripped away certain moral concerns —"

"Thank God for that!" I exclaimed with evangelical fervor. She laughed long and deep, breasts quivering, "I care for you as well. Bridget but –"

"Say no more, William," she smiled an altogether different smile, "not today," she picked up a corset.

"That looks medieval," I remarked to an indulgent smirk.

"Corsets are the last remnants of the Auto de Fey," she stated without expression and wrestled her breasts into the restrictive armor of the corset.

"Auto de Fey?" I asked with more incredulity than intended.

"It refers to the Inquisition," she said offhandedly.

"I don't mean to insult you in any way, Bridget, but –"

"Mount Holyoke, William," she answered the coming question.

"Of course," I said without inflection.

"You're not surprised?"

"No."

"Why not, considering?" She waved an erotically naked arm in the general vicinity of the rest of the brothel.

"Because you're so damn intelligent –"

"And you're one of those for whom the existence of intelligence is bestowed by the existence of a diploma."

"You make me sound –"

"Like the intellectual snob you are," she sweetly finished. Accurately.

"I'm not sure that's fair, Bridget."

290

"Please!" She dismissed it, "I find it somewhat surprising, since your undergraduate school is hardly famous for its liberal arts courses, unless, of course, there's more to your curriculum vitae?"

So much had happened over the past months that the juxtaposition of a beautiful, half nude woman using that term in a brothel did not even cause me to blink.

Instead, I evenly replied, "Are you referring to West Point or my two years at Harvard" I smiled back.

"I should have guessed," she sighed.

"Well, we are all blinded by our preconceptions," I helpfully offered.

"I suppose I owe you an apology."

"I can think of a host of ways for you to effectuate a reconciliation," I said lecherously.

"I have to go," she faced me and volleyed the full force of one of her smiles, "but thank you for the offer," she slinked toward me while I took in her loveliness: white silk stockings, corset halfway up her breasts, squeezing and lifting them, at once offering and protecting.

She reached me, put her hands on my shoulders and straddled me. Her knees gripped my hips, her ass pushed down on my crotch. She moved her hands, clasped them behind my head, bent over and kissed me, hard, our tongues touched electrifyingly.

Abruptly, she sat up straight, pulled my head into her full décolletage and, with her mouth pressed against my ear, said slowly, "How do you like this, William?"

I could do no more than nod. She held my head against her breasts with one hand while the other worked its way down my chest, over my stomach to my maddeningly restrictive, too thick pants. She rubbed, pinched and pushed down my by now prominent, albeit constricted, erection.

She whispered in a voice that would've earned the giblet in early New England, "you see, dear, everything I've done since you came back and watched me dress is all I ever have to do with prim and proper Yankees."

She gave my penis a last squeeze and stood, "I'd show you the rest but you don't want to squish around in messy pants the rest of the day. Do you?"

She shook her head at the foolishness and feebleness of man and walked away, "For this, William, dear," she said over her shoulder, "a quick show, the threat of sex, and quick fingering over a buttoned groin - not needed half the time, by the way – I make far, far more than you do protecting the community from the likes of us."

The lesson ended, she went back to dressing while I breathed rapidly in short bursts to ward off any impending squishiness.

"You are a siren," I exhaled.

She shook her head, "I'm Circe, silly man."

"Marry me," was out before I knew it.

"I think I just told you, you could not afford me," her eyes danced.

"Oh, but I could," I answered to her laughter.

26

I left Olga's in late morning, walked to the rig under threatening skies. A still bleary Charles drove while continuously throwing sly looks my way, a look that did not suit him. I knew he was hiding something and I knew that no amount of cajoling or threats would dislodge it. It merely added to the frustration of the last hours.

Late that afternoon the reason for his self-satisfaction was revealed when he escorted a dazzling Bridget to my sitting room, the two exchanging conspiratorial glances. *Bleak House* suffered yet another rejection.

Bridget stayed the next two days, two days of pouring rain that kept us happily housebound. My siren had clearly enchanted Phelps, he bustled about her like a maiden aunt the bride at a favorite niece's wedding.

Bridget was spirited away by Phelps just after dawn on Thursday, July 18th. The very morning the early papers reported the first solid war news in weeks: McDowell had moved into Virginia toward Beauregard and the showdown fight to end the war. McDowell had little choice, his army was largely made up of state militias called up for three months. All due to expire in a week. The men we were training to replace for the next three years. If we were still needed.

Osgood arrived at the house at 10 o'clock brandishing the *Hartford Courant*, surprised to find Seth, Wycroft and Shay already there, drinking coffee, eating cake, the plates resting on laps covered with copies of the morning news.

"I see you've all seen the paper," he announced to a batch of grins all around. He helped himself to the coffee and joined the others. As he walked by my chair he picked up the like-new *Bleak House* and flipped to the bookmark, "five pages in six days, impressive."

"I've been busy," I said, immediately regretting it.

"So I've heard, although what could be better than a good book?"

"Perhaps he spent much time in bed," Arnold offered, "catching up."

"I'd rather think he spent the time riding," Wycroft added.

"Knowing the good Colonel," Shay said with a degree of maliciousness, "coordinated as he is he managed to combine the two."

I endured the great hilarity that followed without expression, "Very humorous," I said without a shred of humor, "one must normally consort with ten-year-olds to hear this level of sophistication."

A chorus of hisses and boos descended around me, I studiously ignored them.

"I take it," I started when the room quieted, "that everyone wants to discuss the news – I say that because you were each kind enough to come with your own papers."

"We thought you were too busy to see the latest war news," Osgood said with a leer that would have set everyone off again, if not for the fact he had mentioned the elephant in the room.

"McDowell's moving we're not there," I concisely summarized, "see, I'm aware of the events of my time."

"That's great, William," Arnold intoned with a shake of his head, "and while we all admire your grasp of current affairs, I think we are most concerned with how this affects us."

"Afraid we're gonna' miss getting shot at?" I asked with a lightness I did not feel.

"Yes… and, well, no," he sputtered, uncomfortable with the inherent implications, "shit, William, I don't know what to think. We've worked so hard and it's going off without us."

The others nodded, except Shay who stared at me with an unreadable expression.

"First thing we have to do," I said with consideration, "is be prepared to move out in a flash if anything goes wrong down around Centreville or wherever they end up fighting this thing."

"I'll see to it immediately," Wycroft answered earnestly, "you think McDowell can lose?"

"I don't know," I answered honestly, "two armies full of militias with two months training fighting one another – Christ, they could both run away after the first volley."

"It would be interesting to see," Osgood mused aloud.

"I'm sure," I said absently, "I guess we'll hear soon, at least."

"But what if it's a crushing Union victory?" Seth asked the question everyone was thinking.

"That would be fantastic," I replied at once.

"Great," Osgood.

"Wonderful," Wycroft.

"Huzzah," Shay.

"And us?" Seth persisted, "our preparations for naught?"

"I suppose," I deigned to answer, "we'll have the knowledge and satisfaction of a job well done, we did a tremendous job readying this Regiment. And," I made a concerted effort to catch everyone's eye in turn, "we were ready for anything. That's worth something, isn't it?"

"Oh yes," Wycroft.

"Sure," Osgood.

"Amen," Shay.

"Uh-huh," Arnold.

"A Union victory, without us getting shot at, I can live with that. Happily," I went on, "of course, I may have somewhat prematurely retired from my current position."

"And burnt your bridges," Osgood added.

"More like blew them up, thank you for pointing that out. But, like I said, I can live with it."

"Easily," Shay.

"Of course," Osgood.

"As can I," Wycroft.

This time, however, a further echo was not forthcoming from the Colonel in the corner. As one our heads swiveled toward Seth. He sat unmoving, the fingers of one hand massaging his temple, the other hand nervously twirled his coffee cup. He did not look up in recognition of the sudden silence.

"You have a diverging opinion, Colonel?" I asked, gently.

"God forgive me," he started, strange smile playing across lips,

"I will, of course, give Thanksgiving for a quick victory and a short war, but... but, I have to be honest with you all. A strong, strong part of me needs to be part of this. I fear I will wonder the rest of my life at what might have been."

That hung in the air, almost tangible in shape. I could tell at once the others agreed, even Osgood. Perhaps I did as well, although I was loath to admit it.

"I think it important to know," Osgood walked into the breach, "that you were and are ready to lead. And if and when you do, or would have, it will be with great integrity, as we can all attest."

"Thank you," Arnold said with affection, "but this is really a ridiculous discussion, isn't it?" He laughed softly, "five intelligent men sitting over coffee and cakes in a fine home in Hartford depressed because we might not get a chance to go to war."

"We are pathetic," Shay opined.

"Stupid," Osgood.

"Sad, really," Wycroft.

"Perhaps we need hobbies," I observed.

"I think," Wycroft intoned with a measure of solemnity, "it's really just wanting to be a part of something large, world shaking, historic, even if only a small part. It appeals to our sense of immortality – we all want to leave something behind."

"Our number crunching supply genius has a previously undisclosed philosophical bent," I marveled, "and I think I speak for all when I say, very well said indeed, Sir."

'Here, here's' went around my sitting room while our usually reticent quartermaster put a defensive hand up and reddened.

"Shay's father was at Waterloo," I went on, "Seth's great uncle was the hero of the Bemis Heights," Seth nodded gratefully, "my mother's family was represented at Bunker Hill, Trenton, Princeton. They all left something tangible, I think."

"My father was at Trafalgar," Osgood blurted out of nowhere.

"I didn't know you had a father," shot out of me without thought, "In all the time I've known you you've never mentioned him."

"You never asked," he replied with unassailable logic, "my father was on the *Indefatigable* under Collingwood. Commander, believe it or not, in command of the second gun deck. Lost a hand.

"Commander Ransom Osgood, Royal Navy, retired. Should have made captain, but his handicaps forbade it."

"Losing a hand was held against him?" Seth asked, "How? I mean Nelson had one arm, right?"

"One eye, too," I answered, looking at Osgood for a clue as to how far he was going to go with the story, for there was one thing I definitely knew of his ancestry and I was morbidly curious to see if he would reveal it. Osgood met my gaze coolly and I had my answer.

"To put it mildly, my father's loss of limb was hardly his only infirmity. That alone would have been fine. No, he had a far greater handicap. He was Irish. "

The silence was deafening. Osgood shrugged at my look, smiled ruefully.

"Well, I bloody well knew it," Shay, laughing, broke the silence, "there was always somethin' about ya'. I should've known it in the bar tha' night. Always wondered about William an' tha' toast he made. Shouldda' known he had a good coach."

"I make no claim on the manners of this one," Osgood pointed at me, grinned widely, "he had the good sense to do that himself."

"Did he indeed," Shay shot me a rather strange look before training his attention back to Osgood, "well, good ta' know, Osgood, good to have company among the heathen."

"We Irish are everywhere," Osgood said with conviction.

"Ain't we now," Shay toasted him with his coffee cup, "ya' Da was an officer, eh?"

"Protestant as well," Osgood replied without hesitation, "but he had two brothers following Wolfe Tone, both killed at Vinegar Hill."

"A ripe ol'Finian he'd a made then," Shay said with delight.

"You have no idea," Osgood smiled hugely, winked in my general direction.

Seth and Wycroft sat staring at the two Irishmen, incomprehension readily apparent. I endeavored to enlighten.

"Osgood has just explained to Mr. O'Shea that his family, while Protestant, were not landowning bastards that soaked

Catholic tenants to starvation or immigration, they were patriots who died in the 'Ninety-eight rebellion."

"They fought with French troops landed by Bonaparte to –" Shay started.

"That infuriated my father," Osgood interrupted.

"I could see where it would, fightin' the Bonaparte as he was" Shay agreed, "anyway, tha' only thing they accomplished was ta' lead tha' British on a merry chase until they got surrounded at Vinegar Hill. The French were allowed to surrender, then the British opened up with grapeshot and killed 'em all."

"Depriving me of two uncles I never knew," Osgood added solemnly.

"I'll tell you now," Shay sat bolt upright, and looked at each of us in turn, "anyone uses grapeshot on me – us – and I get close enough to tha' bastards, I'll not be taking prisoners."

"Amen," Osgood, just the man to carry out that sentiment, quietly agreed.

27

In days our discussions were rendered moot.

When it became clear that McDowell and Beauregard were sure to clash, Seth and I were invited to the State House. Buckingham had installed a telegraph station in his offices for the occasion. A crowd of notables gathered, refreshments were served, reports received and orated, and a party atmosphere prevailed.

That was supported by the early news from Manassas, all of which indicated that McDowell was on the verge of a great victory. By late afternoon the reports subtly changed and while victory still seemed possible it no longer appeared to be quite as decisive or overwhelming as had been thought a few food courses earlier. It was a nuance not much noticed and even less commented on by the grazers in the room.

Through the evening and into late night the refreshments still came but lay untouched, the news having become dire. On the cusp of victory McDowell had met disaster in the form of Joseph E Johnston's late arriving troops from the Shenandoah Valley. The historian in me noted that those troops came directly off trains to fight, a first.

By early morning – the well-wishers and front-runners having long since gone home – it was clear that McDowell's men were in headlong flight to Washington (and beyond, it turned out). The only force they had been able to fight their way through were the throngs of spectators that had come down from Washington to observe the day's festivities over a picnic.

At that Buckingham ruefully offered his sole comment in hours, "If the rebels could only advance upon the onlookers, perhaps a few more seats will open up for Republicans." It was probably not something he meant to say aloud.

The sun was just beginning to rise when our call up orders came. The terms 'in all haste' and 'by any and all available means' prominent and superfluous.

Almost exactly thirty-six hours later, the 21st Connecticut Volunteer Infantry, men, horses, wagons, ambulances, and everything needed to make mayhem on our southern brothers, was expertly packed aboard a custom train bound for Albany and Philadelphia – Seth and I had decided long ago to avoid the temptations of New York.

We left at dusk, Tuesday, July 23, on comfortably appointed carriages, courtesy of Seth Arnold Industries. The officers rode in the head cars, with legal access to drink; the men in the trailing cars in theory, only, traveling dry. We settled into a pleasantly lurching ride, Seth, Osgood, Wycroft, Shay and I occupied a wide row of seats facing one another, chess set up between Osgood and myself.

We rode in a most pleasant reverie that was interrupted at almost the precise moment we crossed the New York line. Christian entered our car trailed by the ever present James Benjamin and a lieutenant I dimly recognized. Christian, of course, had opted to ride with his men, almost admirable even though the strong smell of alcohol radiated from his every pore.

"Christian, James," Seth bellowed a greeting, "good to have you here, who's your companion?"

"Edwin Fischer," Christian answered. The thin, aesthetic looking man by his side nodded back, "Company B," he finished with emphasis as if the company explained it all. Which, come to think of it, it did.

As I was a piece down to Osgood, a rarity of roughly the same frequency as Haley's Comet, and my position was worsening, I embrace the interruption.

"Captain, Lieutenants!" I yelled, "Great to see you. Please sit down. I'll clean the table for drinks and food." I magnanimously offered.

"Touch a single man on that board and I will run you through," Osgood snarled, "I will hold the drinks."

When none of the trio smiled I knew there was a problem. Not even a fifth of the way to war and already confronted with a problem – it was a fifth further than I thought we would get.

"What is it Christian?" I asked with a sigh – not for the issue at hand, but because Osgood did not have the good grace to be host enough to clear the table of clutter.

"Edwin finds himself in command of Company B, William," Christian announced as the clean shaven Edwin reddened, "He needs to know what to do when we arrive in Philadelphia. He hesitates to tell you, for fear of being labeled an informer, but, after a lengthy discussion, we think it best for you to deal with this now, rather than when we detrain."

"What happened to Captain Huntington?" Seth asked with a good degree of incredulity. Osgood and I looked out the window into the darkness.

Christian, Benjamin, and Fischer exchanged looks. Eventually Christian's elbow found Fischer's ribs – none too gently I noted.

"Sir," he started in a high, thin, nervous voice, "Captain Huntington left yesterday for Washington," sweat beaded on his forehead, he shifted on his feet, "and, well… Sir."

"Easy Edwin," Arnold said in a reassuring voice, "you're in no trouble here, go on."

"Thank you, sir, Captain Huntington ordered me to take the company while he goes to Washington on regimental business. He further forbade me to disclose anything until confronted."

"That it, Edwin?" Seth inquired.

"Well, sir, I didn't know if it was legal order or not, but, sir, Mr. Huntington is my father's employer and –"

"Quite all right, Lieutenant, you've done all you could. Did the captain tell you his plans?"

"Oh, yes, Sir!" Fischer squeaked, "he was very proud, said he had appointments with Cameron, Scott, and McDowell over the next few days. Said he'd have things squared away by the time we get to Washington – said I'd be captain of the company as he'd have the regiment by then," he grimaced, "begging your pardons, Sirs, I would not like to have anything to do with a Regiment that has Huntington in command."

"Think nothing of it," a suddenly grim Arnold whispered, looked over at Osgood and Shay. I continued to stare out the window, "I did not anticipate this, how bad you think…" he trailed off.

"I'm sure," I took over for the stricken Arnold, "he just wants to give those gentlemen the twin benefits of his advice and vast experience."

"No doubt," Osgood agreed, Seth shook his head with a look of absolute disgust.

"You don't seem too upset, William," Christian said with a mixture of perplexity and suspicion.

"I can only hope," I went on, "that they take the time to listen to his fascinating ideas on tactics. Real vision, that man."

"They have to listen," Osgood offered, with great solemnity, "for the good of the country."

"Oh, they will," I answered, "he's too important to ignore."

"That he is," Osgood readily agreed. Our companions watched the exchange as spectators a tennis match.

"And once he finishes with the tactical lecture," I went on unfazed, "he can endeavor to improve the overall political position of the nation."

"Amen to that," Osgood seconded.

"Amen indeed," I looked each of our audience squarely in the eye before focusing on Fischer, "Tell me, Edwin," Fischer jumped at the familiarity, "are you saying that our Captain, lord of the teeming metropolis of Farmington, has meetings with the Secretary of War, the Commander of the Armies of the United States, and the Commander of the Eastern Army?"

"Ah, yes, Sir."

"Please call me William in present company."

"Yes, Sir."

"Excellent," I smiled at my brother, he was just starting to come out of his stunned state, "let me ask you, Edwin, Christian, do you find the itinerary overkill? Perhaps just a bit too much?"

"William?" Christian asked warily.

"Sir... I mean, William?" Fischer repeated.

"What I mean," I elaborated, "is this - you don't find it excessive that a local political hack, albeit a wealthy one, is able to line up appointments with the three highest ranking Army authorities? Does it seem plausible to you?"

"I suppose," Fischer was suddenly, wary, "seeing how he talks.

Seems a little quick, though, at such a bad time for the nation."

"See," I snapped at Osgood, "I told you the turnaround time with everything going on was too quick."

"Nonsense," Osgood retorted, "you heard the Lieutenant, Huntington has an inflated sense of himself, he certainly expected quick reply," he focused on me, "I'm just glad I talked you out of sending an invitation from Lincoln – that would have been overkill."

"Never underestimate the man's hubris," I replied.

"Yes but that would've been a step too far I warrant," Osgood with the closing argument.

"Damn you both," Seth could take it no longer, "no one likes to be outside an inside joke," he sat forward for full effect, "for the first time, and quite possibly last, I order you to tell me what you've done," he sat back looking exceedingly pleased with himself.

"My God," I said with feeling and sat straighter in my seat, "Captain Osgood, I must say that Colonel Arnold cuts quite a commanding figure, don't you agree?"

"I do," Osgood answered at once, "I suggest that the executive officer of the Regiment endeavor to obey that order, before you are brought up on charges."

"Who would prosecute?" I asked innocently.

"Why," as was Osgood, "I believe that you are the only officer in this Regiment familiar with the Articles of War and court martial procedures."

"You are correct, Captain. Just as I believe you are the only member the Regiment with close ties to a Hartford Western Union night supervisor.

"And, in all modesty," I endeavored to look modest, "I am the only member of our Regiment to have gone to West Point with a high-ranking War Department aide, with whom – with who, whom?, I never get that right," I shrugged my shoulders at the groups' unresponsiveness, "I have been in constant correspondence with for the past two months. During which time I may have – no, I think I probably did – mention certain problems with an ambitious, petty underling. Along with the fact that I may need some assistance down the road."

I looked at my fellow officers, my friends, in the spirit of pure bon homme, noted the various stages of comprehension dawning over their faces.

"So gentlemen," I continued, "take those contacts and the inkling of a plan and put it in the hands of a Machiavellian like Osgood and, well, things happen."

"And what has happened?" Seth asked, "Osgood, what did you do?"

"Only that which was requested of me, Colonel," Osgood answered, displaying admirable, if misplaced modesty, "I merely implemented Williams's plan, as I'm sure, William will eventually tell you."

"Well, you see," I took over, "in my ill-advised – I believe you called it, Seth – tete a tete with Captain Huntington at the party he told me, emphatically, that he had friends in Washington. Naturally in the time-honored tradition of all under- qualified, wealthy, self-important, connected officers he would prefer to use influence rather than, oh, say, wait for Seth and I to get shot and earn his promotion the old fashion way."

"So," Osgood could not resist, "it was only a matter of time before he contacted the War Department. We took steps to, ah, monitor his movements waiting for a wire to go out. He did not disappoint. He invoked Buckingham and our senators in requesting – demanding, really – appointments to discuss the situation of the Twenty-first."

"Instead of being ignored," I interjected, "as any wire from a Captain – never mind the Captain of a non-activated volunteer regiment – would be, we saw to it that he got an immediate replies."

"Which, with his opinion of himself, he did not doubt," Arnold offered, the light having burst.

"Obviously," I agreed, "not when telegrams arrived from the War Department offering a series of meetings with the powers that be. And if he had bothered to check – he did not, sloppy officer, the man's opinion of himself knows no bounds – he would've found that the telegram really did originate from a Scott aide, one Captain Albert Denton, Regular Army."

"Indeed," Osgood smiled wickedly, "however, when he arrives

at the War Department, he'll find that there, unfortunately, is no record of the transmission anywhere to be found."

Osgood and I waited expectantly. It took only a moment.

"He has his copy of the telegram," my brother said.

"Does he?" Osgood laughed.

"William?" Arnold asked, a wide smile breaking out.

"It is my understanding," I barely kept a straight face, "that the Captain seems to have been relieved of his copy of the telegram, seems he wandered a little too close to a certain former pickpocket in Company F."

"So go the fortunes of war," Osgood intoned as if in prayer.

"In any event," I mused aloud, "it will be a long, long week for the Captain while he sits and sits and sits without an appointment, without a Regiment."

"One can only hope," Shay spoke for the first time, "tha' Huntingdon's patience stretches to tha' point where he tells tha' Army how important he is and insists on action."

"He'll find quickly," I replied automatically, "that a captain of volunteers has less standing in the War Department than a Confederate private."

To further illustrate the point. I pointed to my own shoulder straps and the 'V' between my maple leafs, "Behold, men, the Scarlet letter," I chuckled to amused faces, "Captain Huntington will find himself Hester Prynne in short order . . .come let us not praise him but bury him," I finished to applause and a self-satisfied grin.

"My God," Seth spoke above the merriment, "brilliant, bloodless, efficient. Utterly fantastic, my compliments gentlemen!"

"I could never have done something like that," Christian added in a voice that approached reverence.

"That's why I'm always after you to learn chess, little brother."

Seth leaned across the table, picked up Osgood's queen, "I, for one, would very much like to start lessons."

28

When we could forget why we were so urgently riding South, the trip was most enjoyable. I, along with every other member of the 21st, chose to engage in disbelief and do just that. A party atmosphere prevailed throughout the night. Groups formed in our car to drink, chat, sing, smoke, boast, insult, and commiserate, the members changing gradually as men dropped out from fatigue or alcohol poisoning while others, forgoing sleep, took their places.

I eventually fell off into that always interesting mixture of half-awake, half-asleep dreams, snatches of song and conversation intruding uninvited. I woke up every twenty minutes or so slightly disoriented with no memory of the dream that had just ended.

I set a Provost guard at our many layovers in obscure New York towns, some of them with names out of Washington Irving stories. We were successful at both stopping our more adventurous comrades from sampling the local drinking establishments and preventing the export of our particular brand of hilarity to individuals content in their self-contained communities.

We arrived in Philadelphia just after dawn. Although early by any standards, wartime animated the station even as the first daylight illuminated it. At least two other trains disgorged blue-clad cargo; porters rushed about as if skirmishers; horses unhappy with their accommodations snorted, loudly, lashing hooves at their perceived malefactors; officers impotently yelled conflicting orders; stevedores sneered and sniped at soldiers attempting to unload their own equipment for both their ineptitude and infringement on their tips; amused engineers and conductors, their work done, stood aimlessly, free to take in the entertainment; severely dressed women with even more severely drawn hair handed out flyers offering legal and non-toxic refreshments to the heroes detraining.

I took it in, the last to leave our train, acting the Captain of a sinking ship. I stood on the car's rear platform above a sea of heaving humanity and angry equines and breathed deep the wartime air.

I was about to wade down into it when our conductor, a tiny, nervous man with square glasses and mousy mustache approached me in what appeared to be something of a panic.

"Thank God you're here," he shouted, unnecessarily, "I thought you'd left, Lieutenant Colonel"

"You address Lieutenant Colonel as Colonel," I snapped, there was something utterly unctuous about the man that had I found instantly disagreeable hours earlier.

"I have something for you, Sir," he said coolly, reached into his great pockets and pulled out a gray- white linen envelope of evident quality. I took it with a sense of dread and certainty.

"What is the source of this letter," I said in my best command voice.

The conductor, the longtime object of similar toned voices from business magnets, judges, Congressman, merchants, and well-dressed, self-important louts, blinked for several seconds before replying in a perfectly vacuous voice, "a gentleman in Hartford, Sir, who merely requested that I deliver this to you upon arrival in Philadelphia."

"Name?" I asked without hope.

"He did not offer it," he shrugged.

"What did he look like?"

"He was tall, Colonel, as tall as you," he replied as if already tired by his ongoing association with me, "but I did not get a good look at his face."

"You remember the money he gave you though, don't you?" I observed with an edge, my temper rising.

"I do not know what you mean, sir," he said with practice ease, spun and waddled away.

I tore the envelope open and pulled out an ornate letter with familiar, flowing handwriting.

William,

I regret very much that you will be out of town for such an indefinite, yet necessary time.

Be assured, however, that I will continue my pursuit with my customary zeal in your, I sincerely hope, brief absence.

Perhaps our paths shall cross at some point if, as you have no doubt accurately predicted, the current unpleasantness continues for an extended period.

I must admit that I am curious to experience the sensation of killing at a distance. I envy you the experience.

Have no fear, Bridget, while lovely and certainly worthy, does not quite meet my criteria for selection. Pity that, though I would think long and hard before depriving you of her pleasures.

Take care of yourself, William, I would hate to have to finish my work without you.

Yours,

None of it surprised me and I believed, however irrationally, his claim of Bridget's safety. She did not fit his bizarre needs, whatever they were, I knew that, just as I knew that I had I stayed in Hartford I would somehow have grown to know him. Perhaps he wanted that.

Regardless of how sure I was, I wired Bridget - an innocuous note telling her we had arrived in Philadelphia and I was thinking of her. Through Osgood's auspices it was delivered by an off-duty Hartford cop. For the next two years Hartford police kept an eye on the house on Asylum Street on the chance my judgment was ill-founded.

It was not. One of few over the next years to prove so.

AUTHOR'S NOTE

The Hanlin Books were conceived as a trilogy, *The Ceremony of Innocence*, *The Blood Dimmed Tide*, and *The Rough Beast*, the exigencies of editing and transcribing (and transcribing and editing) a few thousand handwritten pages – on every conceivable type and size of paper, in every conceivable color of ink (and pencil), have proved daunting, even in this era of Dragon and Scrivener.

Somewhere along the way it occurred to me that three 600 page books might be somewhat daunting to the reader as well – I am a huge fan of Neal Stephenson's Baroque Cycle and have recommended it often, only to have the 'recomendee' take one look at the 900 page *Quicksilver* and . . .

The novels, then, have been broken down, basically halved where there are natural 'endings'. I was initially somewhat concerned about these endings until Richard Slotkin was kind enough to advise: "accept the logic of your own creative act."

Each volume, however, has been designed to stand alone, in or out of the preceding narratives – for the most part. While a fan of the Sharpe series, the constant repetition of Sharpe's back-story – which frequently ran from his birth to the present novel – were at best irritating. Patrick O'Brien got it right, I think, dive in anywhere, be swept up, figure out who's who, what's what later.

Finally, this is a work of fiction – as told by an eighty-something year old man with – well, a few problems. William, his brother, family, and the 21st are fictional. (The 21st here is not, in any way, a reflection of the real 21st Conn. Vol. Inf.). The locations in Hartford and descriptions of its denizens are a combination of fact and fiction, well within historical context though some liberties have been taken – the Hartford Club, for instance, did not exist until the 1880s or so, but the building is special and right around the corner from Williams (fictional) home .

The state of the Connecticut Armory is indicative of the state of armories throughout the North in 1861; most state governors had lists of West Point graduates on hand and tripped over themselves trying to recruit them after Sumter; as the indomitable Bruce Catton put it — every regiment represented 30 political plums for each governor to hand out.

Governor Buckingham is, of course, real and if you think William's opinion of him is too harsh, all I can say is wait, William's opinions of people are always a work in progress.

Throughout the Hanlin Chronicles, historical characters are, mostly, credited with their own words and attitudes, sometimes modified in the vernacular instead of the words they would like us to believe through their memoirs (such a literate war) they spoke in the heat of the moment. While they would very much like us to believe they saw the enemy and orated ala *Henry V*, they most assuredly did not. Case in point, for a later volume, Winfield Scott Hancock — general, *the* hero of Gettysburg, 1880 Democratic nominee for the presidency — is described in more than one journal as a world class 'profaner' — "the air was always blue around him" to quote from one. Hancock's creative use of profanity was legendary then, lost in all *The Killer Angels* —like historical fiction since.

In short, historical figures are not constrained to speak within the confines of conventional Civil War Novels, they are true to their characters, letters, journals, memoirs, etc. . . . but more on this as the story moves on.

Events, however, are all too real

ACKNOWLEDGEMENTS

The Litchfield Monument that inspired the series

Thanks to early readers and encouragers – George Jung, Patrick Clyne, Geoffrey Hooker, and Pat Reilly.

George Jung introduced me to Dominic Streatfeild, a terrific UK writer and BBC producer who was kind enough to read some of my stuff, commented favorably, helped out with a book proposal – and much more.

Richard Slotkin, Piper Kerman, Christopher Dickey, Professor Peter Carmichael of Gettysburg College's Civil War Institute, and Stephen Sears are all respected, bestselling authors and each took the time to correspond with me on several issues.

Special thanks to Rich Slotkin who not only read *The Ceremony of Innocence* but took time out of a busy book tour for *The Long Road to Antietam* (highly recommended) to meet with me for several very entertaining hours.

Tony Horwitz – I have recommended his *Confederates in the Attic* to more people than I can count, it is that good and more relevant than ever in the midst of Andrew Napolitano-type Lost Cause tirades – took a few hours out of his schedule to talk Civil War and publishing. All of it invaluable.

This edition and its follow-ups (due out shortly) would not have been possible without the support – in many forms – of Fred Schott, Bob Dell, R. Bruce Hunter, Dagny Griswold, and the (very) extended Miller family of Avon, Connecticut – especially Sandi, Cal, Capri, Cam, and Sam.

RR Hicks has a law degree, writes, consults, edits, blogs, and has survived and thrived through an innate ability to shoot a basketball - a story for another day.

A soccer and rugby player most of his adult life, he is also a history 'buff' (though he despises the term).

He will defend to the death the simple truth that Shelby Foote's one and one half page, almost stream of consciousness, description of The Bloody Angle at Spotsylvania is more moving, powerful, and visceral than any novel, movie or television show about the Civil War. Ever.

He dearly hopes Tennyson was right:

> Made weak by time and fate,
> but strong in will
> To strive, to seek, to find, and not to yield . . .

For more about Roland please check out his website at
Rolandrhicks.wordpress.com

Upcoming Releases:

The Falcon August 1861 - June 29, 1862

From Washington D.C. to the Jamestown Peninsula; A friendship with royalty; a dead senator and an imprisoned general; disloyalties; disillusionment in Yorktown; The Chickahominy; Seven Days and the White Oak Swamp ...Out -Fall 2014

A Widening Gyre July - December 13, 1862

A view to murder; a Medieval travel tale through Northern Virginia; a comet and defeat; Antietam and end of a friendship; The Bloody Lane; 'Poor Burnside'; Falmouth; the sack of Fredericksburg; Marye's Hill' Out Fall 2014

The Center Cannot Hold January 1863 – July 1863

Hospital and a friend; the politics of the home front; a changed Hartford; a job offer; a body; the Court Martial of General Porter; news from the front; Lee invades; a tavern in Maryland; the Wheat Field; the Immortal. Out Christmas, 2014

The Blood Dimmed Tide August 1863 – June 3, 1864

A fruitless chase; the streets of Washington; a visit from the past; the Address; Hancock's Ball; Grant takes command; a death in the Wilderness; madness at the Bloody Angle; rivers; new men; return to Cold Harbor.

Early Spring 2015

Pitiless as the Sun June 1864 – November 1864

Doctors; Fort Stevens and an army of clerks; Jubal Early; a most miserable camp; Sheridan arrives; Up the Valley; farms, crops, & terror; a throat slit, a mercy given; the Electioneers; Cedar Creek.

Early Summer 2015

The Rough Beast December 1864-1866

A brief return to Hartford; a death penalty case against John Rock; the siege of Petersburg; Sheridan and Five Forks; the chase across Virginia; the last battle line;
Home; the Know Nothing Killer; a trial of opposites. Fall 2015

Made in the USA
Charleston, SC
09 September 2014